PENGUIN

DIV...

YASHPAL (1903–1976) began to write while serving a life sentence for his participation, as a comrade of Bhagat Singh and Chandrashekhar Azad, in the armed struggle for India's independence. What he wrote formed his first collection of short stories, *Pinjare ki Udan*, published in 1938. After his release Yashpal dazzled Hindi readers with the political journal, *Viplava*, which he founded and published with the help of Prakashvati, a revolutionary, whom he later married in prison. He wrote more than fifty books including collections of short stories, novels, essays, a play and memoirs of his revolutionary days.

Yashpal died in 1976 while writing the fourth volume of his reminiscences.

ANAND has translated Yashpal's novels and short stories into English and French. He has also translated the works of Alice Munro, Mordecia Richler and Hugh McLennan into Hindi. He lives in North America.

NAMITA SINGH is the editor of the leading Hindi literary magazine, *Vartaman Sahitya*. She is the author of seven short story collections and one novel. Her stories have been translated into English, Urdu and other regional languages. She has also edited a book on historical, cultural and feminist readings of *Divya*.

Divya

YASHPAL

Translated from the Hindi by
ANAND

Foreword by
NAMITA SINGH

PENGUIN BOOKS

PENGUIN BOOKS
Published by the Penguin Group
Penguin Books India Pvt. Ltd, 11 Community Centre, Panchsheel Park,
New Delhi 110 017, India
Penguin Group (USA) Inc., 375 Hudson Street, New York, New York 10014,
USA
Penguin Group (Canada), 90 Eglinton Avenue East, Suite 700, Toronto,
Ontario, M4P 2Y3, Canada (a division of Pearson Penguin Canada Inc.)
Penguin Books Ltd, 80 Strand, London WC2R 0RL, England
Penguin Ireland, 25 St Stephen's Green, Dublin 2, Ireland (a division of
Penguin Books Ltd)
Penguin Group (Australia), 250 Camberwell Road, Camberwell,
Victoria 3124, Australia (a division of Pearson Australia Group Pty Ltd)
Penguin Group (NZ), 67 Apollo Drive, Rosedale, North Shore 0632,
New Zealand (a division of Pearson New Zealand Ltd)
Penguin Group (South Africa) (Pty) Ltd, 24 Sturdee Avenue, Rosebank,
Johannesburg 2196, South Africa

Penguin Books Ltd, Registered Offices: 80 Strand, London WC2R 0RL, England

First published in Hindi by Viplava Karyalaya 1945
First published in English by Sahitya Akademi 2006
Published by Penguin Books India 2009

Copyright © Viplava Karyalaya 1945
Translation copyright © Anand 2006, 2009
Foreword copyright © Namita Singh 2009

ISBN 9780143103127

Typeset in Perpetua by Gurutypograph Technology
Printed at Chaman Offset Printers, Delhi

To you
In whose heart the glow of love
has never been dimmed by unremitting
suffering and hardship . . .

CONTENTS

Foreword	ix
Translator's Note	xxv
Preface	xxviii
The Festival of Spring	1
The Palace of the Chief Justice	14
Prestha	40
Acharya Pravardhan	71
Self-surrender	82
The Harsh Reality	94
Grandsire Chief Justice	133
Dara	138
Anshumala	164
Sagal	211
Prithusen and Rudradhir	229
Mallika	253
Divya	260

Foreword

ONE OF THE REASONS YASHPAL STANDS OUT FROM HIS contemporaries is that he is a writer of ideological conflicts. His social commitment and objectivity influence his works very apparently and provide an ideological base to Hindi fiction. Most of his novels either have a political background or his characters are politically conscious and active. *Dada Comrade, Geeta, Manushya Ke Roop, Deshdrohi, Meri Teri Uski Baat* and his most acclaimed novel, *Jhootha Sach*, which ranks among world classics, all have the socio-politically charged pre-independent India as a backdrop.

Yashpal witnessed India's freedom struggle and the county's partition thereafter. He was a part of an extremist organization and worked with great revolutionaries like Bhagat Singh and Chandrashekhar Azad; he was even imprisoned for a long period, due to his anti-British activities. It was in prison that he started to write and later decided to make writing a full-time career. *Jhootha Sach* is a comprehensive account of Partition and the great human tragedy that followed in its aftermath. It is a saga of love and hate, political ambitions and the pressure of society and, above all, the suffering of the common masses, be they Hindu or Muslim.

Women are another focus in Yashpal's novels as well as stories. In his novels *Divya, Amita, Apsara ka Shap, Dada Comrade, Geeta, Jhootha Sach* and his last one, *Meri Teri Uski Baat*, women play an important role. His women characters are not passive but energetic and conscious about their identity and dignity as human beings. Both *Dada Comrade*, Yashpal's first novel and *Divya*, published in 1945, are women oriented. So contemporary are the themes and issues addressed in these books that though published before Independence and set in completely different times, they hold true even today.

Divya is set in the first century BC. Though the novel has a historical background, Divya is not a historical character but represents a woman of the era who is in quest of her identity, her desire to be accepted in society on equal terms—as a human being.

Yashpal raises basic questions of woman's empowerment in a society segregated by caste and colour (*varna*). He goes back in time, delving deep into history to trace the roots of the oppression of women. History, for him, is not merely a repertory of past events. It provides an insight into the present and allows us to visualize, even prepare for, changes in the future. For any society, logical analysis and an evaluation of history are essential for its polity. Distortion of history by parties or people who have vested interests often becomes a tool for power and ultimately strengthens the divisive forces, especially in a multicultural, pluralistic society.

When Yashpal started writing, it was a time of great turmoil. In the preface to *Divya*, he says, 'History is not a matter of belief, but of analysis.' Belief expands into faith and faith into blind adoration. History is important because it gives knowledge of the process of development of human civilization so that one can analyse the present composition of society and indicate the future course of development. From a historical perspective, the life portrait of Divya throws light on the socio-political structure of India at the time. It also depicts the plight of women, their social and religious bondage, and their struggle for independence.

In Indian literature, ideological discussions on women-related issues started taking place in the early twentieth century, but murmurs could be heard even in the period known as the Indian Renaissance. The impact of reform movement during the Indian struggle for freedom was significant on various social groups. There are diverse images of this period. On one side, the oppressed working classes, artisans and peasants were opposing British exploitation; on the other, revolutionary groups were fighting for independence. In addition, the leaders of the reform movement were fighting against inhuman Hindu customs like sati and child marriage. The Brahmo Samaj of Bengal and its leaders Raja Ram Mohan Roy, Ishwar Chandra Vidyasagar, Keshav Chandra Sen among others, worked relentlessly and succeeded, with the help of British governance, in enforcing laws, banning sati and raising the age of consent. After much work, the law allowing widow remarriage was also enforced. These were steps to ameliorate the agony and misery of Indian women. Orthodox upholders of religion vehemently opposed these actions. A section of the educated public and those who were enlightened or sensitive also resisted these reforms because they considered them to be British interference in the traditions and culture of India. These reform movements all over the country also raised voices in support of female education, supported the Hindu Widows' Remarriage Act and opposed child marriage.

The national freedom movement was not only for the end of British rule. It also called for women's liberation and the upliftment of untouchables and dalits who were denied basic human rights by the caste-ridden Hindu society. The growth of Western education was creating an atmosphere of enlightenment among the emerging middle class and people were getting acquainted with terms like equality, freedom, fraternity and democracy. Mahatma Gandhi had emphatically declared that a freedom which does not carry the participation of half its population should not be contemplated. It was due to Gandhi's charismatic influence that a large number of womenfolk came out of their confinement and participated in the various phases of the freedom movement. The change in attitude was visible. Contemporary newspapers and magazines were highlighting women's issues. They were showing concern about the miserable condition of widows and the repercussions of child marriage. Some of the magazines had women editors and others had regular women contributors writing on various gender-related subjects.

In the south the task to educate the downtrodden and girl children was initiated by Jyotiba Phule and his wife Savitri Phule. Later, it was taken over by Ambedkar who introduced an aggressive socio-political agenda for the emancipation of untouchables. In Maharashtra, Mahadev Govind Ranade and his associates also made efforts for women's education through a social movement called Prarthna Samaj, which supported widow remarriage while opposing child marriage. Similarly, Sheikh Abdullah was a pioneer in establishing the Female Education Association in Aligarh. Through his efforts, veiled Muslim girls came out to attend the school started by him in 1905, which is now a part of the renowned Aligarh Muslim University and a centre for Muslim girls' education. So, it was the beginning of the twentieth century when gender issues became a focus and the meaning of equality, self respect and self-sufficiency were introduced.

Yashpal entered the world of literature during this time of great upheaval. Before he wrote his first novel, his contemporary, another renowned Hindi writer, Jainendra, wrote *Sunita*. The novel revolves around the protagonist Sunita who, obeying the dictates of her husband, undresses and offers herself to his best friend who is supposedly a revolutionary and is in a state of depression. Jainendra set out to create a bold image of a new Indian woman, but without a deep understanding of social realities, the end result seemed absurd. In the early fifties, another famous novel, *Nadi ke Dweep*, written by the acclaimed writer, Agyeya, was published. It created a storm because it presented a totally new image of the empowered modern woman. Here too the story revolves around a female protagonist, Rekha, who is quite eccentric and individualistic. She is married but offers herself to her beloved Bhuvan. Later, separated from her husband, she declines to marry her lover because she does not want to lose her independence and freedom again. She becomes averse to the role of a wife. This was yet another image of the liberated woman.

Yashpal tries to find a meaningful reading of women's emancipation in *Divya*. He visits history to trace the ancient social order. The questions that arise are whether the history of human civilization is one of women's subjugation. Are the roots of women slavery found in the history of religion and culture? With the discovery of agriculture, the primitive communalistic society started transforming into an organized social system. The growth of private property was a consequence of surplus agricultural produce. Thus emerged, on the ruins of an egalitarian society, the system of monarchy.

In the meantime, the greed for hoarding the surplus grew so much so that it demanded better methods of agriculture. Now the collective ownership of land became impossible, and the concept of private property was ultimately accepted. This new situation demanded free labour which came in the form of slaves. It was the beginning of a new chapter in history.

With these developments was born the consciousness of the difference between the sexes, and eventually the custom of pairing was established and accepted. Domestic affairs became the responsibility of women. The practice of hoarding and the system of private property gave rise to slavery. At the same time, women were given a new place and confined within the boundaries of four walls. As the feudal system became stronger, not only the land, but slaves and women also became part of the private property of men. A new caste-based society began to be formed, in which four varnas, depending on the nature of the profession, became the four castes that could not be changed. The caste or profession became hereditary. This was supported by the Upanishads, and stringent social laws were framed against slaves and women in various Samhitas. This Brahminical social order was convenient for the upper crust of the society. The Puranas, Upanishads and Samhitas defended the varna system, slavery and upper-class tyranny as absolute. This caste-based social order is what is responsible for inequality, injustice and inhuman conditions of the Sudras and subjugation of women in Hindu society.

Yashpal peruses history to trace the roots of slavery in order to offer some solution. He succeeds, with beauty of language and craft, in *Divya*.

The first century BC was the period in Indian history when Buddhism was confronting the old Brahminical social order and was being widely accepted by a large section of the masses. It did not intend to disturb the monarchical system of state polity and therefore became the religion of a number of independent states. This was also a time of various socio-political conflicts. Reincarnation stories were created by the followers of Gautama Buddha through a series of Jataka tales to glorify him. The idea of rebirth in Brahminical philosophy had been rejected by the Buddha, but after his death his followers preached the same beliefs. The Greek emperor, Alexander, invaded India during the time of Chandragupta Maurya and these attacks continued up to 200 BC. A considerably large area in the north-west region remained under these Indo-Greek rulers for about two hundred years. Some of them embraced Buddhism and some were also attracted towards Vaishnavism and the Krishna cult because, when compared to the Brahminical Hindu order, these were more liberal and social in nature. Buddhism advocated an egalitarian social order and rejected the theory of dividing human beings on the basis of birth and heredity. It was a path of salvation for the oppressed and downtrodden. Buddhist philosophy delivered a message of love, equality and fraternity. Thus it was also a period of serious conflict between the supporters of the Brahminical order and the followers of Buddhism. There was great discontent among the Brahmins and Kshatriyas belonging to the nobility and they wasted no opportunity in attacking Buddhism and its followers. The last king of the Maurya dynasty was assassinated by his Brahmin chief commander Pushya Mitra Shung, who ultimately made all efforts to wipe out the Buddhist monks and re-establish the Brahminical social order of *varnashram*. Yashpal uses these incidents from history to construct the foundation of his narrative, voicing contemporary concerns in a historical setting.

What was the status of women during all these conflicts? The Brahminical social order refers to Hindu scriptures to establish that a woman must remain veiled and that her place is within four walls. She is ruled by her master, who may be her father, husband, son or anybody else, and can never be independent. She may be called *Rajmata,* Queen Mother, or *Kuldevi,* Divine Goddess, but cannot enjoy her freedom or be treated equal to the man in actual practice.

Buddhism revolutionized Indian society as it rejected the supremacy of a certain class and opposed the varnashram system which was based upon unequal social laws. However, it does not accept the independent status of woman. Buddhist philosophy says, 'Brahmin not by birth but by his deeds,' but accepts that a woman must have a guardian in a father, husband, son, or, in the case of a slave, her master, whom she belongs to. In fact Buddhism did not touch the basic structure of the feudal social system and could not give any revolutionary verdict regarding the status of women or slaves. The same phenomenon occurs in the medieval period. The Mughals never intended to disturb the basic social structure of Hindu society and thus the plight of women and slaves remained unchanged.

Divya deals with all these aspects. Yashpal tries to remind us that in the feudal system no religion is liberal and friendly

towards women. In his novel he investigates what can be an
ideal or healthy relationship between a man and woman. He
creates the character of Marish to explore this. Marish seems
to be a bit bohemian in his behaviour but he is very serious
about his outlook towards life and society. He is a follower of
the *Charvak* school of thought. He rejects the idea of 'another
world after death' which forms the very base of Hindu religion.
He is impressed by some tenets of Buddhism but opposes the
philosophy of Nirvana or renunciation. Buddhism says that
monarchy, social tyranny, slavery, inequality all are temporary
and salvation of the soul is the attainment of a changeless state
of eternal rest. After Buddha, his followers introduced the
philosophy of reincarnation, a typical Brahminical thought that
was vehemently opposed by Gautama Buddha in his lifetime.
Marish opposes this too. Primitive Indian materialists, known
as Charvaks, who came before Buddha, believed in the sanctity
of human life and its progress. They said that life evolved from
an inanimate substance and there was no other world after
death because matter is the ultimate reality. Marish supports
the philosophy of *Lokayata* (religion of the common masses).
The feudal social system was totally male dominated; a woman
had no space of her own. But Marish believes that man and
woman are both integral parts of a unit. Love and respect for
each other is the only way for a meaningful union. It seems
that Yashpal puts his own philosophy and opinions into the
words of Marish. He wants to establish the dignity of human
life above all else. A religion that makes human life beautiful
and distinguished is the best religion.

Another important question raised by Yashpal in this
novel is the perception of a woman's independence. There is

a misconception that a prostitute is a liberated woman. Being mistress of her body and soul, she is an independent entity. Alas, it is not so simple.

It is true that, in ancient history, prostitution was an integral part of the feudal system and operated under state patronage. Prostitutes were well-connected with the royalty and upper strata of society; they were respected by them. Honours and titles were conferred upon them by the state. A part of their wealth went to the state revenue. Their lifestyle was opulent, and they led independent lives. But the question still arises, whether a prostitute, irrespective of the high-profile life she leads, is an independent, liberated woman. It is true that when compared to an ordinary woman, who is confined within the four walls of her house, she is much better off. She is free to take decisions on her own because she is economically independent. In spite of these privileges, she is not a liberated woman. She is not really a mistress of her own body. Prostitution is supposed to be the oldest profession in the world. It is an entity of the market, and the market has its own rules and regulations. If a woman is a commodity then she cannot refuse a buyer. Hence it is a false belief that if a woman is mistress of her own body she becomes the mistress of her destiny as well. This thought-provoking discussion is beautifully woven into *Divya*.

Yashpal also points out in this novel that it is very difficult for a low-caste individual to survive in the Brahminical social order, no matter how virtuous he is. Even if he is leading a fabulous life he cannot get respect and honour. Society can never forget his lineage. Prithusen excels in martial arts and is appointed chief commander of the royal army. His father is a wealthy trader and very close to the king. Even then his lineage is never forgotten by the aristocratic society of Sagal. He is hated by them and is called *daas putra* (son of a slave). It has been a unique feature of Indian polity that people never forget caste—even of their rulers. Any religion which is not judicious, cannot defend the interests of the masses and cannot make the majority of the people happy, is not worthy to be worshipped.

Yashpal's writings are thought provoking. He never spares the conservative and orthodox value system attacking them in his stories and novels. When he picks up a historical theme, it is not only a journey through history to investigate the past, he puts forward an advanced, modern outlook. This objectivity elevates him much higher among his contemporaries. It is for this reason that he discusses different aspects of the *Lokayata* philosophy.

In *Divya* Yashpal also writes about the relationship between the ruling class and its subjects. Even when preparations are going on in Sagal for a war against the approaching Greek ruler of the neighbouring state, in such a crucial atmosphere, highly placed military commanders indulge in nepotism and merriment. There is also the additional burden of war tax on the subjects as also the forceful recruitment by military officials. Traders have a good time, as such territorial wars always provide a golden opportunity for business, while the sufferings of the common people go unheard. Dangers of war loom large, but conspiracies are hatched in the palace. There is a state of total anarchy and the disgruntled class tries to cash in because the Indo-Greek ruler of Sagal, Mithrodus, has embraced Buddhism. He is very old and is involved in religious discourse most of the time.

Social realism is an important feature of this novel.
Yashpal goes into minute details and presents a complete picture
of the complex situation. He gives a comprehensive account of
the slave trade. In his preface he declares that it is a fictional
tale. That may be true, but the political scenario, social system
and historical events are borne out of real life. Though there
are certain rules and regulations in every territorial war, they
are invariably flouted. A pregnant Divya is sold to a slave
trader, Pratool. The fact that Divya is pregnant and belongs
to a respectable Brahmin family is concealed by him because
a Brahmin could not be sold as a *dasi* (slave), but everything
seems fair in trade.

There are research documents which give proof of human
trafficking that took place in the thirteenth century. Contract
papers prepared at the time of sale show that everything was in
favour of the buyer, who was the master of the slave. These
historical documents also show that the master had the right
to keep him or her at his will; to punish, torture, mortgage or
re-sell as per his desire. On possible suicide by the slave, a very
clear note states that the master will not be considered guilty.
He would remain as clean as he would be after having taken a
bath in the Ganges. The document cautioned the slaves that if
they committed suicide they would be reborn as very lowly
creatures—dogs, asses, *chandal*s (untouchable among
untouchables, those who carry dead bodies). The intent was
to use religion to frighten them to such an extent that they
dare not even think of dying. After all, the traders and masters
had spent money to buy them.

Yashpal attacks this sort of religious exploitation and
hypocrisy not only in *Divya* but also in his other novels and

short stories. *Apsara ka Shap* is based on the famous Sanskrit epic *Abhijnana Shakuntalam*. It exposes the hypocrisy of the ruling classes and their attitude towards women in ancient India. Stories like *Karva ka Vrat* and *Gyandan* are also known for this kind of exposé. His characters are humane, with capabilities, strengths, a fighting spirit as well as weaknesses and frailties. His female characters are in search of their identity, social respect and equal status. Shail is a representative character of his first novel, *Dada Comrade*. She is energetic, bold, politically conscious, and participates in the Trade Union Movement. She is sympathetic to a group of young revolutionaries and extends a helping hand when required. She has a soft corner for Harish, a revolutionary and a trade unionist. A time comes when Harish is in extreme desperation, and to give him a healing touch and solace, she offers herself to him. Later on when Harish is given a death sentence, she decides to carry on with her life and gives birth to his child. Shail and Divya are two of Yashpal's immortal characters .

Yashpal encourages his readers to be critical. He makes it clear that no institutionalized religion is ready to give equal status to women. The novel gives an insight into understanding the true spirit of feminism and meaning of the liberated woman. The three main male protagonists Rudradhir, Prithusen and Marish represent three different schools of thought, that existed during that time—the Brahminical Hindu religion, Buddhism and the materialistic Charvak philosophy respectively.

In all his writings Yashpal aims for social change. He targets the middle-class readership. Though he is critical of the opportunistic mindset of this class—which is hypocritical in its behaviour and attitude—at the same time he has faith in its capabilities. It may be a superficial class but it has created history a number of times. It has been instrumental in bringing about revolution that has ushered in social change in different societies of the world. Yashpal also knows that a writer, however committed, cannot bring about a revolution through his/her writings alone. But it is possible to influence people, to get people to change their attitude and mindset to form the basic foundation of a social system and this in turn creates a congenial social environment for further change. For this reason his readership primarily constitutes the educated middle class. The question of women's independence becomes more pertinent through Divya's portrait and her life. There are two options for her to choose from: one, a right to self determination and the other, a path of self-sufficiency. The former is the key to an independent entity which is next to impossible in a patriarchal system. Divya is well aware of this position. There comes a situation when she is ready to denounce the Hindu religion and expresses her desire to embrace Buddhism and lead the life of an ascetic. To her dismay she is denied her wish, as she is asked to get permission from her father, husband, son or master.

Divya insists on her economic independence, even if it is as a prostitute. There is an interesting instance in the novel when Divya, in the guise of Anshumala, returns to Sagal, her birthplace. Devi Mallika invites her and offers her the honour of being the state courtesan. Just as she is about to be crowned, her identity is revealed by a group of people. Amidst the chaos, a verdict is issued that a Brahmin cannot become a state courtesan. Through this Yashpal exposes the double standards of caste-ridden Hindu society. Nobles of Sagal, whom she entertained in the guise of Anshumala, now oppose her being crowned as the state courtesan. She may be honoured as the *Kulmata*, the female head of the family, but the status of an independent woman, who has the right to take her own decision, is not possible in the varnashram social order.

Divya may be a tale of ancient Indian society but the gender issues it raises are still relevant today. Empowerment of women is possible only when there is social development. The feminist movement in the West has had an impact here as well. Capitalism in its initial stages had a liberal outlook on social issues. This was why the British government enforced laws to ban customs like sati and child marriage. Today with the emergence of educated middle class women, gender issues are occupying centre stage. By the end of the twentieth century, the ideals of an egalitarian socialistic society had been overpowered by a new political and social order. A 'slave' woman, once confined within four walls, stepped out to breathe fresh air, but her path deviated, and she transformed herself into a commodity. *Divya* is an answer to some pertinent questions that are extremely relevant even today.

Yashpal reflects his own ideology in Marish. The author did not support the Buddhist philosophy of renunciation because he believed it led to a passive, non-productive lifestyle. He was for a relationship between man and woman, where no one is a master or a subject. He was a follower of the *Lokayata* philosophy which opposes division in society along any lines whatsoever. Believing in the equality of people ought to be the religion of the masses. Yashpal wants to establish that only this kind of religion based on materialistic philosophy can assure equality and honour to women.

The essence of Yashpal's stories and novels makes him a writer of great stature. His personal life too had its vicissitudes; he observed life closely and critically analysed its pros and cons: whether of the revolutionary movement, Gandhism, the politics of the Congress and other political parties; the communist movement and the emergence of communal forces and their politics of hate and subversion. He vehemently opposed all anti-human action and philosophy with conviction and courage and attacked those tenets of Indian culture that were responsible for the plight of women and untouchables. Yashpal stood by what he believed and he expressed himself sincerely and passionately. That is why his novels and stories are universal and why they endure.

Namita Singh

Translator's Note

WHEN YASHPAL WROTE *DIVYA* IN 1945, HE HAD ALREADY PUBLISHED two novels, five collections of short stories, two collections of socio-economic essays, a book on the basic tenets of Marxism, and one of his best-known works *Gandhivaad ki Shav-pariksha* (Post-mortem on Gandhism). It was an impressive performance for a writer whose first book had been published only seven years previously, and even more creditable for one who had been released from prison in 1938 after serving seven years of a life sentence. Yashpal's creative spirit, cramped by the constraints of his detention—for his role in the revolutionary movement to oust the British from India—was clearly ready to spread its wings. *Viplava*, the pioneering Hindi political monthly journal that he launched with his wife Prakashvati within months after his release, received an unprecedented welcome.

Up till the writing of *Divya*, all of Yashpal's published work had dealt with contemporary social, economic and political issues. The literature of social reform and social protest in Hindi had found a worthy advocate in the author, who wielded a sledgehammer when writing about the exploited and the economically deprived. Therefore, when Yashpal began writing *Divya*, one of his motives may well have been to write about a different world, that of the remote past, a world away from the one he was familiar with. Although the world he had chosen to write about was perhaps not greatly different from the society in which he lived in terms of conflict, strife and oppression, in its portrayal he was free to exercise his imagination, and not simply to limit himself to the realities of contemporary society.

Yashpal was fascinated by that period in the history of ancient India known as the Classical Age. In each of his sixteen collections of short stories, there is at least one tale about that era, in a language and style similar to that of *Divya*. Yashpal's novel based on historical imaginings, *Amita* (1956) is about Ashoka the Great's conquest of Kalinga, circa 260 BC, the conqueror's change of heart and his subsequent conversion to Buddhism. The novella *Apsara ka Shap* (1965), a retelling of Kalidasa's *Abhijnana Shakuntalam*, is a tale from the Epic Age (c. 900–520 BC).

Since its publication more than sixty years ago, *Divya* has had a chequered history, not dissimilar to the tumultuous story of its eponymous heroine. Assertions by Divya such as 'the mistress of a noble family is not a free woman; she is not independent like a disreputable courtesan' outraged many of Yashpal's contemporaries. Others tried to ignore it because they felt that a story about India's so-called Golden Age could not be considered 'literature' if it expounded an unacceptable political ideology. Fortunately, a core of young critics and scholars of successive generations has continued to stand—and even swear—by Divya's yearning for independence when she decides to be a prostitute, so as to be a free woman and have ownership rights over her body. Such thinking is clearly behind the general acknowledgement of the novel's importance and of its impact on Hindi literature.

This translation, too, has a chequered history. Although the final draft was ready by 1988, the manuscript languished with literary agents in North America for several years, including one in Hollywood who, in the wake of the success of various television mini-series on the Orient in the eighties, took an option on *Divya* with a view to marketing it in the media as a similar US production. It also survived suggestions by two publishers to rewrite Divya's story in a less literary language so as to make it more accessible to the average reader.

I acknowledge my indebtedness to Bernard Queenan for his valuable assistance in the work of editing this translation and in retaining the classical flavour of Yashpal's highly literary Hindi. Bernard's versatility, flair for phrasing and mastery of idiomatic English underlined his insistence upon the comprehensibility of the final text, and saved this translation from being—to borrow a phrase from Yashpal's foreword—unforgivably full of errors.

Anand

Preface

THE BASIS FOR *DIVYA* IS HISTORY, BUT HISTORY COLOURED BY imagination. It is an endeavour to portray the motives of man and the dynamics of his world. I have attempted, as a literary experiment, to add realism to a fictional tale played out against a historical background. That this portrayal may contain errors is entirely possible. We do not have extensive knowledge of that period of history, nor can I lay claim to any store of scholarly learning. I, therefore, approached the historical setting with an imagination restrained by an awareness of my shortcomings, but impelled by my fascination with this classical period of the history of India. This may not be acceptable to knowledgeable readers, who may be turned off by any resulting inaccuracies.

We study and analyse our past with the idea of learning about our future. In spite of our failings in the present, we find clues to our capabilities in our past. History does not repeat itself as individual incidents. History means change, but individual and collective striving for survival and progress has always been present in the sequence of change; it is the moving force behind all change.

The study of history analyses the creative urges of an individual and his society as circumstances change. Human beings not only change their existing circumstances, they also strive to create new circumstances. Just as man changes his natural and material conditions, so also he creates his social conditions.

History is not a matter of belief, but of analysis. History is the self-examination by man of his past. Just as the constant flow of fresh water in a river does not change the nature and the name of the river, in the same way a people does not change because of the changes brought about by the process of life and death, and social organizations. From their collective creative forces and their past attempts to alter their circumstances, they learn to resolve the present and find inspiration to create the future.

The most spectacular truth to emerge from efforts made by man to learn from the analysis of history was that man is a creator and not a creation. The world is man's creation. Our own sages realized this when they said: Nothing is greater than man.

Even more powerful than man himself are his beliefs and the social structure he creates. He can be defeated by his beliefs and the social system. Then again it is in the power of man to change it. *Divya* is an attempt to portray that truth, by the power of imagination, playing on the background of a colourful period of our history.

I am painfully conscious of the lack of depth in my knowledge of history. If I had not received generous help from Shri Vasudev Sharan Agarwal, PhD, Director, Lucknow Museum; Shri Moti Chand, PhD, Head of Archaeology, the Prince of Wales Museum, Bombay and Shri Bhagwat Sharan Upadhyaya, this book probably would have been full of unforgivable errors. I am also obliged to Bhadant Bhodhanand, senior monk of the Buddha Vihar in Lucknow, through whose kindness I was able to learn about the religious practices of Buddhism.

A visit to the caves of Ajanta and Ellora was especially helpful in understanding the dress, mannerisms and the intellectual climate of the Buddhist period in our history. Art lovers of the world will forever be indebted to the artists and sculptors of Ajanta and Ellora, but I am further indebted to my friend, Dr Prem Lal Sah, for the opportunity of studying this artwork. For several years I had been planning to visit these caves, but I had felt discouraged and reluctant because of the difficult conditions of the times. The good Doctor dragged me along to see them, and this was the catalyst that gave final shape to the ideas in my mind.

I am most grateful to the source of my inspirations, my readership, without whom no art or literature can be created.

To preserve the atmosphere of classical times, it has been necessary to use some unusual words and verbal forms. The meanings of these words are explained in footnotes, and may add to the reader's comprehension.

19 May 1945   Yashpal

The Festival of Spring

DEVI MALLIKA, THE COURT DANCER AND LAUREATE OF ART, STRICKEN with grief at the sudden death of her grown-up daughter, Ruchira, withdrew from art and society. For a long time she led the life of a recluse. The town of Sagal,[1] sharing Mallika's pain, remained dismal and gloomy, wearing the appearance of a place plunged in darkness. In those dark days, only her steadfast devotion to Saraswati, the goddess of dance and music, sustained Devi Mallika through her suffering. At last, after nearly two years, on the night of the full moon in the month of Chaitra she resolved to appear before the public.

Awaiting the appointed hour, in much the same way as the waves rose in the water of Pushkarni—the broad and beautiful lake of Sagal—the crowd of people swelled on its bank long before sunset.

In the surging throng of men and women, the pavilion erected for the festival appeared like an island surrounded by the swollen waters of a stream in the rainy season. The marquee was bedecked with spires, plantain stalks, archways and festoons of newly sprouted mango leaves and garlands of flowers. The air was heavy with the scent of blossoms and incense. Militiamen in their tall helmets, with shields on their backs and lances in their hands, stood on duty around the marquee thronged by the enthusiastic crowd as well as inside, where seats had been reserved for the members of the Republican Council, feudatory chiefs, nobles, prominent merchants, leading citizens and ladies of the noble families.

[1] Later known as Sialkot.

As the sun sank below the horizon, the gentry made their way towards the marquee through the throngs of people teeming the roads lined with guards. They moved along on chariots drawn by powerful horses, on palanquins shouldered by nimble-footed bearers in colourful livery and on horseback. As the members of the Council and the gentry entered the theatre, before being ushered to their seats, their arrival was heralded first by trumpets and then their names along with the names of their clans and their status were announced. The chariots and palanquins, emptied of their occupants at the gate, were taken by fan-bearing slaves and personal attendants towards the southern part of the arena, where they were parked in orderly rows.

The nobility were dressed according to their family status and in keeping with the festive occasion. Brahmin men wore red silk turbans embroidered with gold threads, with crescent marks in sandalwood paste glistening on their foreheads. Their heads were clean-shaven and around their necks they wore strings of black rudraksh beads and pearl necklaces. From beneath the silken shawls cascading from their shoulders peeped the yellow sacred thread of their caste. Their starched, milk-white dhotis reached the feet, brushing their sandals.

The soldierly Kshatriyas were in brilliant white costumes that were embroidered with gold thread. Under their aquiline noses their moustaches pointed upwards, like the tails of scorpions. They wore ornaments studded with diamonds in their ears, round their necks and on their arms and wrists. The upper part of their body, from the broad chest down to the narrow waist, was clad in close-fitting garments. From waist to knees, they wore dhotis, while the lower parts of their legs and feet were encased in thonged sandals. The swords

that hung from their waists had diamond-studded hilts.
The merchants were dressed in expensive but rather shabby
clothes. The members of the Republican Council were in
saffron-coloured gowns. Some of the Greek nobles had on
plumed hats, with flowing, knee-length woollen gowns over
loose trousers. On their feet they wore slippers. Others had
adopted the Aryan dress.

The women of the nobility were dressed exquisitely. In
their hair, set in different styles with the help of pearl strings,
they wore crescent-shaped coronets of flowers, while *chandrika*[1]
ornaments, necklaces, garlands, bracelets, bangles and rings
bedecked their bodies. Under the flimsy stoles thrown over
their shoulders, their tight bodices stretched over the swell
of full-rounded breasts. Firm breasts matched firm hips
accentuated by three strings of diamonds, tied to the shining
navel-stud and encircling the waist. They moved to the tinkling
of tiny bells strung together by girdles around their waists.
Their saris spread out at the back like the tail feathers of
peacocks, brushing the carpet as the women walked, and
hiding from view their feet painted with red *alakta*[2] paste
and covered with ornaments. The air around them was heavy
with the fragrance of different flowers. Nearly all the Greek
women wore the Aryan dress.

Soon the Chaitra sky lit up with the light of the moon.
The light of torches fell on all sides of the arena and along the
path. The illustrious Mithrodus, who had served as Commander-
in-Chief during the reign of the righteous Greek king, Milinda,
and had afterwards accepted the office of the President of
the Republic of Madra, took his seat. Festive music and songs

[1] Ornament in circular and semi circular shape.
[2] Red dye used by women to paint their feet.

began. A herald, poised on the steps of the stage, announced the arrival of Devi Mallika, the Court Dancer, Light of the Town and Laureate of Art.

The concourse swayed in enthusiasm at this announcement like the sea when a strong wind blows. People craned their necks towards the western entrance. An escort of torch-bearers on horseback was followed by chariots, which in turn were followed by more mounted torch-bearers. Soon the chariots approached the pavilion, passing through the turbulent stream of people. A storm of cheers greeted the arrival of Devi Mallika. Flowers and garlands were showered on her chariot, some of which fell to the ground after barely touching its sides, while others added to the heap already formed inside. With bowed head and folded hands, eyes filled with gratitude and a smile playing on her lips, she acknowledged the greeting of the people surging on all sides as far as the eye could see. When she entered the marquee and walked towards her place of honour near the President, she acknowledged the salutations of the dignitaries. In the wake of her chariot came six more chariots, carrying the troupe of her prize pupils who were to take part in the dancing competition.

Once again the herald blew a fanfare. The festive music ceased and the kettledrums began to roll. The dance and music events were to be preceded by a contest in martial arts for young men who had returned from Taxila and Magadh, after completing their education in the scriptures and in the art of warfare. It was on the basis of their performance in this contest that young men from noble families were to be selected for posts in the army of the Republic.

The names of the contestants were announced:

'Vinay Sharma, grandson of Mahapandit Dev Sharma, Chief Justice of the Republic; Indradeep, son of Sarvarth, the feudatory chief; Vasudhir, son of Acharya Pravardhan, Chairman of the Republican Council; Sakrid, son of Kartavir, Election Officer to the Council; Vrishnesh, son of Samarthak, the merchant; and Prithusen, son of Prestha, the business magnate.'

The six young men stepped on to the platform with quivers filled with arrows on their shoulders, swords hanging from their waistbands ánd lances held upright in their hands. They wore breastplates and helmets.

One by one, they went up to the aged Mithrodus, saluted him, with bowed heads and swords held before the face, proclaiming, 'I, resident of the town of Sagal in the Republic of Madra, having completed my education in the scriptures and the arts of warfare do hereby offer my services to the Republic. May the Republic test my ability and grant me whatever military rank I may be considered suitable for.'

The President commanded the young men to prepare for a contest of marksmanship. Arrows were drawn in the taut bows. At being signalled a soldier standing nearby began to toss balls of various colours high in the air. The spectators held their breath in suspense, as they watched the arrows strike the targets or stray off into the darkness. The balls had to be hit while in the air. The President and the judges watched intently keeping a tally of the balls each young man hit. Thereafter, the President raised his hand to indicate the end of the archery contest.

The President then ordered the young men to take off their breastplates and arm themselves with a weapon of their choice. Indradeep and Vinay Sharma picked lances while the others chose swords.

'Each warrior,' declared the President, 'shall regard the others as aggressors, and while defending himself against them attack them too. Care should be taken to ensure that the person attacked is not seriously injured. No one should play foul or be partial to anyone. Both these practices are culpable offences under the law of the Republic.'

The President then waved the *uttariya*[1] covering his shoulder to signal the beginning of the contest. Weapons flashed like lightning. The six young men, standing apart from one another, were ready to attack. Their bodies poised, taut like bows, they clenched their fists and bared their teeth like tigers. Each kept his gaze trained on the others. Their weapons for a moment emitted flashes of light under the awning and, like the trembling flame of a lamp came to rest again in their hands. With bated breath and eyes riveted on the young men, the vast multitude of people eagerly watched every move in the combat. Time and again the warriors would charge at their adversaries, sending a chill through the audience. Positions would change and the contestants would stand trembling like blades of grass under a soft breeze. Perspiration ran down their taut necks, bare arms, hairy chests and broad backs. Here and there, streaks of blood mingled with sweat appeared on their bodies. It seemed as though their bodies had been painted with ochre.

At a signal from the President, the herald blew out his trumpet to announce the end of the contest. The young men lined up before the President for appraisal. Both Sakrid and Prithusen had only two streaks of blood on their bodies, Vrishnesh had three; the remaining young were marked with four streaks of blood.

After consulting other members of the Council, the President declared, 'May the members of the Council and those present listen to what I have to say. Sakrid and Prithusen

---

[1] Large scarf worn over shoulders, and by women over the head; similar to Spanish mantilla.

have distinguished themselves in the use of weapons. Prithusen would have won the first place, had he not wasted much of his energy hitting aimlessly on his left side. Because of this lack, the honour of being the best swordsman goes to Sakrid.'

Then pointing to a coronet of green leaves interwoven with white flowers, the President said, 'We shall now start the music and dance contest. The girl who, among the pupils of Devi Mallika, wins the title of Daughter of Saraswati, shall have the honour of crowning the best swordsman with this coronet.'

The herald sounded the trumpet. There was a shout of joy from the spectators. The young men paid their obeisance before climbing down the steps of the platform. Prithusen, however, did not move.

Holding his sword straight in front of his face and bowing his head a little, he said, 'I, Prithusen, son of Prestha, the merchant, seek your permission to say something.'

The President looked at him curiously.

Prithusen continued, 'With Your Honour's permission, I beg to submit that I did not waste my energy in aimless backhand blows. I was fighting not five enemies, but six; the sixth being the plantain tree. If you permit, sir, I shall prove it.'

And so saying, he moved towards the left side of the arena, straight to the pillar against which the plantain tree stood. Doing so he struck at it with all his might. The severed pieces of the tree fell in a heap.

There was a gasp of admiration from the audience, impressed by his dexterity and unique swordsmanship.

Bowing before the President, Prithusen said in great humility, 'Sir, I have overpowered that enemy too. I would now pray for Your Honour's judgement.'

The President, too, was impressed by this amazing display. He got up and, placing his hand on Prithusen's shoulder, said, 'I erred in my previous judgement. It is Prithusen who is the outstanding swordsman of Sagal.'

'Yes, yes . . . this is as it should be,' uttered the members of the Council, nodding assent.

The spectators were thrilled.

However, the Chairman of the Council, Acharya Pravardhan, stood up to object, 'Sir, I would request the members of the Council to give this matter serious thought. Can a judgement, once given by the President, be reversed?'

The members of the Council, the nobles and other spectators, struck dumb with surprise, looked at the Acharya.

Before resuming his seat, the President raised his hand again and said to the audience, 'Members of the Republican Council, honourable lords of the nobility and citizens of Sagal, I ask you to reflect on the objections raised by Mahapandit Acharya Pravardhan, Chairman of the Council. I have admitted my error of judgement. In my old age my eyesight is not what it used to be. It is not proper that injustice should be done to a young man on account of my failing eyesight. If the Republic has faith in me, I should be permitted to rectify my mistake.'

The members of the Council looked at each other while the crowd looked at the nobles. The President remained standing on the platform.

Addressing the audience once again, he said, 'I would like the Council to give its decision in the matter. Shall I take it that the Council will give me a chance to rectify my mistake?'

Noticing that many people nodded their heads in agreement, the President went on, 'I, Mithrodus, President of the Republic of Madra, do hereby accept the rectification in the judgement given by me as the Commander-in-Chief. If any honourable member has any objection, he may speak up.'

He then resumed his seat. A hush fell over the Council, as an indistinct hum arose from the audience, indicating approval of the President's action.

Once again the trumpet rang out, and the sound of numerous musical instruments—the lute, veena,[1] flute, kettledrums, cymbals and tambourine—filled the air; the dance and music performances were about to begin. When the instruments were tuned, Mallika, surrounded by her large troupe of pupils, looking resplendent like the moon among the stars, sang the prelude in a voice that would have been the envy of a nightingale. As the prelude came to an end, her pupils joined in, and the marquee resounded with their song. Devi Mallika conducted their choral cadence with arms as graceful as lotus stems. The crowd seemed borne aloft on the waves of music. Even when the raga came to an end, the crowd sat silent and transfixed like Sheshnaag, the thousand-headed serpent.

The orchestra started to play the *shataji* raga. At a sign from Mallika, Madulika began to sing. She was followed by Kusumsena, Divya and Vasumitra the dancer, accompanied by her group. The audience sat on in quiet, collective enchantment.

Devi Mallika rose from her seat, and in a voice ringing with gratitude, said, 'With the permission of the distinguished and appreciative audience, we would now like to end the music event and move on to the dance contest.'

Released from the spell cast by the music, the audience breathed more easily. The torches had dimmed, but the people were so lost in the music that they did not notice the failing

[1] Stringed musical instrument, similar to a sitar.

light. The torch-bearers found time to replenish the oil and the
stage was again filled with bright light. The instruments broke
into a different tune. Flanked on both sides by her pupils,
Mallika stepped to the front of the stage. The eyes of the
spectators were riveted on her. She started her recital with the
raas[1] dance. It seemed as though a constellation of stars had
begun to swirl. The next dance was of an allegorical nature,
with Mallika as Indra, the Lord of Rain, and her pupils enacting
the role of the rain-thirsty earth, the plants and the living
creatures of the world.

The pupils prayed for rain by adopting different dance
postures, making their Lord the centre of their devotion. In
the beginning Indra remained unmoved. But soon, their
supplications enhanced by their grace and beauty, aroused such
irresistible compassion that Indra relented and burst into rain
showers. Mother Earth and her children were satiated. The
spectators, surrendering their senses to the magical spell of
art, sat with their mouths open, silent and still.

After a brief interval, during which the audience relaxed a
little, Madulika presented a dance titled 'The Maiden Keeping
her Tryst', which she had specially prepared for the occasion.
This was followed by Kusumsena's rendering of 'Urvashi's Love
Plaint' and finally Divya stepped forward to present 'The
Swan's Surrender'. Since a fortnight, Devi Mallika had been
preparing Divya for the dance, while training the musicians in
the intricate modulations of the musical accompaniments.

Divya was dressed in a white costume resembling the
plumage of a swan. Her diaphanous stole hung on her soft,
shapely arms, like the wings of *marali*, the swan maiden.

---

[1] Circular dance, associated with Lord Krishna.

Her searching eyes looked anxious and perplexed. Thrilled at her beloved's presence, the marali, flapping her wings in impetuous enthusiasm, rushed in the direction of the swan's call. But hardly had she gone a few steps when she got caught in the net of a hunter.

The swan continued to call. Each note made the imprisoned marali restless and desperate. She struggled with all her might to free herself. But despair and helplessness were her only rewards. Still she struggled, in a bid to throw off her bindings. But to no avail. The call of the swan, once so thrilling and provocative, now became a source of intense suffering to her. She would feebly raise her head every time the call was heard, and merely flutter her wings in helplessness.

The swan then appeared on the stage, played by Devi Mallika herself. Ignoring the net in which the marali was held, the male glided into it, getting trapped. The marali was overwhelmed. In the ecstatic moment of reunion, they forgot their captivity in sweet abandon. A brood of young swans, born of this union, flew out in different directions.

The sky rang with the enthusiastic applause of the audience. The roof of the marquee shook and the flames of the torches trembled. From among the audience, a Buddhist monk, dressed in russet robes, stood up with his hand raised and cried, 'May the wise ones see and understand. Caught in the throes of maya, the individual has a false sense of happiness.'

Devi Mallika stood near her seat acknowledging the ovation of the audience. She looked at the bhikshu without much interest. The members of the Council, the distinguished guests and others, all turned their eyes towards him.

In the ensuing silence, a loud voice was heard, 'Even when the individual has a false sense of sorrow, the eternal activity of life continues in much the same way. Renunciation is nothing but self-deception by the timid. Life moves on; this is the irrevocable and indubitable truth.'

The arena echoed with laughter. The person who had thus replied was none other than young Marish, the master sculptor of Sagal—son of the trader Pushyakant—who had been censured for his public profession of atheistic and immoral views.

After consultation with Devi Mallika and the Council, the President awarded the title of Daughter of Saraswati to Divya, the great-granddaughter of the Chief Justice of the Republic. In turn, Divya presented the flower coronet to young Prithusen, the best swordsman. Both the prizewinners, in their distinctive costumes, looked the embodiment of their respective arts.

The fanfare was sounded to signal the end of the festival. Though it was nearing midnight, the spectators were not tired and showed no intention of moving away. In the clear, star-spangled Chaitra sky, the full moon floated. A crowd of enthusiastic spectators blocked the path reserved for Devi Mallika and the contestants. It was with great difficulty that the state officers managed to clear the way.

It was a custom in Sagal for young men of the nobility to carry to her home, the flower-bedecked palanquin of the girl honoured as the Daughter of Saraswati. Divya stepped shyly into the palanquin after receiving the blessings of her paternal great-grandfather, as also of her uncles and other relatives. The young nobles rushed towards the palanquin, whose four poles had room for only sixteen bearers.

Prithusen had already put his shoulder to the front pole of the palanquin, when Vasudhir pushed him from behind, wanting to take his place. But Prithusen refused to move.

At this, Rudradhir, son of Acharya Pravardhan and older than Vasudhir, shouted, 'The son of a slave has no right to put his shoulder to the palanquin along with the young men of noble birth.'

Infuriated, Prithusen drew his sword and held it ready, 'My sword will determine my right,' he cried. Many swords flashed out of their scabbards on all sides.

Alarmed by the uproar, a number of dignitaries intervened, and disorder and bloodshed were averted. The palanquin of the Daughter of Saraswati, carried on the shoulders of the young nobles, moved towards the town, followed by Devi Mallika's chariot. The palanquin went rocking over the heads of thousands of cheering people like a boat moving on the waves of the sea.

Trembling with anger like a wounded tiger, Prithusen remained standing in the limpid moonlight. The anger raging in his heart made him restless and agitated. The accident of birth! Is that a crime? . . . If so, how can it be set right? No power on earth, neither the force of arms nor the power of wealth or knowledge, can alter the status of one's birth. Should man seek revenge from the gods for the injustice of his birth, or from those who, for their own selfish ends, have instituted the unfair law? Seething with hatred and not finding an outlet for his feelings of revenge, Prithusen clenched his teeth and set out in the direction of his palace, avoiding the crowd.

The Palace of the Chief Justice

HUMANITY IS LIKE A FOREST ON THE EDGE OF THE RIVER OF TIME;
inundations enrich the soil of a forest. Similarly the floods of
change, which, from time to time, swept the city state of Sagal,
left behind rich layers of thought and experience. In this little
forest of Sagal, the aged scholar Dev Sharma, Chief Justice of
the Republic, stood like a great banyan tree for many years.
Every hair on his head had turned white. With the passage of
time, the vigour in his body dried up, but his faculties, fed by
more than a hundred years of living, were still active and alert.

The eminent scholar was still young when the powerful
Greek king Milinda, at the head of a mighty army, invaded the
kingdom of Madra—then ruled by the Paurav dynasty—and
established his own imperial rule in its place. On the death
of Vagish Sharma, who had held the office of the Chief Justice
during the reign of the Paurav dynasty, Milinda appointed his
son, Dev Sharma—gifted with rare talent and wisdom—to
the same post. For many years, Dev Sharma administered justice,
giving to the traditional policies and organization of a caste
society, the flavour of a Greek way of life. When the mighty
King Milinda embraced the Buddhist faith, justice in the
state became charged with humanism and a feeling of universal
compassion. It was during Dev Sharma's lifetime that the
righteous King Milinda gave up his throne, renounced the world
and took to the path of Nirvana. As Milinda was childless, a
republican state of the dynastic order was founded and in the

new regime, Dev Sharma continued to discharge his office in accordance with the new concepts of justice.

Dev Sharma had three sons by his three wives. Of these, one died. From the other two sons he had four grandsons. The wife of one of these grandsons, the eldest, gave birth to a baby girl. The birth of a girl child in the family, already well provided with sons and grandsons, occasioned great joy, just like the appearance of the half moon, on the eve of a waxing lunar month, holds out the promise of resplendent moonlight, even as the glow of the setting sun still pervades the sky. She was given the name of Divya, the radiant dawn, showing the faith that people had in her bright future and, like the crescent moon, her effulgence only increased with the passage of time.

As ill luck would have it, Divya's grandfather and both her parents succumbed to a fatal disease and met with untimely deaths. The girl was left to the tender affection and caring of her great-grandfather and thus became the apple of his eyes.

The stately palace of the Chief Justice, surrounded by ramparts and gardens and looked after by a large retinue of servants and maidservants, was a centre of learning and culture. In its meeting halls, votaries of the caste system, Greek philosophers and Buddhist monks freely discussed and argued on matters of all kinds, both to quell their doubts and for the sheer joy of debating.

Here, the love of knowledge and discussion was far greater than addiction to wine or women. The guests, lost in argument, would be oblivious to the dark and tawny-complexioned slave-girls who stood before them, holding on silver trays, crystal cups brimming with the famous *kapisha* wine. Even the parrots and the mynahs of the household, in their silver or copper cages hung from the arched doorways in different chambers of the palace, would in that atmosphere of learning mimic the speakers by uttering maxims, aphorisms, precepts and the like. Sometimes, to shake off their drowsiness, one of them would cry out a sutra from the Vedas, or some such religious or philosophical saying.

In the house of the Chief Justice all subjects were discussed: religious rituals, text of the scriptures, jurisprudence, logic, law, the Vedic concept of 'the one without a second'. There was room here for investigating the absolute truth beyond the world of appearances, as enunciated by the Greek philosopher Plato, and the cycle of birth after birth, as preached by the Buddha. The doors of the house were open even to the atheist Marish, who held in contempt the Vedantic concept of salvation and of Nirvana. Marish had been censured and denounced both by the Brahmins and the votaries of the Buddhist faith for his views. He believed that there was no world beyond the visible one, regarded the palpable world as the true one and dismissed the belief that reward for one's deeds awaited one in the next life. Even though twice punished by the Chief Justice under the law of the state, Marish continued to be welcome in the palace.

After his return from Taxila, where he had gone to study sculpture, Marish was given the assignment of engraving scenes from the life of the Buddha on the façade of the main gate of the Milinda monastery. One day, however, he suddenly declared that there were no grounds to believe in the previous incarnations of the Buddha, and refused to engrave the scenes any further, thereby breaking the agreement entered into with the head of the monastery. Next he was asked to engrave scenes demonstrating the dictum that sensual attachments were false and illusory. Marish did not agree to do that either. Thereupon, the head of the monastery lodged a complaint against him, accusing him of having broken his contract. The Chief Justice punished Marish with a fine. The same evening, however, he invited Marish to his house and seated him next to himself.

The Chief Justice was a man with a reflective bent of mind, hence Marish was not treated with disrespect in his house. The eminent scholar was not overzealous in regarding any system of thought as completely true, nor did he declare any world view to be totally false. He held the liberal view, which is expressed in a precept of the Vedas: 'The wise ones say the same thing in many different ways.'

Having been brought up in such an atmosphere, Divya was imbued with the spirit of learning, art and culture, much as a lotus contains moisture within itself, even though it may not be steeped in water. Her main interest lay in music and dancing; her knowledge more in the form of feeling than of words. However, living in close proximity with her aged great-grandfather, she was not ignorant of intellectual issues.

Divya had been delayed for some time at the Festival of Spring on the previous night, so she emerged from her bedroom a little later the next morning. She went about her work in an unhurried manner, in delightful lassitude. By midday, the consciousness grew that a large number of guests would come in the evening to congratulate her. The very thought of the approaching evening thrilled her.

Divya recalled that on the previous night, the Acharya's son, Rudradhir, had drawn his sword for the honour of being one of the bearers of her palanquin. Rudradhir had often been seen in the reception room of the palace, or at the evening

gatherings. He always found the presence of Marish insufferable
and would inject his conversation with bitterness. Her great-
grandfather shut his eyes to this. Her grand-uncle, Vishnu
Sharma, disgusted with Marish's impertinence, would remain
silent, and a smile of amusement would begin to play on the
face of her uncle, Prabuddha Sharma. In his arrogant
indifference, Marish would just laugh. Divya was both annoyed
and curious at the antagonism between Rudradhir and Marish.

Rudradhir had been married two years earlier, but had
later developed an infatuation for Divya. Though she held the
Acharya's family in great regard, Divya was not pleased at
the prospect of becoming a mere second wife. Absorbed in
such reflections, she waited for the evening.

A maidservant approached her and said, 'Grandsire has
asked for you, my lady.' When Divya went to meet her great-
grandfather the old sage fondly put his hand on Divya's head
and said, 'Shrambak, the doorkeeper, informs me that someone
has come to meet me in a chariot, and is presently waiting at
the gate. I am somewhat tired after the strain of working late
into the night. Can you go and receive this visitor and enquire
from him the purpose of his visit?'

Divya proceeded directly to the reception room, followed
by a maidservant carrying the welcome offerings and *tambool*[1]
on a silver platter. A tall, well-built Kshatriya youth, fair-
complexioned like a Greek noble, but with eyes dark like
those of a Brahmin, entered through the main gate, looking
solemn and serious. He was dressed rather carelessly in expensive
silken clothes. Divya did not take long to recognize him. He

---

[1] Green beetle leaf eaten with beetle nut.

was none other than Prithusen, the champion swordsman of the previous night's contest.

Divya greeted the youth by holding her palms together and touching her forehead. 'Pray, come in,' she said, and taking the platter from the maidservant's hand, offered it to the visitor, 'Please, Arya, partake of these.'

The visitor, looking distraught, acknowledged the greeting and before accepting the offering, said, 'Gentle lady, I am Prithusen, son of Prestha, the merchant. I have come to beg for justice at the hands of the Chief Justice.'

From a cage hanging in the entrance of the reception room, a mynah cried out, 'Men of firm resolve never stray from the path of justice!'

The hospitable smile on Divya's face broadened into laughter at the words of the garrulous bird. 'Pray, do partake of the offering,' she said reassuringly to the visitor. 'You will not have to return disappointed from the House of Justice. Even the unlettered mynah bears testimony to this.'

'I have complete faith in the assurance given by you,' said Prithusen in a voice tinged with humility. Sitting down on a seat indicated by Divya, he took the betel nut from the platter.

'I hope you will not mind, but my great-grandfather's health does not permit him to see you at present,' Divya said, taking a seat near him.

Prithusen expressed concern for the health of the aged Chief Justice and got up in confusion. He again expressed his satisfaction at the assurance given by the Chief Justice's great-granddaughter—that justice would not be denied to him. Asking for permission to visit again, he took his leave. As he was about to go, Divya's grand-uncle, Pandit Vishnu Sharma, and her uncle Prabuddha Sharma entered the reception room. Both looked grave and were deep in conversation.

Prabuddha Sharma greeted the visitor, saying, 'Prabuddha Sharma offers his salutations.'

Vishnu Sharma, on the other hand, threw a sidelong glance at Prabuddha Sharma, and gave the minimum salutation. 'Greetings to the visitor,' he said, and turned away.

Prithusen had already paid his respects. Seeing that the elderly gentlemen looked preoccupied, and not wishing to intrude, he simply acknowledged their greetings and left.

'You honoured the son of a slave-charioteer with an offering?' Vishnu Sharma said, addressing Divya. 'You do not deserve to be a Brahmin but a disciple of the Buddha like your uncle Prabuddha Sharma.'

Divya was crestfallen at the reproachful remark of her grand-uncle, but Prabuddha Sharma retorted to the sarcasm. 'Father, Prithusen's father was at one time a slave. Today he is the owner of many slaves. Besides, he is the biggest merchant of Sagal and chief adviser to the President of the Republic. Who is there that can ignore him in Sagal? And Father, Prithusen carries with him not a fan, as slaves do, but a sword! What do you say, Divya? I think he fully deserved to be honoured, dear.'

Vishnu Sharma was agitated. 'He deserves to be honoured, does he? Simply because he has accumulated wealth? It is because you move in the company of Buddhist monks and the Greeks, because of this pride in wealth,' Vishnu Sharma's voice grew sharp, 'that this son of a slave had the audacity, last night, to compete with the sons of the twice-born Brahmin nobles and to put his shoulder to the palanquin of the Daughter of Saraswati. When Rudradhir tried to prevent him, he pulled out his sword ready to fight. To think that a slave can have the effrontery to draw his sword against a Brahmin! It is such wickedness that reduces the caste system and our dynastic rule to dust.'

'But, Father,' replied Prabuddha Sharma, smiling, 'change comes in the life of man as well as in the status of his dynasty. Even the imperial Mauryas were at one time a family of barbers. Later, the whole of India bowed to them, and the most eminent Brahmin, Chanakya, served as their minister.'

'The earth has been cleansed of that wickedness,' said Vishnu Sharma. 'It was to raise his own worthless position and to degrade the caste system that Ashoka joined the ranks of the tonsured Buddhists. If the deity is more powerful than man, and Brahmins who bear the sacred fire are a part of the deity, then they cannot be on the same footing as Sudras. In the yore when the fire-bearing Brahmin pronounced his curse, sinners were destroyed and the earth was rid of sin. Yesterday, while daring to compete with the sons of the nobility, this son of a slave pulled out his sword. If he had not withdrawn, he would have paid with his blood for his arrogance. This problem has arisen because of lack of understanding on the part of the President of the Republic. This kingdom belongs to the caste dynasty of Madra, not to the Buddhist dharma-chakra[1] of that Greek, Milinda. How dare the low-caste wretches say: "It is by his actions that a man becomes a Brahmin." Only the Creator, who has conferred the divine nature on him, can deprive a Brahmin of participation in His divinity. No mortal can do that. Will these close-shaven Buddhists dislodge Indra, the God of Rain, too from his place, if ever the rains are delayed? Will

[1] The wheel of law. It is a Buddhist emblem of Hindu origin. It resembles a wagon wheel with eight spokes, each representing one of the eight tenets of Buddhist belief. The circle symbolizes the completeness of the Dharma, the spokes represent the eightfold path.

they say: "It is by one's actions that one attains godhood?" Such
heresy will not be tolerated in Sagal any more. We shall pull
out the tongue of the sinner. Very likely, Prithusen came to
seek justice at the hands of grandsire, didn't he . . .?'

'But, Father,' said Prabuddha Sharma, speaking in a tone
of mild amusement, well hidden out of regard for the old
man, 'Just as proof of the deity's existence is not absolute, the
conception of the deity is also a matter of faith and inference.'

'That is the absurd reasoning of the close-shaven Buddhists,'
replied Vishnu Sharma agitatedly. 'What is proof? The utterance
of a sage is proof enough. The word of one who knows is proof
for one who does not know. The proof of a Brahmin's authority
lies in his power.' Then, pointing to the diamond-studded
bracelet on Prabuddha Sharma's arm, he said excitedly, 'Why
wear these ornaments?' He pointed to the uttariya covering
Prabuddha's shoulder and said, 'Why these costly clothes, when
even slaves and Sudras go about wearing such, nay, even costlier
clothes and ornaments? Do these serve today as an indication
of caste, family or authority? If rubies can be had for the
asking, then why wear them on your forehead? If the Sudra
and the slave can also acquire the same rights and privileges as
the twice-born Brahmin, then wherein does greatness of
Brahminism lie? Is the power of the Brahmin's mantra and of
the Kshatriya's sword meant only to serve the Sudra?' Face
flushed with anger, he strode off towards his own chambers.

Embarrassed at the anger of her grand-uncle, Divya stood
gazing at the floral pattern drawn on the floor, twisting a
corner of her dress between her fingers.

'You need not feel depressed, my dear,' said Prabuddha
Sharma reassuringly. 'A guest must be treated with due honour.
Your grand-uncle did not want to greet the son of a slave, but

he too acknowledged his greetings. How could he be indifferent
to the prevalent customs of Madra?'

Touched by her uncle's sympathy, Divya became even more
agitated. She covered her face with her stole, so as to hide her
tears, and stood there with her head bowed.

'Silly girl,' said Prabuddha Sharma, affectionately stroking
her back. 'Why should you feel hurt that your grand-uncle
holds such views? Have you ever seen intellectuals agreeing on
anything in the gatherings arranged by your great-grandfather?
And are they all fools? Will you call Acharya Pravardhan a
fool, or Pandit Ikrid or the venerable Buddhist, Dharma Rakshit,
or Cheebuk or Marish?'

Divya wiped her eyes and said in a faltering voice, 'Yesterday
evening, it was the Council that gave Arya Prithusen the title of
the best swordsman. How am I to blame for that?'

'Of course, you are not to blame,' agreed Prabuddha Sharma
playfully. 'That young man, to have the chance of demonstrating
his regard for you, was ready to shed the blood of Rudradhir,
the Acharya's son. Why shouldn't you respect him? The people
of Madra do not have ungrateful blood in their veins.'

Taking Prabuddha Sharma's sinewy hand tenderly into hers,
Divya said, 'Uncle, was it Prithusen, then? Is my grand-uncle
annoyed with him because of that? The palanquin was high up
and there was a crowd of people, so I couldn't make out.'

'Yes, yes. Let's go in,' he said and putting his arm tenderly
round Divya, moved towards the door, which led to the interior
of the house. 'No wonder. Those who ride in palanquins are
never able to see the bearers. Dear girl, tell the maidservant
to prepare my bath. I perspired greatly on the way and
am covered with dust.'

Divya could not directly go and convey the news to her

great-grandfather about the purpose of Prithusen's visit. Night came, but the Chief Justice, preoccupied with numerous matters, was still surrounded by visitors. The subject kept working in her mind the entire evening. She would begin to ponder on it for a number of reasons, among them the attitude of her grand-uncle Vishnu Sharma, and her own involvement in the incident. She knew that the news of Prithusen's untowardly behaviour must have already reached her great-grandfather, surrounded as he was by numerous guests. More than telling him about Prithusen's visit, she wanted to know his views on the matter.

Divya's anxiety caused her to vacillate. Had she conveyed the news to her grandsire before brooding over it, there would have been no difficulty. But now she felt a certain reticence in broaching the subject; it was not proper to keep quiet about it either. She had assured Prithusen of justice, had given him her word. How could she remain indifferent? She had never paid much attention to the discussions on the subject of justice that went on around her great-grandfather. But now there was no excuse for passivity.

Divya went to her great-grandfather only next day at noon, when she found him alone, resting in his room. The elderly sage was reclining against a pillow on his bed. Stroking his snow-white hair, Divya gave him news of Prithusen's visit, and also casually mentioned the attitude of her grand-uncle, Vishnu Sharma.

With his hand to his forehead, the old man listened to all that she had to say. When Divya fell silent, he looked up, and seeing that she was waiting for a reply, said, 'My child, I believe Devi Mallika has recovered from her grief and is once again devoting herself to her art.'

'Yes, Grandfather,' answered Divya, her eyes resting on his hair. 'Now there is regular training in her palace. She has also taken on a few new pupils.'

'There is nothing more paralysing than grief at the death of one's own child,' said the old man, heaving a deep sigh. 'Which of her pupils does Mallika propose to appoint as her successor? Does any one of them have the same talent as Ruchira? Mallika used to say that you and Ruchira were to her like her own two eyes.'

'I think she will select Madulika . . . but she is not fully satisfied with her yet. Madulika lacks the ease and grace of movement that Devi Mallika has.'

'Yes, you are right, I think. It is asking a great deal of Mallika's successor to have the same talents as she has. Nature does not always manifest itself in the same way. In her time, Mallika even excelled her teacher, Indira. People completely forgot Indira . . .'

Divya was feeling restless. Her great-grandfather had not paid any attention to the question that she had, with difficulty, put before him. 'Grandfather, isn't it true that all citizens are equal in the eyes of the law?'

Removing his hand from his forehead and placing it on Divya's head, he said in an amused tone, 'Child, why must you bother about these complicated things when you have your garland-weaving, painting and music to occupy you?' But then his voice changed, 'Divya, there was one kind of justice during the reign of King Paurav and a different kind in the days of the victorious King Milinda, and now we have yet another one in the kingdom of the caste dynasty.' After a slight pause he continued, 'Justice is not an independent and self-existent entity. It is a manifestation of the aspirations of a society and the system prevailing in that society. Having administered justice for such a long time, I have come to the conclusion that justice is subservient to the ruler. During the days of my father, may his memory be revered, the verdicts of the Paurav dynasty and of its nobility, and the system that protected their rights and privileges, represented justice. In the days of the victorious King Milinda, justice meant divesting the Pauravas of all their power and protecting the rights of King Milinda and his nobles. At that time, in the kingdom of Madra, the Buddhist tenets constituted justice and animal sacrifice became a crime. Under the present rule of the caste dynasty of Madra, the power of the noble families forms the basis of legislation. The caste system once again is being given the place of honour.'

'But, Grandfather,' said Divya, not getting any reply to her question, 'the family of Prestha has been emancipated from slavery. Prithusen has been honoured by the Republic itself.'

Glancing at the mynah in the cage hanging by the door, the aged Chief Justice said, in a voice heavy with anxiety, 'You are quite right, my dear. Therein lies the intricacy of the problem. Prestha has been emancipated. Prithusen has been honoured by the Republic, or he would never have come to raise the question of justice. Those young colts who were snatched by Prestha from their mothers and sold in the market, or those slaves in whom he trades, do not raise the question of justice. Dear girl, it is not difficult to satisfy the demand for justice made by one individual. Young Prithusen can try to protect his rights with the power of his sword. But the question is not only of his honour or of his rights. The problem is a far more intricate one. He has applied to the Council for a commission in the army and he deserves it too. His father is ambitious; he can spend a thousand gold pieces. If the law court grants him the same rights and privileges as are enjoyed by the high-caste members of the nobility, then he automatically becomes entitled to a commission in the army. And if the Council grants him the right of a commissioned rank in the army, he automatically becomes entitled to the rights and privileges of the high-caste nobility.'

The Chief Justice's gaze was still on the bird in the cage, 'For Prithusen to secure a commission means his stepping onto the first rung on the ladder of nobility. If every caste can acquire the status and the rights of noblemen, then there will be no authority left with the nobility. Had the Republic consisted only of the twice-born Brahmins, the situation would have been different, but the Republic is not a homogeneous society. It now consists of Greek and many Kshatriya and Vaishya nobles who have been influenced by Buddhist faith and in whose eyes, therefore, purity of caste and caste privileges have no significance. Nevertheless, they are jealous of the power of the caste nobility. That is why the Chairman of the Republican Council has been shelving the issue all along in the Council. The question before the law courts is a challenge to the basic structure of society.'

'But, Grandfather,' said Divya, discouraged by this answer, 'what about the principle in the law courts of the Republic of Madra, of the lion and the deer drinking together at the same stream?'

A smile lit up her great-grandfather's face with its snow-white beard and moustache. 'The metaphor of the lion and the deer drinking together is needed to inspire respect for the law,' he said. 'The lion and the deer can drink together only if they are subservient to someone else. That person is free who can force them to drink from the same watering hole, and that ability and desire of his, in itself, forms the basis of law. The atheist Marish was punished by the law for having broken his pledge to engrave scenes from the Buddha's previous incarnations. It was necessary to do so to safeguard the system. But would it have been proper for Marish to act against the dictates of his conscience? Daughter, justice can have many forms.'

Her great-grandfather kept stroking Divya's hair, but in her vexed state of mind, this show of affection appeared futile and even irksome to her.

Almost every evening, Divya was present at the gatherings in the garden of the palace, which were attended by her great-grandfather, her uncles and the ladies of the house. The elderly guests would compliment her for her exquisite mastery over art. The young men and women of the nobility would also praise her lavishly. This gave her fresh courage and a sense of satisfaction.

Rudradhir never showered her with praises. Divya was quite satisfied that it should be so. To receive compliments from him or to acknowledge them made her feel uncomfortable. The same could be said about Marish too.

One day Marish said something rather strange: 'Your art is only the blossoming forth of your power of attraction, which is the primeval force of creation in woman.' These words from the cynic Marish, who had been censured for encouraging immorality and wickedness, the tone of his voice and the expression in his eyes, had sent a shiver through her body.

Divya would often remember what Marish had said. Those words were charged with meaning. She would try to unravel their significance, the suggestion that lay hidden in them. There was sweetness in the words, as also a sense of pride, hope and enthusiasm, but whenever that crazy young man, who had been censured and denounced, was nearby, she felt unsure and apprehensive. She would say to herself: 'The best swordsman, Prithusen, had not expressed any opinion about my art . . . That he should have drawn his sword to lend a shoulder to my palanquin . . . that itself was an expression of opinion.'

Even before Divya's birth, her mother's health had been frail. The day Divya was born, she was given a wet nurse, who had an infant of her own clinging to her milk-heavy breasts. The people in the palace, forgetting the nurse's real name, began calling her 'Dhata', meaning the nurse of the newborn baby. The nurse too, proudly accepted the name and thought of herself as taking the place of the child's mother. Divya's mother, on the other hand, looking upon the wet nurse's child as the 'shadow' of her own daughter, gave her the name of 'Chhaya', and this name struck.

As she was the only girl born in the family after three generations, Divya was everyone's favourite. She was from the bloodline of the eldest son and the eldest grandson and the first great-granddaughter of the Chief Justice, and was, therefore, the recipient of special love and affection from the members of the family. She lived with her grandmother and her nurse in the same part of the palace as the Chief Justice, but the living quarters of the other elders too were always open to her. Like a butterfly she flitted about in the garden, followed by Chhaya and the nurse. Up to the age of ten, Chhaya was merely Divya's playmate. Thereafter, she began to be assigned simple tasks, now in one part of the palace, then in another.

Just as when the crescent moon slowly waxes and attains its full form in the sky, its reflection in a shallow pond below waxes with it, in the same way did Chhaya, Divya's shadow, grow into womanhood alongside Divya. The sky-faring moon goes on its journey at a calm, steady pace, but not so its reflection. The water below gets ruffled by the slightest draft. Chhaya, by serving young couples in the interior of the palace and living in close proximity with them, soon came to understand things that eluded Divya, especially about the growth of her body and its purpose.

One day, Vinay Sharma's wife was enraged to find Chhaya in her son's room at an odd hour of the day. She dismissed her from all household work and yoked her to the task of fetching water from the water tank. Fate proved to be kind, however. Youth bloomed unbridled in her person; her face acquired a new lustre and charm. With the help of Bahul, the chief-slave, Chhaya secured for herself the job of serving wine to the guests in the reception hall. Compared with the interior of the palace, which was infested with dwarfs, factotums, decrepit old guards and jealous maidservants, service in the reception hall was much more attractive. There was variety to it, and freedom too. And above all, Bahul, the chief-slave, looked kindly upon her.

Chhaya sometimes longed to go near the reception hall, but the thought of the Greek women guarding the door, sword in hand, would make her blood freeze. Separation from Bahul made her very restless and she wanted to break her body to pieces by dashing herself against the walls of the palace; to tear her body to shreds by plunging headlong into thorny bushes. For a long time she remained depressed and in the end resigned herself to her plight, regarding it as the will of fate.

Divya came to know that Prithusen was in the house, that he had come to present a petition to the grandsire. Etiquette did not permit her to find out more and her mind was in turmoil from curiosity and indecision. She knew that the grandsire was not unfavourably inclined towards Prithusen, but she was eager to speak to the latter herself. What exactly did she want to tell him? She did not know . . . maybe something in the way of sympathy, consolation.

Everywhere, whether in the palace of her great-grandfather, or at the houses of her acquaintances, at Devi Mallika's or Vasumitra's, at drinking or gambling parties, whenever any mention was made of Prithusen, Divya listened eagerly. Something kept gnawing at her heart all the time. Her mind troubled by uncertainty, Divya became listless and uncommunicative. She could find no satisfaction in anything. Her great-grandmother, Mahadevi, drawing near the end of her life's journey, was, in the light of her beliefs, approaching the other world, and had, to all intent and purpose, turned her face towards it. She had been unable to make up her mind as to which was more preferable, salvation or Nirvana. Therefore, in a confused state she strove hard to win both, by trying to secure the blessings of the cleric-sacrificers, the priests, the sages and the Buddhist bhikshus. Concern for her large family had become a source of annoyance to her.

Dhata drew Mahadevi's attention to Divya's languid and depressed state of mind. Mahadevi felt angry. The girl was of marriageable age, she said, and yet neither the great-grandfather, nor any of the elders were paying any attention to this. She, however, as a remedy to Divya's distraction assigned a number of tasks to keep her occupied, such as preparing different kinds of dishes in the kitchen, weaving special garlands for the guests, and making pictures and drawings. She also ordered Chhaya to work once again as Divya's personal attendant and companion.

One day, Divya and Chhaya sat weaving garlands in an arbour in the inner garden of the palace. Before them lay a mixed heap of flowers. Chhaya's fingers moved nimbly, but her eyes would often rest on Divya's face. Divya sat on a low stool, her eyes downcast and her fingers hardly moving. Throwing the half-woven garland to Chhaya, Divya let out her suppressed vexation. 'I can't do this silly work,' she said and covered her face with her stole.

For a few seconds Chhaya gazed at Divya's face, and then said, 'My lady, the other day I heard Mahadevi say to my mother: "Why don't the elders pay any attention to Divya's age? She is depressed because of her youthful desires, like the birds and beasts in season . . ."'

Divya lowered the stole from her face and said angrily, 'What a shameless creature you are! Have you no modesty? Aunt Amita must have dismissed you from her service because of such brazenness.'

'No, my lady,' said Chhaya, looking boldly into Divya's eyes, her fingers still working on the garland. 'Do you know the fault for which mistress Amita dismissed me? That evening, her husband, Arya Vinay was in the room. He asked me to fetch the vessel of *kadambini* wine. When I brought it to him, he playfully pressed my bosom with his hand. I shrank back. At this, mistress Amita was offended and called me a deceitful hussy; that I was only a maidservant and yet pretended to be modest, like high-born ladies; that I was trying to entice her husband.'

'Enough!' Divya said in disgust, turning her face away. But Chhaya continued undaunted; she was the same age as Divya and had been her childhood friend. 'Mahadevi has instructed Mother that in the evening when Acharya Pravardhan's son Rudradhir comes, you should attend to him. Mistress Amita was telling Mahadevi that Arya Rudradhir is deeply attracted to Divya.'

'Keep quiet, you chatterbox!' exclaimed Divya. Frowning, she rose from the stool and went towards her room. It depressed her to hear such gossip about herself. To quieten her mental turmoil, she lay down on her bed and covered herself with a silken sheet, but Chhaya's words kept ringing in her ears, 'Mahadevi has instructed Mother that you should attend to Arya Rudradhir.'

Divya had often attended on young nobles—twice-born Brahmins and Greek youths. She had greeted Rudradhir too, several times. Arid now, guessing the purpose of these instructions, she grew annoyed. Rudradhir's face and figure appeared before her mind's eye—his luxuriant hair tied with a red cloth interwoven with gold thread, a red mark on his forehead in the midst of a white, sandalwood crescent, a part of his sacred thread peeping from under his shirt, and sword in hand as he tried to prevent Prithusen from putting a shoulder to Divya's palanquin. As she lay deep in thought with her eyes closed, Divya's mind was filled with a sense of fear and revulsion.

She sat up, throwing the silken cover from her. 'Listen, Chhaya, what is the time now?'

Chhaya had followed her mistress to the bedchamber. She was still weaving her garlands, reclining against Divya's bedpost. Her eyes rested on the flowers, but she was lost in her own thoughts. Hearing her name called so abruptly, she roused herself with a start, and looked out of the door. She said, 'It is nearly sunset, my lady. Shall I dress you now?'

'No. Well, yes . . . you may,' Divya replied, absent-mindedly, her eyes half-closed, her chin resting on the palm of her hand.

'My lady, will you be so kind as to permit me to accompany you to the reception hall? I shall carry the offerings,' Chhaya said, an appeal in her eyes.

'You're really shameless,' said Divya, heaving a deep sigh and getting out of bed. 'Go to the doorkeeper and tell him to get the chariot ready.'

Without waiting for the chariot to be brought to the gate, Divya left the interior of the palace and passing by the reception hall, went straight towards the main gate.

'Tell Mahadevi that I am going to Devi Mallika's,' she told Chhaya, as the latter followed her carrying a silken shawl and a few garlands on her arm.

On her way to the main gate, Divya met Taruk, an aged, dim-eyed servant.

'I hope you are in good health, Uncle?' she asked smiling, feeling his intent gaze upon her.

'May you live long, Mistress,' stammered Taruk, his voice breaking with affection, as he recognized Divya. 'May you reign supreme in your father-in-law's house. It is many days since I set eyes on you. In which direction are you going?'

'I am going to Devi Mallika's, Uncle.'

Stepping close to Divya and gazing intently into her face, his eyes feeble with age, Taruk said, 'My little mistress is looking very tired and depressed. Is it because she has kept away from dance and music for a long time?'

Divya did not know what to say. Glancing towards the reception hall she said abruptly, 'Where's Chhaya, I wonder?' Then her eyes fell on Chhaya who stood concealed behind a vine arbour. Bahul, the chief-slave was with her, standing close to her. Turning her eyes away from them, she said, 'Why is the chariot so late in coming, Uncle?'

'Shall I go and find out at the gate, Mistress?'

Without answering or looking behind her, Divya proceeded towards the gate. Chhaya hastened after her and in order to help her mistress onto the chariot, she gathered and held Divya's flowing garments as she climbed in.

The road was uneven and the horses galloped at top speed, the chariot swaying from side to side. 'You must be happy at heart, my lady, that you are going to Devi Mallika's after such a long interval,' Chhaya said, trying to divert Divya from her listlessness. Lost in her own thoughts Divya took Chhaya's words as a link in the chain of her own, and as though talking to herself, said, 'Yes, but I don't know whether he will be there or not.'

'Who, my lady?' asked Chhaya in a tone of intense curiosity, raising her head.

Encouraged by Chhaya's intimacy, Divya replied, 'Prithusen.' Just then her eyes fell on the attendant sitting at the back seat of the chariot. Confused, she somehow managed to complete her sentence, 'Arya Prithusen has submitted a petition through me in my great-grandfather's court. That's what I am going to discuss.' And again Divya lost herself in her train of thoughts.

Devi Mallika was at her toilette, getting ready for the evening's recital when the maidservant came to tell her that the Chief Justice's great-granddaughter had arrived at the gate in her chariot. Beside herself with joy, and impatient like a cow eager to meet her calf, Mallika rushed barefoot towards the main gate. The two women met on the path leading to the inner courtyard. She took Divya in her arms, and according to the custom, smelt her hair. Tenderly lifting Divya's chin, she said reproachfully, 'Should you have forgotten me for so long? Ruchira has abandoned me; will you leave me too?' Mallika wiped her tearful eyes and, looking closely at Divya's face, said, 'You are looking so pale! Why, I hope you are in good health? May Ashvini Kumar, the Physician of the Gods, protect you. You are looking worried. It is almost two months since the Festival of Spring. You haven't even bothered to enquire about your aging mother.'

Mallika said all this in one breath. Overwhelmed, Divya could not utter a word in reply. She put her head on Mallika's breast, and shut her eyes in sheer contentment. But as soon as she opened them, they began searching for someone . . . Hadn't Arya arrived yet? Wasn't it time that he did?

Moving towards her chamber, with her arm round Divya, Mallika continued to reproach her, 'You are my only hope, my dear, you are the child of my soul. Fate snatched Ruchira from me. Having you, I thought I would be able to forget Ruchira. But you are so callous. You may not fear me, child, but you should at least respect Saraswati, the goddess of dance and music. Daughter, it is after the penance of many births that the goddess grants the boon of rare talent. But the recipient, who is indifferent to this gift, incurs the curse of the goddess. To you the goddess granted a portion of her own self.'

Mallika had dressed herself with particular care that evening. With unusual enthusiasm she ordered flagons of kapisha and kadambini wines for the guests. She informed the aged musician, Vabhru, about Divya's arrival and instructed him to play his best. When the guests were seated on soft mattresses against heavy cushions, Mallika appeared before the gathering with Divya by her side. Then signalling the musicians to play the *gandhari* raga, she herself sang the first few notes. When the singing was over, she instructed the musicians to play the tune for the *chhalika* dance.

Divya could not ignore Devi Mallika's invitation, but her heart was not in her dancing. Her eyes wandered again and again towards the door and the garden path beyond. The guests cheered the Daughter of Saraswati as the most skilful dancer in Sagal. Presents were offered to Mallika as a token of their satisfaction at the performance. Mallika remained silent. But when the performance was over, she turned towards Divya, 'Lack of practice is the worst enemy of art. Is there anything on your mind, my child?'

Divya admitted her fault and apologized, 'Mother, I am not feeling well. I just came to meet you.' Tenderly stroking her pupil's back, Mallika sat down by her side. Time and again, Divya's eyes turned towards the main gate and the garden path.

Just when the function was about to end, Prithusen came into view. A wave of satisfaction swept over Divya, but thereafter she could not look in that direction. She knew, however, that Prithusen had sat down in one of the back rows. He looked worried and tired. Divya felt the injustice done to him like a stab of pain in her own heart.

At a sign from Devi Mallika, the maids in attendance again placed flagons of wine, cups and betel leaves before the guests. Soon the room began to ring with laughter. But Divya, not being able to participate, felt awkward. She noticed that Prithusen, too, sat disconsolate at one side. He had acknowledged Mallika's hearty greeting with a faint smile and had remained silent and reserved.

Before the guests dispersed, Mallika proposed a round of the raas, the circular dance performed by Lord Krishna with

gopis.[1] Because of Divya's indisposition, Mallika did not ask
her to join in, but she urged Prithusen to participate. She was
a great admirer of his nimble footwork. But he begged to
be excused and remained seated.

For the performance of the raas it was necessary to make
some changes in the seating arrangements. While this was
being done, Divya stepped out of the hall for a breath of fresh
air. As she passed by Prithusen, she greeted him and enquired
after his health. He politely rose from his seat and while answering
her query, accompanied her into the garden.

'My great-grandfather is taking a keen interest in your
petition,' Divya said with feeling. 'He is probably waiting for
the decision of the Council.'

With a vain effort to smile, Prithusen said, 'I have lodged a
petition with the grandsire to hear the verdict from him—the
verdict of law—not to know the decision of the Council.'

'Yes, you are quite right,' Divya said in a voice full
of sympathy.

'The justice which you had assured me, with a mynah
as your witness,' Prithusen said, in a grave voice, 'was not
the justice of the Republican Council, but of the court of law.
Gentle lady, I do not want to be judged by caste, but by the
law. The Council is nothing but an arena of debate for vested
interests, while the court is the seat of justice itself.'

'You are perfectly right,' Divya replied, studying
her fingernails.

'And, my gentle lady,' Prithusen continued, 'I shall
feel little gratitude for the justice that is meted out to me by
the law court at the insistence of the Council. That won't be
justice but an obeisance to the powerful.'

---

[1] Specifically any of the herd-girls of Brij who were in love with Krishna.

Divya was hurt by Prithusen's words and by the tone of his utterances. With her head bowed, however, she said, 'You are quite right in what you say.'

'The function of the Chief Justice is not to carry out the instructions of the Council, but to show the Council the path of justice,' said Prithusen. Finding Divya silent, with her head lowered, he said with a soft smile on his lips, 'Is my eagerness to shoulder your palanquin a crime in your eyes too?'

'No, Arya,' replied Divya, trying to raise her eyes, but finding that they had filled with tears, she kept her head bowed. 'I am grateful for the honour,' she said, and her head bent still further.

For a few seconds they remained silent. Then Prithusen said, 'For cool fresh air, it would be better if we sat down near the pond in the garden.'

Without answering, Divya followed him with a bowed head.

Prestha

THE RULER OF MADRA, THE GREEK KING MILINDA, A MAN OF GREAT integrity and righteousness, became a convert to the Buddhist faith. A little later, he renounced the royal palace and the throne and took his vows as a monk. He set free thousands of slaves—men and women who had been owned either by the state or by himself. When granting freedom, he gave the slaves generous sums of money to build a future free of serfdom. After that, for some days the streets, lanes and marketplaces of Sagal became the scene of much turmoil caused by the newly emancipated slaves. The slaves, unused to saving or handling money, spent the bounty on drinking excessively, wearing expensive clothes, and making a nuisance of themselves. Soon the money was exhausted and they took to borrowing. And when they could not repay their debts, they were again sold back into slavery, to Brahmins and other wealthy people. Some of them, finding both slavery and freedom equally strenuous, took refuge in the monastic way of life of the Buddha and attained peace by adopting the yellow robes and the begging bowl of mendicants.

Prestha, the veterinary doctor and palace slave, had come with the king from the land of the Greeks. Being exceptionally clever, humble and adept in the breeding and rearing of horses, he became a favourite with the king. As he was a royal slave, he was well looked after. When the king renounced the world, besides granting him freedom, he gave him as a special favour a large number of pedigree horses which had been brought from such faraway places as Kapisha, Kamboj, Valhik and Sugam.

With these valuable horses, Prestha went, along with the other horse dealers, trading and dealing, to the east and west, north and south. He bought chariots and horses in one place and sold them at a higher price in another, and thereby, in course of time, accumulated thousands of gold pieces. He then settled down in Sagal like any other rich merchant while his agents continued to attend to his extensive trade. He bought a poor but pretty Brahmin girl and married her. He built himself palaces and gardens, purchased men and women slaves, and began to live like one of the nobility.

King Milinda had established his kingdom in the land of Madra by routing the royal dynasty of the Pauravs. During his long reign, he granted rights and privileges to numerous families of the deposed Paurav dynasty and to many noble Brahmin families, thereby making them his associates in administering the kingdom. Likewise, he made royal gifts of land to numerous Greek military commanders and turned them into feudatory chiefs. At the time when he renounced his throne, King Milinda did not leave behind any successor. The wealthy and powerful noble families of Madra did not want to put anyone in his place. Instead, following the practice of the republics of the eastern Jambu Dweep,[1] they began to administer the kingdom in the style of a republic. Mithrodus, an aged and experienced statesman and the erstwhile Commander-in-Chief under the Greek king, having held the reins of the military forces, was nominated President of the new republic and chief of the armed forces, while the king's minister, Mahamati Acharya Dev Mitra, was appointed Chairman of the Republican Council.

[1] Ancient name of India.

Even though Prestha the merchant had amassed wealth and enjoyed the respect of the people, he could not become a member of the Council, since he did not belong to a high caste. But with the power of his wealth, his ingenuity and humility, he succeeded in becoming a trusted confidant of Mithrodus, and thereby exercised great influence. The only son of Mithrodus had died young. To the grief-stricken President of the Republic, Prestha became his right-hand man.

Prestha, the magnate, brought up his son, Prithusen, in the same manner as children in noble families, and like them he had him trained in the use of weapons and in the scriptures. While Prithusen was in his teens, he was also sent to Taxila for higher education, along with Vinay Sharma, grandson of Dev Sharma, the Chief Justice; Sakrid, son of the feudatory chief Kartavir; Indradeep, son of Sarvarth; and Vasudhir, younger son of Acharya Pravardhan, Chairman of the Republican Council.

Having enjoyed a significant status since his childhood days, Prithusen had more self-esteem than his father and was less adept in the art of humility. He was more inclined to breaking down barriers than to bypassing them. Being wealthier and more talented than his contemporaries, he could not bear to be considered their inferior in public esteem.

Highly coloured reports of the murder of Vrihadrath, the last king of the Maurya dynasty in Magadh, at the hands of his Brahmin Commander-in-Chief, Pushya Mitra, followed by a revolt in that nation, reached distant Madra. It was strongly rumoured among the families adhering to the caste religion system and among the common people of Madra that Commander Pushya Mitra was none other than an incarnation of Kartikeya, 'the invincible commander of the gods', who had taken birth to rid Jambu Dweep of the lowly 'Sudra kings of the Maurya dynasty' and of the curse of the atheistic Buddhist religion, and that it was for this sacred mission that the great Brahmin sage, Patanjali, had performed for him the holy Rajasuya yajna[1] and rendered him invincible.

With the banning of animal sacrifice in Madra under the orders of the righteous King Milinda, the charm and importance of yajna had diminished considerably. But when the caste system was revived in Magadh, the long-abandoned ritual of blood sacrifices was again observed in Madra with great enthusiasm. Once again the Brahmin priests, long since unused to performing and conducting sacrifices, donned the marks of their caste—the top knot, the sacred thread and the tilak[2] on their foreheads. The air of Sagal was thick with the smell of the oblations in the sacrificial fires—barley, sesame seeds, coriander, ghee and the flesh of sacrificial animals. Once again the air resounded with the sounds of musical instruments of worship—the conch shell, the gong, the cymbals and the kettledrum.

In reaction to the revival of the caste system, the Buddhist monasteries began to hum with activity like disturbed beehives. They were thronged by the landlords, who had been the recipients of gifts of lands from the righteous King Milinda, and by the thousands of Buddhist mendicants receiving alms from the Nirvana-aspiring votaries of the Buddhist faith. In the monasteries, chants in front of the Buddha grew louder and were heard for longer periods of time. To awaken the citizens who had strayed on to the sinful path of animal sacrifice, hundreds of bhikshus began to walk through the streets chanting

---

[1] Religious ceremony, often includes sacrificial acts.
[2] Ornamental or ritualistic mark on forehead.

religious verses and delivering the message of their faith: 'Come to the fold of the bhikkus, for the good of many, for the comfort of many, for the compassion for all.'

It was the month of Shravan and the sky of Sagal was overcast with monsoon clouds. A heavy downpour resulted in waterlogged streets and the life in the town became sluggish. After the rains, the scorching heat made the stone houses and streets unbearably hot. Oppressed by the heat and unhappy at the lack of social activity, the inhabitants of the city, rich and poor alike, headed towards the groves and parks. But rain clouds would gather again and sudden showers would force people to run for shelter to their houses.

The mental state of the people of Sagal was much the same. Many were perturbed by the daily wranglings between the Brahmins, eager to resurrect the caste system through the power of religious sacrifices, and the adherents of Buddhism. Men of higher castes were apprehensive lest the spread of what they considered to be irresponsible doctrines, such as disbelief in the other world, preached by men like Marish who had shed their fear of god and of divine retribution, should lead to improper conduct by the people. There was an uneasy calm in the public when Marish raised his voice against a levy for animal sacrifice and when he was punished by the Chief Justice for refusing to carve the images of the Buddha in accordance with the instructions of the head of the monastery.

The judgment, therefore, on the dispute that had taken place on the evening of the Festival of Spring between Rudradhir and Prithusen was virtually shelved for fear of serious consequences. The question of the appointment of new officers in the army of Madra had also been put on hold in the Council, because of rivalries among some of the prominent families. But the main cause of tension was the news that the state was about to be attacked from the north-east by Kendras, the Greek ruler of Darva.

During the long reign of King Milinda, and also afterwards, for well over half a century the people of Madra and the citizens of Sagal had had no experience of invasion or a state of war, so much so that they had forgotten the very feel of war. Their minds were occupied with such things as the performance of religious rituals, accumulation of wealth, establishment of monasteries, prosperity through trade with foreign countries, realization of rent from peasants settled on their fiefs, importation of able-bodied slaves and buxom women, and with rivalries among themselves for right and honour through membership of the Republican Council.

When the administration of the mighty King Milinda passed into the hands of the dynastic families, the military organization in Madra also underwent a change. In the reign of King Milinda, the treasury of the state had been emptied in the service of Buddhist monasteries. There were no means, in those days, of maintaining a strong army of twenty thousand men, built during the early period of his reign when he had been ambitious of conquests. The professional soldiers of Madra, dissatisfied with the king's pacific policy, left to join the armies of other kingdoms or took up different professions. Many donned saffron robes and took up the begging bowl in place of the bow and the sword. Seeing the exhausted nature of the state treasury, Mithrodus, the President and Commander-in-Chief of the Republic, transferred the organization of the army into the hands of the noble families. Every noble who was a member of the Council was allotted the task of equipping five hundred to one thousand soldiers for the Republic, while every plebeian member had to supply for two hundred. In accordance with their position and authority, the noble families were granted fiefs of five to twenty-five villages, in recognition of the services rendered to the army.

And now, when the invasion of Kendras was imminent, the mobilization of the army by the noble families existed merely as a resolution on the palmyra leaves of the scribes of the Council and in the imagination of its members. The rent exacted from the peasants in the fiefs was not used for the maintenance of soldiers but was squandered in the pursuit of pleasures.

The aged Commander-in-Chief, shaken by the death of his young son, was trying to seek solace in philosophical detachment, as preached by the Buddha. But conscious of his duty towards the defence of the Republic, he instructed Acharya Pravardhan, the Chairman, to call a meeting of the Republican Council.

The Chairman, in turn, issued similar instructions to the feudatory chiefs through Kartavir, who was responsible for convening the meetings. Eventually, the Council assembled after a long delay.

'The army of the Republic is a joke,' said the Commander-in-Chief. 'For the purpose of defence, the Republic must raise a suitable army forthwith.'

Acharya Pravardhan issued a decree for an increase in state revenues, in order to replenish the treasury for the conduct of war and mobilization of the army.

In the oppressive heat of the monsoon season and with alarming reports pouring in each day about the fast-advancing cavalry of Kendras, the inhabitants of Sagal felt weary, dejected and hopeless. The streets, lanes and marketplaces lost their bustle and liveliness. The fear of invasion became all the more oppressive because of the manner in which the officers of state went about extorting taxes for the war.

People had no strong inclination to resist the enemy; rather terror reigned in their hearts. An uncanny suspense pervaded the atmosphere. What would happen when Kendras arrived? Would there be any respite from the terrors of the nobility in this dynastic republic, from the ever-increasing war taxes, from the conscription of citizens, craftsmen and peasants by the soldiers of the feudatory chiefs? Or would there be worse repression, massacre and looting by the soldiers of Kendras? In the drinking booths and market squares, greatly exaggerated reports of the awful might of tyrant Kendras, as also of his kindness and his love for the people, were spreading. There was a feeling of helplessness and of submission to the inevitability of fate.

Out of sheer panic, bankers, transport contractors and traders were transferring their money to the nearby states of Malla and Katha, and towards Shursen and Magadh. In the palaces of the feudatory chiefs, Sarvarth, Kartavir and Acharya Pravardhan, discussions went on till late in the night. Acharya Pravardhan had sent a number of secret messages to Shursen and Magadh. These nobles were hoping that the great Brahmin commander Pushya Mitra, the saviour of the caste system, by sending an army for the defence of Madra against Kendras, would not only crush Buddhism in Madra but also reinstate the caste system. They wanted to discuss this strategy in the Council, but refrained from doing so as they feared opposition from the Greek nobles, the President who was drawn towards the Buddhist faith, from the feudatory chief, Indrasen, and from Dev Sharma, the Chief Justice of the Republic.

The feudatory chiefs, Sarvarth and Kartavir, had begun to raise an army so that, while defending the state against Kendras, they might at the same time install on the throne some survivor of the Paurav family, and thus establish once again the rule of the Paurav dynasty. The magnates, merchants and traders were minting money by supplying foodstuffs, clothing, chariots, horses and other goods to the army at exorbitant rates, and were sending it out into the hinterland to such markets as Taxila, Pushpapur and Mathurapuri.[1]

In Sagal, inhabited as it was by people of different generations, only a few aged persons, like Dev Sharma, the Chief Justice; Mithrodus, the President of the Republic; and Prestha, the magnate, had any memories of war. The President's memories were those of a victor, while the memories of the Chief Justice were of one who had suffered defeat. The news of the advance of Kendras brought to the mind of the Chief Justice pictures of disaster, of elegant mansions falling to the ground in raging fires, of clouds of smoke hovering over the town making it impossible to breathe, of streams of blood coagulating in the lanes and alleys, of the wailing of women, of the humiliation of the nobles treated as prisoners. Time and again, the Chief Justice would ask the President—who had not been able to overcome the shock of his son's death and was lost in the pursuit of detachment from worldly things—to convene a meeting of the Council, so that matters relating to the defence of the state might be discussed. And every time such a meeting was called, it would end in pointless wrangling and debate.

Prestha, the magnate, did not remain indifferent to the situation. He contributed to the mobilization of the state army by securing from neighbouring areas hundreds of horses and chariots which he sold to the state, and thereby made a profit of thousands of gold pieces. Knowing that both the Chief Justice and the President were anxious about the war, the

[1] Now known as Mathura.

magnate voluntarily contributed a thousand gold pieces to the treasury. This gesture earned him not only the confidence and respect of both dignitaries, but also the right to participate in the secret councils of the state. The magnate was of the view that control of the army should be entrusted to well-known and tried senior officers and such army commanders as had lately proved themselves worthy of confidence. The Council met again to examine the question of military organization, but because of the intrigues of Acharya Pravardhan, the distribution of senior posts and the selection of commanders could not proceed smoothly. On the insistence of Kartavir, the feudatory chief, Arya Indradeep and Arya Vrishnesh were appointed the new commanders of the cavalry, while Arya Vinay Sharma was appointed commander of the chariot-borne army.

Little attention had as yet been paid in the Council to Prithusen's petition for justice, and for a commission in the army. His father would often try to encourage and reassure him, saying, 'Son, an opportunity is soon to come your way. Be ready and alert to take advantage of it. The wise men of Greece have a saying: "The god of opportunity has his face hidden behind his forelock. It is difficult to recognize him, but you can overpower him only by catching him by the forelock. The back part of his head is bald. It is easy to recognize the god after he had passed you by, but you cannot grab him by his bald pate." Therefore, it is necessary to be prepared and alert in recognizing your opportunity. Son, if you have courage, valour and intelligence; if you have money, then your worth will be recognized in this very crisis. Have courage and gain the confidence of the people who matter. Go and wait on the aged Chief Justice and the President; establish personal contact with the feudatory chiefs, Okris and Indrasen . . .'

Despite his father's advice, the thought of going to beg for acceptance and favour was unpalatable to Prithusen. He felt the cold silence of indifference and disdain towards him and found no satisfaction or sympathy anywhere, be it in the company of friends or in drinking booths or gambling dens. He no longer had any interest in high living or dancing. When time hung heavy, he would sit under a tree in the garden of his palace and shoot arrows at the fluttering leaves of trees, or play chess with the slave Shwang, who was his personal attendant.

In the evenings, Prithusen would sometimes go to the mansion of Mallika or of Vasumitra, but it would be mainly in the hope of meeting Divya there. It gave him great consolation to be near her because she shared his despondency—the one person who befriended him, looking upon him as an equal, who offered her heart to him despite the numerous obstacles in her way, who was his only support, and whom he could truly call his own. He yearned to take Divya away to some unknown place, to some secret hideout, and there, make a new home for himself with new friends; a new world, in which he would not be penalized for his birth; where he would not be a helpless victim of unknown deeds from his past lives; where he would have the freedom to act as he liked; where his energy and his talent would not be futile because of his being the son of a low-born father.

News reached Sagal that the forces guarding the frontier had been routed by Kendras. Panic gripped the town. Everywhere people began to talk of war. Devi Mallika too had contributed money and had thereby participated in the war effort. In the concert hall of her palace, in the midst of the performances of song and dance, the state officers charged with military duties and administration would begin to talk of war. Wine cup in hand, they would ignore the graces of art and get involved in the discussion of the horrors of war. The joys of life were there, no doubt, but concern for its security was stronger. And when the wine took effect, discussion would give place to sheer babble. Prithusen felt irritated by their stupidity and cowardice, but he kept his mouth shut.

Indradeep, deep in his cups and with his chest stuck out, said, 'Wars are won by the physical prowess of the Brahmins. You need the drive and fortitude of a Pushya Mitra for it. How can our ancient Commander-in-Chief, whose head shakes all the time because of the confusion inside, lead us in battle? . . . These petty victories and defeats mean nothing. In my veins flows the blood of the Paurav dynasty. Even the Greek king, Milinda, was scared of this prowess and could not rule, although he had come as a conqueror, and renounced everything and took the beggar's bowl. You will see what happens to Kendras the day Indradeep, the great commander, takes into his hands the reins of military command.' He burst out laughing and stretching out his arms, he pulled to himself the slave-girl who was standing in front of him, with the wine tray in her hand. 'On that day, the wives of Kendras will drop into my lap in the same way, ha, ha!'

Terrified at Indradeep's wildness, Magga, the slave-girl, trembled from head to foot. Mallika put her finger to her lips indicating that he should not frighten the girl.

Irked by Mallika's censure, Kedar Sharma, son of feudatory chief Shrimukh Sharma, who was sitting next to Indradeep, exclaimed, 'Is it for such subservience as this that we shall bare our chests to the sword-thrusts of Kendras?' and holding out both his hands, he looked at all those sitting round him, confident of their approval. 'See? A noble's son is helpless even before a slave-girl! He cannot do as he pleases even with a slave-girl! Should we have to seek the consent of such an inferior creature? Should insolent upstarts go about insulting and challenging the twice-born Brahmins in the streets and lanes of Sagal? Should weavers and menials sit next to us as our equals? Do we count for nothing in the administration of Madra, such as it is? And shall we shed our blood in its defence? What do you say, Udaya Bhanu?' he cried loudly, turning for confirmation to the merchant.

'It's all the same to me,' replied Udaya Bhanu in a tone of listless unconcern. 'The Republic extorts the bulk of my earnings from me in the form of taxes. Kendras too will rob me of my wealth. The Republic has taken from me a hundred gold pieces as my contribution to the war fund. Will the Republic give me hundredfold protection too? . . . Is my body a hundred times bigger than that of other citizens?' he asked, patting his rotund belly. 'Why should I annoy anyone, brother? They are all alike, so far as I am concerned. I'm only a Vaishya, a humble trader. Let that man go to war who thinks that he deserves to sit on the throne. A Vaishya is only a humble servant.'

'Devi,' Indradeep said, turning to Mallika, 'I swear by the beauty of your art, I swear by Goddess Saraswati when I say that the Republic of Madra has been eaten to the core by the Buddhists as a wooden column is eaten up by white ants—it is all hollow inside. One-third of the state revenue is spent on the Buddhist parasites. What is then left behind? Is it not armed soldiers that will face Kendras? Will these young fawns of the Buddha, the yellow-robed bhikshus with begging bowls in their hands protect Madra? This is what comes of denying food to the hound and feeding the fawn instead. Send Cheebuk, the Buddhist monk to face Kendras; send the head of the monastery to face the sword of Kendras,' he said, roaring with laughter.

Mallika could not join in. 'Arya,' she said to Indradeep, 'will these mutual rivalries not lead to our surrender to the enemy? . . . When Madra and Sagal are reduced to rubble, who then will be left to listen to the others' accusations?'

Such boasting by the sons of the nobility was too much for Prithusen to bear. Making a sign to Divya he left the hall and headed towards the pond, which was situated in the midst of a grove of trees. Divya followed him soon after.

Taking Divya's hand into his, Prithusen said in a depressed voice, 'Did you see that, my love? Such are our war preparations! The mighty Kendras has his heels on the throat of Madra, and here are its leaders scheming against one another.'

Confused, Divya covered her eyes with her stole.

Putting his arm around her, Prithusen said, 'In the eyes of these people, this invasion is a kind of punishment for the sins of Buddhism. Under the cover of war, Acharya Pravardhan is conspiring to re-establish the caste system. It doesn't occur to anyone that neither Pushya Mitra nor Kendras will come here to shed his blood for the sake of establishing the caste system in Madra. They are interested in the expansion of their empire, in the wealth and resources of Madra. These people think that Kendras, after conquering them, will begin to venerate them, and recognizing their birthright of Brahminism, will set to worshipping them.

'The vanquished are never worthy of respect. Kendras considers himself a god. This "holy sacrifice of war" is for his own satisfaction; it will turn the whole of Sagal into a sacrificial pyre. And in that fire, the bodies of these Brahmins, these nobles and their possessions will serve as oblations. Only those people will survive who, bereft of self-respect, will kiss the foot that kicks them. Do you call that survival? Their high-born ladies, whose feet had never so much as touched the ground, will become a reward for the hungry, lecherous soldiers of Kendras. People proud of their aristocratic ways and noble birth will go about with fetters on their feet, like slaves. Ladies of the nobility and Brahmin virgins, shrieking with terror, will be gathered up in the spoils of victory. In that fire of utter ruin all our hopes will be consumed.'

Lost in that nightmare of his own thoughts, Prithusen's eyes gazed at the reflection of the stars swirling in the water of the pond. His hand slipped out of Divya's and rested on the hilt of his sword hanging from his girdle. He did not notice that Divya was staring hard at him. Lost in thought he continued to murmur, 'In the light of burning palaces, the arrogant soldiers of Darva, drunk with victory, will put their hands on you, and I, chained and fettered, will look on, helpless. But rather than such a moment should come, I shall have lost my life by the enemy's sword, or shall have killed myself with my own hand. To imagine that such a thing can happen to you even after my death is a thought I cannot bear.'

Prithusen was interrupted in his thoughts by the sound of Divya's sobs. He put his arm around her and pressed her tightly to his chest. He kissed her on her forehead, her cheeks, her mouth, and then, holding her face between his hands, said reassuringly, 'What do we gain by fear and panic, anyhow? It is far better that we live to the fullest, the moments of life that are given to us and then put an end to it with courage.'

In his effort to console Divya, he himself began to seek comfort in her lithe body. Her arms became limp and he gathered her waist more closely in his embrace. Her breasts swelled in her bodice, as if to comfort his pounding heart. His chin rested on Divya's head. The intoxicating fragrance of Divya's hair was driving him wild. The terrifying flames of destruction and war receded farther and farther from his eyes, as the wick of a lamp grows dimmer and dimmer when the oil runs out.

Prithusen's eager soul, seeking fulfilment, yearned for her lips, and finding them, clung on in ecstasy. His unruly hands in search of her throbbing heart became restless on her bodice.

Divya trembled and shrank away from him. Torn between the pleasure of surrender and the instinct for self-protection, she held Prithusen's hand in hers. Prithusen heaved a deep sigh and restraining himself, bit into his lower lip. The terrifying spectre of war which, for a moment had disappeared from his eyes, returned once more. He swallowed hard to cleanse his mouth of the bitterness born out of frustration. Resting lightly one of his hands on Divya's shoulder and the other on her waist, and turning his eyes once again towards the reflection of the stars in the pond, he said, 'I am not afraid of death, Divya . . . what is death? The end of one's being. He who has no being, who is devoid of feeling, cannot feel fear either. If I am afraid, it is of being alive to bear the pain of subjugation, the lifelong agony of subjugation. To have you in my arms and then die will satisfy my desires. Then what is there to be afraid of? That will be a happy end to a happy existence. I cannot bear the thought of being conquered and overpowered in war, and then to die a slow death. The fulfilment of life lies in power and affluence. For these people, war is only an opportunity to carry out a treacherous conspiracy. They look upon one another as enemies but regard their real enemy as a potential friend and accomplice. Mourning the death of his son, the Commander-in-Chief has become a recluse from the world, and wants to follow in the footsteps of King Milinda. For hours he listens to the discourses of savant Dharma Rakshit about the joyful path of Nirvana and draws

comfort from them. The Chairman of the Council will gladly
see Madra in ruins, if thereby, like his predecessors, he can
obtain some position of power under Kendras. The life of the
entire population of the Republic is dependent on the selfish
intrigues of these people, whose petty interests are dearer to
them than the lives of millions of people,' Prithusen went on,
his eyes still resting on the starlit water in the pond.

Divya took Prithusen's hand and placed it on her cheek.
She said in a pleading voice, 'Why don't you go and speak to
my great-grandfather, dear? He is as much worried about the
dreadful consequences of the war as you are. He saw with his
own eyes the devastation of Madra at the hands of King Milinda
and he took a vow that he would rather die than live to see that
holocaust again. He can do a lot. Neither the Commander-in-
Chief nor the Acharya can afford to disregard his opinion.'

Gazing deeply into Divya's eyes in the darkness, Prithusen
said, 'Dearest, even now, if I am given a chance, I can block the
way of the barbarian, Kendras. I am sure I can. But what can
I do if I have no support?'

Divya took Prithusen's hand in hers and insisted, 'You
must go and meet great-grandfather. You must. Just go once
and you'll see. I'll speak to him myself. I must go now,
my love, it's getting late . . . the attendant is waiting.'

Paying little attention to the groom waiting for him at the
main gate of Mallika's palace, Prithusen set off on foot towards
his own house. He left the main street and took to the weavers'
lane. The lane was almost deserted. But for a glimmer of light
here and there it was dark on all sides. The lane, paved with
flagstones, rang with hoofbeats as the groom led the horse
behind his master. Prithusen walked on, lost in thought.

From the narrow weavers' lane he came to the comparatively broader blacksmiths' lane. It was late at night and most of the shops were closed. The lane was almost deserted. Dim lights could be seen, however, in a few shops from which came a strong reek of cheap liquor. Here and there meat and other foodstuffs were being roasted. At one place there was more light and the sound of many voices. Hearing the clop of horses' hoofs, the knot of people turned towards Prithusen. As their eyes fell on his clothes, they became confused and a hush fell on them. Being the centre of attention, Prithusen came to himself with a start. He realized that here too people were talking about war.

Prithusen moved on, and after a little while removed his turban and gave it to the groom, telling him to return home, taking the horse with him. He then covered himself with his uttariya and went on alone. Only a close look at his jewelled earrings, swinging under his curly hair, revealed that he belonged to the upper class.

At the end of the blacksmiths' lane he came to the prostitutes' square. Light fell from the terraces of the houses of the prostitutes on the group of people standing below. Some boys and girls went about selling garlands and flowers, shouting loudly that the garlands were just the thing for lovers and amorous men. One boy, in a shrill, loud voice, was inviting bystanders to taste soft roasted meat. An old woman stood in front of a wine shop, holding onto a drunkard's shirt and demanding money. A large number of people gathered around, laughing at her.

'No, no, I won't let you go from the shop without getting my money,' said the old woman in a sharp irritated tone. 'What if you have become a soldier? That has nothing to do with me. Tomorrow you may be packed off to Darva, then who will pay me my money? Is wine made without money? You are a clever one, aren't you? Came along to have a few drinks without any money in your pocket. What do I care if you've enlisted as a soldier? Get your liquor from the noble lord who has recruited you into his army and whose life you're going to guard! Why should you cheat a poor old woman like me? The tax collector has already grabbed two gold pieces from me for the war fund, and here you are, refusing to pay for the drinks.'

'Give money to the war fund and make the officers rich! Ha, ha!' someone shouted, interrupting the old woman. 'Of the two gold pieces you've given, Grandma, one will go to the treasury while the other will find its way to the officers' pockets. There will be little left for Kendras to loot! Grandma, you serve wine free of charge and cheerfully to state officers who extort money from you by force, but from us poor folk you charge double the price for thimblefuls of wine which is one-half water, anyway!'

'Such is the way of the world, friend,' laughed another drunkard, slapping the speaker on the back. 'One dog bites another and protects the wealth of his master. You and I will kill one another at the whim of some civil servant. Friend, if you had an officer's belt round your waist, you too would growl at every passer-by, just as a dog tied to his master's porch barks at every dog passing in the street. Feeding the Brahmins is a greater virtue than having your own dinner. Do you know why? Because the Brahmin is the dog of the gods.'

Prithusen, standing in a dark corner on one side, recognized the voice of the speaker: it was Marish, the sculptor–philosopher. Marish's clothes and hair were so dishevelled that it was difficult to recognize him. To what depths of poverty had Marish sunk after having been dismissed from his assignment, Prithusen thought. Just then, his attention was again drawn towards the old woman, who was holding onto the shirt of the errant customer and was still berating him.

'You old miser,' someone was saying to the woman, 'don't be so hard on the poor fellow. What if he has drunk a couple of glasses to drown his sorrow after being forcibly recruited into the army?'

Another old boozer, holding his earthen wine bowl in one hand and some food in the other, stepped forward and said, 'Friend Shandeya, I shall pay for your drinks. Drink as much as you like.' He put the bowl to Shandeya's lips. Then smashing the empty bowl on the ground, he said, 'Of what use is money? The food I eat or the wine I drink, that alone is mine. I stand in front of a scorching fire the whole day long and forge swords. With my sword in hand the state officer drove my son into the army. My son will go to the front line to bear the brunt of Kendras's attack, while the priest and the sacrificer, with the money I've paid in taxes, will drink the wine sanctified by mantras and devour the meat offered in sacrifice, and pray to the gods for protection by chanting hymns. The great warrior, the feudatory chief, will show his prowess by carrying off to bed slave-girls of fair and dark complexions while my son, trembling under the sword of his enemy, will be dubbed a coward. Oh, it would have been far better if he had become a Buddhist monk and thereby gained a longer lease of life!' The old man sat down on the ground with his head between his hands.

Shandeya pulled away his shirt from the hands of the old woman and sitting down beside the old man began to console him. 'No use crying, Uncle. Fate is all-powerful. It is fate that saves, and it is fate that kills. Man's actions are of no consequence. Have no worry. Uncle, I am myself a mercenary soldier of a feudatory chief. I'll look after your son. Do you know wherein lies the heroism of a mercenary soldier? He's the last among those who fight and the first among those who run.'

'Will some Arya pay for a bowl of wine?' shouted another drunkard, paying little attention to what Shandeya was saying. 'My grandfather used to make swords for King Paurav; my father made swords for the Greek king Milinda. I make swords for the two hundred rulers of Madra. With the swords that I make, empires are won. With the swords I make, countries are ruled, while I don't have enough to buy myself a bowl of wine. Will some kind friend stand me a bowl of wine?'

Many of them went on shouting, without listening to the others. Prithusen could hear only those who spoke louder than the rest. A middle-aged man raised his bowl above his head and said, 'Yesterday, all my three horses were taken away by the officers of the government. Prestha, the king of horse dealers, gets five gold pieces for every horse from the treasury, but for my three horses they paid me four gold pieces. My horses are needed for war. Sarvarth, the feudatory chief, rides in a chariot driven by four horses, blocking the whole road. The state needs my horses but not the horses of the feudatory chief. Ha, ha!' He burst out laughing.

The swordsmith who had been begging for a bowl of wine went over to him and putting his mouth close to his ear, said in a very loud voice, 'Friend, spend the four gold pieces on wine. Stand drinks for your friends. Sleep with Aloma, the pretty strumpet, and then put on the yellow robes of a monk, take the begging bowl in hand, give blessings and receive a bellyful of food in return. The world is nothing but maya. Desires lead you nowhere. Come, friend, let's drink!'

A young man was trying to console the disconsolate old woman who had not received payment for her drinks.

'Don't deny drinks to the good citizens, Grandma. Once the demons of Kendras are here, they will not only drink up your wine, but every second day they'll break your pitchers and also torture you.'

'Hey, you're only a greenhorn. What do you know?' another said, interrupting the young man. 'Why be afraid of Kendras? The rule of one king is better in every way than that of the hundred kinglings of a republic. We shall have peace in Sagal of the kind there was before, in the time of the righteous King Milinda.'

A youth sprawling on the road exclaimed in a louder voice, 'Stand me a drink, friends! This is the last day of my free life. The officers of the nobles came to draft me into the army today. My wife is clever. She said to them, "He's gone to the weavers' shop on an errand. Come tomorrow." They will grab me tomorrow. This is the last day of my life. Friends, buy me a drink!'

'Why do you want to die as a mercenary, you fool?' said a fellow sitting next to him, slapping him on the thigh. 'Why don't you just run away? Hundreds have saved their lives that way. Go away to the Republic of Katha. The feudatory chiefs don't rule there. There, all men are equal and free.'

'How can I run away?' the youth replied despondently. 'What will happen to my devoted wife, to my little boys? The priest says that the person who doesn't obey his master will be born a dog in his next birth and will again be forced to serve his master. Haven't I suffered enough in this life that I should wreck my next birth too?'

Licking the drops of cheap pungent wine from his lips, Marish said from among the crowd, 'Stupid man, have you seen the next world? Has your master seen it? This belief itself makes a slave of you. You acknowledge the authority of

your master over you; this is what binds you to slavery. You
seek safety by running away from danger and in that lies your
weakness. Danger will dog your footsteps wherever you go.
Conquer danger. To be vanquished is, in itself, a sin. You will
suffer the consequences the very next moment. You are a
free agent. To feel the breath of freedom is life itself. The one
who admits defeat is already dead, even though his body may
be living. Cast off fear. Fight for life. Death is the end of
fear. Live in a spirited way. Don't be a coward!' Marish put
the wine bowl to his lips again, took a gulp and handed the
bowl to the frightened youth.

Shaking off from his neck the arm of the whimpering
swordsmith, Shandeya addressed Marish, 'For whom shall we
go to war? For whom shall we lay down our lives? For the
glory of the feudatory chief Sarvarth? For the religious sacrifice
of Acharya Pravardhan? For the Buddhist Dharma Rakshit?
It's all the same to us. He who, by reason of his past actions
has to serve others, can serve anyone and everyone.'

'You too are a fool,' said Marish, licking his wine-soaked
lips. 'You think that you've been born to serve others, that you
are destined only to serve. You were not born to serve as a tool
for the satisfaction of other people's interests. For that there
are animals. Fight for yourselves. The feudatory chief and the
Acharya fight for themselves. You too should fight for
yourselves—for your food, for your clothing, for your wine,
for the woman you take into your arms and who gives you joy,
for the child in whom you see the perpetuation of your life.
Die you must, but at least die for the right to live. One who
allows himself to be used by others is a lump of dead flesh,
worse than an animal. Under a feudatory chief you are only
partly human; try to be a human being. In despair and out of

sheer laziness, don't accept the position of animals. Kendras is barbarous. He is greedy for the wealth which is the essence of your life. Powerful is the man who kills, weak is the man who fears,' Marish said, getting up and walking off.

One of the drunkards suddenly noticed Prithusen and said, 'Why are you so glum, friend? Are you stricken with fear? Marish says there is no truth in fear. Of whom are you afraid? Are you afraid of war? Go and become the slave of some noble! The officers of the state won't even be able to touch you. Are you annoyed with your wife? Then go to the prostitute, Aloma. She's smooth and sleek like an ivory statue. Aloma is not greedy. Come, friend, acquaintance in a drinking parlour is the beginning of friendship.' He put his own bowl of wine to Prithusen's lips. Prithusen pushed it away and quietly walked off into the darkness.

Even after he had gone some distance, Prithusen could hear the wailing of the old swordsmith.

The waiting attendant led Prithusen to his bedchamber. Ill at ease, he sat down on his high bed. Like moths that come fluttering round a flame, cares and worries came crowding into his mind—the menacing enemy advancing on Sagal, the all-pervading panic, the intrigues of the nobles, the dissatisfaction and indifference of the populace, the unconcern of the nobility—what would all this lead to? He remembered how Divya had grown limp in his arms and had abandoned herself, and then suddenly trembling all over, had begun to resist. She had been so loving, then why did she reject him? Would they be allowed to marry each other? What will happen before that, under Kendras's invasion? Should he go away from Sagal? Marish was right, after all. Who will stand up to Kendras? How would any resistance be possible without the support of the people? Resting his chin on the palm of his hand, he remained sitting, lost in thought, unmindful of the soft pillows. He was unaware of the slave-girl standing behind him, fanning him softly to drive away the mosquitoes that had appeared with the stifling air of the rainy season.

'Arya!'

Prithusen raised his eyes. Another slave-girl, Vapa by name, stood before him.

'The master has enquired after your health. He hopes that you are well and in good cheer,' said the slave-girl.

'Convey my salutations to my father. I am in good health.' Then, lying down on his bed, he said, 'I don't need the light.'

Of the five earthen lamps burning with scented oil, the slave-girl extinguished four. Only one was left burning and its light fell only on the carpet below. Seeing him motionless, Vapa went away. The other slave-girl softly stepped to one side, so as not to be seen by Prithusen, and continued to fan him.

Prithusen turned from side to side, put his arm under his head, now in one posture, then in another, but could not sleep. A long time passed. Through the door and casements came strong gusts of wind, followed by the sound of pattering rain. The air became cool and laden with moisture. The slave-girl put down the fan and stood motionless. A little later she picked up the silken sheet lying on a stool by the bed and covered Prithusen with it. Rain and cool air brought some relief to his troubled mind. He tossed aside the covering and turned on his side. After a few seconds, he pulled up the sheet again over his body.

Seeing that her master was not able to sleep, the slave-girl went out into the corridor and told the attendant to send for the slave-girl who knew the art of inducing sleep.

Smooth and glossy as a plantain tree, a fair-complexioned slave-girl tiptoed into the room. She had a pleasant face and had dressed with care. A pearl necklace and garlands of fresh flowers swayed over her shapely bosom, covered with a pink silken bodice, tied at the back. Below her small bare midriff her well-rounded hips swelled voluptuously. Round her waist she wore a skirt of pale yellow silk held in place by a girdle of pearls. On her soft, bare arms she wore pearl armlets and bracelets. Her perfumed hair, plaited with strings of pearls, hung loose. She did not wear any hard metal like gold; only pearls which were cool and soft to the touch.

Prithusen's eyes fell on her as he turned again on his side. The slave-girl was bending over to touch his body. There was a look of uncertainty and hesitation on her face and in her large eyes: 'Will it please the master if I smile or should I continue to look solemn out of sympathy for him?' Prithusen felt uneasy at the girl's perplexity. He turned his eyes away. The slave-girl began to massage his feet. The touch of her hands did not afford any pleasure to Prithusen, and he pulled his feet away. Thinking that the master was feeling cold, the slave-girl took another silken covering from the stool and spread it over him.

With one covering already over him, Prithusen felt warm enough. When a second sheet was put on him he looked at the slave-girl. The hair on her uncovered skin stood on end from the gusts of cool air coming through the door. Her body had been bared for the gratification of her master. Looking at her, it occurred to Prithusen that Sagal was similarly being pushed into the abyss of ruin for the gratification of the feudatory chief, Sarvarth, and of Acharya Pravardhan. The gentry of Sagal, the commonfolk, his own family that had attained a measure of prosperity through the untiring efforts of his wise father, he himself, his Divya . . . How could he feel indifferent towards any of them? Father is perfectly right, he thought. This is the proper time to remove those who are vying with one another in self-destruction. He wants me to win the confidence of the Commander-in-Chief. Divya wants me to go to her great-grandfather, the Chief Justice. He turned and his eyes again fell on the slave-girl who stood waiting in doubt and uncertainty, her chilled body covered with gooseflesh. He made a sign to her to go away and kept on tossing and turning, troubled in mind. Later, sleep brought him some relief.

When he woke up, his usual slave-girl was there with a water pitcher, basin and towel. Prithusen looked out of the door. The sky was still overcast with heavy clouds, and a light drizzle was falling. It seemed to be already long past daybreak.

'What's the time, girl?'

'Past first quarter of the day, Arya.'

Prithusen washed his face and rinsed his mouth. The slave girl handed the towel to him and said, 'The master has asked twice about Your Honour, since morning. When he learnt that Your Honour had gone to bed rather late, he decided to wait for you in his own room.'

Prithusen got up, changed his clothes, and went to meet his father. Prestha, the magnate, looked solemn, but acknowledged the greetings of his son with a smile and a blessing. Putting his hand on his son's shoulder, he spoke in a low, confidential tone, 'Perhaps you know about the army and the situation in Sagal? News came last night that the army of Madra has been routed a second time by the forces of Kendras. This news is being kept secret from the President of the Republic. Secret treaties exist between Acharya Pravardhan and the rulers of Shursen and Magadh. I have obtained positive proof of this by spending a great deal of money. Son, take this· information, together with the documentary proofs I have, to the President. On the strength of these you will be able to win his confidence and respect. A golden opportunity has come your way. It's also your duty to defend the state.'

For a few seconds Prithusen was lost in thought. Then he said in a voice equally secretive, but despondent, 'You're right, Father. But the time for defence is almost gone. What can the two or three hundred families of the nobility do, ensconced in their palaces? And they don't agree among themselves on anything either. The vast population of Madra is terribly disheartened and dissatisfied. It's only waiting for Kendras to march in. Last night, I heard with my own ears the views of the poor and the low-caste people. They are disturbed, frightened, disappointed and terribly dissatisfied. Father, the orders of commanders have their importance, no doubt, but it's the ordinary people who do the fighting. They're waiting to welcome Kendras. There's no way left to us except either to leave Sagal and seek shelter elsewhere while there is still time, or die fighting and save ourselves from disgrace.'

The magnate was pleased ·to find that Prithusen was not as indifferent to the situation as he had been earlier. He made his son sit next to him and said, 'If the people are dissatisfied they can be satisfied too. It is important that people should be contented, that they should cooperate, but their satisfaction and cooperation should be drawn not towards the feudatory chief Sarvarth or Acharya Pravardhan, but towards the President, towards Prestha, towards Commander Prithusen. Do you follow me, my son?'

And for a long time, the magnate went on explaining to his son the fine art of diplomacy.

The army of Kendras reached the bank of the Tavisha river after defeating the forces of Madra. The terrible news coming from the frontier frightened and discouraged the inhabitants of Sagal greatly. Before they could overcome their earlier fears and regain composure, more terrifying news would come to increase their panic. In such circumstances another unexpected incident occurred which bewildered them all the more. Stunned, they began to conjecture about its causes and possible consequences.

Dev Sharma, the aged Chief Justice, seldom stirred out of his palace. Similarly, Mithrodus, the aged President of the Republic and Commander-in-Chief, led the life of a recluse. One day, however, the aged Chief Justice got into his palanquin and went to the palace of the President. The same evening, the palanquin of the aged President was seen going to the palace of the Chief Justice. Both times, Prithusen, the outstanding swordsman of Sagal and son of Prestha, the magnate, mounted on his agile white horse, was seen riding besides the palanquins of both the Chief Justice and the President.

The same day, the chariot of Prestha, was many times seen standing at the gates of the palaces of both the President and the Chief Justice. Besides, the chariots of the feudatory chiefs, Okris, Meghavritta and Indrasen, and of Samarthak, the merchant, were seen moving about in mysterious haste on the roads of Sagal.

These comings and goings continued for three days. The curiosity of both the gentry and the ordinary people reached a high pitch of excitement. On the evening of the third day, the President summoned the Republican Council to an urgent meeting. Until late that night, people kept waiting to know the results of the Council's deliberations. Sagal had learnt nothing new when its inhabitants retired for the night.

Next morning, even before the sun had risen, the streets and lanes of the city resounded with the sound of kettledrums. Many a timid citizen, having lived under the shadow of imminent disaster, and thinking that the armies of Kendras had entered the city, cried out in consternation. A lot of them, holding up their clothes with one hand, reached with the other for the weapons to which they had so far remained indifferent. The majority of them, however, were simply bewildered, and began peeping through doors and windows and from behind terrace walls, out of curiosity and fear.

When the sound of the kettledrum subsided, the notes of the military bugle were heard. Men on horseback made the announcement:

'Under the orders of the Republican Council, the President of the Republic of Madra, the Most Honourable, the Most Valiant, the Chief Noble Lord, the Commander-in-Chief Mithrodus hereby assumes full control of the administration of the Republic of Madra for the duration of the war. Under orders of the Council, the ownership of the entire wealth of the noble families now rests with the state. All the subjects of the Republic of Madra shall be regarded as equals in the eyes of the law and the state. No officer of the state shall levy contributions to the war fund by force. No citizens will be bound, under duress, to offer his services for the war.

'Any person taking out of the country, or dispatching to another country any wealth produced within the boundaries of the state, such as gold, foodgrains, clothing or cattle, in any form whatsoever, shall be punished by death. Half of the hereditary unearned income of the noble families, half of the money donated towards monasteries and monastic organizations, and the entire income from the grant-lands shall be payable to the war fund. Weapons of war, horses and chariots, belonging to families and to individual citizens shall become the property of the state for the duration of the war. All arable lands belonging to persons who voluntarily offer their services to the army of the republic, shall be free from taxation. Slaves who offer their services voluntarily shall be freed from bondage, along with their wives and children. The state shall look after the families of soldiers who die on the battlefield. The said order has been issued by the Most Honourable, the President of the Republic, the Commander-in-Chief and great feudatory chief, Mithrodus, with the assent of the Republican Council. It is the bounden duty of every citizen of the Republic to obey and carry out the said order.'

The nobles as well as the commonfolk were struck with amazement at the proclamation. As time went by, people began to talk about it, at one place with enthusiasm, at another with vexation. In the twilight of hope brought in by the new social order, the views and attitudes of people began to undergo a change. People with foresight began to make conjectures as to who would be appointed the new army chief and senior commanders.

Acharya Pravardhan

IT WAS PAST MIDNIGHT. AFTER A DAY OF APPREHENSION, PANIC and bewilderment, the town of Sagal was breathing heavily under the cover of darkness, silence and sleep. Every few minutes, the thick pall of silence was broken by the shouts of the guards at the ramparts and gates of the town. Armed soldiers, taciturn and alert, stood on duty in the streets and lanes. Orders had been issued to the effect that after midnight anyone whose identity could not be established, or anyone found in suspicious circumstances, would be arrested and brought before the officers of state. As a result, the clamour in the drinking parlours and in the prostitutes' quarters, which used to go on until late in the night, began to subside soon after sunset.

Besides the ramparts, the only other place where any activity or glimmer of light was to be seen was the palace gate of Acharya Pravardhan. There weary charioteers, grooms and attendants were trying to ward off sleep by making banal conversation. The tired horses, standing in front of the main gate, beat the cobblestones with their hoofs, to register their nervous restlessness. Some of the visitors to the palace had already left. The expectant eyes of the attendants and horses that remained would time and again look to the palace gate, and turn back disappointed. They were uncertain whether their masters had simply forgotten them.

In the past, too, on many occasions their masters had kept them waiting until late in the night at the gates of many

palaces, but then the situation and the prevailing atmosphere
had been different. This time there was neither the jingle
of dancers' anklets nor the resounding beat of the mridang[1]
to be heard. The sweet notes of music and guffaws of laughter
were missing and so were the pleasant odours of food and
wine. No one had remembered to send out bowls of wine
or the coarse *meraya*.[2] The five sentries standing at the gate,
armed and alert, were not there for mere show, as had been
the case on previous occasions. Their suspicious alertness was
such as to make the waiting grooms and attendants feel uneasy.

Similarly, in the corridors of the reception hall, armed
soldiers were keeping guard, instead of the usual torch-bearers.
Light was to be seen only in the assembly chamber.

Acharya Pravardhan looked extremely perturbed. By
his side sat Rudradhir, motionless, with his head bowed, looking
like an image carved in wood. Around them sat the feudatory
chiefs, Kartavir and Lakshman, the merchants Dharmajit and
Balbhadra, as also Pandit Vishnu Sharma and Vinay Sharma, the
son and grandson of the Chief Justice. They all sat with their
faces drawn and heads bowed reclining against cushions.

On the terrace the sentinel struck the gong announcing
the end of the third watch of the night. Realizing how late it
was, Pandit Vishnu Sharma sat up and, addressing the feudatory
chief Kartavir, said, 'The Commander-in-Chief suddenly
came to his senses and summoned the Council. As you know
they made a proclamation in the city. The fears aroused by
his actions have become a reality.' He looked at the Acharya
who sat in anxious contemplation, with his head bowed.

[1] Cylindrical drum, played on both ends.
[2] Coarse wine, toddy.

The Acharya only heaved a deep sigh. Others now sat up from their cushions, and began to stretch their limbs. Anxiety was writ large on every face.

The doorkeeper of the inner palace came up and announced that the ladies were arriving. The ladies entered, and each sat down by the side of the man related to her.

Stifling a yawn, Kartavir straightened his heavy back and said, 'In the present circumstances we can do nothing but wait. The Commander-in-Chief and the Chief Justice are but the arrows of crooked diplomacy, the men shooting them being the feudatory chiefs, Okris and Indrasen and the jumped-up groom, Prestha. By replacing all our military officers and commanders through fresh appointments and by winning over the public through this proclamation, they have virtually crippled us. There is none to beat Prestha in the game of intrigue; he is as cunning as Kautilya. And it is certain that the son of this groom will soon occupy the position, not just of a senior military officer, but of the Commander-in-Chief. This proclamation is just a lead-up to his appointment.'

Vishnu Sharma interrupted to say to Rudradhir, 'Young man, the best thing for you to do is to go straightaway to the city gate, and as soon as it is opened, get out of the city and take the road to the east. Go to Valka and stay with your maternal uncle. You should travel through other towns of the Republic and acquaint yourself with the prevailing conditions. After a few weeks or months, when these low-caste atheists have been crushed, the time will be ripe for you to come back to Sagal.'

Vishnu Sharma fell silent, seeing that the Acharya was shaking his bowed head in disapproval and clasping his hands tightly in an effort to control his feelings. His head still bowed, the Acharya said in a faint and hopeless tone, 'I am of the view

that Rudradhir should travel about in Magadh for a period
of two thousand days. For some time to come, Madra will
perforce suffer from the intrigues of Prestha and his band
of low-caste people. Valka is an utterly unprotected town.
In such circumstances, if Rudradhir falls a victim to some
conspiracy, we may not even know about it. I have a stomach
ailment and my health is failing. I would like Rudradhir to
receive his initiation for the redemption of the caste system
in Magadh, at the hands of sage Patanjali, and from the great
Brahmin commander and statesman Pushya Mitra. Madra will
not always remain under the heel of the low-born . . .' He
could not say more and fell silent.

'What a bizarre judgment the Chief Justice has given,' said
the merchant, Dharmajit, leaning back against his cushion.
'The incident of the Festival of Spring has almost been forgotten.'

'This is exactly what I was saying,' said Kartavir,
bending forward.

Another feudatory chief, Lakshman, took up the thread
of conversation and said, 'This is not the result of what happened
at the Festival of Spring; this is wartime diplomacy. At its root
lies the Chief Justice's faith in the system of government
that prevailed in the time of Milinda and his faith in the
Greek President of the Republic. Moreover, it is a form of
punishment to preserve discipline. Friends, this proclamation
of the President, that all the citizens of Madra are equal in
the eyes of the law and the Republic is a proof of this. It is
a way of winning over the people . . .' He glanced at Vishnu
Sharma and stopped.

Vishnu Sharma was not embarrassed. 'No,' he said, 'my
father himself holds in great regard the Buddhist tenet that "It

is by one's actions that one becomes a Brahmin." But I believe little can be done about his views at his age . . .'

'The Acharya's suggestion that Rudradhir should go away to Magadh is a good one,' said Balbhadra, the transport contractor, putting his hand to his mouth to stifle a yawn. 'I have contacts in every town on his route. He will have no difficulty. It is only when he is in Magadh that he can take the necessary steps for the liberation of Madra. Our hope lies in Pushya Mitra, who has been installed in his office by the proper rites of mantras.'

Noticing that the Acharya was again shaking his head, everyone became quiet and turned to look at him. 'We have not been able to get help from the ruler of Magadh at this juncture because of the shortage of time,' he said. 'It was not right to keep on waiting, pinning our hopes on the Brahmin commander. Valuable time has been lost. Instead of getting help from him, we got entangled in the intrigues of the low-born people. Commander Pushya Mitra could easily have given instructions to Ravi Sharma to send forces from Shursen. He himself is perhaps pre-occupied with the struggle for power in the south. He does seem to regard Shursen as the limit to which Jambu Dweep extends. This policy of our President for the defence of Madra will result in the subjugation of the nobility, and the unrestricted tyranny of the low-born people. A country without a proper government is like a cornfield without a watchman.'

The Acharya took a deep breath, and without looking at anyone in particular, thanked all the guests for their kind consideration and urged them to go home since it was getting very late. He himself got up from his mattress and the guests followed suit. Unable to speak any further because of the tears choking his throat, he merely folded his hands in salutation to the guests, and headed towards the interior of the palace.

Rudradhir's eyes were bloodshot and his face as immobile as a statue. He paid obeisance to the elders, but he and his friends remained standing where they were.

One by one the ladies of the nobility blessed him, applying the auspicious tilak on his forehead and offering him coconuts for good luck. Then as a propitious offering, each lady took out a gold coin, touched it to Rudradhir's head and threw it into a vessel to be given away in charity to the priest. After wishing him long life, success and fame, the elders and their ladies proceeded towards the main gate along a path lighted for them by the torch-bearers.

After the departure of the elders, the remaining four young men sat down in a relaxed fashion around Rudradhir. Rudradhir's younger brother, Vasudhir, out of respect for his elder brother and his friends, sat some distance away. Indradeep yawned and asked Vasudhir for a round of drinks.

Rudradhir sat with his elbow on the cushion and his head resting in his hand. Three quarters of the night had passed since he had returned from the House of Justice, and not a single word had passed his lips. The fires of ignominy and humiliation raging in his heart had consumed his power of speech.

When the sentence was pronounced in the House of Justice— a thousand days' banishment for insulting the son of a slave— Rudradhir felt so angry that he forgot all decorum due to the law and the government of the state. His eyes became bloodshot and his hand went to the belt where his sword usually hung. As within the precincts of the House of Justice only state officials could carry weapons—the plaintiff, respondent and other people were not permitted to do so—his hand could not grasp his weapon. Finding himself thus thwarted his anger and irritation increased. He raised his head contemptuously to look squarely into the eyes of the aged Chief Justice and say, 'Does the government of the caste nobility exist only for the glory of slaves?'

Not a muscle moved on the face of the aged Chief Justice at the youth's impudence; only his lips, surrounded by his snow-white beard, did. He said, 'Rudradhir, son of Acharya Pravardhan, the Chairman of the Republican Council, has been punished for his offence of insulting Prithusen, son of Prestha, the merchant, in public. He is now being further punished for contempt of this law court of Madra by an addition of another thousand days to his period of banishment.'

Silence fell on all sides. 'In view of the status and high birth of Acharya Pravardhan, the Chairman of the Council, a period of one day and one night is hereby granted to Rudradhir to prepare himself for his banishment, failing which the state officials shall force obedience to the order.'

As soon as Rudradhir stepped out of the House of Justice, he was greeted by Indradeep, Sakrid, Vinay Sharma, Balajit and other high-born young men. They seated him in a palanquin and carried him on their shoulders to the palace of the Acharya. That he should have accepted the insult to his caste and family, and should still be alive, was a thought too terrible for Rudradhir to bear. 'I should have killed Prithusen and thereafter killed myself,' he kept repeating to himself.

After drinking some wine, and taking Rudradhir's hand into his, Indradeep said, 'My friend, a man must submit to the will of the gods. The gods act according to their own purposes, which the mind of man cannot comprehend. A Brahmin has been banished, while a Sudra has been honoured—this in itself will prove to be the instrument of emancipation of Madra.' Taking another bowl of wine he went on, 'The Brahmin commander, Pushya Mitra, has not been able to grasp the significance of the Acharya's message. The day you come back, holding aloft the banner of the caste system, riding at the head of the Magadh army, the destroyer of the low-born, that very day, all the conceited, low-born Sudras of Madra shall atone for their sins by serving as the animals of sacrifice.' Raising the bowl of wine above his head, he continued, 'I swear by my noble birth, that for the insult suffered by my friend, I shall not rest content till I have plunged into flames the entire family of Prestha. May the gods bear witness to my vow.' At this, his listeners also raised their wine bowls and drank, to show their participation in his vow.

Sakrid sidled up to Rudradhir, almost touching his shoulder, and said in a conspiratorial whisper, 'Friends, we lost one good chance by waiting for Pushya Mitra. Are we going to waste all our opportunities by hanging on like this? I am of the opinion that instead of going to Magadh, Rudradhir should proceed to Darva. He should try to force an alliance with Kendras. Kendras wants to extend the bounds of his empire. By coming to an understanding with him, we can divide the kingdom in half, and set up in the other half the rule of the Paurav dynasty, the protector of the caste system. In the course of time we can take over the rest of the kingdom also. The great sage Chanakya was right when he said, "A wise man will give up half for fear of losing the whole and preserve the rest."'

'What did you say?' asked Rudradhir, coming back to himself. 'Will the conquering Kendras seek our assistance to administer his empire? Once he captures Madra, he will destroy, body and soul, every possibility of the establishment of an independent state, either of the Paurav dynasty or of the twice-born Brahmins.'

'What Rudradhir says is quite correct,' said Vinay Sharma, putting down his empty wine bowl. 'If the Greek Kendras has any sympathy, it will be for the tonsured Buddhists. They will honour the low-born Kendras with the title of the "Righteous King" as they did Milinda, and he in turn will grant these wretches his protection and support. Once again the religion of holy sacrifice and of the caste system will stand to lose. It goes without saying that the Greeks will oppose the caste system. Our only hope lies in Pushya Mitra.'

'We have lost a golden opportunity because of the policy of the elders,' said Rudradhir, trying to shake off his depression. 'We showed weakness before Kendras; we weakened the Republic. Because of Sarvarth's policy of capturing state power, we have entirely lost the confidence and respect of the people. If we had removed the aged President by force, at the right moment, and had taken over the control of the army . . .' Finding everyone silent, he changed the subject, by saying, 'But let that be. I think the venerable Vishnu Sharma is right. It is better that I reach the city gate before sunrise, rather than expose myself in daylight to the jeers of the masses. The longer I delay, the more painful will be my departure, since the news will have spread. If I continue to live and breathe, after putting up with that insult hurled at my caste, my family and myself, it is with the hope that one day I may be able to take revenge.' He bowed his head.

Having gone without sleep for so long, his friends were feeling weary. Only the eyes of Rudradhir and Vasudhir remained alert and thoughtful. Putting his hand to his mouth to mask a yawn, Sakrid said to Vasudhir, 'Have all the preparations been made for the Arya's departure?'

'Yes, Arya,' replied Vasudhir. 'He is thinking of going on horseback instead of in a chariot. Only Mathura, his trusted attendant, will go with him.'

At a sign from Indradeep, Vasudhir asked the attendant to bring the wine tray again. Indradeep filled a bowl with his own hand and put it to Rudradhir's lips, saying, 'Friend, we are parting today with the pledge that we shall fight unto death for the protection of our blood and race and our sacred rights. The day of reunion will come soon.' All the friends drank again after Rudradhir had emptied his bowl.

'We shall all accompany Rudradhir to a distance of one *yojan*[1] beyond the city gate,' proposed Vinay Sharma. In support of this proposal, they drank again. With drink, Rudradhir's voice, which had been restrained, became normal, and then hardened somewhat. Holding Vinay Sharma by the arm, he took him to one side and said, 'What do you think is going to happen to Divya?'

Blinking his drink-heavy eyes, Vinay Sharma replied, 'There is no check on her movements, since our grandfather is extremely fond of her. My elder, Prabuddha Sharma, encourages Divya in her self-willed way of life, firstly because of grandfather's indulgent attitude, and secondly because he himself is inclined towards the faith of the tonsured ones. The period of two thousand days is surely very long. To

[1] Ancient measure of distance, roughly thirteen kilometres.

make the girl wait for so long . . . The family will doubtless be distressed on account of this.'

'What about the groom's son, Prithusen?' asked Rudradhir, looking into Vinay Sharma's eyes.

'There is some slanderous gossip rife about the two of them,' replied Vinay Sharma vaguely, dropping his gaze.

Yawning, Balajit called to Rudradhir, 'It won't be long before the sun rises. You will need time to bid farewell to your father and mother, and to the rest of the family.'

Self-surrender

MITHRODUS, THE AGED PRESIDENT AND COMMANDER-IN-CHIEF, realizing the magnitude of the problem, resolved to mount a determined resistance to Kendras. He entrusted the treasury and the department of war supplies to Prestha, the magnate, and the department of war strategy to Okris, the Greek noble. The task of fighting off the enemy in the impregnable mountain passes by the Tavisha river was entrusted to Prithusen with his army of freshly trained soldiers. The President took upon himself the work of general coordination and supervision. The internal administration of the city and of the state was left to the Chief Justice.

This new arrangement soon dispelled much of the fear and panic that had prevailed among the populace, and aroused a new enthusiasm for the war effort. Inspired by the thought of defending their country, groups of citizens began to offer their services voluntarily. Production of the weapons of war increased fourfold.

The President, feeble with age, could not travel widely over the country's rough roads. He could be seen, however, in his palanquin at all hours of the day in parts of the capital or its suburbs, engaged in inspection work. Prithusen was often seen riding by the side of his palanquin, on his agile white horse, its neck bent almost double by the tightly pulled reins, or he would be seen galloping, swift as an arrow, through the streets and lanes, followed by a detachment of cavalry. From dawn to dusk he was busy training the infantry and the cavalry in tactics of attack and defence. He spent days in the forests and in the lowlands of the Apaga river training his men in jungle warfare.

Prithusen was well liked by the Chief Justice, and also by Prabuddha Sharma and Dhriti Sharma, yet he never went to the palace of the Chief Justice, conscious as he was of the silent hostility of Vishnu Sharma and Vinay Sharma towards him. With his father's permission, he made one visit to the Chief Justice to ask him for the hand of his great-granddaughter. The old man's reply was, 'My son, at this time you have taken upon yourself a very heavy responsibility. You should attend to that, heart and soul. There is a time for everything.'

Divya's heart, already laden with worry, had now, like a flower, begun to wilt under the heavy weight of another anxiety. She would have to wait for days on end for a mere glimpse of Prithusen. She went to the palaces of Mallika and Vasumitra looking for him, but would come back disappointed. Unable to restrain herself any longer, she went to the palace of Prestha, the magnate. Prithusen's father and mother greeted her warmly, took her into their arms and smelt her hair according to the custom, but there was no sign of Prithusen. Sick at heart but with a smile on her lips, she went home and in utter despair shut herself up in her room. Mahadevi would scold her for her listlessness and apathy, but Divya could give no reply except to shed tears. Now and then, when he had some free moments from his work, Prithusen would send a message to Divya through Vapa, the old maidservant, and they would meet for a little while, either in the seclusion of a grove by the side of the lake, or in the palaces of Mallika, Vasumitra and Prestha. Overwhelmed by emotion, Divya would throw herself into his arms, with tears streaming from her eyes. Prithusen would himself grow extremely restless and, in turn, seek comfort in Divya. Divya would be obliged to resist his advances by holding his hands in hers and this would make him languid and absent-minded. It caused Divya much suffering to see him in this state.

Prithusen said one day, 'I shall soon be leaving for the battle front by the Tavisha river. You have accepted my love, yet you continue to spurn me. I shall carry with me only the painful memory of your rejection. What if I don't come back and it is my dead body that is brought back to Sagal!' He clasped his arms tightly, in an attempt to restrain himself. Divya put her hand on his mouth and burst out crying.

Prithusen had spoken out of frustration, mingled with self-pity. But when Divya burst into tears, his heart was filled with remorse. Holding her in a close embrace, he began to kiss her hair, her tear-stained eyes, her cheeks, consoling her and begging her forgiveness for his harsh words. On her part, Divya was swept away by her desire to soothe his unrest. Oblivious of their separate identities, their hearts merged in a flood of mutual passion.

The moment was, for Divya, the culmination of a long period of distress and despair. Whenever she reflected on her suffering, the words of the physician Cheebuk, the Buddhist monk, would come to her mind, 'Joy and sorrow are interdependent. They exist only in so far as we give credence to thought and feeling. At the root of sorrow, in every situation, lies desire. The satisfaction of one desire gives birth to another. Real happiness lies not in the satisfaction of desire, but in ridding oneself of it.' The monk's sermon now irritated her. It would be a lie to say that the Chief Justice's verdict in Prithusen's favour and his promotion to the rank of commander had not elated her for until a few days ago her only wish was

the fulfilment of that desire. Any reference to his abilities
and his performance would thrill her and make her all the more
eager to be near him.

Divya regarded Chhaya's mother, Dhata, as her own mother
and, accordingly, called her 'Amma'. Chhaya had been Divya's
playmate in childhood and was the same age as Divya, hence
her love for Divya knew no bounds. She would put up with
Divya's rebukes, given with or without reason, and would
never harbour any hard feelings. At times, when Divya was
upset, she would rail at Chhaya and say harsh things, but
even then Chhaya would remain by her side. Divya too was
fond of Chhaya. A friendly informality existed between the
two girls. Divya took her attendant as much for granted as the
clothes she wore every day. Bahul, Chhaya's lover and the
chief-slave of the household, had gone away. Of his own
will, he had enrolled as a soldier to obtain his freedom. In
Divya's dejection and lassitude, Chhaya felt her own hidden
sorrow. The measure of each girl's suffering was in her capacity
to bear and to express it.

Chhaya always sat by Divya's side, wherever she was.
With her hand resting on Divya's foot or some other part of
her body, she would go on talking of this, that and the other to
distract Divya's mind. She would tell Divya about Mahadevi's
constant concern for Divya's marriage; about the numerous
worthy suitors; about Prithusen's request for Divya's hand
and the grandsire's reply to it; about the indignant remarks
made by Vishnu Sharma and the usually reticent Bhrigu Sharma,
in the privacy of their rooms.

Divya felt furious at the disrespect shown towards Prithusen
by her family. 'Let my great-grandfather know, let the whole
palace know, that I shall not marry anyone except Prithusen.

Arya Prithusen has expressed before the grandsire not only his wish but mine too. This and this alone will satisfy me. There is no question of my marrying anyone else. Only when my great-grandfather knows this, will he pay any serious attention to Prithusen's proposal. And the marriage must not be delayed. I would like it to take place before the Arya leaves for the battle front.' She spoke her mind before Chhaya without let or hindrance, knowing that her views would be conveyed to Amma, and through her to the whole household. 'What then? Let them all know,' she said to herself.

One day Tara, wife of Prabuddha Sharma, her paternal uncle, took Divya into her arms and said tenderly, 'It isn't proper to be so impatient, dear. The grandsire cannot deny your wish because he loves you so deeply. But in these disturbed times, people will not think well of you, if you marry in such haste. Besides, the judgment given by your great-grandfather in Prithusen's favour will be construed as scandalous partiality.'

The news that Kendras's army was bearing down on Sagal had brought terror and panic into the innermost recesses of the city palaces. 'There is no reason for alarm,' said Prabuddha Sharma reassuringly, both to his wife and to Divya. 'Our new army, so well organized by Okris and Prithusen, will march into battle after viewing the eleventh moon, on the auspicious day determined by Vikram, the astrologer. The fortunes of war will surely take a favourable turn. There is a world of difference between mercenary soldiers forcibly conscripted, and those engaged in the defence of their motherland.'

Divya learned that after midnight on the fourth day, Prithusen would leave for the front with his army, and she felt a stab of pain in her heart. Divya had had no direct experience of war, but she had heard a great deal about it: that hordes of men, with deadly weapons in their hands, attacked one another, that rivers of blood flowed, that thousands of wounded lay screaming on the ground, that war always meant peril and disaster. In her mind's eye she saw Prithusen, mounted on his horse, plunging headlong into the slaughter. Under instructions from Mahadevi, Divya was required to help in numerous household duties, to divert her mind from thoughts of disaster and depression. Thus, while her hands were engaged mechanically in household tasks, her mind would see visions of battle: of Prithusen, seated on his white horse, his sword raised high, charging into the jaws of danger. Such visions sent a shiver through her body.

Bahul, the chief-slave and Chhaya's lover, had now been posted as foot soldier in Prithusen's army. Separated from him, Chhaya was miserable. Divya would make Chhaya sit by her side and talk to her about Bahul, thereby seeking consolation for herself. Chhaya had procured an amulet for her lover's safety from Baikunth, the tantric pandit. Divya, too, parted with a gold ring to obtain from the pandit an especially powerful talisman for Prithusen's protection.

On each of the three days before his departure, Divya managed to slip out of the palace in search of Prithusen. She went to the palaces of Mallika and Vasumitra, to the garden by the lake and to the palace of Prestha. But each time she came back disappointed. She learned from Dhriti Sharma that Prithusen, as commander of the armed forces, was extremely busy, that he knew no rest, that he was spending day and night on horseback, and that if one horse got tired, he would call for another.

'What if he is so busy? Can't he spare even a few moments for me?' she would say to herself. 'Had he thought of me, he could easily have sent Vapa to me . . . But this is as it should be, I don't deserve any better. When have I ever provided any comfort to his tired body or to his anxious mind? I have always thwarted him by my harsh indifference. If, in this struggle, he has chosen to blot me out of his mind, then I have fully deserved it.'

Her eyes filled with tears. But she was not free even to cry. She could not give vent to her feelings as freely as Chhaya could. Her throat so choked with tears that she would find it hard to breathe. In her mind's eye would appear the same sequence of events: Prithusen, tired, weary and eager, seeking rest and solace in her arms and then, frustrated by her rejection, plunging headlong into the thick of the battle. 'From which, very likely, only my dead body will come back,' he had said. Prithusen's dejected face rose before her eyes and her soul felt crushed.

She began to imagine the worst. She saw Prithusen, falling from his horse, covered in blood. She saw a troop of soldiers, stricken with grief, standing round a dead body. With such scenes as these, she also saw visions of her own death. She recalled the discussions about life, death and the thereafter in her great-grandfather's assemblies, and she would imagine that she and Prithusen would be born again, to be united forever. She remembered the utterances of Buddhist sages, that it was the keen desires and mental restlessness of mankind that made death so painful.

Prithusen's eagerness and longing came back to her. She became restless, and kept repeating to herself, 'My body belongs to him, my mind belongs to him, my whole being belongs to him. Why should I see him suffer? Whatever he desires shall be his. But where can I meet him before he sets out for the battlefield? There is only one evening left.'

Divya held in her hand the all-protecting amulet that she had procured from the tantrik. She would not let Prithusen go to the battlefield until she had tied the amulet around his arm with her own hands. Though she appeared calm, inwardly every fibre of her being trembled with anxiety, like the swings of a veena.

In the temple of Brahma, the Lord of Creation, a grand yajna was organized by Prestha, the magnate, to offer prayers for the well-being of his son and for the victory of the forces of Madra. In the holy monastery of the Buddhists, the magnate organized for the chanting of hymns by three hundred monks before the image of Lord Buddha, and afterwards he fed a thousand bhikshus. While in the temple of the Greek god Zeus, he arranged for the sacrifice of a horse with great pomp and ceremony. Taking Chhaya with her, Divya went to all three places, but Prithusen was nowhere to be seen. She learned that he was in the military camp. She turned back disappointed, but the disappointment made her all the more restless. She begged Dhata to go to the palace of the magnate and sent Guha, a slave, to the military camp to find out where Prithusen was.

Divya was perplexed. On one hand, each moment she spent without Prithusen seemed to be as long as a lifetime, on the other, the sun sinking towards the west, made her feel that time was rapidly slipping out of her hands. Neither had Dhata come back from the palace, nor had Guha returned with any news of Prithusen. The setting sun illuminated only the treetops now. To Divya its fast-fading rays seemed to be carrying away with them her last hopes.

The light died on the treetops. Struggling against her despair, Divya turned her eyes towards the north, and the mountain range that towered above the palaces of Sagal, on which the last rays of the setting sun still lingered. Solace and relief seemed as far from her as the mountain tops. Dhata came back to tell her that she had failed to locate Prithusen. Just then, the last light on the mountain also vanished.

Divya could not sit still any more. She got up from her bed and sat down beside it, only to get up again and walk up and down the room, before going out into the garden. After a few moments, she came back inside. She had no respite. Feeling thirsty, she asked Chhaya many times for water, but when it was brought, Divya put the cup down by her side and forgot to drink.

Just then Mala, another maidservant, appeared at the doorway and said, 'Vapa, the maidservant from the palace of Prithusen, has brought gifts from the auspicious yajna, and is at present in Mahadevi's room.'

'What? When did she come?' exclaimed Divya, jumping up from her bed.

'This very moment, Mistress.'

Divya felt abashed at her excitement and lay down once more, but she could not take her eyes off the door. Nor could she keep lying in bed after the maid had left. She got up and began pacing up and down the room once again. When it became impossible for her to suppress her excitement, she turned to Chhaya, 'Go and see if Vapa is still there or has left.'

Just then old Vapa entered the room. Greeting Divya and praying that Divya's afflictions be transferred to her own worthless aged person, she sat down by her side and began giving a long description of the yajna ceremony. Her eyes turned again and again towards Chhaya, who was listening intently to every word that she uttered. Turning to Chhaya, Divya said, 'Go to the kitchen, Chhaya, and bring some sweets for Vapa.'

When Chhaya had gone, Vapa whispered into Divya's ear, 'An hour after sunset, in Mallika's palace.'

Divya's eyes sparkled. She took off a diamond ring and handed it to Vapa. Then, getting up eagerly, she began to change her clothes and make herself beautiful. In her excitement, she broke out into sweat repeatedly and her hands trembled, slowing down her preparations. She could not talk to Chhaya who was standing there to assist her, or speak in her natural voice. She was getting ready to set out on her triumphal expedition of self-surrender. These preparations were a necessary ritual for that expedition.

This self-surrender was an offering to prepare Prithusen for his departure to the battlefield to defend Madra and to appease the goddess of victory. Divya, therefore, got ready to become his beloved in his hour of trial and danger, to give him courage and strength by offering herself to him, by making her way into his heart. He alone was the one nearest to her in the whole world. She was ready to sacrifice her family, her social position, her very being for his sake. She took into her hand the all-protecting amulet and asked Chhaya to get the chariot ready.

A month had passed since the infantry and the cavalry of Madra had left for the Tavisha river, under the command of Prithusen. The news that began to pour into the town was that Kendras was no longer advancing. His forces had begun to withdraw towards Darva. The whole town of Sagal was thrilled to hear the news, and Divya more than anyone else. She began to hope that in another month's time Prithusen would return home, holding aloft the banner of victory. In her imagination she saw scenes of her wedding ceremony. Time passed more quickly now, as she was filled with pride in his victory, praying for Prithusen's well-being and hoping for an early reunion. Mahadevi felt relieved at heart that with Prithusen away from the town, the girl had finally calmed down.

The second month was soon over. The army of Kendras had been defeated and was now retreating, while Prithusen, in hot pursuit of the enemy, was penetrating deeper and deeper into the territory of Darva. That the territory of the Republic was being extended filled the hearts of the citizens of Sagal with great enthusiasm. Divya was happy and proud that she too had a hand in that victory. She grew more tranquil, content to spend her days just awaiting his return.

She would shut her eyes and recall the night when Prithusen had set out for the battlefield. When she relived the feelings of that night, a wave of excitement would pass through her body. Finding that her despair had turned into victory, she was filled with a sense of achievement and pride. Her heart leapt with joy at the thought that within her she was carrying the presence of Prithusen. As her joy mounted, it turned to restlessness; she wanted Prithusen to come back immediately, fearing that further delay in his return would become a source of shame.

At the end of the fourth month the news came that Prithusen had conquered half the territory of Darva, that Kendras had been killed at his hands with a sword thrust and that Prithusen himself had been wounded in battle. The victorious army was returning home, carrying with it jewels, treasures, herds of horses and cattle, besides two thousand sturdy slaves and beautiful slave-girls. Hearing this news, Divya clasped both her hands to her bosom, and unable to control her tears, covered herself with a silken shawl and lay down in bed.

She began to feel embarrassed at the change that was taking place in her body. Although no one else had noticed or even suspected her condition, Divya, pretending to be unwell, spent most of the time confined to her chamber. Every moment of the day, her soul would call out for Prithusen, 'Come back soon, Arya! Come back and take care of your Divya, and of that part of yourself which you have committed to her.'

The Harsh Reality

LONG BEFORE SUNRISE THE STREAM OF PEOPLE MOVING DOWN every road and path had become a sea of eager citizens headed for the northern gate of Sagal. A large number of people had passed the night or much of it at the gate itself. In their hands they carried garlands of flowers and in their pockets and uttariyas, flowers and rice-confetti. Under the festooned and garlanded gateway, musicians sat playing auspicious music, accompanied by the beat of kettledrums. Even the trees standing by the city wall and on the northern road were crowded with people bursting with eager curiosity. In their enthusiasm, many had set out along the road to the north, to meet the soldiers returning in triumph.

Runners brought news that the victorious army of Madra, with their wounded commander, Prithusen, was slowly moving towards Sagal. The previous night, the army had camped at a distance of two yojanas from the city. The commander was unable to travel more rapidly on account of his wounds. As soon as the news of Prithusen's injuries reached Sagal, the aged physician Cheebuk, with a number of other eminent and experienced physicians of the town were sent post-haste on chariots drawn by the fastest horses.

Shading their eyes with their hands from the glare of the sun, and looking out towards the north, the crowd noticed a cloud of dust rising on the horizon. The sound of musical instruments was drowned in the loud cheering of the crowd.

Weary with pain and fever, surrounded by a slow-moving army carrying cartloads of gold, jewels, precious stones and valuable articles captured from the conquered territory of Darva, together with two thousand men and women slaves, Prithusen at last arrived at the city gate.

A delegation of happy high-born matrons welcomed the victorious commander and performed the arati with a hundred and one lighted lamps, their wicks burning in ghee, around Prithusen. Seero, the granddaughter of Mithrodus, the aged President of the Republic and Commander-in-Chief, anointed him as victor, and in accordance with the Greek custom, placed on his head a coronet of green leaves.

The President pressed the young commander's head to his beard and remained standing in silent rapture for some time. Dev Sharma, the aged Chief Justice, supported by slave-attendants, stepped down from his palanquin and putting his hand on the head of the wounded commander showered his blessings on him. The feudatory chief, Sarvarth, Acharya Pravardhan and members of the Republican Council and other prominent citizens welcomed the young commander in a similar way.

The city of Sagal went wild with the joy of victory. Festivities continued day and night, in the streets and in the lanes. The booty captured in Darva, including male and female slaves, was put up for auction by the state officials to replenish the government treasury. The President distributed compensation in the form of money and slaves to those families whose breadwinners had been killed in the war.

Prestha, the magnate, organized a grand yajna for the propitiation of the gods. Acharya Pravardhan agreed to act

as the Chief Priest of the yajna. A thousand priests chanted
mantras and performed the religious rituals. In the holy Buddhist
monastery, the magnate engaged a thousand bhikshus to chant
the sutras before the image of the Buddha and thereafter gave
them large donations in gratitude of their prayers for deliverance.
He also offered a sacrifice in the temple of the Greek god Zeus.

Prestha's palace resounded with rejoicing and merrymaking.
The only section in the palace where silence reigned was
the one in which Prithusen lay. The eminent physician, the
aged Cheebuk, was in attendance. A competent surgeon, he
stitched Prithusen's wounds with strands of *kausheya*[1] grass and
bound them up with herbal dressings. He also prescribed a
restorative, and ordered him complete rest. Through sleep
induced by sedatives, Prithusen began to recover his health.
Seero, the granddaughter of Mithrodus, the Commander-in-
Chief, stayed day and night with the victorious commander,
attending to his needs.

Divya heard from the mouths of Chhaya and other
maidservants as well as from Dhriti Sharma and the children
of the palace the accounts of the festive reception given to
Prithusen on his entry into the town. She herself had not gone
to the city gate because of a sense of embarrassment at
her condition. Her position made her feel miserable. It filled
her with a sense of pride that Prithusen had been received
in triumph, but the news that he was wounded and suffering
made her anxious and uneasy. 'Had I been married before
he left for the front, I would have gone to the city gate in a
palanquin in whatever condition I was,' she said to herself,
feeling bitter. 'I would have put his wounded head on my lap

[1] Sacred grass used in religious ceremonies.

and brought him into the palace.' That Seero should be by his bedside was a cruel irony. In that state of helplessness, she kept her body well covered, and guarding her secret with all possible care, lost herself in the contemplation of that moment when Prithusen would recover his health and their marriage would be duly solemnized with proper ritual and ceremony.

Divya grew impatient as she waited daily for the old maidservant Vapa to bring some message from the palace of Prestha. A moment came when she could not restrain herself any longer. After sunset, she wrapped herself up well, and taking Chhaya with her, went in a palanquin to the magnate's residence.

Her heart pounded within her breast as she was ushered along the path leading to Prithusen's room by the slave-girl. The slave gently pushed back the door leaf. There lay Prithusen, weak and emaciated, his head and shoulders heavily bandaged. Near the sick man's bed sat Seero, fair-complexioned, her golden-yellow hair falling down her back, and on her head was a coronet of jewels, in the Greek style. With the help of a maidservant, she was preparing a potion for the patient in a vessel which stood on a pedestal before her.

As her eyes fell on Divya, Seero, with the authority of the mistress of the house, gestured her to sit down on a seat near Prithusen's bed. Then, putting her mouth close to Divya's ear, she whispered in a barely audible voice, 'He is not to be disturbed. He is sleeping, and these are the physician's orders. It is too exhausting for the patient if visitors talk to him.'

From where she sat, Divya could see only Prithusen's bandaged head and shoulders. He was asleep. To be so near him and yet not be able to utter a word to him or touch him and to have a third person standing as a barrier between them, exasperated Divya. She yearned to take him in her arms. The passage of the last six months vanished from her mind, and the feel of his touch on the night of his departure came back to her. Seero's presence and her discouraging attitude kept Divya from taking Prithusen in her arms. She looked at him with wide-open eyes and her gaze took in all of him. As her emotions could find no outlet, they flowed out as tears.

Seeing her agitation and sorrow, Seero came over and with a show of civility began enquiring after the health of the Chief Justice and the family. She also described in detail the critical condition of the patient and the heavy responsibilities that lay upon her, how night and day she had to be in constant attendance, how despite the insistence of friends and relatives she found it impossible to leave the wounded hero and join in the festivities.

To Divya, Seero's behaviour appeared to be intolerably haughty and conceited. She seemed to be making fun of her unfortunate situation. She could say nothing in reply but only lower her eyes and remain silent.

'You too seem to have missed the festivities, my dear,' Seero said, her eyes opened wide with curiosity. 'Without you it has been so dull in the cultural programmes. Devi Mallika is always looking for you and thinking about you.' Her searching gaze travelled over Divya's body, and the effort to suppress her smile made her full red lips quiver. She covered her lips with a corner of her stole.

Divya could not bear to wait for Prithusen to wake up. As politeness demanded, she somehow managed to express her wishes for the speedy recovery of the wounded hero and came away.

When he woke up, Prithusen learned from a maidservant about Divya's visit and her departure. At the city gate, when the ladies and young women of the nobility had anointed him, his eyes had been searching for Divya, and his ears had been eagerly waiting to hear her voice. Whenever his pain subsided a little, his thoughts would turn to her. That she should have come after such a long time, and then gone away without even waiting for him to wake up, caused him great grief. As he was himself unable to go and see her, he became all the more restless. Troubled by her apparent indifference, he was at a loss to understand what could have occasioned it. He asked Seero why Divya had gone away without even waiting to speak to him.

An ironical smile hovered on Seero's lips. With a pout of her thick red lips, she said disdainfully, 'How can I tell what was on her mind, Arya? Maybe the great-granddaughter of the Chief Justice did not have enough time to wait until the patient woke up. What else can I say?' Prithusen did not have the courage to ask any more questions to Seero.

His anxiety, since he was not able to allay it, became all the more oppressive. However hard he tried, he could not imagine what could have happened during his six months' absence. 'Can it be that Divya's ardour has cooled towards me out of pride for her high birth? Can it be that she has grown afraid of her family? Or perhaps she has been drawn towards someone else, someone who is more attractive? Why is she unwilling even to see me now?' Lying alone, he would spin all kinds of dramatic explanations.

The treatment administered by old Cheebuk proved highly effective. With his medicines and the life-giving virtues of rare fruits from Kandahar, Prithusen's health soon recuperated. This in turn led to an increased eagerness for Divya. He had gambled his life in order to achieve success. Now, in the absence of Divya, that very success appeared meaningless.

Prestha, the magnate, was overjoyed at his son's recovery. But when he learned that Prithusen had become sad and listless, he made arrangements to provide dance, music and other entertainment to divert him. But these distractions only jarred on Prithusen's senses. Impetuously, he would dismiss the performers from his room with a wave of his hand and lie by himself in silence. Sometimes, the magnate himself would sit at his son's bedside and make small talk to divert his son's mind. But Prithusen took no interest in such talk either. He kept thinking of how best he could broach with his father the subject that was uppermost in his mind, but he could not summon up the necessary courage.

With his hand resting on the shoulder of a newly bought slave-girl, dark and beautiful, who held a veena in her hand, the magnate entered his son's room. He sat down by the bed and said, 'My son, your health has been making satisfactory progress, thanks to Cheebuk's remarkable medicines. But why do you look so despondent? There is nothing more injurious to one's health than depression. Cheer up, son, and try to take an interest in things. You have a fine ear for music. This slave-girl, Ulka, comes from Dakshinapath,[1] and is an excellent veena player. She will play for you, and I am sure you'll find her music very soothing to your troubled mind.'

The magnate signalled the girl to begin playing. At the first touch of the strings Prithusen was filled with a sense of weariness. He raised his hand for the girl to stop, and then, turning towards his father, said, 'Father, I wish to go in a palanquin to pay a call at the palace of the Chief Justice. Do I have your permission to do so?'

[1] The southern route, from Mathura towards Avanti (Malva) and Gujarat, along the edge of the Vindhya mountains.

'In this state of health, when you are so weak and feeble? Why, what is prompting you to go there?' asked the magnate in surprise, passing his fingers through his grizzled beard, now yellowing with age.

'Before I left for the battlefield, I had asked for the hand of the Chief Justice's great-granddaughter. I want to seek his approval now without delay,' Prithusen replied, with his eyes cast down.

The old magnate continued to play with his beard. With a distant smile, he said, 'Son, the gods have been pleased with you and have blessed you with knowledge, talent, aptitude, wealth and victory in battle. In due time, the gods will be generous in granting you the joys of matrimony. Besides Divya, there will be many a beautiful and cultured damsel whom you will find pleasing. A patient man who feels the pulse of time and acts accordingly is blessed by the gods with joys in this world as well as in the next. Wait for the opportune time, my son.'

Out of regard for his father, Prithusen made no reply, but began to feel all the more restless at heart. Divya would appear before him in many enchanting images: Divya dancing, her arms weaving sinuous gestures, her full bosom heaving above her slender waist, her shapely, supple thighs, showing under a tightly wound silken sari, her soft, oval face, her curved red lips, her sensitive nostrils, her large, trusting eyes; Divya on the day of their first meeting, her easy amiability; Divya with her eyes moist at finding him restless and impatient; Divya putting her head on his chest and murmuring words of reassurance. How his heart would throb at the touch of her limbs, her devotion and surrender on the night of his departure for the battle front! And his whole body would quiver with desire.

He yearned for Divya's company, but then like a wave that breaks against the shore and then recedes, his mind, frustrated by his helplessness, would drift off to other things. 'Why has she become indifferent to me? Was there such callousness behind that tenderness and grace! Her charm and softness, then, were as meaningless as the beauty of the moon reflected in the shallow waters of a stream.'

Seero was very loving towards him, yet he ignored her. Sometimes this indifference would embarrass him. But, then he would tell himself: 'No, no, Divya must become mine.' With his eyes on the ceiling he would think again and again of those moments of intimacy, when he was eager and Divya reluctant, and later, when she gave herself up to him, in his moments of extreme agitation. He would recall those times and ask himself: 'How could she be so fickle?'

His father praised Seero to him, for was she not the granddaughter of the President of the Republic? Prithusen guessed his father's intentions and one day said despondently, 'Father, I have pledged my word to the Chief Justice's great-granddaughter and I love her deeply. It is not possible for me to think of any other woman.'

The old magnate's hand paused in the act of combing his beard. The furrows on his forehead deepened, tightly set in determination, but a smile still played on his lips. Turning to Chir, the attendant slave, who was fanning them with a large palmyra leaf, he said, 'Let Vak take your place now.'

Vak, another slave in the household, was both deaf and dumb. He was kept to act as an attendant whenever confidential discussions took place. Prithusen sensed that his father proposed to discuss the subject seriously. He decided to remain firm in his resolve.

As the magnate talked, a smile continued to flicker in his eyes and on his lips, 'My son, with young men, passion for women is always strong. But passion is one thing, and life quite another. Life is like a vessel full of water, whereas passion is like the bubbles that rise in it. To achieve success in life, it sometimes becomes necessary to suppress passion, similar to a medicine that may be unpalatable, but still has to be taken in the interest of health. You have abundant means at your disposal, and can pay court to any number of pretty women for the satisfaction of your desires. But let marriage be an instrument for the achievement of success and power. It is power alone that gives a man the right to enjoy and desire.'

The magnate paused for a moment to give his son a chance to reply, but seeing that he sat silent with his head bowed, he continued, 'My son, a woman is not the only fulfilment of life; she is only an instrument for the realization of something greater than herself. A successful man, a man of influence can have any number of women, but not many opportunities present themselves to achieve success in life. Son, it is power alone that matters; the power of wealth and the power over men. Do you intend to turn your back on the favours of the head of state, the President of the Republic, and live merely on the aged Dev Sharma's graces? Son, you understand politics. Just think, by marrying the granddaughter of the Greek President, you will, without any effort and without any opposition, become one of the high-born nobles; but by marrying the great-granddaughter of Dev Sharma, even if the liberal Dev Sharma does not oppose it, you will turn the entire Brahmin clan against yourself. The power of the Brahmins lies in the subjection of the common folk, in their right to secure the services of the people. If commoners were to become their equals, what special privileges would be left for the Brahmins to enjoy? They will never allow the common people to become powerful, but at the same time, they cannot ignore the influence of those who wield power. Why should we turn anyone against us? Son, it is friends and supporters that we need, not enemies.'

The magnate paused for a moment and glanced at his son, hoping that he would express agreement. But finding him silent and sullen as before, his voice softened, 'Son, it is from the position of a common slave that I myself have risen, and have acquired a position where my son, an army commander, can aspire to become the Commander-in-Chief. What you have already achieved is not the peak of your possible success. The value of wealth and position does not lie in foolish self-indulgence, but in the power that they bring.

'Son, the height of enjoyment lies in the exercise of power. It is time that you won the confidence of the President of the Republic and acquired the rights and privileges of a noble. Then, with your resources, you can raise an army of your own for the defence of Madra. That army will be your strength. You will be able to change the very face of the Republic of Madra. I want to see you in the seat of supreme power, as President of the Republic. I want to see you on the throne of Madra. If in Magadh, the rule of the Maurya dynasty, who were Sudras by birth, can be established, why can't the rule of the Prestha dynasty be established in Madra?'

He looked again at his son, but Prithusen still said nothing. He continued to sit as before, his hand on his chin. His father had pushed him into the waves of ambition and aspirations and had left him there. He felt bewildered at finding himself in that vast expanse. The force of the current was proving too strong for his willpower. He had difficulty in just keeping his head up and catching his breath.

Resting his elbow on the cushion, the magnate turned aside. Prithusen thought that his father was about to leave. Fearing that his silence might be misconstrued as agreement, with his head still bowed, he made a bold attempt to speak his mind, 'But Father, I have given my word to Divya. I have already accepted her as my wife. That would be a violation of trust.'

The old man's brow darkened, his eyebrows dropped lower over his eyes, and the ironical smile deepened on his lips and in his eyes. 'Son, this is no violation of trust. After some time, if you so desire, you can even marry the great-granddaughter of the Chief Justice. A man in authority has a need for many women and many marriages. But not at this stage. You did not give your word in order to betray her. The situation was different then. If the situation changes after a pledge is given, then the pledge loses its validity. At that time, marriage with Dev Sharma's great-granddaughter would have been the right thing to do. Now a better course has opened before you. Your future lies in marrying the granddaughter of the President of the Republic.'

Thinking that Prithusen's bowed head meant a refusal, the magnate said in a voice touched with self-pity, 'Son, do you want to throw overboard my efforts of a lifetime and the future of our family, for your infatuation with a girl? The great sage, Chanakya has said, "Always protect yourself with your wife and your wealth." Son, a woman is for man's enjoyment. It is only when he is blinded by his emotions that he begins to sacrifice his whole life for the sake of a girl. My boy, it is in situations like this that the sages have termed women as the door to ruin, both for the man who aspires to rise high and for the man who wants to attain the other world.'

Prithusen remained silent as before.

'Son, I am confident that you will save my honour and your own future prospects,' said Prestha, after a moment's reflection. 'On the night of the last full moon during Mallika's performance, the Chief Justice enquired after your health and made mention of the feelings that existed between you and Divya. At that time I told him that in view of my race and family, it would be very thoughtless of me to seek a wife for my son in the family of twice-born Brahmins; that having been a slave, I could not risk inviting on myself the wrath of the entire Brahmin community of Madra. I also told him about the tender feelings that Seero, the President's granddaughter, had for you my son, and that caste was no obstacle there. I told him that I was an applicant for the hand of the President's granddaughter in marriage with my son.'

Prithusen's head bowed even lower. Without looking at his father, he turned aside and laid his head on the pillow.

It did not take Prithusen long to recover his health completely, but his mind was still troubled. He would sit in the visitors' hall staring vacantly into thin air, at other times in the interior of the palace, looking sad and disconsolate. He showed no particular enthusiasm when Seero came to him. Seero found Prithusen's solemn bearing even more attractive. On her insistence he went out with her in a palanquin, once to Mallika's palace and another time to the palace of the President. There was only one question weighing on his mind: Would he be able to have Divya even after marrying Seero?

He brooded long and hard over the question and then, with a resolve in mind, began to show interest in

Seero and pay attention to her. One day, in an emotional outburst, he took Seero into his arms and begged her to accept Divya as a co-wife.

Seero gave a hiss like a startled snake. She wriggled out of his arms and stepped away from him. Her full red lips curled and twisted; hot tears of rage welled from her eyes.

Later on, clinging to Prithusen's shoulder, her face streaked with the tears and kohl from her eyelashes, Seero expressed her contempt for the custom that permitted the Aryans of Jambu Dweep to have more than one wife, 'Among the Aryans, a woman is only a slave and an object of enjoyment. I cannot share my beloved with anyone else. I want to be the only queen of the heart of my beloved and the sole mistress of my household.'

Prithusen recalled his father's arguments and brooded long over the question. He began to regard all women with indifference, as unpleasant intrusions into the serious business of life. He was steeling his mind for the struggle ahead, and his father's advice appeared to be a sound guideline, reflecting intelligence, foresight and much experience.

He felt that he was a mere pawn in Seero's love game, and love, all of a sudden, seemed to be nothing more than a charade. He compared his own situation with that of the helpless and beautiful slave-girls in the households of rich nobles, who were treated merely as instruments for the satisfaction of their lust.

Divya had left Prithusen's side in a mood of utter despair. Neither had she had a good look at him, nor exchanged a single word. 'It will take another two or three months for him to recover,' she said to herself, numb with apprehension. 'What will become of me?' Ever since Prithusen's triumphant return, the subject of Divya's marriage was being broached in the Chief Justice's house as an unpleasant but unavoidable topic. Chhaya would bring her news of this. In the chambers of Pandit Vishnu Sharma and her uncle, Prabuddha Sharma, Prithusen's family background would be discussed; her other grand-uncle, Bhrigu Sharma, adopted an attitude of cold neutrality. Mahadevi was indifferent, though she kept quiet because of the grandsire's approval. Divya was only too willing to accept all the opposition and ill will and regard it as a blessing, but little could be done while Prithusen was on his sick bed.

Without being joined to him in wedlock with the proper ceremony, how could she protect from hostile eyes that part of Prithusen that she carried within her? What had been the grandest and sweetest thing in her life was now turning into a matter of shame and ignominy. How proud and happy she had felt to shelter and receive the agitated and restless Prithusen! That pride had now turned into a dark abyss, which was about to swallow her up. 'Only a miracle can save me now,' she told herself. 'I want to be married to Prithusen, to bear his children. Then why has the prospect become so terrible now?'

Divya kept to her bed most of the time, listless and depressed. Mahadevi again grew anxious about her health. She appointed Dhata to look after her, and every now and then enquired about her. Knowing that the situation would arouse suspicion and make her face perilous consequences, Chhaya and Dhata, out of love for Divya, would tell Mahadevi and others that Divya was merely indisposed.

Chhaya's lover, Bahul, had been killed in the battle of Darva. Having lost her lover, Chhaya had become all the more attached to her mistress suffering the pangs of separation. She had literally become Divya's shadow. At night, unsure if Divya was asleep or brooding over her plight, Chhaya would keep a watch on her mistress, and doze off leaning against the bedpost.

Every day, under Mahadevi's instructions, Assa, another maidservant, would go to the temple of Prajapati and to the Buddhist monastery to make offerings for Divya's health. On her return she brought all sorts of news, which Chhaya passed on to Divya. Assa once said, 'Just as offerings are being made for Divya, they are also being made for Prithusen's health, and at the same temples and monasteries. And do you know where the offerings are being sent from? From Prestha's palace and from the palace of the President.'

Then one day Chhaya said excitedly, 'Arya Prithusen has recovered completely.'

Divya could not share Chhaya's enthusiasm. Her thoughts had turned in a different direction ever since she had learned that offerings for Prithusen's recovery were being sent from the palace of the President. She recalled how possessively Seero had sat by Prithusen's bed, as though she was the mistress of the house.

Chhaya also brought another piece of news from Assa— Prithusen and the granddaughter of the President had been seen going together in a palanquin to the palace of Mallika, to lake Pushkarni and also to the palace of the President. Divya fell into a fit of deep despondency. 'What is the matter with him?' she said to herself. 'He used to be so sensitive and so strong, a victor in battle, one who would set his life at naught for the sake of honour. For him, life without me had no meaning; he went smiling to face death on the battlefield in the assurance that I would be his. Was his declaration of love and passion mere deception and duplicity? Has he forgotten me altogether? Where shall I seek refuge now? If only the earth could open and hide me in her fold! I was not destined to have abiding love, otherwise why should my mother, who gave me birth, have vanished from this earth? The one person whom I regarded as my very own—the only one in the whole world—has turned his back upon me. And Rudradhir? He was banished by my own great-grandfather and has gone far far away.'

At midday, finding Divya lying on the mattress with her eyes closed and thinking her to be asleep, Chhaya went away to Mahadevi's chambers to spend some time with her mother. But there she heard some news that made her rush back to Divya. Divya lay motionless with her face towards the wall. Chhaya could not contain herself. How could she let her mistress remain ignorant of the terrible news she carried?

In order to get over her mental agitation, Chhaya busied herself in tidying up the room. While doing so, her foot struck the metal lamp-holder, which fell and the whole room rang with the noise. Divya sat up startled and looked at her. Humbly apologizing for the disturbance, Chhaya faced her mistress and said in a tremulous voice, 'An invitation has come, to attend the ceremony of Arya Prithusen's betrothal with the granddaughter of the President. Both the grandsire and Mahadevi are terribly worried. There was a heated argument between Arya Dhriti Sharma and Vinay Sharma . . .'

Divya lay motionless on her bed, staring at the ceiling. For a long time she lay still. Stifling the cries that rose in her throat, Chhaya silently wiped the tears from her eyes and gazed at her mistress.

Late that evening, Chhaya helped her mistress prepare for bed. Despite the winter cold, Divya had not thought of covering herself warmly. Chhaya covered her with a quilt and a shawl, and sat down on the floor beside the bed, her chin resting on the bedstead.

Divya's eyes were dry, but Chhaya's were red and swollen.

'Chhaya,' Divya said looking at her without raising her head from the pillow. Chhaya looked up eagerly. 'I would like just once to meet the Arya,' said Divya in a feeble but determined voice.

'Mistress,' said Chhaya in a hushed tone, drawing close to Divya, 'the President's granddaughter has bewitched the Arya by some tantric spell. There is no doubt about it. If you will permit me, I shall go to Baikunth, the tantrik, and get a mantra from him to undo the spell cast by her. I will also get a magic charm to put the Arya in your power.'

'Do whatever you like,' said Divya, in a faint despairing voice. 'God knows what has come over him. Even if he is so attracted to Seero, why is he turning away from me? I would willingly live with Seero as a co-wife. In every noble family of the Aryas there are several wives. Can't Seero accept other women as wives of the Arya? Many a creature finds rest in the shade of a single tree. The king elephant has many wives. Surely, both of us could live together in the shelter of the arms of the Arya.'

Divya had begun to feel uncomfortably warm under the quilt and the shawl. She suddenly threw them aside. 'There's a cold wind blowing, Mistress,' Chhaya said, as she drew up the shawl again, leaving only the feet uncovered. 'You could catch a chill.'

Still feeling uncomfortable, Divya let down her hair, spread it on the pillow and said, 'There are dozens of maidservants in his palace. Can't there be a place for me?'

Chhaya could no longer hold back her sobs. It was impossible for her to answer. Muffling her mouth with a corner of her shawl, and covering her face, she huddled up on the floor against

Divya's bed, feeling as if her heart would burst. She remained
for long in that position. Fearing that her sobs and cries might
add to her mistress's grief, she did not look into her face to
see if she was asleep or awake. At last she dozed off. The cold
wind blowing through the vents, made her clasp her arms
round her knees, and like a dog attached to its master through
bonds of love, lay down on the floor by her mistress's bed.

When she woke up, it was already broad daylight. Ashamed
of having slept so long, she sat up. The bright, cheering rays of
a frosty winter sun lit up Divya's pale face. She was in a deep
sleep, breathing evenly. Careful lest she should wake her up,
Chhaya tiptoed out of the room and made for Dhriti Sharma's
quarters across the lawns to tell her mother of Divya's anguish.

Dhriti Sharma's young wife, Moksha, was passing through
the travail of her first childbirth and, therefore, Dhata, the
experienced midwife, was in constant attendance. In the fresh
light of the early morning, drops of dew glistened on the
grass and the arbours. To the depressed Chhaya it seemed as
though, like her mistress and herself, nature too had been
shedding tears all night.

Moksha's condition was serious. Mahadevi and the other
ladies of the household, Amita, Tara and Uma, had gathered
in the chambers of Dhriti Sharma. Outside, Dhriti Sharma
was anxiously discussing something with Vinay Sharma. Dhata
was holding Moksha in her arms, attempting to comfort
her as each convulsion of pain gripped her. Wrapped in a
silken shawl, Mahadevi sat on a low stool nearby. The young
matrons, unconcerned with Moksha's pain, were deeply
engrossed in conversation, as though glad to use this occasion
to exchange gossip.

'And what have you to say about Divya's so-called
indisposition? All the symptoms point to pregnancy,' Chhaya

heard Amita say, in a secretive tone, yet loud enough to be heard easily.

Chhaya had bowed her head to touch the floor in salutation to Mahadevi, when these words fell on her ears like a thunderbolt. She raised her eyes, and saw that Mahadevi had forgotten to acknowledge her salutations and was staring hard at Amita's face with her old lustreless eyes, her mouth agape.

Holding her breath, Chhaya quickly returned to Divya's room. Her mistress lay peacefully asleep as before, her rounded bosom rising and falling with her quiet breathing. In her agitation, Chhaya went round Divya's bed and stared at her face. She had no heart to awaken her. Yet how could she keep from her this terrible news?

Chhaya went out of the room, but came back after a few seconds and again stood looking at her mistress's face. She sat down, holding her head between her hands, leaning against the bed. Unable to control her agitation she again left the room re-entering it after a few seconds. She brought with her a jug of water, with basin and towel, and put them near her mistress's bed. Divya was still fast asleep. Every fibre in Chhaya's body was trembling with anxiety and foreboding.

At last Divya opened her eyes. Chhaya wanted to tell her about the disaster, but words failed her. What should she say? How should she say it? Instead of pouring out water for her to wash her face, Chhaya handed her the towel. As she stood silently, tears streamed down her cheeks.

When Divya asked why she was crying, Chhaya almost broke down. Fearing that the water jug might fall from her hands, she put it on the floor, and covering her tear-stained face with her shawl, sat down beside the bed. Divya had to ask her several times before Chhaya could answer in a voice choked with tears.

'In Lady Moksha's apartment, Lady Amita said in front of Mahadevi and for all the other ladies to hear, "What have you to say about Divya's indisposition? All the signs point to pregnancy."'

Divya's eyes remained wide open and motionless as though carved in wood. Her face became extremely pale and expressionless. Suddenly, there was a sound of something falling. Chhaya looked up to find that Divya had fallen back on the bed in a dead faint. Greatly alarmed, she tried to lift up her mistress.

In her distress, Chhaya had stopped crying. She sprinkled water on Divya's face to bring her round, fanning her with a piece of cloth and rubbing the soles of her feet. It was some time before Divya opened her eyes. Moistening her dry lips with her tongue, she asked for water.

Keeping herself well under control Chhaya tried to divert Divya's attention, lest she should faint again. For the rest of the morning her mistress lay inert, her eyes gazing unseeingly at the ceiling, the walls and the garden outside the window.

At about midday, Assa, the maidservant, appeared with food. After intense pleadings from Chhaya, Divya swallowed a morsel or two. When Assa was about to return, Chhaya told her that Divya wanted Dhata to be sent to her immediately.

In the afternoon the whole palace began to ring with the sound of music, played upon the shehnai and the mridang. Trying to smile, Chhaya said, 'A child has been born to Lady Moksha.'

Divya merely heaved a deep sigh. She thought to herself, 'Moksha's child is an occasion for rejoicing for the whole family, whereas my pregnancy is an occasion for ignominy. This is because my child has no father. I shall take my child to his father. Had I been in the palace of Prestha, would my pregnancy have been regarded as a source of disgrace? I belong there, with the father of my child.'

'Call Amma,' she said, turning to Chhaya, 'I am going to the palace of Prestha.'

Though the palace resounded with joy and excitement, the Chief Justice and Mahadevi had shut themselves up in their rooms, lost in anxious and dreadful thoughts. In the confusion caused by rejoicing on one side and anxiety and apprehension on the other, Divya, without informing anyone, covered the shame of her condition under a silken shawl and taking Dhata with her, set out in a palanquin for the palace of Prestha. Preparing herself for the worst, she prayed silently to the gods that Seero should not be present in the palace when she arrived. If this prayer was granted, she was ready to wash Seero's feet for the rest of her life, like a common slave.

When she saw the palanquin of the Chief Justice's great-granddaughter after such a long time, the Greek female doorkeeper of the inner quarters of the palace, holding a sword in her hand, respectfully bowed to Divya and said, 'The Arya is at this time in the pleasure grove with Seero, the President's granddaughter.'

Divya was dumbfounded. There was no point in going back. But how long could she go on waiting at the gate, and to what purpose? 'Let the Arya know of my arrival,' she said.

Divya sat in her palanquin waiting for an answer, like one in a daze.

The answer brought by the maidservant was conveyed to Divya by the Greek doorkeeper, 'The Arya begs to be excused. Because of indisposition he regrets his inability to have the pleasure of receiving you.'

Divya's ears heard the answer but her mind did not accept it. Still in shock, she stared at the doorkeeper, waiting for an answer. She was unable to think of anything to say. The tiny flame of hope which she had carried with such care, sheltering it from the winds that blew on all sides, had been extinguished by a mere puff of wind. Her eyes were wide open but they saw nothing.

Noticing Divya's expressionless eyes riveted on the door leading to the inner palace, the worldly-wise Dhata was filled with apprehension. She ordered the bearers to take back the palanquin, lest some discourtesy be shown to Divya. It was only when the palanquin had reached the main road that Divya came to her senses. The realization of her situation brought a fresh flood of tears to her eyes. Dhata immediately lowered the curtains of the palanquin; she did not want passers-by to witness a high-born girl crying on the highway.

This action had its effect on Divya. She remembered the day when, on the evening of the Festival of Spring, she had been crowned the Daughter of Saraswati and had proudly been carried on the shoulders of the high-born young men. 'Has it come to this that I should seek shelter behind closed curtains?' she said to herself. Heedless of the tears that flowed down her cheeks she threw open the curtains, and wiping her eyes with a corner of her shawl, lifted her head proudly.

The highway was brightly lit and Dhata told the bearers to take the palanquin home by some other route.

The bearers left the brightly lit main street, with shops and houses crowded with people and took to a dark lane, which passed through a poorer district. The lane was almost deserted, as the business of the day had ceased with sunset. The bearers had no torches and had to shout as they went along, 'Look out! Clear the way! Step aside!' to the strollers who were walking right in the middle of the road.

Suddenly, someone was heard calling, 'Who's there who wants us to get off the road?'

Right in the middle of the dark, narrow alleyway, a shadowy figure stood with head erect and his chest thrust out. In his outstretched right hand he held a bowl of wine and with his left hand he beat his chest again and again, as though challenging someone. Two more men, with wine bowls in their hands, swayed on unsteady legs on either side of him.

'Captain Vrik . . . here's a p-pretty damsel . . . a palanquin-riding p-prostitute!' shouted one of them with glee.

The palanquin-bearers pricked up their ears. '*Matals*![1] A band of matals! There will be trouble!' they whispered to one another.

Dhata too shrank within herself with fear, but admonished them in a firm voice, 'Leave the road for the palanquin of the noble lady to pass, matal!'

Instead of withdrawing, the matals, attracted by the female voice, moved towards the palanquin. Tottering under the influence of wine, they yelled lustily, 'Friend Vrik . . . a . . . p-pretty girl . . . pretty!'

Twirling his long moustache with his left hand, Vrik said, 'Vrik was only looking for you, my pretty, after drinking a few bowls of wine . . . And you refused to take him in your arms because he had no money, eh?'

A shiver ran through Divya's body. Dhata rebuked the man more harshly than before, 'Matal, make way for the palanquin of the noble lady!'

Emboldened by Dhata's voice, Divya too called, 'Leave the path, citizen!'

'Matal? Who is a matal?' Vrik shouted back. 'Captain Vrik drinks good wine, high-class wine, in the company of friends and then sleeps with high-class prostitutes.'

[1] Hooligans.

'Matal, you will pay dearly for your insolence to the high-born lady!' Dhata's voice shook with fear.

Vrik, with his friends, advanced towards the palanquin and said jeeringly, 'Ha, ha, the high-born! . . . Money alone is high-born! Who dares call the soldiers of Commander Prithusen low-born? These soldiers bared their breast to the swords of the enemy. What does a woman's family matter? A woman takes the family name of the man who enjoys her. Vrik has put his heel on the throats of the high-born nobles of Darva and has snatched a hundred gold pieces from them.'

He gulped a mouthful of wine. 'That money is not yet spent. Vrik has enjoyed the high-born beauties of Darva, trembling in their own silver bedsteads! Tell me your price, high-born woman! Even if you are Vasumitra or Mallika, the power of my gold will disarm your sword-carrying doorkeepers. You will yourself come begging for my favour. Pretty one, my mouth does not smell of cheap meraya. It has the sweet odour of wine made of the finest grapes, as sweet as the scent of your body after you are bathed and sprayed with perfume.'

The second matal, tottering on his feet, threw back his head and shouted drunkenly, 'Oh! A high-born beauty!' He made a sucking sound with his lips and started beating the ground with his feet.

'Come, my beauty! Give joy and get money!' said Vrik opening his arms wide towards Divya.

Dhata again shouted, her voice trembling with fear and anger, 'Insolent matal, you will have to pay dearly for insulting this girl from a noble family!'

The matal on the right of Vrik, took an unsteady step forward and said jocularly, 'High-born girl!' while the other, rolling the words round his lips, drawled, 'For Captain

Vrik, a high-born lass with a juicy body!' And raised the wine bowl to his lips.

Divya could bear it no longer. Although very frightened, she hardened her voice and said, 'Soldiers, this insolence will have grave consequence.'

'Look at the conceit of the woman!' growled Vrik, throwing the bowl on the ground and advancing towards the palanquin. 'What is the price of your pride? Are you puffed up because some high-born noble enjoys you? Vrik, the captain, has trampled upon the heads of many a noble in Darva,' and he struck the cobbled street with his heavy Greek sandal. 'You are full of pride because rich fellows of high families sleep with you on silver bedsteads and silken mattresses. Vrik has rolled on the bodies of many a palanquin-riding, proud girl like you.' With an oath, pulling out a heavy money-pouch from his waist-belt and dangling it aloft, he shouted, 'I can pay for your pride,' and then stretching his arm towards his companion he ordered, 'Varan, present the high-born lady in the palanquin to Vrik, the battalion commander!'

Divya was trembling from head to foot. Dhata raised both her hands and stood in front of the palanquin. 'Beast! Ruffian! Help! Help, citizens, help!' she shouted, and called upon the palanquin-bearers to save the girl. The bearers hastily put the palanquin down on the ground and came forward.

Suddenly on the cobbled street, the sound of fast-approaching horse hoofs was heard. At the bend in the street a glow of light appeared, moving towards them. A rider, accompanied by a torch-bearing slave and an armed attendant, was racing towards them.

'Help, Arya, help! Save the great-granddaughter of the Chief Justice from these ruffians!'

The rider reined in his horse. All three matals stood stupefied.

'Ajeya Verma, son of Sarvarth Verma, the feudatory chief, is at your service, lady!' said the youth, drawing his sword and edging his horse close to the palanquin. 'How did you come at this untimely hour to this wretched place?'

'Arya, she is returning from a visit to a friend's house to which she was invited,' Dhata replied, bowing low. 'The main road was too crowded, so we decided to return by this secluded road, when these ruffians blocked our way.'

Ajeya Verma looked at the matals with fire in his eyes. Both the companions of Vrik were trembling with fear. Vrik tried to run away but was quickly seized by the armed attendant. Seeing his military uniform, Ajeya Verma said angrily, biting his lip, 'Who else but the soldiers of Commander Prithusen, the slave-born, would dare to do such a thing?'

He placed the three matals under arrest and ordered his attendant to hand them over to the authorities. He then ordered the torch-bearer to proceed towards the palace of the Chief Justice. He himself rode alongside the palanquin. 'What else can be expected, when low-caste people are encouraged to occupy posts meant only for the nobility?' he asked contemptuously. 'Perhaps the next thing will be that we shall be turned out of our palaces and made to rub shoulders with the populace, losing our identity altogether.'

After the palanquin had gone some distance, Divya said, 'Many thanks for your timely help. The Arya need not trouble any further. I gave my word to Devi Vasumitra that I would pay a call at her palace. That was one of the reasons why this route was chosen. It won't be difficult to get a torch-bearer from her palace. It's a safe road from there on.'

Dhata glanced at Divya in surprise but did not contradict her mistress. 'My lady is awaited at the palace of Vasumitra. Greetings to the Arya from this humble servant,' she said.

On instructions from Ajeya Verma, the torch-bearer changed direction. At the brightly lit entrance to Vasumitra's palace, Ajeya Verma offered his salutations to Divya and took his leave.

Divya stepped out of her palanquin at the gate of Vasumitra's palace. Instead of going towards the reception hall, she entered the garden. Not understanding her mistress's intention, Dhata followed her closely. Divya went to a thick grove of trees and sat down on the ground in the dark. 'Amma, you may go now,' she said. 'Take the palanquin and go back to the palace. There is no place for me there any more like I have no place in the house of Prithusen. I have been cast out. And I don't know which way to turn, where to find refuge——on the roads, in the city streets, under a tree in the forest or in the waters of the Apaga river. You may go, Amma. You nursed me on your breast like a mother. It is customary for a mother to bid farewell to her daughter when the latter goes to her husband's house. Bid me farewell in the same way. My husband has played me false. And now there is no place for me either in the house of my great-grandfather, or in the house of the father of my child. I don't know which way I shall go.'

Tears welled up in Dhata's eyes. She had once suckled Divya, had held her to her breast. And Divya, though her mistress, in this unbearable crisis had become for her like her own daughter, a part of her very heart. She sat down by her side and putting her arms round her said, in a voice choked with emotion, 'What are you saying, my child? How can I leave you? Where will you go?'

Divya's eyes were dry and her voice firm. 'Amma, how can I live in the grandsire's house, now that I have become pregnant before marriage? When there is no place for me in the house of the man who is responsible for this pregnancy, from whom else can I seek shelter? I belong where my child belongs. If I don't find a place, I shall work as a drudge somewhere, sell my own body and somehow save the one who is lodged within me. Whatever god wills . . .'

'What are you saying, child?' Dhata repeated, clasping Divya to her heart, her tears wetting Divya's hair. 'Will you pass your life on the roads and in the streets? You have never so much as touched a pot or a pan with your hand; your feet have never trodden on the ground; you have never experienced heat or cold—and you will work as a drudge? My precious one, the world is full of ruffians and dangerous people. How can you live alone in the street or the desolate forest?'

'What way out is there for me, Amma?' Divya asked. 'I don't have to fear anyone. And who is there that I am afraid of? To be afraid of Vrik, the matal? I was not afraid of Prithusen. Why should I be afraid of Vrik? What is a woman, after all? Vrik was right, Amma. All men are alike, so far as women are concerned—tough and unbending Rudradhir, sensitive Prithusen, the outspoken Marish and Vrik the matal. Who can a woman depend upon, when she is born to serve merely as an object of enjoyment? She will continue to be merely an object of pleasure. My great-grandfather, my grand-uncle wanted to marry me off to Rudradhir. I, of my own accord, surrendered myself to Prithusen, and this is the result. What is the way out for me, Amma?'

Holding Divya close to her breast, Dhata went on weeping silently. Then, her voice cracked with tears and broken by sobs, she said, 'My child, my mistress, how can I let you go alone in this world inhabited as it is by wild creatures? My jewel, your servant will follow you about like a shadow. For a girl as tender as you are, childbirth will be an ordeal. The servant's place is always with her mistress. How can I leave you in misfortune and suffer for this sin in the next life? I've seen something of the world; I've seen good days and bad; I've seen a great deal of craftiness and duplicity. You are very innocent, child. Your mother left you in my care. In your days of difficulty, your Amma will always remain by your side, sheltering you as best as she can.'

Divya and Dhata sat in the garden for an hour or so. Then, when the concert at Vasumitra's palace was over and the assembly dispersed, they left through the back door, avoiding the palanquin-bearers at the main entrance, and once again plunged into the labyrinth of the dark lanes of the city. Divya finding it difficult to walk because of her delicate condition soon expressed the desire that they should go and spend the night in some inn.

'Child, without a man to accompany you, it is risky to go to an inn,' Dhata explained. 'The state officials may put inconvenient questions to you. Moreover, when the bearers take the empty palanquin back to the palace, a desperate search will begin for you.'

It was nearing midnight and a pall of darkness covered the town. Only occasionally, through windows and from terraces, glimmers could be seen. There was light, however, in front of wine shops and in the prostitutes' quarters. Divya and Dhata were afraid that they might be recognized. In the darkness, fear of the unknown troubled them. Fear, in fact, surrounded them on all sides—fear of man! At that hour of the night, only men were to be seen on the roads; men such as those who could only bring trouble for women. If there were any women, they were prostitutes. To stop at any place in the street would arouse curiosity and suspicion.

Though extremely tired, they walked on. It was cold, yet Divya was perspiring under her clothes. Whenever a gust of wind blew in her face, she would shiver, from head to foot. They were in search of shelter, but didn't know where to find it, and in what form.

Wandering without any clear sense of direction, Dhata and Divya once again found themselves in the prostitutes' lane. From the terraces light fell on the road below. Under the lamps sat the prostitutes, their hair decked with flowers, their cheeks rouged and eyes lined heavily with kohl. They were trying to attract the attention of passers-by, by calling to them. From some of the terraces music from the veena, flutes and drums could be heard.

In the roadway too stood a number of prostitutes, wearing garlands, their lips red with tambool and their eyes bleary with drink. Some of them pretending to be in the throes of passion were inviting men to join them. Others strolled about in the streets, hanging onto the arms of their customers.

'This is a brothel area. Let's get away immediately,' Dhata whispered into Divya's ear.

'Amma, I can't walk any more. Let's sit down and take a little rest somewhere,' Divya replied, showing no embarrassment or fear.

They were passing by a drinking parlour when a drunk called out to them, inviting them to join him. Finding his invitation ignored, the man stepped forward, put his hand on Dhata's shoulder, and said, 'Auntie, who is the lucky fellow to whom you are taking this beauty, ignoring all her admirers waiting here?'

Earlier in the evening Divya had felt fear at being accosted by Vrik, the matal, even though she had been sitting in the palanquin and had the bearers to protect her. Now, though unprotected, she spoke fearlessly, 'Citizen, we are not prostitutes; we have forgotten our way to the inn. We don't belong here.'

A few more men emerged from the parlour. Just then an old woman, who had come out from a nearby lane, stepped into their midst and raised her arms to protest in a loud voice, 'What scandalous behaviour is this, citizens of Sagal? You don't know the difference between ladies of a good family and common prostitutes?'

'Why are you butting in, Auntie Jaya?' the drunkard said to the old woman.

'Am I butting in, you young imp?' She replied in a hurt tone, raising both her hands in protest. 'Am I butting in? They are my sister's daughters who have come from Valka and I'm taking them to my place. Don't you see, they aren't used to walking? How weary and tired they look!'

The old woman stroked Divya's head and Dhata's back tenderly.

'If you want to go to prostitutes, why, go ahead, who's stopping you? Go to Vasa's. She's got two new girls from the hills. Why, you're so drunk, you can't even keep your eyes open.' To Divya and Dhata she whispered. 'Come on, let's go.'

After they had gone a few steps, the old woman said in a voice full of sympathy and concern, 'How wicked these men are! What would have happened if I hadn't come across

you? Your feet must be sore with walking. What if you have
lost your way! What if the inn is so far away! I'll take you
there in the morning.'

Dhata touched Divya's arm and made a sign to her. Divya
looked at her enquiringly, but could not make out anything in
the dark. The old woman kept on, 'The gods have given me a
house of my own. It may not be a mansion like a magnate's, but
it provides shelter all right. There is food and clothes. I too
have a daughter like you.'

The old woman's eyes fell on the metal ring on Dhata's
ankle, an indication of her being a slave attendant, and turning
to her she said, 'How devoted you are to your mistress, you
are certainly blessed with a great soul.'

'You're very kind, Auntie, but it's necessary for us to go
to the inn. Our relatives are anxiously waiting for us there . . .'
Dhata was saying when Divya spoke up, 'But I'm very tired,
Amma. It is so difficult for me to walk.'

Dhata once again pressed Divya's arm, but again Divya
failed to follow her cue and only kept staring at her face.

The old woman sized up the situation. She put her hand on
Divya's head and said in a kind voice, 'You shouldn't have stirred
out in your condition. A girl from a noble family should't be
out on the streets full of strangers. Daughter, a young girl can
never feel safe with men. I'm an old woman now. Yet, whenever
I see a man on a lonely road, I tremble all over. This town of
Sagal is more dangerous for young women than a jungle full of
beasts. The men here are forever on the hunt for women.' She
did not even pause for a breath. 'I am worn out with age, and
sometimes I can't find my way in the dark . . .'

They crossed a dark lane and the old woman stopped
opposite an ordinary-looking house and knocked at the door.

A few seconds later, the door opened. An elderly man stood before them. As soon as Dhata and Divya had entered, the door was shut and locked behind them. The sound of the key turning in the lock sent a shiver through their bodies.

As they passed through the door, they faced the inner courtyard of the house, beyond which was a veranda with a row of rooms behind. The doors of the rooms were shut. At one end of the veranda stood a lamp while at the other end was a low bed with a white mattress. Near the bed sat a slave-boy, huddled up in the cold. As she stepped into the inner courtyard, Divya heaved a deep sigh and a question rose in her mind: Have I walked into a haven of rest or a prison? She looked into the eyes of Dhata. There, too, she saw fear and uncertainty.

In response to the enquiring look of the man, the old woman said, 'See, this girl is from a noble family, and she and her maid have lost their way. They were in such trouble that I couldn't bear to see their plight. I felt like she was my own daughter. Poor girl! My heart bled for them. And what horrid men these matals are. Anyway, give them a place to sit down, and let them have something to eat.'

The elderly man nodded his head as he took in the situation, and sitting down on the mattress he clapped his hands and made signs to the slave-boy, who looked up, to spread something on the floor and bring food for the visitors. The old woman sat down on the floor close to the elderly man and they began discussing something in hushed voices.

A little later the boy came back carrying a rolled-up mat under his arm, and a wooden bowl in his hand. Dhata took the mat from the boy and spread it on the floor. When Divya had sat down, Dhata took a seat on the bare floor near her, but Divya pulled her onto the mat and snuggled close to her.

The boy put the bowl, full of roasted grain before them. Pushing the pot away with the back of her hand, Dhata told the boy to bring some water.

Although the elderly man was still engrossed in conversation with the old woman, Dhata's voice drew his attention. He again made a sign to the boy, who then went out through the door opening into the inner courtyard but soon returned, followed by a young woman.

The young woman was pretty, with a fair complexion, wide dark eyes, and a lively and confident countenance. She must have been of the same age as Divya. She wore gold ornaments round her neck and on her arms, and was wrapped in a warm shawl. With a sidelong glance at Dhata and Divya, she looked at the elderly man.

To her he uttered a few words in some dialect, unknown to Divya and Dhata, and then reverted to familiar speech and said, 'Anjana, this noble lady and her maidservant are our guests. Bring something for them to eat.'

The young woman nodded and withdrew, casting another meaningful glance at the visitors. She returned shortly after, with the boy carrying a bronze vessel in one hand and in the other a flagon of wine and cups.

'Lady,' she said, placing the dishes before Divya, 'this is all that we have in the house at the moment. Pray, partake of it. It will refresh you.'

Divya expressed her unwillingness to eat, at which Dhata again asked for some water. At a sign from the young woman, the boy brought water in a copper pot. Not being used to drinking from pots, Divya held the heavy vessel to her lips with some difficulty and took a few gulps. The cold water sent a shiver through her body.

'Eat, child, eat something,' the old woman said, pressing Divya to eat, 'you will feel better for it. The meat is very soft and tasty and the wine is of an excellent vintage. Feel at home, child; don't be shy.'

The old woman had been conversing with the elderly man in low tones and in an unintelligible language. Suddenly her voice now grew loud and fretful. She got up in a huff and went grumbling towards the door. The elderly man also got up, and in an attempt to pacify her, took out a gold coin from the waistband of his dhoti and offered it to her.

The old woman pushed his hand away, and the coin rang loudly as it fell to the ground. The man picked up the coin and putting it into her hand again, accompanied her to the door, continuing to utter words of reassurance in the same incomprehensible language. He unlocked the door, and after the old woman stepped out, locked it again, and tucking the key into the waistband of his dhoti he went out through another door.

The boy sat against one of the pillars of the veranda, his arms wrapped round his dark legs, his chin resting on his knees, while continuing to gaze at the two women. Even though Divya was looking away she was acutely conscious of the locked door. She felt imprisoned and helpless.

'Mistress!' whispered Dhata into Divya's ear, leaning close to her, 'I don't think we have fallen in with good people.'

'Whatever it may be,' Divya replied, heaving a deep sigh, and resting her head on Dhata's shoulder, 'there is no way out.'

The beaten earth of the courtyard was plastered with cowdung, and the walls were painted with whitewash tinged with bluestone. From the lamp in the veranda, a dim light fell on the courtyard and the lower part of the walls. The upper parts seemed to blend into the dark sky above. Since their eyes were accustomed to light, the sky looked all the more dark and through the mist, the stars flickered like water at the bottom of a well. Divya and Dhata sat silent for a long time. They had begun to regard themselves as helpless prisoners thrown into a dungeon.

In the troubled state of their minds, the long-familiar stars too began to look strange. For some time Divya gazed at the sky, then resting her chin on her knees, said to herself, 'Where have I landed? What will become of me now? There was everything for me in the house of my great-grandfather. But there I was looked upon as a sinner who had disgraced the family. I am ready to work as a drudge, a slave, only if I am not regarded as a criminal, as a disgrace to the family. I am about to become a mother. I want to be a good mother.'

In her mind's eye, Divya saw the palace of her great-grandfather. Moksha, Dhriti Sharma's wife, had given birth to her first child there and the whole palace was ringing with celebrations; whereas she, for the same reason, was wandering from pillar to post in search of shelter to protect the child in her womb. She let out a deep sigh. Oh heartless Prithusen! The very pregnancy that should have been an occasion for joy and pride, had become a source of ignominy and irredeemable disgrace. She also saw the solemn authoritative face of Rudradhir, and of Marish, the caustic atheist. She remembered the words of praise which Marish had uttered, 'Your art is only the blossoming of your power of attraction, which is the primeval force of creation in woman.'

Divya felt bitter at heart. What preparation had she ever had for all this? Such was the will of fate.

The elderly man returned, followed by the young woman. 'It will be uncomfortable here, daughter, it is so cold,' he said, addressing Divya, and putting out his hand, added, 'Here, hand over these ornaments of yours. I shall put them away in a safe place.'

Divya lifted her eyes to look at him. Dhata looked up too. Without uttering a word, Divya took the pearl necklaces from around her neck and handed them over.

The young woman standing by could not restrain her curiosity. She snatched the necklaces out of his hands and took them over to the lamp where she began to examine them with admiring eyes. Paying little attention to her, the elderly man said to Divya, 'And that armlet too, daughter.'

Divya put out her arm towards Dhata. With trembling fingers, Dhata untied the jewel-studded ornament from Divya's arm and put it into the man's outstretched palm. The young woman snatched the armlet away too. The elderly man again said, 'It's too open and cold here, daughter. You won't be able to sleep on the floor. Come and make yourself comfortable in the room.'

Silently both Divya and Dhata rose and followed him. They passed into a bigger courtyard, which had rooms on all sides, the doors of which were also shut. Only one room in the southern corner had a light shining from its open door. The elderly man moved towards it. Outside the room stood a man, wearing the shabby uniform of a guard, with a sword hanging from his waistband and a whip in his hand. Three men emerged from the room. In their ragged and grimy clothes, they shivered from the cold. They looked like slaves. The guard led them off in another direction.

The dumb boy, carrying a mat under his arm and holding a lamp in one hand trailed behind the elderly man. At a sign from him, the boy put down the lamp in one corner of the room and spread the mat on the floor. 'Daughter,' said the man to Divya, guiding her by placing his hand on her back, 'it won't be cold in there. You can go in.'

Dhata too was about to step into the room when the elderly man blocked her way with his arm and said, 'For you there is a separate room.'

'Let Amma come in here,' said Divya, sobbing loudly. But the door of the room had been closed. Divya heard the bolt slide home.

A muffled cry rose from Divya's throat, and Dhata too cried out. Realizing the futility of their situation, both shed tears of helplessness and despair.

Grandsire Chief Justice

LATE THAT NIGHT, THE ASSEMBLY IN VASUMITRA'S CONCERT HALL
dispersed. The guests got into their chariots and palanquins
or mounted their horses and headed home. Seeing the guests
depart, Divya's palanquin-bearers also shook off their sleepiness
and stood up, waiting for their mistress to appear. But of
Divya and her attendant, Dhata, there was no sign. The night
watchmen of the palace shut the main gate and put out the lights.

The palanquin-bearers made enquiries about their
mistress, but were told that she was nowhere to be seen—
neither in the concert hall, nor in the gardens. They then
returned to the palace of the Chief Justice, bewildered and
trembling with fear.

The elders of the household and the ladies were already
worried that Divya had not returned at so late an hour of the
night, when they were informed by Taruk, the old slave, that
Divya's palanquin had been brought back empty.

Arya Prabuddha Sharma, Vinay Sharma, Dhriti Sharma,
and last of all, Pandit Vishnu Sharma went into the sitting
room. The ladies of the house followed them. In a short time,
except for the Chief Justice, Mahadevi and the children,
practically every member of the family had assembled.

Pandit Vishnu Sharma learned from the attendants and
the doorkeepers of the reception hall, the gardens and the
main gate that a little before sunset, Divya had been seen
leaving in her palanquin with Dhata to attend a concert, either
at Vasumitra's or at Devi Mallika's, and since Mahadevi

was indisposed and the rest of the family was engrossed in the festivities occasioned by the birth of a child, the delay in Divya's return had not be reported earlier.

Pandit Vishnu Sharma at once gave orders to have fast horses saddled up and made ready. Riders dispersed at top speed in search of Divya towards the palaces of Vasumitra, Mallika, Prestha and Sarvarth.

The palanquin-bearers and Dhata's daughter, Chhaya, were put under guard. Orders were given to the doorkeepers to take the palanquin-bearers separately into isolated rooms and beat the truth out of them. Slaves, female attendants, factotums—all sat in separate rows, trembling with fear, their hands outstretched on their knees. Armed guards stood over them, whip in hand. Such events had never been seen before in the palace of the Chief Justice, even though it was common knowledge that in many a mansion and palace, servants were beaten and tortured in different ways.

One by one, the riders came back to report that they had been unable to trace Divya. The atmosphere of confusion and despair thickened. Not getting any information out of the palanquin-bearers, Vishnu Sharma ordered that they be immediately put on the rack and tortured.

Since Dhata had gone out with Divya, Vishnu Sharma suspected that her daughter, Chhaya, must have been a party to some intrigue. He asked the ladies of the house to retire to their respective chambers. When the women had gone, he called two of the doorkeepers, Vakkat and Dhwaj, and ordered, 'Get the truth out of Chhaya. Subject her to the severest torture.'

Stricken with fear, her tear-stained face touching the floor, Chhaya expressed ignorance and in a trembling voice

pleaded for mercy. At a sign from Vishnu Sharma, the
doorkeepers put their hands under Chhaya's arms and dragged
her away. As they were leaving, Vishnu Sharma shouted, 'Bring
her back after she has confessed the truth.'

He learnt from some of the female attendants that
Assa, the maidservant, had taken food to Divya's chamber at
about noon. He ordered two other doorkeepers to take Assa
away and make her confess to whatever she might know.

A little later, Prabuddha Sharma and Dhriti Sharma retired
for the night. Vishnu Sharma sat on a low couch, his elbows
resting on his knees, his chin on the palm of his right hand,
sunk in deep thought. Vinay Sharma stood near him. On either
side of the couch stood two doorkeepers waiting for orders.
The remaining servants of the household were sent back
to their respective duties.

The gong had been sounded to announce that it was past
midnight. Twice a doorkeeper was sent to find out if any
information had been extracted from Chhaya and each time he
returned with a negative reply. This only further depressed
the already weary Vishnu Sharma.

Suddenly the voice of a Greek female guard rang through
the corridors: 'Attention! Attention! One and all! Grandsire,
the Chief Justice is coming!'

Vishnu Sharma raised his care-worn face. The Chief Justice
was approaching slowly, his hands resting on the shoulders
of two attendants, walking with great difficulty. Vishnu
Sharma stood up, greeted his father with bowed head, and
respectfully offered him a seat.

The old man continued to stand, however, leaning on
the shoulders of his attendants.

'I have heard loud cries coming from one of the rooms. Where is the girl, Chhaya? Let her be brought before me.

At his command, a doorkeeper immediately left the room. The grandsire's head and limbs were trembling with age, but he continued to stand with the support of the attendants.

The doorkeeper came back, made his obeisance, and said, 'May Your Honour live long! The maid, Chhaya, is not there.'

'Not there? What do you mean?' the grandsire asked in a quavering voice.

'May Your Honour grant mercy! Chhaya is no longer alive,' explained the doorkeeper with bowed head.

The grandsire began to breathe rapidly. His knees buckled. Both his attendants put their arms round him and laid him down on the couch.

His breathing was fast and obstructed and he could not speak. Vishnu Sharma, Vinay Sharma and the two attendants bent over him. The old attendant, Vilhan, pillowed the grandsire's head on his knees.

At a sign from Vilhan, the other attendant ran off and brought water and some strong wine. A few drops of water mixed with wine eased the rattling in the Chief Justice's throat. Motioning Vishnu Sharma to draw near, the grandsire said, in a weak voice, 'Son, in your zeal to avenge injustice, you have committed another injustice. This will set off a chain reaction. Son, retaliation and revenge are not justice. You are angry because our daughter has gone. Whose fault was it that she went away? Mine? Yours? Our society with all its rules . . .'

Once again there was a rattle in his throat and he began to choke. Vilhan put some more drops of water mixed with wine into his mouth. In a voice feebler than before, the grandsire said, 'Chhaya suffered . . . because her mother was devoted to her mistress! I wish I would die and thereby atone for this injustice!' During pauses between gasps for breath, the grandsire said, 'Son, do not . . . be angry . . . with our daughter.'

The grandsire could not swallow the wine. To ease his breathing, Vilhan raised the old man's head. However, when he gazed intently into the eyes of the Chief Justice he caught his breath. Then, lowering the grandsire's head to the couch, Vilhan beat his head with both hands and burst out crying.

The sitting room was once again filled with men and women. The palace rang with cries of lamentation. The grandsire's sons, grandsons, great-grandsons, ladies of the house, attendants, doorkeepers, maidservants, porters and chamberlains, all cried bitterly.

In the misty sky of late winter, even the stars appeared to have blurred in sympathy.

Dara

THE SHATUDRI[1] RIVER FORMED THE SOUTH-EASTERN FRONTIER of the Republic of Madra. On its western bank, the caravan of the slave trader Pratool had been camping since the previous evening. Two more caravans were also awaiting clearance from the state tax authorities, in order to be allowed to cross the river. Before traders crossed the frontier, and went over to foreign territory, the customs officers of the state checked their possessions and levied whatever taxes were due.

The slave trader Pratool had dined and drunk the previous night with the Chief Customs Officer. Since Pratool frequently travelled the route, he was well acquainted with the officer and was on friendly terms with him. Seven months earlier, while bringing dark slaves from Dakshinapath into Madra, Pratool had presented the customs officer with a Sinhalese pearl ring, and had promised that while returning from the north, he would bring him back a sapphire from Kashmir. But despite the friendly relations that existed between the two and the previous night's carousal, the necessary formalities expected of a tax collector had to be observed.

Seven months earlier, Pratool had imported one hundred and thirty-five slaves, both men and women, from Dakshinapath. On his return he brought with him one hundred and sixty-five slaves. There were Greeks, Kashmiris, some fair-complexioned

[1] Later known as Sutlej.

slaves from Uttarapath,[1] but the majority of them were female slaves from the newly conquered territory of Darva—light-eyed, fair-complexioned, with curvaceous bodies. After every battle on the frontiers, there would be a boost in the trade in slaves. The tax collector examined the palmyra-leaf document containing details of every slave, and satisfied himself that none of them was a runaway, had been kidnapped or was a Brahmin by birth.

Holding the seal of the Republic of Madra in his hand, an assistant examined the manifest, and drew the attention of the customs officer to one of the entries, 'Seven months ago, the trader Pratool entered the territory of the Republic with one wife, six slave-porters and two slave-attendants, a boy and a youth. Now, while returning from the state, he has with him two wives. Besides, he is travelling with a fair-complexioned slave in place of the dark-complexioned slave. The trader has sold within the borders of Madra the dark slave whom he brought as a personal attendant. No tax was levied on that slave. Since the slave has been disposed of, tax to the amount of one *nishk*[2] must be paid.'

'What the diligent officer says is perfectly correct. It was my mistake. Please accept one more nishk,' Pratool replied laughing.

The assistant with the state seal again spoke to the customs officer, this time in a conspiratorial whisper, 'Is this second wife a bought slave or a formally wedded spouse?'

Overhearing the whispered question, Pratool laughed jovially and said, 'The young officer's vigilance is truly

[1] The northerly route of east–west transit and trade, extending from Punjab and the upper Indus to Bihar and the lower Gangetic plain.
[2] Gold coin of the Vedic era.

commendable, but this trader does not cheat for the sake of one nishk. Among high-born people, transactions in slaves are always made in writing, whereas marriage——the giving away of a daughter and her acceptance as wife——are executed by word of mouth only, holding the invisible gods as witness. For that reason, a document on palmyra-leaf cannot be produced. My friend, the aphorism "You as wife, I as husband" explains the traditional mode of marriage among the Aryas of Jambu Dweep. I was enamoured of the beauty and accomplishments of the daughter of a high-caste tradesman of Sagal, Naimityak by name, and I took her in marriage. And look at the superior worth of a high-born girl; she is already bearing in her womb the continuity of my family. My first wife, despite three years of married life, is still childless. That's why a second wife . . .' He laughed again.

'May fortune smile on you! May your family prosper,' the customs officer said, also laughing. 'But how can we expect your fortunate wife to be happy, away from the free land of Madra and its cool climate, in areas where the climate is so sultry and hot and where princes rule with an iron hand? But of course, the poor girl couldn't know anything about foreign places where people suffer under tyrants and the climate is so much harsher than our own. It all shows that man is only a plaything in the hands of fate!'

On the veranda of the Customs House, Divya sat with Anjana——the wife of the slave trader, listening to the pleasantries being exchanged between Pratool and the customs officers. She felt a stab of pain in her heart. She was being pulled away from her motherland——the free state of Madra, the beloved city of Sagal——where she had spent her carefree childhood. Divya knew that she had only to cry out in protest and she would be free, free from the clutches of the slave trader, free from bondage. But then, where would she go? Was there anywhere that she would be truly free? Where would she find shelter and security? Where would she get protection for her child? Freedom had little meaning for a person who did not have the means to survive!

Pratool was saying to the customs officer, 'Love of land and country is linked with life. My motherland is wherever I can earn my living. And what do you say to love? Hasn't lover's feeling any importance?'

To Divya, the word 'love' connoted terror and dread. Love was what had brought on her predicament; her deception by Prithusen. From the elderly Pratool too, she had known nothing but terror. He had called her 'daughter' but had been nothing but a tyrant. He had snatched Dhata, her only support, away from her. Since the night Divya had been locked up alone, she had heard nothing of Dhata. Whenever she cried or complained, Pratool would pretend to be kind and sympathetic, and would ask her to have patience. Anjana would again and again show surprise and say, 'Oh! God alone knows where that crafty woman has gone!'

Sometimes, however, Divya would think that perhaps Amma had become frightened and had returned to the palace, and this thought would keep her quiet.

Behind the ostensibly kind behaviour of Pratool, Divya sensed the trickery of the slave trader in keeping his captive safe and contented. Divya realized that Pratool was sympathetic only because he wanted to take her safely across the borders of Madra. Once the border was crossed, the noose of slavery and oppression would tighten around her neck. Her silence was a form of consent. The impulse to cry out seized her once again. One cry, one word, and she would be saved from the agony. But where would she go? Back to the palace of her great-grandfather in Sagal? No, never!

Even though a slave, she still had a roof over her head. Where would she go if she became homeless? Caught in the rain, a homeless person seeks shelter even behind a fence post. Tears welled up in her eyes and she fell silent. 'Pratool and Anjana also know of my plight,' she thought. 'So they don't consider it necessary to use real chains to bind me. Far stronger than any physical bonds are the subtle invisible shackles that have kept me a captive.'

The customs clearance given, the slave trader Pratool's caravan boarded a barge standing on the shallow waters at the bank of the Shatudri river. The boatmen pushed the barge into the current and it began to move swiftly down the river. They then began to ply their oars with full strength, calling out the rhythm of their strokes.

The chorus of the boatmen as they swung their oars, the conversation among the passengers about the situation in Madra—Divya was oblivious to all that she heard or saw. Her eyes saw the vast stretches of the sandy bank on either side of the river, but she felt nothing. She was thinking to herself, 'I have, with my own hands, pushed the boat of my life into the fast current . . . Who knows where it will carry me?'

The barge moved slowly eastwards and the shore of Madra receded into the distance. Though she had suffered greatly there, separation from it tore her heart. Her agony struggled to express itself in one word 'Mother!' Would she have left that country in her helpless state, if her mother, who had given her birth, had been alive? And her second mother, her Amma, Dhata's face appeared before her eyes. 'All daughters leave their mothers one day or the other to go and live with their husbands in the house of their in-laws,' Divya thought, 'but they are content to go, they are even eager at heart, to be starting a new life in marriage.'

The thought of a husband brought Prithusen's face before her eyes. 'What is the difference between the deceiver Prithusen and the slave trader Pratool?' she thought and a shiver ran through her body. She felt as though her teeth had closed on a mouthful of grit. Of what use was her love for the country where she had been treated so shabbily? With a deep sigh, she closed her eyes.

Anjana, the wife of the slave trader, was sympathetic towards Divya. She had taken for herself Divya's jewellery, which in value, was worth more than four slaves. And Divya had not uttered a word about it. Anjana could not help feeling touched by this silent generosity on Divya's part. Divya's pearl necklaces, jewel-studded armlet and the clothing of silk had convinced Anjana that the girl belonged to some noble family. She also understood that Divya's pregnancy was the reason behind her choosing the path of suffering and poverty. Out of sympathy as well as curiosity, she tried to find out the secret. All that she could get out of Divya was the brief timid reply, 'I am an unfortunate deserted woman. In my father's house there was everything, but I couldn't stay there. In this condition I couldn't expect any help from my family. While going about in search of a refuge I fell into the hands of your husband. Now I am at the mercy of fate . . .'

The slave trader Pratool was hoping to sell Divya to some rich, pleasure-loving customer of Magadh and earn a lot of money. For a slave of such beauty and elegance, even four hundred gold pieces would not be too high a price. However, by the time they reached Mathurapuri, in the kingdom of Shursen, Divya's condition did not permit her to travel any further. She was not used to rough journeys, and found it uncomfortable even to travel in a chariot. On uneven roads there was always the danger that she might collapse.

If her child could be taken from her after birth and she could be fattened up for four or five months, to bring her back to the bloom of health, then any connoisseur would readily buy her, without thinking twice, and willingly hand over fistfuls of gold. But Pratool could not afford to stay on indefinitely in Shursen for the sake of one female slave. There were no fewer than one hundred and sixty-five slaves in the new batch— male and female—and he would not want to feed them to no purpose for a very long time. Moreover, that would delay him from the slave fair which took place in the month of Chaitra in Dakshinapath.

Since he was an experienced trader in human beings, Pratool was well versed in the subtle qualities of different individuals of different categories, just as a potter understands the quality of clay from different soils, and the characteristics and the value of vessels made from them. In his house in Pataliputra[1] in the kingdom of Magadh, Pratool kept four female slaves. These four did not merely do domestic work or were hired out to make money by their master. Each one of them would produce a child every eighteen months. Instead of selling the women, Pratool would sell their children. After the first few separations, they became inured to the pain of losing their children. Their grief was made more bearable by one or two babies which were left for them to rear. With good food, the debility caused by pregnancy and childbirth disappeared.

[1] Later known as Patna.

But Pratool knew he could not hope to exploit Divya in this way; childbirth would deprive her of much of her charms for a long time to come. And if her child was taken away from her, she might not even survive the loss. Slaves can be tamed with the whip and through starvation, but in some situations force is of no avail. Pratool, therefore, decided to remain content with the ornaments that he had taken from Divya and to sell her off in Mathurapuri.

Pratool met another slave dealer, Bhoodhar, in Mathurapuri. He spoke to him about the problems he faced in travel, and offered to sell him an extremely beautiful, though pregnant, slave-girl from Kashmir. 'I purchased the girl—Dara is her name—from a noble's palace in Pushpapur for a hundred and fifty gold pieces,' Pratool said. 'I can easily sell her to the royal palace of Magadh for four hundred, but there is the inconvenience of travel and the girl is of a delicate constitution.'

Bhoodhar had a good look at Dara and offered to buy her for twenty pieces of gold.

'What?' Pratool protested, his eyes wide open in amazement at this barefaced unfairness. 'Can't you see the curve of her fine limbs? That smooth, pale complexion like a champa flower? What if it is a little faded because of her pregnancy? Don't you see that for the price of one you are getting two people? And for how long will her complexion remain faded? A ruby remains a ruby even though it may be covered with dust.' Then, putting his mouth to Bhoodhars ear, Pratool whispered, 'Look at her eyes and her face; the marks of a thoroughbred. How is she inferior to any princess? I can tell you, four months hence, you will receive five hundred pieces of gold for her.'

'Yes, yes, I can see how she looks,' replied Bhoodhar, stroking his greying moustache. 'I don't deal in cattle and

horses, I deal in human beings. I can see her bloodlines. She has
been brought up on a soft bed. It's obvious that she's a Brahmin
girl, and it's her first pregnancy too. On top of that, she's still
weak after a long journey. But she has only to miss her footing
once and my twenty gold coins will go down the drain.'

And whispering into Pratool's ear, Bhoodhar said again,
'Friend, gone are the days of the low-born rulers, Ajatshatru
and Vrihadrath. It is Pushya Mitra, the Brahmin, who is ruling
in Magadh now, and the governor of Shursen is the dreaded
Ravi Sharma. If some Brahmin falls for her beauty and declares
her to be a member of his family, then I am done for. I will
spend my last days in prison and the state officials will torture
me until they leave me just a bag of bones. Anyway, it's unwise
to take her to Magadh; you'll be running a grave risk.'

Dara, the slave, had hardly recovered from the travails
of childbirth when fate sent her to a new master.

Chakradhar, a priest and cleric-sacrificer of Mathurapuri, had
an ailing wife. Soon after giving birth to a baby boy, she
developed a serious fever. The physician forbade the mother to
feed the infant with her own milk, and the boy was too frail to
digest the milk of the cow kept in the house.

Chakradhar came to know that Bhoodhar, the slave
dealer, had a slave who had recently given birth to a child.
He purchased both the mother and the child for fifty gold
pieces. With her own child in her lap, Dara took over the
priest's son too. She was thankful to the gods for at least being
permitted to feed and bring up her own child. She was happy
at the thought that besides her own, she would also be able
to assist in fostering the life of another newborn baby. When
the priest's wife recovered from her dangerous illness, she

found that her breasts had run completely dry of milk. So Dara continued to nurse both the children and tried not to make any distinctions between them.

But Dara's joy was short-lived. Soon enough her feelings underwent a change. Her mistress's bidding was that she should suckle the mistress's child first, and then her own. This order pierced Dara's heart like an arrow. But she had no choice. After suckling the son of the Brahmin priest, there would be little milk left in her breasts for her own child. She would cry her heart out when she saw her own child hungry. She was always on the lookout for a chance to give the breast to her own child when the Brahmin's wife was not looking. She began to cheat with her own milk. When the Brahmin's son was hungry, there would be little milk left in her breasts for him. She began to hate the child of her master. Even when there was milk in her breasts, it would not flow to feed the master's child.

The Brahmin's wife was beside herself with rage at the slave-girl's trickery. She shouted at Dara and scolded her in the most insulting terms. Seeing that Dara was not mending her ways, she warned her that she would take her child away from her and sell it. She ordered Dara to put her own child aside until she had satisfied her master's baby.

Dara's own child would lie on a rag in the veranda, and she would watch him with tearful eyes, while the other baby lay on her lap. This irritated her mistress all the more. She accused Dara of all kinds of duplicity and of disloyalty to her master.

It was unbearable for Dara to give the breast to her mistress's child and see her own son crying for milk. She would turn her eyes away, and milk would stop flowing from her breasts. The Brahmin's son would tug at her nipples with his toothless gums and start crying, waving his fists in the air. The Brahmin's clever wife knew how to handle the situation. She would order Dara's son, Shakul, to be brought before his mother. Milk would start rushing to Dara's breasts and tears to her eyes when she saw him.

A similar scene was enacted every morning and evening with the cow in the cowshed. Before milking the cow, its little calf was let out to suck its mother's teats. Feeling the mouth of the calf on her teats, the cow would release all her milk into the udder, but just at that moment the calf would be pulled away and tied to a stake nearby. The cow was then milked by the Brahmin's wife or a slave-girl. Dara would watch this without batting an eyelid.

'You are so devious and crafty,' the Brahmin's wife would scold Dara. 'In this lifetime you are suffering as a slave because of your past misdeeds. And in your future birth too you will suffer because of the sin of treachery that you are committing against your master now. The cow is only a beast, yet it is more honest than you.'

Dara would keep quiet, but in her own mind her situation appeared to be quite like the cow's. The only difference was that there was no halter round Dara's neck. In other respects she was just as helpless. 'Does the cow feel any sense of injustice or wrong?' she would ask herself. 'If not, why not? Why do I feel this way? Why do I feel that I alone have the right over my body?' To be a slave and yet regard her body as her own was, in Dara's eyes, a sin, but she could not think otherwise. 'Why doesn't my child have the right to nourishment so that it may live and grow?' she would ask herself.

Her imagination would take possession of her mind. Had her child been born in Prithusen's palace, instead of in these conditions, the walls of the palace would have shaken with the sound of rejoicing and merrymaking. As Prithusen's son, everything would have been available to Shakul. But since he was a fatherless child, there was no place for him. Dara felt that her son was like water that had overflowed the vessel and had fallen on the scorching ground, only to evaporate. But, no, she would not let Shakul be regarded as the neglected castaway of that wicked Prithusen. For her child she would do all that was possible.

At her own birth, her mother had fallen ill. She too had been breastfed by a wet nurse. 'Is this the consequence of that deed?' she would ask. 'The Buddhist monks say that man suffers as a result of his own misdeeds. What are my child's misdeeds? He has only just come into the world. Can it be that even before his birth his fate was sealed? He does not even know for which sin he is undergoing punishment or that he is being punished. If I am the one who is guilty, she thought, I am fully prepared to bear the punishment. Why should my son go hungry? . . . Was my love for Prithusen a misdeed? . . . Was bearing a child a sin? . . . The whole creation bears progeny. What have I done that others do not do? I conceived without the approval of the society of twice-born Brahmins; is my suffering the result of that misdeed? Are Brahmins alone the disburser of rewards and punishments?'

The Buddhist monks who came to the door of the house for alms would deliver pious utterances, 'Our actions and our life are a chain of sorrow. Happiness is only a transient feeling.'

The words of the monks would have a ring of truth for Dara. When had she experienced happiness in her life? It had always been as fleeting as the shadow of a passing cloud . . . The day she was elected Daughter of Saraswati . . . The ecstatic moment in the arms of Prithusen . . . Memories of things before and after that fateful encounter! In misery she thought, 'The world is for the strong. For those who suffer, happiness lies only in renunciation. It is futile to have any attachment for life.' But Shakul's existence was not just a creation of her own imagination.

The yellow-robed monks who went from house to house begging for alms used to call upon unhappy worldlings to seek sanctuary in the Buddhist faith, 'O suffering men and women, come into the fold of the Buddha! Come into the fold of the Faith! Come into the fold of the Monastic Order! He who is Mercy Incarnate will relieve you of all your troubles!'

In the early hours of the morning, before daybreak, little Shakul, lying on the ground by his mother's side in the courtyard, began to cry. Dara took him to her breast. Shakul took his fill of milk and went off to sleep. A little later, the mistress and her child woke up and Dara was summoned to feed the other baby. Not finding any milk in the nurse's breast during the very first feed of the day, the priest's wife lost her temper. She screamed and berated and then set Dara to the back-breaking job of pounding rice to separate the grain from the chaff.

At midday, Dara was sitting in the veranda eating food from an earthen bowl, with Shakul on her lap, when Loma, the old maidservant of the house, came over to her. 'You haven't acted wisely, child, in annoying your mistress,' Loma said pityingly. 'The master and the mistress have decided to give Shakul away. Go to your mistress, you unfortunate girl, and beg for pardon.'

Dara could not eat anymore. Only one thought possessed her mind: What now?

In the afternoon, the priest and his wife were taking their siesta. Old Loma too had retired to a shadowed corner of the house to lie down. The baking hot afternoon of the month of Jyeshtha was as still as a winter night. The eye-searing rays of the sun left one as sightless as in the pitch darkness of the

night. To escape from the scorching dust-filled wind hitting
one like the waves slapping the side of a boat, the townspeople
had withdrawn into their houses. And birds and animals
had sought whatever shade there was to be found. Dara sat
motionless, her hand on her forehead, fearing that her son
might be snatched away from her at any moment.

The voice of a Buddhist mendicant, returning late from   his
round, was heard in the street, 'O suffering men and women
of the world, for peace and relief, come into the fold of
the Buddha, into the fold of the Faith, into the fold of the
Monastic Community!'

Dara, eager for shelter above all else, saw the mendicant's
offer of safety as a ray of hope.

In that blistering heat, dust rose on the roads of the town
like grey flames. Even the hot air seemed to be rushing towards
the forest for relief. In that dreadful time of the day, clasping
little Shakul to her breast, Dara left the house of the priest
and stepped into the cobbled street, which was burning like
plates of metal. To protect the tender skin of the child from
the scorching rays of the sun, she wrapped round him a dirty,
threadbare piece of her stole.

On Dara's body, there was just a rag of a bodice, which she
tied at the back, and a thin well-worn piece of sari, wrapped
round her waist. In the haste to get away from the Brahmin's
house, her tangled hair had come loose and was being blown
across her face by the wind. She tripped again and again on the
dangling end of her sari, tearing it further. The rays of the sun
stabbed into her head and every pore of her sweat-covered
body. Hot cobblestones burned her feet.

But Dara was oblivious to all this. In her ears rang the
compassionate words of the mendicant's invitation: 'O suffering
men and women of the world, for peace, come into the fold

of the Buddha.' Her eyes were fixed on the tall spire of the Mahabodhi Monastery, rising into the hot, dusty sky, above a cluster of pipal trees.

For more than a hundred years the spire of the monastery had stood as a symbol of the merciful sanctuary of the holy faith to suffering humanity. With her eyes on it, and holding her baby tightly to her breast, Dara headed straight to the monastery, in the howling wind that seemed to echo the mendicant's message.

The great doors of the main entrance to the monastery were shut. Behind those closed doors was the abode of mercy and shelter. Dara raised her hand and struck the clapper of the large bell hanging at the main entrance. The hushed silence of the summer afternoon was broken by a deep resonant sound. To Dara, the reverberating notes seemed to be shedding drops of mercy.

A small panel slid aside in the door. Through it a young monk looked at Dara curiously, his eyes heavy with sleep. Dara implored, 'Reverend sir, I have come to beg for shelter. I seek the protection of the Buddha, of the Faith, of the Monastic Community.'

The eyes of the young monk disappeared behind the door, and the peephole was closed. Dara, trembling all over in eager expectation, rested her head against the door. A short time later, a part of one of the door opened and a kind-looking, elderly monk emerged.

'Shelter, kind sir, grant me succour, holy father!' Dara said, her voice and her limbs quivering.

Raising his hand in benediction, his face radiant with peace, the monk said reassuringly, 'Calm yourself, my daughter.'

The young monk appeared with a small mat of kausheya grass, which he spread on a stone platform in the shade of a pipal tree opposite the door of the monastery. The elderly monk sat on the mat, and making a sign to Dara to sit in front of him, enquired, 'Tell me what is on your mind, my daughter.'

'O Fountain of Pity, reverend sir, grant shelter to this unfortunate child and its mother!' Dara said beseechingly, her eyes filled with tears.

'Lady,' the elderly monk spoke after some thought, 'the solutions that you desire are not ones that can be found on the path leading to the shelter of the Buddha, of the Holy Faith, of the Monastic Order.'

'No, Father, your humble servant desires nothing,' Dara cried out. 'She only begs for shelter from tyranny. O Ocean of Compassion, grant that at the feet of the Buddha your humble servant may be able to keep her child with her.'

A smile of pity illuminated the calm countenance of the monk. 'Lady,' he said, 'all worldly relations are nothing but infatuation, a source of pain. A soul disturbed by infatuation cannot achieve peace.'

Dara was left staring at the face of the monk. Despair stifled her eagerness. Picking up courage, she said again, 'Holy Father, your humble servant begs to be admitted into the fold of the all-pitying Buddha, in this monastery. Under its threefold shelter, your humble servant shall conduct herself with propriety and humility and shall thereby be redeemed from attachment.'

The calm countenance of the elderly monk remained unruffled. She laid down her son near the monk's feet and bending her forehead so as to touch the stone platform, implored once again, 'It is for the sake of this helpless creature that your humble servant seeks refuge in the Holy Faith. She will act upon the commands of the Faith and freeing herself from attachment, shall enter the sacred fold.'

Feeling the hard stone beneath him the child opened his mouth wide and began to cry.

'Lady, take the child in your lap,' the elderly monk said, turning his eyes away from the pathetic sight. 'Who are you that is so desirous of adopting the Buddhist Faith?' he asked.

'Holy Father, I am the mother of the helpless child,' Dara replied.

'Do you have the permission of your husband to adopt the Buddhist Faith?'

'I have no husband, Father.'

'If you have no husband, do you have the permission of your father to join the Buddhist Faith?'

'I have no father, either,' Dara said, shaking her head.

'If the husband and the father are not there, do you have the permission of your son to adopt the Buddhist Faith?'

'Holy Father, your humble servant's son is in no position to grant permission,' Dara again replied, shaking her head.

The monk remained unmoved, as before. 'If you are a slave, do you have the consent of your master to embrace the Faith?'

'No, Holy Father,' Dara replied timidly. 'It is on her own account that your humble servant is begging for asylum.'

The monk raised his eyes. 'Lady,' he said looking at Dara, 'according to the laws of the Faith, the Monastic Order cannot grant shelter to a woman without the approval of her guardian.'

Dumbfounded, Dara stared at him again. Seeing him about to rise from the mat, she folded her hands and said in a tearful voice, 'But Father, Lord Buddha once granted shelter to Ambapali, the prostitute!'

'Lady, a prostitute is a free woman,' the monk replied and rose from the mat.

Stupefied, Dara stared open-mouthed after the monk as he walked back to the monastery and disappeared behind the door. The young monk came out, rolled up the mat and went back inside. The doors of the monastery were shut. The sweltering air kept ruffling the foliage of the pipal tree in search of shelter from the sun. Dara, her face reflecting the rejection she felt, still sat on the platform. She was unable to think or understand anything. Only the words of the monk kept ringing in her ears: 'Lady, a prostitute is a free woman!'

Shakul's cries shook her out of her reverie. She gave the child her breast to stop him from crying. But finding the breast empty of milk, the child cried louder than before. Dara was not permitted even the comfort of forgetting herself for a while, or of remaining oblivious to her surroundings. It was necessary for her to feed herself in order to be able to nurse her baby. She felt no appetite, but the thought that her son was hungry made her stomach twist with hunger.

She got down from the platform. Her legs shook under her from fatigue and exhaustion, and her arms felt limp under Shakul's weight. She fought hard to regain control of herself and hold on to her child lest he should fall. Leaving the shade of the pipal tree, she went back to the scorching heat of the road, with blasts of hot air beating against her face.

Dara dragged her steps along the road which, a little while earlier, had held so much promise. Driven by panic, she had run away from the priest's house to find some safe place for her child. Now both mother and child were destitutes. Her mind went into a daze, from pain and shock. Only one thing flashed across again and again, that a prostitute was a free woman. That as a slave, as a dependent, as a woman, there was no place for her.

'Was there ever a time when I was free?' she asked herself in desperation. She had accepted slavery so that she might be free to keep her child. By enslaving her body, she had hoped to preserve the freedom of her mind. But she did not succeed in getting the freedom she wanted. A woman from a high family is not free. Only a prostitute is free.

Dara decided, that for the sake of her child, she would become free.

Late in the afternoon, as the sun dipped behind the tall buildings of Mathurapuri, the lanes and alleys became shaded. Dara, bedraggled and exhausted, holding Shakul to her breasts, bereft of milk, once again wandered the streets and lanes of the city. In the shade of the tall buildings, the roads had come back to life.

'Citizen,' Dara stopped a passer-by and asked, 'could you tell me the way to the prostitutes' quarter?'

'Why would you be interested in prostitutes, woman?' asked another man jocularly, as he overheard her question.

'I want to become a prostitute,' Dara replied, trying to hold up the child in her tired arms.

At this, the man, seeing the expression on Dara's face, fell silent. But another passer-by, hearing this, pointed to Dara's shrunken face and unkempt hair, her sunken eyes and threadbare, dirty clothes and roared with laughter, 'Surely, she will make a fine prostitute! What beauty! What charm! What class! If she becomes a prostitute, the lovers of beauty in Mathurapuri will forget all about Ratnaprabha, whom they just idolize.'

The one who had jeered at Dara earlier came closer to her and said, 'Do you really want to be a prostitute? But you are a mother! You have gained a position that entitles you to honour and respect, and you want to give it up and become an enemy of society? You want to sell your body and the virtue of your motherhood for money? You're done for. Someone has sucked

you dry and thrown away the husk of your body. You have no
attractions left; all that is there is your misfortune. Why cling
to life? You've been drained of all spirit. You are unfit to go on
living. The meek have no right to live. Your destiny is to drown
yourself in the Yamuna river . . . Go!'

Dara had not recognized the speaker at first. His face
was covered with dust and a growth of beard after a long
journey. But she identified him from his voice. She wanted to
call out his name, but the young man did not give her the
chance and went on speaking in a disgusted tone, 'If you want
to sell your body just to be able to feed your child, then go
you ill-fated soul, go to the banks of the Yamuna. The rich
merchant, Padmanabh, who has made a fortune out of people
such as you, only to leave them destitute and hungry, is handing
out free food and is earning through it good deeds for his
rebirth. Go and take food in charity and give him another
chance to earn spiritual reward through meritorious actions.'

Dara opened her mouth to call out the man by his name,
but he had already turned his head in disgust and walked away.
Holding up Shakul, who had cried himself to sleep, Dara set
out towards the riverbank, enquiring from those she met the
way to the charity centre of the merchant Padmanabh. With
every step she took, her limbs became weaker with fatigue.

Evening came. The bank of the Yamuna, paved with
flagstones, was crowded with people. From the charity centre,
the sacred smoke from the yajna fire was rising. Crowds of
paupers surrounded the centre and were jostling one another
to reach the door where food was being distributed. Dragging
her feet, and making desperate efforts to hold up her baby,
who had begun to howl again, Dara was also trying to push
her way through the crowd towards the door. Suddenly, she

heard someone shouting behind her, 'Grab her! Grab that woman! She's my runaway slave!'

Dara knew that voice. It was that of her master, the priest, shouting at the top of his voice.

Others took up his cry and began to yell, 'Catch her! Grab her!' The pursuers were closing in on her. Seeing a clear space towards the river, she rushed in that direction, clutching Shakul. The priest's shouts drew nearer. Standing on the high bank of the river, and not knowing what to do, Dara considered it more desirable to die than to fall once again into the hands of the priest. Holding Shakul tightly to her breast, she jumped into the water.

The Yamuna river was a favourite resort for the nobles, state officials and wealthy merchants of Mathurapuri. The relentless Jyeshtha sun turned their houses and palaces into hot ovens, and seeking to escape the heat and yearning for relief, they went for leisurely cruises and pleasure rides on the river in the cool of the evening. Near the spot where the runaway slave-girl had jumped from the high bank, the barge of Devi Ratnaprabha, the Court Dancer and Laureate of Art in the province of Shursen, happened to be passing. She immediately ordered her servants to rescue the drowning girl and haul her into the barge. Even at that moment the baby was tightly clasped in her arms.

Devi Ratnaprabha's heart melted with pity. She took the child from the arms of the unconscious woman to find that it was dead. Putting the child aside she took the slave-girl's wet head, covered with weeds, on her lap, caring nothing for her expensive silken clothes. Her female attendants put smelling salts to the slave-girl's nostrils and fanned her with a large fan, to bring her round. Many other crafts rushed towards

Devi Ratnaprabha's barge and surrounded it. There was a great clamour, from the boats and from the crowd along the riverbank.

Dara regained consciousness. Opening her eyes, she asked for her son in a weak but anxious voice. 'Calm yourself, girl, your child is safe!' Ratnaprabha said tenderly, putting her hand on Dara's forehead.

At this unexpected and unfamiliar sign of affection, Dara opened her eyes wide and looked around her. Could it be that she had returned somehow to the house of her great-grandfather? Was she dreaming?

Chakradhar, the priest, was still shouting on the river-bank, 'That girl is my slave, my property! Give her back to me. I shall bind her hand and foot and drag her to the law court. She is a thief! I bought her for fifty gold pieces from Bhoodhar, the slave dealer.'

Dara trembled from head to foot, and clutching at Ratnaprabha's arm with both her hands, said between sobs, 'Noble lady, save me! Save me from this butcher priest! He will kill my child. He will kill me. Lady, I shall become a prostitute and pay back the Brahmin's debt. I know the art of dancing. I beg you, noble lady. Slavery is unbearable . . .'

Chakradhar was still protesting and demanding that the girl should be returned to him. Suddenly, above the tumult on the river and its bank, rose the piercing sound of the state trumpet. A hushed silence fell on all sides. 'Attention, citizens!' a crier proclaimed, 'His Excellency the Viceroy, the Protector of the People, the Defender of the Faith, the Valiant Ravi Sharma is arriving!'

The boats withdrew to make way for the Viceroy's barge. A boat with a golden canopy, manned by sixteen rowers, swept up and stopped near Devi Ratnaprabha's boat.

The people on the bank and in the boats bowed again and again to hail the Viceroy. Reclining against a milk-white cushion, under the golden canopy, Ravi Sharma smilingly acknowledged Ratnaprabha's greetings and asked after her health and well-being.

The herald, wearing a red turban and standing in the bow of the Viceroy's boat, announced, 'His Excellency the Viceroy, the Protector of the People, the Defender of the Faith, has been gracious enough to come here, noticing some restlessness among the people. His Excellency commands that whosoever has been the victim of any wrong or injustice should, without fear, appeal for justice before His Excellency.'

The Brahmin standing on the riverbank bowed, joined his palms and said imploringly, 'Your Excellency, I, Chakradhar, priest and performer of yajnas, son of Varundhar, swear by Lord Indra, and most humbly submit that his slave girl from Kashmir, Dara by name, at present in the boat of Devi Ratnaprabha, is my lawful slave, bought by me with the offerings earned from the sacrificial fires. The slave-girl ignored her duties and ran away from my house. I pray Your Excellency to order the slave to be restored to me.'

Devi Ratnaprabha stood up in the boat and with bowed head, said, 'Your Excellency, I, Ratnaprabha of Shursen, Laureate of Art, pray that I may be permitted to pay the price of this oppressed slave to the Brahmin and buy her from him.'

'Nobody's property can be acquired forcibly just by paying its price,' said the Viceroy, turning towards Ratnaprabha. 'In the court of law, the rich and poor are alike.'

'Long live His Excellency, the Incarnation of Justice!' shouted the priest, raising his arms and blessing the Viceroy. 'This slave-woman is wet nurse to my child. My wife is ill. Protector of Brahmins, order the slave to be returned to me so that the child of your humble servant may live. This slave woman is the chief support of a Brahmin child.'

Devi Ratnaprabha again joined her hands and said, 'Your Excellency, I am prepared to pay the necessary amount of money for the purchase of another wet nurse for the Brahmin child.'

'Justice does not obey the wishes of any individual,' the Viceroy said, raising his hand. 'Its aim is to uphold right conduct. The slave-girl committed a crime by running away from her master's house. She has acted like a thief by turning away from that service. The slave-girl is the property of the Brahmin. By attempting to commit suicide, she has tried to deprive the Brahmin, her master, of his property.'

'Long Live His Excellency! How right his judgment is! The Protector of the Faith, the Incarnation of Justice. Long Live His Excellency!' shouted the Brahmin again, raising his arms in benediction.

The Viceroy turned towards Dara, who sat kneeling on the planks of Ratnaprabha's barge with hands joined, 'Slave-girl, you are guilty of theft having tried to deprive the Brahmin of his lawful property.'

Dara bowed so low as to touch the deck with her forehead, and said, 'Incarnation of Justice, for this crime, may the slave and her son be punished with death. The slave will be beholden to Your Excellency for this act of justice.'

The Viceroy shook his head disapprovingly and said, 'Punishment cannot be meted out in accordance with the wishes of the criminals. The slave and the slave's child are both the property of the Brahmin. It does not rest with slaves to decide the manner of their disposal.'

'How right is His Excellency!' shouted the priest again, 'the Incarnation of Justice! The Image of Truth! The Image of Justice! Long Live His Excellency!'

The Viceroy turned again to the slave-girl, 'Why did you try to commit the sin of suicide?'

'It was the misery of being a slave, Your Excellency, the hunger, and my child's hunger!' Dara said with palms joined together, tears streaming down her cheeks.

At this Ratnaprabha pleaded, her voice touched with pity, 'Protector of the Faith, I am prepared to pay in gold any fine that is imposed on this slave-girl as a punishment for the crime that she may have committed.'

The Viceroy raised his hand asking the Court Dancer to wait and addressing himself to the priest, said, 'Listen, Brahmin, you are well versed in the scriptures and in jurisprudence. The fact that this slave-girl has tried to kill herself along with her child is clear proof of her being oppressed. In the eyes of the law you are guilty of having been cruel to a slave.'

The priest's face turned pale and his voice shook, 'Not cruel, Incarnation of Justice. This slave is an unwilling worker and is hostile to her master.'

'Brahmin,' said the Viceroy, 'a master is entitled to service from a slave, but not to the slave's life.' The Viceroy's voice grew stern, 'It is the gods that grant life to living beings and they alone can take it back. On earth, the king is the representative of the gods, and only the king has the right to take back life. The slave too, like the Brahmin, is the subject of the king.' Then, turning towards others he said, 'Where is the child of this slave?'

'Incarnation of Justice, the child of the unfortunate slave is dead,' Ratnaprabha replied, with bowed head.

Dara fainted and fell back on the wooden planks of the barge. Only the quick reaction of Ratnaprabha and her attendant saved her from rolling into the water. The episode sent a shiver through the crowd. Only the Viceroy continued to sit unperturbed and silent. Turning to the priest again, he asked, 'Brahmin, what price did you pay for this slave?'

'Incarnation of Justice, I paid fifty gold pieces for her.'

'Brahmin, for the crime of causing the death of this slave's child, you will have to pay a fine of two hundred gold coins to the state treasury. The slave-girl will remain in state custody till the time that she is sold again by the state.'

Chakradhar was aghast. 'Have mercy on a poor Brahmin, Incarnation of Justice,' he implored. 'It is impossible for a poor priest who ekes out a living from the performance of religious sacrifices to pay such a heavy fine in his whole life.'

'You are guilty of murder,' the Viceroy's voice grew harsh. 'According to the scriptures, a Brahmin cannot be punished with death and imprisonment. But you will pay the fine, even if you have to beg in the streets in sackcloth and ashes. However, if it is found necessary, money will be given from the state treasury for the maintenance of your family.'

And turning his eyes towards the unconscious slave-girl, he said, 'As for this slave, for the crime of having run away from the house of her master, she shall be punished with four lashes on the back.' The people were horrified at the severity of the sentence.

Devi Ratnaprabha's eyes filled up with tears.

'Keeping in mind the fact that the slave is weak and ill,' the Viceroy said in a solemn voice, 'she shall receive the strokes not with the whip but with a feather fan.'

Anshumala

RATNAPRABHA HAD THOUGHT THAT BY RESCUING DARA, SHE HAD picked a piece of shining glass out of the mud, but Dara turned out to be a jewel.

One evening her star pupil, Muktavali, was dancing the Peacock Dance before a gathering of visitors. Dara, with a platter of tambool in her hand, was attending to her mistress.

Without taking her eyes off Muktavali, Ratnaprabha stretched her hand towards Dara for a tambool. When none was given to her, she turned her head to see that the slave-girl was watching the dancer, her eyes following every movement and gesture in a frown of rapt attention. Amused by the slave-girl's reaction, Ratnaprabha kept her eyes on Dara.

'Oh, no! She missed a beat,' Dara exclaimed suddenly, and the platter dropped from her hand.

Muktavali stopped short. The clang of the fallen platter woke Dara from her reverie. Embarrassed and frightened, she humbly apologized, both to Ratnaprabha and the dancer.

Waving aside the apologies, Ratnaprabha asked Dara to continue the Peacock Dance in the correct form. Dara, with the utmost humility, expressed her lack of ability and her ignorance of the dance, and once again begged forgiveness for her unseemly behaviour.

'No, Dara, you seem to be quite well versed in the art of dancing. There is no doubt about that.' Ratnaprabha suddenly recalled Dara's words on the day of their fateful first meeting.

'Didn't you say that day on the river, that you knew dancing, that you would like to become a dancer?'

Upon Ratnaprabha's insistence, Dara had to push aside her embarrassment. She shyly made her way to the dance floor. As the veena and the mridang started playing, her reluctance slowly disappeared and she began to move to the rhythm. From her very first steps, Rohit, the aged instrumentalist, sensed her abilities. He varied the tempo; now brisk, now slow. Dara followed his lead with smooth and graceful footwork, as she gave herself up to the music. Feeling the rhythm flow through her body, she performed the most intricate footwork flawlessly and with such spirit that old Rohit found it difficult to keep up with her. His forehead was covered with drops of perspiration. The spectators watched the performance spellbound.

Devi Ratnaprabha, with her finger on her chin, sat transfixed.

Dara finished the dance, then came and stood before her mistress and bowed to her. Ratnaprabha rose from her seat, and taking the jewelled necklace from her own neck, put it around Dara's and then swept her into her arms. 'Nowhere else, except in Sagal, Magadh and in Taxila, is such artistic perfection to be seen,' she said. 'My friend, such a level of art is not attained without the dedicated counsel of a teacher and the blessings of the Goddess Saraswati. You have something of the style of Devi Mallika, my own teacher, in you. Tell me, truly, where and how did you get this priceless training?'

Bowing her head in humility, Dara replied in a voice tremulous with gratitude, 'I am also beholden to that very lady, the favoured devotee of Saraswati.'

Ratnaprabha had already been kindly disposed towards Dara. Now, discovering her great talent and her secret,

she became deeply attached to her. She even gave Dara a
new name: Anshumala.

With the change in her name, Divya's world changed
once more. Once again she began to glide, like a young swan,
free-spirited on the current of gaiety and luxury, in a stream
of music and dance. But no droplet from this torrent could
penetrate the wall of sorrow that surrounded her.

The smiles and charm she radiated around her were in
the nature of an obligation towards her art. As soon as she
was away from the public, she would withdraw within herself
and become indifferent to everything around her; just as a
young swan shakes its wings to shed every drop of the water
over which it has moved. The wall of agonizing memories that
enclosed her mind was impenetrable. The loss of little Shakul
overwhelmed her.

The connoisseurs of art waxed ecstatic over Anshumala's
charm, her amazing skill and grace as a dancer. After a
performance, precious gifts would pile up before Ratnaprabha's
seat. Anshumala had no eyes for these tributes. Her conscience
would eat into her thinking about the hungry innocent eyes
of her baby son, Shakul. Her pain would translate itself into
exquisite rendering of songs of sorrow, and the audience, not
knowing the truth, experienced it as true and brilliant artistry.
Such feelings as she could express in her dance performances
had never been seen before.

Ratnaprabha's mansion had been a place of pilgrimage
for the lovers of art, not only in Mathurapuri, but also in
the entire territory of Shursen. But now its fame spread to
Magadh, Kuru, Katha and Madra. In the evenings, connoisseurs
would vie with one another for a seat in the concert hall.
Whenever Anshumala gave a performance, it became necessary

for the state officials to post guards on the roads to maintain order. With such popularity, Ratnaprabha's wealth doubled and tripled in a short time. Earlier, at the performances of Muktavali and Ratnaprabha, garlands and silver coins were the usual gifts, whereas now gold coins, precious gems and jewelled necklaces were showered on her. The glory went to Ratnaprabha, but Anshumala was the reason for it.

Anshumala's magnetism yielded yet another result. Young merchants, nobles and state officials began to flock to the palace carrying bouquets and garlands. They made handsome gifts of money to Ratnaprabha and offered to escort Anshumala on excursions along the river or in the forests. Those who used to plead for Ratnaprabha's favours, now came to the palace with their hearts aflutter for Anshumala. The riches poured at the feet of Ratnaprabha ceased to have any attraction for her. Conscious of her own waning attraction, she began to find everything around her dull and insipid.

Instead of being the focus of attention for visitors, Ratnaprabha had become the protectress, the mistress and the guardian of the new public idol. The money and the gifts that were offered in appreciation of Anshumala's art belonged to Ratnaprabha. She would look at the mounting riches and often ask herself, 'What has been the purpose of being attractive? Money I have plenty. But there is something which is lacking now.' This sense of loss would depress her, 'What is the use of money? Is it meant to be used for enjoyment? But then how should I enjoy it? By wearing beautiful clothes and ornaments, by living in a palatial house? Yet, what lasting comfort do they give me? Such worldly possessions are not the aim in themselves, but only the means. Even if the cage is made of gold, it is the mynah that attracts attention, not the cage.'

Eighteen years before, when she had finished her training under Mallika and had come to Mathurapuri, the people had welcomed her performances with delirious enthusiasm. Kaumudi, the reigning public favourite, had been so jealous. Such is the irony of a courtesan's life. The courtesan gives up her private existence for the sake of success, affluence and self-dependence. But a wife, in giving up her independence in marriage, gets a man in return. The life of a courtesan is like a meteor, which gives a brilliant display of light for a little while, and then plunges into darkness. The life of a housewife, on the other hand, is like a lamp that burns dimly but for a long time. There are sheltering hands to protect it when the strong winds of adversity blow. Before her extinction, she is able to light other lamps from her being, and is able to see her own light in them. Even when she is extinguished, her light glows on. Ratnaprabha would often remember Marish's words; he used to say, 'In such continuity lies man's immortality.'

Ratnaprabha frequently recalled Marish's comments, and the memories connected with them. The first time the atheist artist—a young man with prematurely grey hair—had come to her house, had been three years ago, when he was on his way to Sagal from Dakshinapath. He had attended a concert. Ratnaprabha had seen nothing in his face or his dress to attract her attention. Even after the assembly had dispersed, he had lingered on in the hall. When Ratnaprabha was about to retire for the night, he asked for an audience with her. But she had declined to meet him. Discouraged, he had sent his reply through her maidservant, 'Yes, the lady's behaviour is in keeping with her vocation. I only wanted to have the pleasure of her company, but I cannot pay for that pleasure with money. But, there are other things in the world besides money.'

The remark had intrigued Ratnaprabha, and she had agreed to see him, though not very willingly. She had found that there was something in Marish's behaviour, which commanded attention. In the end, he had stayed on as her guest for some weeks. At first his utterances would only rouse her curiosity, but later she had begun to reflect on them, and had found some truth there.

Her heart was not at peace, but she still had faith and hope. A significant portion of her earnings went for religious offerings. She believed that the deeds of her previous life had resulted in her present fame and wealth, but that she had been deprived of life's real fulfilment. And that by performing meritorious deeds in this life she would attain life's consummation in her next birth, and also in the other world.

'Devi,' Marish had said in a bantering tone, 'would it give you greater satisfaction if you touched your nose, not directly, but circuitously by stretching your arm round the back of your neck?'

'What a curious question! Why do you ask?'

'Because abstinence in this world, in the hope of getting greater opportunities of enjoyment in the next one, is no abstinence at all,' Marish replied. 'According to your way of thinking, abstinence is the price you are paying for the pleasures of your next birth. If you wish to indulge yourself in the pleasures of life, then do so while you still have the means. There is nothing to be gained by depriving yourself. The next world is only a figment of the imagination. No one has ever seen it. The person who assures you about its existence is only repeating what others have told him, and those others too have been doing the same. No one has given evidence of its existence after seeing it with his own eyes. In everyday life, we do not accept such evidence. Is it wise, therefore, to sacrifice the tangible for a figment of our imagination?'

Ratnaprabha had simply stared at Marish. She could not say anything in reply. 'How will you attain the next world after your death?' Marish went on. 'Through the medium of your soul? Devi, the individual soul, of which the sages talk, has no existence. That too is mere conjecture and a mental invention. The ability to feel and think with which man is endowed, is a subtle attribute of the physical body alone. It exists in man as fragrance exists in a flower or light in a burning lamp. Where does the light of a lamp go after the lamp is extinguished? Can light have an independent existence separate from the sun or the lamp? It is the same for the individual soul. How can there be any soul without the body?

'Devi,' Marish's voice grew more excited, 'is it reasonable and prudent to regard the experience of the palpable world, which all living beings are aware of, as illusory, and to regard the eternal spirit and the individual soul as realities, when they are only the product of some sage's imagination? Instead of putting blind trust in another man's word, you should rely upon your own experience and reason. This life alone is real. This world alone is real. Attain whatever you feel you have to, in the lifespan you have before you.'

Ratnaprabha looked at him with wide open eyes. 'But, Arya,' she said, doubtfully, 'this body is transient, and the happiness obtained through it is also transient.'

Marish looked at her through his half-closed eyes, with an ironical smile on his lips. 'Is the body transient? Devi, do you want immortality? Tell me, of all the things that you see around you, how many remain without change, in shape and form, taste and odour? What we call death is only change. Imagine a situation in which there is never any change in

the world. Would such a world have any charm or attraction?'
He looked at her inquisitively.

'You're right, Arya,' Ratnaprabha replied after some
reflection. 'A world without change would not be a happy
place to live in.'

'And man is surely immortal,' said Marish. 'His immortality
lies in the continuity of the human race, which has gone on
for thousands and thousands of years.'

Under Marish's influence, Ratnaprabha ceased to be
preoccupied with immortality and the other world, and
began to think about the meaningfulness of the present. Even
though she had acquired wealth, she did not consider her life
to be meaningful, since she was merely a source of distraction
and enjoyment for the community. The life of a high-born
housewife held the ultimate attraction for her, but she felt
that she had lost the chance of becoming one herself. Who would
accept her as a wife? Into whose hands could she entrust
herself? Her life, at best, stimulated the desire for life in others.

Even though she had all the gifts to earn a fortune as a
courtesan, Anshumala was not vain. She was indifferent towards
her own self, but for Ratnaprabha she felt a profound attachment
and gratitude. From the very beginning, Ratnaprabha had
displayed sympathy and affection for her. And on learning that
she was the pupil of Mallika, her own teacher, and that the girl
loved her and looked upon her as her saviour, she began to dote
on her. Anshumala addressed her as 'mistress' while Ratnaprabha
called her 'sister' or 'friend'. Already in her forties, Ratnaprabha
had come to regard Anshumala not as a rival who challenged
her place and position, but rather as a worthy successor who
would perpetuate her art and her tradition. Out of a sense of
pride, admiration and love, she took to calling her not Anshumala
but 'Anshuprabha', commingling both their names.

At the appearance of Anshumala in Ratnaprabha's concert
hall the pleasure lovers of Mathurapuri went into ecstasies
over her. But Anshumala was not thrilled by such adulation;
she remained as distant and unapproachable as before.

Anshu's aloofness merely heightened the ardour of her
admirers. They showered presents on her in the hope of
ingratiating themselves. But that did not work either, and
soon her indifference began to turn them off.

Rumours spread in the town, that she was no courtesan
but a mere performing doll; that she was more like a marionette
who went through the motions of ritual dances before the
image of a god than a real dancer; that her alluring smiles and
bewitching glances were mere formal gestures of art and carried
no genuine feeling for anyone. She had nothing inside her and,
therefore, she could give out anything. She was devoid of
that warmth which is the essential quality of a desirable woman.
She was only a jointed puppet whose strings were pulled
by Ratnaprabha.

Such comments would reach the ears of Devi Ratnaprabha,
and she herself would observe the behaviour that led to the
rumours. She would worry about Anshu's depression and
become anxious about her future. Neither could she say anything
directly to Anshu for fear of hurting her feelings, nor could
she remain silent.

She even called in Prithvi, the well-known tantrik, to
exercise his skills to find out what was ailing Anshu, but to no
effect. Hesitantly, she broached the subject with Anshu one
day. 'Death comes to us all, one day or the other,' she said.
'Why go on this way, with a half-dead, half-alive existence? Is
it proper to ignore the wishes of those from whom we receive
the means of subsistence? People come to us to forget their
sorrows. If we too offer them sadness and dejection, then what

can they expect from us? Art without purpose is like a beautifully coloured artificial fruit, which can give no real satisfaction. Why offend the feelings of those who offer their love in the hope of receiving the same in return? Love is nothing but regard given active expression. You wanted once to become a courtesan in order to be a free woman. You must have faith in and respect for your vocation. It's a duty one owes to one's profession . . .' There was so much more that Ratnaprabha wanted to say but she could find no words for it.

Anshu joined her hands and said in the subdued tones of a supplicant, her eyes brimming with tears, 'Mistress, you have purchased this body of mine. My mind is not under my control. You have shown me nothing but the greatest kindness. I wish to submit my mind also to your bidding. I am most grateful.'

Seeing that her advice, however well-meaning, had troubled Anshu, Ratnaprabha did not return to the subject. Had Marish been there, she thought, he would probably have brought Anshu around with his arguments and lifted her out of her despondency. She would have listened to him with attention, and very likely, changed her outlook. Ratnaprabha often thought about Marish, but now she felt she needed him as an adviser.

Marish was in the habit of arriving unexpectedly, like some bird landing for a rest on its migratory flight. When he wearied of Sagal, he would proceed to Magadh by way of Shursen; spurned in Magadh he would again return to Shursen; and when Shursen palled on him, he would again set out for Sagal.

Every year, in the month of Shravan, a Festival of Swings was celebrated in Vrindavan, a suburban district of Mathurapuri. Pleasure-loving men and women assembled there in large numbers from all corners of the land. The common people would go there for entertainment, while the connoisseurs of art would meet for argument and debate on aesthetics. There would be a rich variety of performances: displays of musical virtuosity in the well-tempered voices of experienced singers and the graceful performances of dance by troupes of young trainees. The best artist would be honoured by the audience, and honours would be conferred on the state to which the artist belonged—Magadh, Kuru, Madra, Malla, etc. But for the last three years in succession, ever since Anshu had appeared in Ratnaprabha's troupe, the honour had been won by Mathurapuri. On account of the Festival of Swings, Anshumala's fame had spread far and wide.

The festival took place during the rainy season. A large number of devotees of the performing arts flocked to Mathurapuri. Their arrival would cause a rush in Ratnaprabha's concert hall, so much so that there would not be enough seats. Even a heavy downpour in the evening did not discourage people from attending her concerts. After the month of Shravan, rains continued far into Bhadrapad. Only during the worst of the monsoon rain showers, when the roads became impassable, did Ratnaprabha and Anshumala get some respite.

On one such evening, Ratnaprabha sat alone in the veranda of her house, musing over her life and the future of her friend, Anshu, when suddenly Marish appeared, escorted by a maidservant. Ratnaprabha's eyes lit up with joy at the sight of her long-awaited friend. It also flashed through her mind, that, very likely, Marish would be able to dispel Anshu's gloom.

It was raining heavily. Ratnaprabha and Marish sat on the veranda reclining against cushions. The pouring rain looked like a sheet of water before them. In Ratnaprabha's concert hall, the tambourine and the kettledrum were silent. Across the sky, dark and heavy thunderclouds billowed with rumbling sounds that seemed to parody the silent tambourine and kettledrum.

Caressed by a soft breeze, the trees appeared to wave their limbs in imitation of the resting dancers. Ratnaprabha asked the slave-girl, who stood waving the fan behind her, to call Anshu and to bring the wine tray.

At the mention of Anshumala's name, Marish felt curious, 'Devi, good luck has brought you a pupil who has spread your fame far and wide. I would certainly like to see her and also to have the pleasure of watching her performance.'

'I called Anshu because I want you to meet her. But my friend, don't be disappointed if you find her poor company. Off the stage, she spends all her time wrapped up in her own thoughts; dance and music for her are merely a means of earning a livelihood.'

Marish waited with eager curiosity.

Anshumala came, dressed in an expensive but casual white dress. She wore no ornaments, not even a flower. Sad and listless, she had little consciousness of her charm, only heightened by her careless dressing.

With a flicker of a smile, Anshu joined her hands in greeting to the visitor, 'The humble servant to the Court Dancer offers her salutations to the honoured guest.'

Marish found himself staring at her petal-like lips. He raised his eyes and felt a flash of recollection. In the sad, set features of this timid woman he recognized the young dancer in the white costume of the lovelorn swan-maiden who had danced five years before in Sagal's Festival of Spring.

At a sign from Ratnaprabha, Anshu sat down on the mattress, and as desired by her mistress, filled a bowl with wine and held it out with both hands to the visitor.

Marish continued to look at Anshu with astonishment. Anshu, finally recognizing him, sat petrified under his piercing gaze.

Ratnaprabha sized up the situation and put her arm round Anshu in reassurance. Noticing the extreme bewilderment in Marish's eyes, she smiled and with a corner of her stole screened Anshu's face. 'Arya,' she said jokingly, 'you will frighten my gentle friend by staring so hard.'

Lost in memories, Marish's gaze remained fixed on Anshu. Then his lips moved, 'Kumari Divya!' he muttered.

Speechless, Anshu lowered her eyes.

Ratnaprabha looked at Marish and then at Anshu. The faces of both had darkened like the overcast sky before rainfall. For a few seconds she hesitated, and then, taking with her the slave-girl who had been waving the fan all the while, and issuing a string of instructions to her, she moved off the veranda.

'Kumari Divya,' Marish muttered again, after a few seconds.

Anshu sat motionless, holding the bowl of wine in her hands. She lowered her head still further. 'Arya, I am no longer Divya,' she said in a faint voice. 'I am no longer a kumari (virgin) either. I am Anshumala now, dancer–courtesan and the bought slave of Devi Ratnaprabha. Do, pray, accept this bowl of wine.'

With a deep sigh, Marish took the bowl, but put it back on the tray. His mind, soaring on the wings of memory, once again flew towards the past. 'How did you happen to come here, to this far-off place?'

'Fate brought me here, Arya, my karma,' Anshu answered in a firm voice, raising her eyes and looking at Marish in the dim light of the cloudy evening.

This mention of fate and karma exasperated Marish. He felt as though he had been rudely jolted out of his reverie. 'What has fate or karma to do with it?' he said. 'Fate is nothing but an expression of human helplessness. And to blame your present way of life on karma, as the result of your deeds in a previous life, means nothing but blindness to the cause of suffering and helplessness. Dear girl, fate and karma are nothing more than this.'

'Arya, that is what your humble servant meant. I feel completely helpless, and I am ignorant of the cause of my helplessness.'

Marish felt relieved by Anshu's answer, which seemed to reflect his own ideas. But her resignation hindered further conversation on the subject. Marish sat silent, his eyes fixed on the bowl of wine on the tray. Anshu once again picked up the bowl and dutifully offered it to the guest, 'Pray, do have some wine.'

Marish, without raising his eyes, quietly accepted the wine and gulped it down like a bowl of medicine. He turned his eyes towards the curtain of driving rain, which seemed to fill the gap between heaven and earth.

'Several years ago,' Marish said, his eyes still turned away, 'at the time of the death of the Chief Justice, I had occasion to hear some stray mention of you. It was said that the Chief Justice's great-granddaughter had died of some serious ailment. There was suspicion of suicide . . . And I find you here, under a different name. Am I dreaming now, or was I dreaming then?'

Hearing something like a stifled sob, he turned to look at Anshu. Her face was covered by her stole. 'This subject has pained you. I'll say nothing more about it,' Marish said sympathetically.

Struggling to control herself, Anshu said humbly, 'Arya, separation from dear ones does cause pain. The grandsire was the only person I could turn to.'

'Of course, separation causes great sorrow, but, lady, death is the law of life. The Chief Justice's death caused much sorrow to the people of Sagal. For more than a hundred years he had been the pride of Sagal, the very soul and spirit of justice. His sacred memory will continue to be a source of pride. When the light of his life was extinguished, Sagal was plunged in gloom. But, gentle lady, such sorrow too falls to the lot of fortunate people, just as anxiety for the health of one's children contains within itself the joy of being a father or mother.' Marish and Anshu were silent for some time.

Ratnaprabha returned with the slave-girl, carrying a lamp. Finding Marish and Anshu sitting in silence in the dark, she tried to lighten the mood, and said jocularly, 'Those gifted ones who can read each other's thoughts without uttering a word, have no need to go on sitting in the dark at such a late hour.'

When neither of them gave any answer, Ratnaprabha touched Anshu on the shoulder and said, 'Get up, my dear, it is already late. Arrangements have been made for the guest in the guest house. He must be tired after the long day's journey.'

The memories of the past were like a nightmare to Anshu; bringing back so much horror and pain. And the future was a void. She did not think about the past any more, for there was hardly a time in it which did not move her to tears. She found herself unable to think of happiness. What was happiness? A rich family, a loving husband, beautiful children? She had had her chances for all of these and lost them, and in consequence found only pain. She remembered the words of the Buddhist monk, Cheebuk. He had been right when he said, 'Joy and sorrow cling to each other. Pain comes only when one desires happiness. There is much more pain in the world than there is happiness. When the world is so full of sorrow, how can anyone escape it?' Anshu had gone through so much that 'she had become indifferent to pain and happiness alike. By making herself insensitive to feeling and by accepting her situation with resignation, she had attained a certain peace of mind. Her physical activities were mechanical and devoid of any purpose. Her mind, no doubt, could respond, could think, but it stopped prompting her to act, to take an initiative, to strive or to construct. She had become fixed in the tendency to withdraw from life, a detached observer who could see only futility on all sides.

Anshu spent a restless night. When the water in a pond is disturbed, it stirs up the mud and brings up the weeds from the bottom. So the contact with Marish had brought to the surface the horrible memories from her past. The peace of mind achieved in three years had been shattered in a few seconds.

She asked the maidservant to remove the light from her room, and kept tossing and turning in her bed for a while. She recalled the kind of life she used to lead in the house of Chakradhar, the priest. Lying on the bare stone floor, she would be so sleepy that she did not know where she was. She would wake up only when the mistress shouted for her, or when little Shakul woke up crying. The mistress would scold and curse her for having such sound sleep.

The drumming of rain was so incessant that it dulled all other sounds of the night. Anshu thought, 'Every drop of rain makes its own little sound as it falls to the earth but taken together, they become just a dull monotone. Even so, each sorrow produces its own pain, but innumerable sorrows, all coming together, incapacitate a person from feeling anything, from experiencing pain.

'Arya Marish kept me company in silence, as if he was sharing my grief. Why should he feel anything towards me? Hundreds of pleasure seekers come here for entertainment. They are concerned only with that side of my existence, which they see before their eyes. Perhaps Marish had eyes for the inner reality, and could not remain indifferent to what lay hidden behind the appearance.

'Five years ago, I had found Marish's remark flippant; his words had filled me with revulsion and disgust. That prophecy of Marish, which was more like a curse than a prediction, has proved only too true. Why do these admirers flock to my mistress's concert hall? In Sagal, what was the purpose of those grand festivities held in Devi Mallika's palace? Did the audience come to take pleasure in a woman's charm, to take in that primeval force of creation in woman? . . . They come, amuse themselves and go away, but Marish is looking for sorrow in a shop where only entertainment is on sale. It is not entertainment but pain that gives him satisfaction; pain and sympathy in pain . . . Everything is futile, there is nothing but futility all round . . .' And she lay wide awake, lost in the maze of her thoughts, with the rain still pattering away in the darkness.

On the other hand, Marish, who had made a practice of remaining indifferent and unconcerned, felt very disturbed at finding Divya in Ratnaprabha's palace. He kept tossing and turning in his bed till late in the night. Divya's face, bereft of hope, overwhelmed with grief, devoid of interest, lingered before his eyes. Divya in her white clothes, looking the very picture of sorrow, sank deep into Marish's heart. At one

moment he would picture her as he saw her on the veranda of
Ratnaprabha's palace. At another, it would be Divya vibrant
with life, full of hope and zest, like a newly budding flower, as
she used to be in Sagal, in the house of her great-grandfather.

His heart melted with pity for her, and he lost hold
over himself as wax, once molten, cannot be held in the palm
of the hand.

In Sagal, Marish had felt attraction towards Divya, but it
had been one of admiration, rather than desire. He was well
aware of his lack of resources and lowly social status. He knew
that a wide gap existed between him and Divya. But here, in
Ratnaprabha's house, Divya was no longer living on those
inaccessible heights of pride and grandeur. She had fallen from
there and was now at the same level as he was, and therefore,
she had come within his reach. He had only to stretch out his
hand in sympathy and he would be able to touch her.

This attraction, reinforced by a feeling of sympathy, grew
very strong. He became restless, yearned for her company,
yearned to have a glimpse of her, but his references to her past
had upset and pained Divya. He had no wish to distress her.
One thought constantly irked him: Would she continue to
despair and indefinitely isolate herself from the world? He
was still consumed by his concern for Divya when, in the
evening of the following day, he attended the performance in
Ratnaprabha's concert hall.

Anshumala got up from her place near Ratnaprabha and
began her performance. Her make-up was simple yet effective,
and a smile enlivened her features as she drew inspiration from
the music. Marish could not concentrate on her singing and
dancing. He kept thinking to himself: Compared to this artificial
and vivacious Anshumala, the Divya of the previous evening,

clad in white, serious and without any embellishments looked much more beautiful. Last evening she had been free to voice the sorrow in her heart. At this moment she was obliged to be a purveyor of entertainment, an object of enjoyment with the admirers drinking in her beauty through their eyes.

The smile of humility that Anshumala gave in return for the thunderous ovation became unbearable for him. He waited impatiently for the spectators to disperse.

The performance was over. Tired, Anshumala withdrew into her room and with the help of Vrinda, her maidservant, began removing her make-up. The doorkeeper slave-girl swung a fan of peacock feathers to cool her perspiring body. Vrinda untied her bodice, and putting Anshu's arm on her shoulder, was removing the armlet when suddenly Marish appeared at the door to the room. Not finding the doorkeeper, Marish had walked in, without giving any notice. Anshu shrank back as the maidservant hastily covered her shoulders with a stole. Anshu's eyes were half-shut with shyness and her cheeks flushed deep red with embarrassment.

Marish turned back, with his head bowed. As he stepped into the veranda, he heard someone saying behind him, 'Arya, the mistress conveys her greetings to you.' Somewhat nonplussed, he went back into the room.

Anshu's clothes were in place. Some of the ornaments had been taken off; others she still wore. Though her face was still flushed and her eyes shone with the embarrassment of having been seen partly dressed, a smile of welcome played on her lips. 'Pray, come in, Arya.' She received him with her hands together and head bowed.

Strings of pearls were still woven in her hair. She had the crescent mark on her forehead, and her lips were painted red. Her curving neck, luminous as a seashell, looked all the more lustrous, set off by strings of pearls. The tight cloth of her red bodice restrained her full breasts like the bridles on a pair of horses. Below her waist, her smooth light-green sari clung to her firm round hips and her long, shapely thighs still quivered faintly from the strain of her performance. Between the bodice and the sari, the skin of her bare midriff had a natural glow that outshone the lustre of the red silk above and the light-green below.

Marish's mind was still troubled and he could not acknowledge Anshu's greetings with due formality. His lack of courtesy, however, did not annoy Anshu. What did irritate her a little was the attempt he made to maintain his usual air of nonchalance.

'Pray be seated, Arya,' she said, pointing to a seat.

Marish sat down, without replying to the greeting. Anshu, unmindful of the maid who was removing her ornaments, came closer to Marish and said, 'Arya, I hope you are feeling well, both in body and mind?'

'Yes, I am quite well, lady. Did my sudden entrance into your room cause your embarrassment?' He was trying to control his feeling, but signs of discomfiture appeared on his face. Anshu understood the reason for Marish's discomfiture, but trying to keep a smile on her face, assured him, 'There was no inconvenience, Arya. Your humble servant is at your disposal.'

Marish was silent for a moment, and then said in a grave voice, 'I came because I could no longer bear to keep my thoughts from you.'

The words reverberated like drumbeats in Anshu's mind. Clasping and entwining her fingers in an effort to control her agitation, she suddenly realized that it had been improper for her to permit a man into her chamber without the permission of her mistress. 'It is stuffy inside the room, Arya. If it is not too much trouble, let us go into the garden and talk in the open air,' she said.

The slave-girl whose duty it was to fan her mistress was so taken aback by the entrance of a man into the chamber that she had neglected her task. At a sign from her mistress, however, she had resumed it. 'That will do,' Anshu said, 'we don't need the fan. Take the Arya to the garden seat under the *bakul*[1] tree.' Then turning to Marish, said, 'Arya, I shall follow you there in a moment.'

'What should I tell her and how should I put it?' Marish was thinking as he sat down under the bakul tree, on a seat carved from stone. In a moment of agitation, he had gone into her room. The recollection of that mistake, however, induced him to reason things out with himself rather than feel disturbed. He saw Divya coming towards him. She had changed out of her dance costume and was once again dressed in white clothes, without any jewellery. The smile too had disappeared from her lips. She sat down beside him. 'I am listening, Arya,' she said, after a little while.

'Is this the life for you? Is this what you wanted from your life?'

Anshu was silent for a few seconds, trying to grasp the purpose of his question. 'I have not accepted anything, Arya, of my own accord. I did not have to reason out what was proper or improper. It is all the doing of fate.'

'Fate?' Marish sat up. 'Devi, to speak of fate is nothing but an admission of helplessness.'

---

[1] Flowering tree, *Ninsops dengi*.

'Yes, Arya, it is helplessness,' Anshu admitted.

'Fate means lack of fortitude,' Marish said again.

'Yes, Arya, it is a lack of fortitude,' Anshu admitted again.

Marish did not know what to say. 'But that means you have no wish to change anything, you want to make no effort to have any kind of life,' Marish said intently, after a moment's thought.

Anshu was not put out by the remark. Her eyes, with their pupils flecked with blue, looked squarely into Marish's, 'No, Arya, I made all possible efforts and endeavours. I strained to my utmost capacity, and it was when I realized my inability to control things that I admitted my helplessness.'

'Lady, effort and endeavour are natural functions of life. As long as life is in you, it is only natural to keep on trying.' Marish's voice was no longer agitated and provocative, but low and persuasive. 'The disappointment in your attempts at one stage of your life cannot decide things for the rest of it. The other end of life is never visible; life is limitless. Why should we, then, put limits to our efforts and striving? To admit one's lack of strength means to give up, to lose interest in living.'

Anshu lowered her eyes as she heard the ring of sympathy in Marish's voice. 'Arya, it was this very impulse that led me to venture into the unknown. I knew that my way would be difficult. Yet I went on, till at last I found that I was lacking in the necessary strength.' She heaved a deep sigh. 'Whatever had to happen has happened. Why should I worry now? Why have any regrets? The wise ones say that hope and desire are at the root of suffering. I found it so, too.'

Anshu's despondency pained Marish even more. 'Nothing much has happened. Whatever did happen, affected only a period of your life. As long as there is life, there is a possibility of change in it, and consequently, of effort too.' To emphasize his point, he looked deep into Anshu's eyes as he said, 'Divya, life is limitless and so is a person's capability.'

At the utterance of her name—Divya—Anshu's whole body trembled. 'Arya, the proud great-granddaughter of the Chief Justice is dead,' she said, trying to suppress her agitation. 'In her dead body, Anshumala is passing the rest of her days, as a dancer–courtesan who earns a living by her art. I am deeply obliged to you for your kind sympathy.'

'I am not saying this merely out of sympathy,' Marish said, trying to swallow the lump in his throat.

'Then, the dancer is grateful to you for your charitable attitude.'

'No, Devi, I am saying this out of love for you,' Marish replied.

Anshu felt the rush of blood through her veins. The almost full moon of the month of Bhadrapad was playing hide-and-seek in the sky dotted with clouds. In the absence of any human sound, crickets and beetles filled the moist air with their incessant buzz. To Anshu's ears, however, more piercing than these sounds were the words uttered by Marish. They rang in her ears till they deprived her of any ability to react.

In the wake of her great popularity, Anshu had been pestered by many a lover pleading his suit. She had politely warded all of them off, without paying much attention. Those confessions of love were directed towards the favourite performer of Mathurapuri, the dancer Anshumala. But it was to Divya, not Anshu, that Marish had addressed his words. It was difficult to ignore them, but to respond to them was even more difficult.

Under the moon disporting itself among the clouds, sat Anshu with her head bowed, surrounded by the murmuring plants and trees that were being gently tickled by the wind, and the chirping and buzzing of the rain-happy insects, terrified by Marish's declaration. In her imagination, she saw Marish coming towards her with outstretched arms, advancing towards her, as once, on a night as bewitching as this, Prithusen had advanced towards her . . . Anshu shuddered all over as she recalled that terrible night. Its memory brought a bitter taste to her mouth. Her womanly coyness, meant to excite and invite an impetuous lover, turned into a feeling of revenge. Her mind swiftly cleared of its numbness. With it vanished the meekness in her voice.

She said with a derisive smile, 'The dancer–courtesan Anshumala is ready to entertain any pleasure seeker. Arya, what can I do for you?'

Marish ignored the sarcasm. 'I am a petitioner, lady, not for any flirtation with the dancer–courtesan, but for the meaningful love of a woman.'

'But that woman is dead, Arya.' Looking into Marish's eyes, just as the moon, emerging from behind a cloud flooded the earth with its bright light, Anshumala said sharply, 'Does the Arya remember an evening three years ago, at the close of a hot summer day, when the Arya rebuked a beggar woman, with a child in her arms, who was ready to become a prostitute? The Arya said to her then, "Your shelter lies in the cold waters of the Yamuna river." That very evening, the woman did throw herself into the river, but it cast her out, and she emerged from the water a dancer and a courtesan. What satisfaction will it afford you, Arya, to love that same woman now, when the

Arya had such contempt for the would-be prostitute then? The dancer—courtesan Anshumala is none other than Divya, the woman who died that evening.'

Marish stared hard at Anshu, his eyes wide open in amazement, as the light of the moon once again grew dim. For some time Marish sat thus, breathless and unmoving. When he stirred and heaved a sigh, Anshu said humbly, with down-cast eyes, 'It is already late in the night. It would be better if the Arya retired for rest.'

By asking him to retire, Anshu robbed him of his sleep and rest as much as she lost her own. She had ridiculed his expression of love for her. That gave her the satisfaction of having taken revenge against barbarous men, but hardly had she reached her room, when she was filled with a sense of remorse: Why should I have behaved in that way? Why did I rake up the memory of the beggar woman with her child? Was this the reward for his love and respect for me, for a person who had extended his hand of sympathy, to help and to offer shelter?

At the mere idea of a place in someone's sheltering arms, Anshu felt a delightful lassitude. To sink into accepting arms capable of giving protection——therein lay the fulfilment of a woman's life. And the desire for it reawakened in Anshu's heart the desire to be free from the self-imposed torture of indifference and aversion to the joys of life. 'Why was I so hostile to him?' she asked herself. Unable to overcome her sense of remorse, Anshu felt like crying. There was fulfilment for her in acceptance of the sympathy and love in Marish's heart. In his desire for her lay the possibility of her achievement as a woman. She could provide refuge as well as receive it. 'Ah, but on a night like this . . .' she remembered.

Anshu felt that her body was covered with perspiration. Before her closed eyes appeared the tender Prithusen, the solemn Rudradhir, the matal Vrik, and the scholar Marish, all advancing towards her with outstretched arms, and she thought with disgust, 'I am a woman, and therefore an object of enjoyment for men. Therein lies my only attraction—an object of enjoyment!' She tossed about in bed for a long time, persuading herself that she would never again be trapped into the snare, even to seek shelter.

But her thoughts did not cede. 'Why should I have an aversion for worldly things? Like Devi Ratnaprabha and Mallika, I too should dedicate myself to the service of art and make that the aim of my life. Instead of thinking of protection and pleasing a man, I should become self-reliant. There is nothing to regret. Whatever happened to me was what had to happen.'

Anshumala did not stir out of her room for the next two days, pleading sickness. Ratnaprabha knew that the girl was upset and had been suffering in silence. She went and sat by her bedside for a while. Putting her hand on Anshu's head, Ratnaprabha thought, 'It may be that the grief concealed in her heart has found an outlet now. Perhaps, she will be able to breathe more freely once the load of sorrow is lifted from her mind.'

The usually loquacious Marish, too, had become quiet and moody.

Some days later, torrential rains again made the road to Ratnaprabha's palace impassable. Profiting from this enforced leisure, Ratnaprabha sat on a mattress in the veranda, reclining against a cushion. Feeling a need for company, she sent for Anshu and Marish. They sat together for a while, drinking wine, when the conversation drifted to the Lokayata philosophy of materialism. Ratnaprabha asked Marish, 'If death is the ultimate end of life, and if there is no hope of another birth in this or in the next world, then how can one feel enthusiastic about the present? This life, then, can only be regarded as an accidental occurrence, without cause and without effect, which may or may not occur as a real event.'

Anshumala felt that the question had some bearing on her own state of mind. She looked inquiringly at Marish. 'The mistress is right, I think,' she said. 'What substance can there be in something, which is so transient and of no consequence?'

Marish was slow in reacting to their question. He replied by posing a counter-question, 'How is it that we know about death with certainty even though we have not experienced death?'

'By seeing the deaths of others like us,' Ratnaprabha said.

'Does it mean, then, that we too are a part of that chain of existence, of the unending life process?'

'Undoubtedly,' Ratnaprabha admitted.

'And this chain of existence was present before we were born, and will continue after we're gone, isn't that so?' Marish asked, gazing straight into Ratnaprabha's face with his own tired eyes.

'This is also true,' Ratnaprabha had to admit.

'It means, then, that it is only the individual who is born or dies. The chain of existence or the collective life is unending, even immortal, so far as man's understanding can go. The cause and the consequence of an individual's life are both to be found in this chain of being, in this continuous process of existence.'

'That is true, but death causes fear. That too is a reality based on experience. And unless and until we are freed from that fear, there is little purpose in being attached to life, isn't that so?' Ratnaprabha asked, smiling.

'Would life be happy and free from fear if men became immortal?' Marish asked with a hint of amusement in his tone.

'The desire for immortality is only natural. In the orthodox Vedic view, immortality is the Supreme Bliss; that alone gives freedom from fear.'

Marish sat up, discarding the cushion. 'Devi, what is the difference between the living and the dead?'

'The living has motion, while the dead is immobile.'

'True,' Marish agreed, 'and motion means entering from one point of time and place into another point of time and place. In other words, motion is change. This change is motion, and motion is life. Immortality means changelessness or absence of change. Devi, if the sun were to become stationary, if water and air were to become motionless, if everything were to become still and unchanging, would then life be desirable and happy?'

Noticing that his listeners were somewhat puzzled, Marish continued, 'Devi, if all change is desirable, then death too is a part of that process of change. It is nothing but the arrival of the new in place of the old.'

'Arya has made the incomprehensible reality even more incomprehensible,' Ratnaprabha said, with a slight laugh. 'If you will permit me, I will go and rest. You two can continue the discussion if you are not too tired.'

When Ratnaprabha had left, Marish said, 'Would it be too embarrassing to take up the subject we were discussing the other day?'

'As you wish,' Anshumala replied, demurely.

'Have you given any thought to it?'

'Yes, I have been thinking about it long and deeply.'

'And what have you to say?'

'I feel frightened, Arya. Self-fulfilment is not for me in this life. My days will be spent in the service of my mistress, for the entertainment of the fortunate well-to-do, in the pursuit of art as a vocation.'

This relapse into indifference and apathy struck at Marish's heart. He looked away, to avoid meeting her sorrowful eyes, and said, as though to himself, 'Art! What is art?'

And himself gave the answer, 'Art is only a means. Art is for life, to serve towards the fulfilment of life. Indifference to life, but paying attention to the means of life; such an attitude will reduce you to being a mere instrument for the satisfaction of others without any chance of a full life for yourself. Should the life of such a person remain deprived of its own fulfilment, which—in the case of a woman—lies in creation? That would be like the life of a slave, which is spent as a tool in the service of others. What dreadful self-deception!'

Anshumala's head was reeling. She had been thinking incessantly about her problem, and Marish's logic confused her further. She was not afraid of the advances of dissolute admirers who hungered after her beauty, but Marish's friendly sympathy sometimes penetrated her resolve and left her defenceless. She had decided to remain adamant and not be shaken in her resolve. Trying to hide her nervousness, she said, 'What do you mean when you say that the ultimate fulfilment of a woman's life lies in creation?'

Taken a little aback by the uncharacteristic boldness, Marish looked into her eyes, 'Lady, women are the vessels of procreation. Being the primeval force of creation, a woman is the obvious centre of the family and of the human community. Man revolves around her as the ox revolves around the oil press.'

Marish's words brought back to her mind her resounding success at the Festival of Spring in Sagal, and the compliment Marish had paid to her on that occasion. She felt a thrill running through her body. Trying to remain calm, she replied. 'All that certainly brings fulfilment to a woman's life. It is perhaps a woman's natural purpose, but for that fulfilment she pays with her very existence, by becoming an object of enjoyment for man. How can one have fulfilment when one is merely an object of another's pleasure?'

Her heart began to beat violently, and drops of perspiration broke out on her forehead. Her voice too became bitter. In the dusk deepened by the moist air and the overcast sky her face could not be seen, but in the bitterness of her words Marish sensed her mental anguish and knew that his words had hit home.

He remained lost in thought for some time, then he said, 'What you say is partly true and partly untrue.' The seriousness of what he said kept him subdued. 'Lady, life is a mixture of many contrary elements. With one and the same aim, a man can act in many different ways. Out of love for a woman, and because of her desire for protection, a man wants her to be subservient. He treats her as an object of enjoyment, not by any law of nature, but because of the conventions that regard males as superior. In nature as well as in society, men and women are mutually dependent. By receiving a man's protection a woman does become dependent, but for the fulfilment of a woman's life a man's protection is necessary and so is the support provided by a woman to a man.'

'So where does a woman's fulfilment exist in this state of dependence?' Anshu asked vehemently. 'In man's enjoyment and use of her? Just as a bowl is useful to drink from when a man is thirsty? Arya, a woman is independent only as long as she can do without a man's protection. A prostitute is the only independent woman for that very reason.' Her breathing

quickened and she turned her eyes towards Marish who was
still looking at the clouds.

'How does the freedom of a courtesan–dancer give her
fulfilment?' Marish asked in a calm, serious voice. 'What does
she obtain through her freedom? What has Devi Ratnaprabha
gained? If a respectable housewife is an object of some man's
enjoyment, then a prostitute, a courtesan–dancer, is an
instrument for the satisfaction of the entire community.
She feeds the desires in the community and in return receives
only money, which is nothing but a means of acquiring material
satisfaction. What else, besides this? A prostitute is only a
medium for rousing desire, but her own desire in consequence
remains unfulfilled. Her art is useful insofar as it serves as
a means of satisfying the desire of others, but what does
she gain herself? She is the fuel in the sacrificial fire of desire.
She herself is deprived of the benefits of self-fulfilment.
Her independence is enjoyed by the community, but not by
herself. All that she receives is deprivation.'

With bowed head, Anshu listened to his dispassionate
but forceful words. Her resolve not to yield or be swayed was
crumbling under the impact of his persuasive and apparently
logical arguments, just as the sandy bank of a river crumbles
under the force of a powerful current. She felt as though she
was about to fall into the outstretched arms of Marish, ones
that seemed to offer protection. Her eyes brimmed with tears,
but she made no attempt to wipe them for fear of revealing
her feelings. And since her head was bowed, she did not know
whether Marish was looking at her or at the clouds.

Suddenly, a light appeared in the veranda. Lamp in hand,
Dagdha, the maidservant was coming towards them. 'The

mistress is waiting for the Arya and the Devi to come to dinner,' she said. Anshu, who was losing her foothold in the powerful current, found something to hold onto.

Marish had, on numerous occasions, enjoyed the hospitality of Ratnaprabha's palace, but had never stayed on for so long. Time would hang heavy on him if he had to remain silent and inactive, and he was not the type who could contemplate the shimmering leaves of the trees for any length of time. He now took to sculpting an image out of a piece of rock in the palace garden, under the bakul tree by the side of the ornamental pond. In the hot sun of the month of Bhadrapad, with perspiration streaming down his face, or in pouring rain, soaked to the skin, he was seen with mallet and chisel at the rock, trying to liberate from the mass of stone the image he had conceived in his mind.

Ratnaprabha would come every day in the morning or in the evening to watch the progress of the form that was gradually emerging. When she asked him what it was, his reply was evasive, 'Something that has been on my mind, just a whim.'

Although she hid it behind a smile while talking to Marish, a regret often gnawed at her mind. It had taken her a lifetime of effort to build the shrine of her reputation as a court dancer, but the altar for a god before whom she could make her offerings in that shrine had up till now remained vacant. That bare altar made all her affluence and her success seem pointless. Could Marish not fill that place and give meaning and fullness to her life?

'But what have I to offer him?' Ratnaprabha would ask herself. 'My barren old age? To that self-willed youth, I can only offer my affection. And Anshumala? Like a tortoise, she shrinks within herself, and hides under the shell of her indifference and defeats all his advances. But Marish, like a canny hunter, has now discovered her main weakness and has succeeded in unsettling her inner calm. To save herself, she has retreated further and plunged into the depths where nobody can reach her.'

'Silly girl,' Ratnaprabha would sometimes find herself addressing Anshu in her mind, 'how long will you hide away, ignoring life and suppressing your instincts? The path of life lies open before you and all your urges are pressing you in that direction. How long will you go on fighting yourself? Heaven knows what the future has in store for you.' Anshu was in fact fighting against herself in her resolve not to surrender to any persuasion from others. In the hushed silence of the midday, sitting alone in her room, she heard the clink of the chisel and the thud of the hammer on the rock, and felt as though the blows were being aimed at her heart. But even so, it was pleasant to hear them, and she wanted them to continue. Those blows did not rouse any anger or feeling of revenge in her. She was angry only with herself. 'Why have I begun to feel so restless?' she would ask herself.

On a day of overcast sky and cool breezes, Marish sat listless, ignoring the unfinished work and his tools. 'Why are you not doing any sculpting today, Arya?' Ratnaprabha asked him curiously.

'Devi, my idea has taken its final form,' he replied. Ratnaprabha was surprised at the answer. It was only yesterday that she had missed visiting him at his work. By what miracle, she thought, could the sculpture have been completed?

'Won't you show us the masterpiece that you have created?'

Marish nodded his consent, and Ratnaprabha asked Dagdha, the maidservant, to bring Anshumala and Muktavali to see the sculpture.

The three stood by the ornamental pond looking intently at the sculpture. The upper and lower parts of the rock had been left rough and untouched. Only in the centre, in the right half of the surface, a small area had been cut away, like a window. Framed in that window could be seen the full-grown breast of a young woman, with a depression below suggesting a waistline, and from the navel swelling downwards, a gracefully domed curve.

Ratnaprabha stood there with her companion for a long time, her hand on her chin, contemplating this work of art. Marish, too, stood there in silence.

'Is this work finished, Arya?' Ratnaprabha finally asked.

'As far as my intention is concerned, yes, it is complete. Devi.'

'I think it shows only part of the body of a woman and not the complete woman.'

Running his fingers through his unruly hair, Marish replied, 'You may be right, but that very part of a woman's body invites a man for the fulfilment of her womanhood and, then, nurses the fruit of that fulfilment.'

Ratnaprabha nodded to acknowledge Marish's serious tone. 'Arya, you have tried, then, to express an eternal truth about womanhood.'

Muktavali turned her face aside to hide her smile. Anshumala was looking thoughtfully at the panel cut in the rock. Marish's words rang in her ears, '. . . which is the primeval power of creation in woman'.

That night again Anshu could not sleep, her heart thudding, as she pondered on what had become the fulfilment of her own life and the price that she had to pay for it. Every now and then she would heave a sigh and promise herself that she would remain unshaken in her resolve.

Next morning, heavy and inert from lack of sleep, Anshu went into the garden for a breath of fresh air, and sat down under the blooming *kadamb*[1] tree. Seeing Marish coming towards her, she felt unsure of herself but greeted him politely, 'I hope the Arya is in good health.'

Marish stopped and leaned against the tree trunk. His eyes looked heavy and red. He noticed Anshu's tired eyes, 'Lady, it seems that you've perhaps had too much on your mind to sleep soundly.'

'You've guessed rightly, Arya,' Anshumala admitted, with her head bowed, forgetting to observe the courtesy of a smile.

'But, lady, a conflict never ends unless the problem is resolved. Especially if the problem involves a return to the natural assertion of the normal ways of life. The suppression and destruction of a natural instinct is no solution.'

'For me there is no other way except to suppress my desires and to destroy my inner self.'

'For what reason, may I ask?'

'Arya, I am frightened. All my experiences in life have done nothing but terrify me,' Anshu's voice shook as she looked around nervously.

Marish stood away from the tree and faced her, 'Lady, no experience in life is final. Life is measured in time and time is a continuous flow. All kinds of events—good and bad, pleasant and unpleasant, occur in this flow. This continuity is the only

[1] Flowering tree, *Nauclea cadamba*.

unchanging and certain thing in nature and the universe. But to step out of the current of life and to go against the natural appetite for life, simply because of a sequence of unfortunate occurrences is nothing but obstinacy to my mind.'

'Arya, I tried, but I have failed.'

'Lady, the circumstances in which you failed have all but disappeared. Ceaseless effort alone is the sign of life. The failure of one attempt does not mean the failure of one's entire life.'

Anshu sensed that Marish was waiting for her answer. She looked up, 'You are right, Arya. But I am frightened. I do not want life's fulfilment in exchange for the favour of shelter. I may have failed in life, but I have chosen freedom as a courtesan. Arya, that is still my decision.' She covered her eyes with a corner of her stole.

Marish took a deep breath and waited for a few seconds to steady his voice. 'I've obviously troubled you, lady, but I was hoping to offer you some happiness and perhaps to receive some in return. Now that I know your decision, I shall depart from Mathurapuri today. Pray, accept my good wishes.'

A year and half had elapsed since Marish had left Mathurapuri. Ratnaprabha would often think of him and talk about him. Anshu herself would never refer to his visit. Gradually a change came over her. She came out of her habitual gloom and began to take a more lively interest in her art.

That year, on the occasion of the Festival of Swings in Vrindavan, she presented an original fantasia of dance and music, and named it 'Saraswati Mallika' in homage to her guru. The fame and reputation of this superb artiste from Mathurapuri travelled to the farthest corners of the land.

The citizens of Mathurapuri were elated to find that their pride, the concert hall of Ratnaprabha, would continue to be the showpiece of their city, now that the most-prized blossom in the garden of Ratnaprabha's troupe had opened fully, and its fragrance, in the form of her fame was being spread for all to enjoy. They had only heard of Mallika, who lived in faraway Sagal, as an exquisite exponent of art. Anshumala they could see with their own eyes, and for them it was difficult to imagine artistry more captivating than hers.

Anshumala's leisure time, which used to be spent in solitary brooding and despondency, was now given to learning and mastering the different styles of dance and music. She made no effort to rid her mind of the memory of Marish. He stayed on in her mind, as did her great-grandfather, Prabuddha Sharma, Dhata and Chhaya; only he seemed a little closer. Sometimes she hoped that he would come again and see that she, at last, had found some source of satisfaction in her life.

One night, at the beginning of winter, Anshumala stepped out of the concert hall after her performance and went towards the bower of *malati* vines to rest her aching feet The vines laden with tiny white flowers looked resplendent in the light of the moon. She was still there when a maidservant came to inform her that a foreigner of noble birth was waiting inside, requesting the privilege of meeting her.

It flashed across Anshu's mind that it might be Marish, but the maidservants knew Marish well. In the empty hall, the caller was sitting alone near an oil lamp. Greeting the caller politely from the veranda, Anshu went up to him. She stopped short and caught her breath, but still managed to utter, 'I hope you are well, Arya. I hope everyone at home, your relatives, the ladies of the house, are all well. When did you arrive?'

Rudradhir's demeanour remained as serious and self-important as ever.

'Perhaps you remember,' he said, 'that I was banished from Madra for a period of two thousand days. It is only occasionally that I get any news of Sagal. I spent much of my time in Magadh, and it was there that I heard about the great fame of Devi Anshumala. On my way back home, I thought I would have the pleasure of seeing her. But what I see before me is beyond my wildest imagination.'

Trying to keep the smile on her lips, Anshumala said, 'Arya, the river, when it springs from its source, does not know in which direction it will flow, or with which ocean it will merge.'

Anshumala's coolness nettled Rudradhir and he decided to probe a little, 'News reached me of the marriage of the slave-born Prithusen with Seero, the granddaughter of the President, and also the rumours of your untimely death. Is it that you have been reborn as Anshumala in the same body?'

Anshumala remained unruffled. 'You have guessed correctly,' she smiled.

Her indifference still irritated Rudradhir. 'It must be so,' he said, with his head lowered, then suddenly lifting it and looking straight into Anshu's eyes, he added, 'I also heard that the grandsire, the Chief Justice, died out of grief for the loss of his great-granddaughter.' Then as if feeling ashamed of what he had said, he lowered his eyes and added in a faint voice, 'My father, the Acharya, is also dead. He died of some stomach ailment.'

'They were both fine people,' Anshumala said, after a brief pause. 'Everyone loved them. They were worthy of the respect of the gods, and that is why they were summoned to heaven.' She continued with a slight change in her tone, 'I hope your sojourn here was not too uncomfortable. Magadh is a large and prosperous kingdom known for its grandeur, but naturally, no place can compare with one's home. I wish you a pleasant return journey.'

Rudradhir was overwhelmed on seeing Divya after such a long time, but the same could not be said of his meeting Anshu. Baffled and crestfallen, Rudradhir looked for a way out of the embarrassing situation. 'It is getting late,' he said. 'May I be permitted to leave? If I stay on in Mathurapuri for a few more days, I would like to have the pleasure of seeing you again.'

'That would indeed be very kind of you,' Anshumala replied, joining her palms in farewell. 'This house would always be honoured by serving so distinguished a guest. Your humble servant would only be too pleased at a further visit.'

In Mathurapuri, Rudradhir was staying as a guest in the palace of Acharya Suchit, the savant. One of the reasons for his visit was to see Anshumala, the famed pupil of the court dancer of Shursen. In Anshumala he met Divya, an old love, who had supposedly died years ago, and his feelings for her revived. But her attitude and manner disconcerted him. Beneath her polite smiles and elaborate courtesies, he saw the professional politeness of a courtesan; a demeanour, to his mind, most unbecoming for the high-born Brahmin girl his Divya had been. Rudradhir's mind was torn between love and revulsion.

On recognizing Divya in Ratnaprabha's concert hall, Rudradhir had sat frozen for several moments. When he recovered, his old days in Sagal came back to his mind with extreme vividness. The dances of Anshumala and Muktavali and the singing of Ratnaprabha ceased to have any interest for him. In his imagination, he began to see Divya in the palace of the Chief Justice, in the concert hall of Devi Mallika, and in numerous other places.

He was returning to that very city of Sagal. He had taken a solemn vow to re-establish the eminence of twice-born Brahmins, and end the rule of barbarians, slaves, and men of low birth. Divya herself had been cruelly deceived and cast out by the son of a slave, Prithusen. That affront was symbolic of all the insults hurled at Brahmins. By restoring Divya to her rightful place, he would show Prithusen and the people of Madra who were the victors and who the vanquished.

But Divya's attitude and behaviour demolished the grand design that he was shaping in his imagination. With a deep sigh, he tried to rid himself of the hope that he had been nurturing secretly in his heart. 'That soft-spoken and timid Divya, the high-born Brahmin maiden that I had once desired, does not exist any more,' he tried to tell himself. But this attempt at self-deception could not conceal the reality before his eyes.

In the mansion of Acharya Suchit, the midnight religious service ended to the sound of bells, gongs and conch shells. Soon the household settled into stillness. In every room of the palace, the inmates slept soundly, and the sound of their even breathing filled the air and seemed to deepen the still of the night. This quiet was broken only by the calls of the night watchman, who, in an effort to ward off sleep, shouted to the others to keep awake and alert. For Rudradhir there was no rest. He tossed about in the comfortable bed provided by his kind host. All the means of inducing sleep had proven ineffective. Delicious food and fragrant wines he pushed aside with distaste. Even the services of a supple and experienced slave-girl did not bring rest to his body, tired as it was after his long journey.

He mulled over Divya's professional courtesy and her indifference to her past. That he should have been treated like an ordinary visitor to whom such formal courtesies were extended, seemed like a personal insult to Rudradhir. Again and again her words rang in his ears: 'This house would always be honoured by serving so distinguished a guest. Your humble servant would only be too pleased at a further visit.' It appeared to him as though a brazen prostitute was dancing shamelessly on the dead body of a gentle, pure, high-born maiden.

At Acharya Suchit's palace, he heard frequent praise of Anshumala. Such comments appeared to him to be insulting and demeaning to a noble Brahmin girl. 'A courtesan has to make herself attractive to others,' he tried to reassure himself. But Aniruddha, the son of his host, who was of the same age as Rudradhir, expressed his dislike of her. 'Anshumala is interesting only from a distance,' he said. 'Otherwise she is nothing but a puppet, devoid of human qualities. Her charm and smiles are only a part of her routine. She is too detached and indifferent to be a true artiste. She titillates your senses, but offers no satisfaction.'

Such negative remarks about Anshumala compelled Rudradhir to change his opinion and lapse once again into fantasy. He began to see Divya, the pure maiden, cheated and slighted by the son of a slave, in her bridal finery, standing in all her beauty and gentleness over a dying Anshumala.

Rudradhir had originally intended to stay only a couple of days in Mathurapuri, to rest for his journey, but a full fortnight had passed and he still lingered. Every evening he returned to Ratnaprabha's concert hall to watch the performances, and stayed behind to exchange a word or two with Anshumala after the recital. Invariably, she received him politely and always treated him with respect and consideration. Her behaviour, so correct but lacking in warmth, was distasteful to him. He longed for the effect his dynamic personality had at concerts in

Sagal, when Divya, on meeting him, would became nervous and lower her head with bashful timidity.

In his own eyes, Rudradhir was a privileged person who, on account of his past associations, was entitled to a special place and status with Anshumala. But there, in Ratnaprabha's palace, he was just one of the hundreds of high-born dignitaries who assembled to witness the performances—just an individual, like any other. It was an affront to his dignity and to his family to see that other people received greater consideration because they were able to offer expensive presents. To be passed over as someone in the crowd was like feeling a dagger being plunged into his heart.

Disgusted with such treatment, he would go back to the palace of his host. Alone at night, he brooded over the comments and criticisms he had heard, especially those uttered by Aniruddha: 'Anshumala is nothing but a puppet . . . her charm and smiles are only a part of her dance routine . . . she is not a true courtesan; she is a cheat who promises, but never delivers.' And Rudradhir would add further, on his own, 'She was born into a Brahmin family . . . She must still be a virgin.' He found that his passionate attachment to her was as strong as ever. He would certainly win her back, he promised himself. It became impossible for him to keep away from Ratnaprabha's concert hall even for a single evening.

Rudradhir noticed the presents lavished on Anshumala. He thought, if money has become all-important for Divya, either from greed as a courtesan or from a desire to earn for her mistress, then he too would give her money. He certainly did not lack money; as the son of the Chairman of the Republican Council of Madra, he was the heir to an estate of ten villages, and, in his own right, a noble of a high Brahmin family.

At the time of his banishment, Rudradhir had not carried
much money with him. When he was leaving Sagal, Acharya
Pravardhan, in order to provide his son against want and
difficulty, had with his own hands put round Rudradhir's neck
a seven-stranded necklace of big Sinhalese pearls. That precious
necklace was of the value of almost one village, and was part of
the inheritance of the Acharya family. Rudradhir always wore
the necklace next to his heart, under his clothes.

That evening Anshumala was dancing, enacting the lovelorn
chakore,[1] waiting for her mate, eager to consummate
their love before the setting of the moon. The entire audience
watched her every gesture and step with rapt attention.
In her outstretched arms, in her fingers, eyes, lips, subtle
tremors expressed the agony of the bird. As the performance
reached its climax, the audience held their breath, such was
the intensity of her rendition.

The dance over, Anshu paused for breath. The musicians put
aside their instruments to wipe the perspiration from their
brows. Overwhelmed with the performance, the connoisseurs
began to lay gold coins, jewels and ornaments in front of
Ratnaprabha's seat. With a smile on her lips, Anshu acknowledged
the gifts. Just then a heavy pearl necklace, thrown from one
side of the hall, fell near Anshu's feet.

The audience was struck dumb at the magnificence of the
pearls. Vinayak, the merchant, who sat nearby, stared wide-
eyed. 'Worth at least one thousand gold pieces,' he exclaimed.

Heads turned to look at the person who had thrown the
necklace. Anshu too noticed Rudradhir, who stood with his
chest thrust out in a challenging stance. She had been placing

[1] Bird, *Alectoris chukar*.

the presents from her admirers in front of Devi Ratnaprabha, but she kept the necklace in her hand, after touching it once to her forehead as a token of acknowledgment.

Even after the audience had dispersed, Rudradhir did not address himself to Anshumala. With a drawn look on his face, he remained in his seat.

Holding the necklace in her hand, Anshu went over to him, a smile of gratitude playing on her lips.

'Of course you are satisfied today, now that you have received your price,' Rudradhir said to himself.

'Your humble servant will remain ever grateful to the Arya for this precious gift, offered as a token of his love for art,' Anshumala said politely.

Rudradhir smiled nonchalantly.

'At home in Sagal, you could give hundreds of such gifts,' Anshumala continued, 'but here, in a foreign land and in times of difficulty, I would beg of you not to part with something that you may need.'

'Why, is this small gift not worthy of your acceptance?' Rudradhir asked, with an edge to his voice. He added harshly, 'Or is it that no gift is good enough for a person who has taken up the profession of a courtesan?'

'No Arya,' Anshumala was still smiling. 'Your humble servant is obliged to you for your generosity and kind thoughts. She honours these sentiments,' she said, touching the necklace to her forehead. 'But I am returning the gift, which is only the outward symbol of those sentiments. From a tray of offerings, the offerings are taken away but the tray is returned. I do this also because you happen to be in a foreign country.'

Suddenly Anshu, with her impudent smile and mannered gestures, took on an aura of innocence in Rudradhir's eyes. A

shiver ran along his spine and a lump came to his throat, which
he was unable to swallow. A surge of emotions warmed his
body. Putting his hot hand on the cool arm of a smiling Anshu,
Rudradhir said in a voice thick with passion, 'Devi, to me you
are still the daughter of a great Brahmin family. Seven years
ago, I myself, son of the Acharya and the owner of an estate,
went to your parents and asked for your hand. Devi, since you
are independent now, Rudradhir is asking for your hand in
person from you. He will take back to Sagal what belongs to
Sagal, the light that will illuminate every corner of the city.'

The smile still played on Anshumala's lips. His grip tightened
on her arm. 'Devi,' he said, 'I will return to Sagal only after
you have agreed to be my wife, to be the treasure of my family.
Your place is that of the mistress of the Acharya household.'

Anshu's smile remained unchanged. She answered in a
soft, steady voice, 'Arya, the girl Divya, born into the Shaivilya
family of Sagal, found herself adrift, either from some quirk
of fate or her own errors of judgement, in the current of life
which she had not been trained to cross. From those angry
waters she emerged as you find her today—a dancer and a
courtesan, Anshumala by name. She has lost the purity of her
maidenhood also. She is not committed to a Brahmin husband,
to one high-born noble; she has now become the property of
the community, of all and sundry.'

Rudradhir drew still closer to Anshu, 'Devi, from a gold
mine, iron cannot be extracted. Race and caste are the creations
of god, above the power of man. Man is powerless either to
give or to take away high caste. The blood of Brahmins
flows in your veins. A piece of gold, even if it falls into
mud, cannot turn into stone. Rudradhir takes the vow that when
he occupies the seat of the Acharya of Sagal, he will take you

as his wife.' And he looked solemnly into the guileless, smiling eyes of Anshu.

'Your humble servant is grateful to you for your kind sentiments. But such is her character that she does not deserve the honour of being the mistress of a noble family. She has passed through the fire of misfortune and evil days and emerged from it with the marks of ignominy. But for all the shame, she has also passed through the fire to become a free woman. That freedom is what she prizes above everything else.'

'What are you saying, Devi? You are a Brahmin born,' Rudradhir's voice was shaking.

'Arya,' Anshumala replied, smiling, 'the water of a stream, once it overflows and spreads into the fields cannot again return to the limits of its two banks.'

Rudradhir was reduced to speechlessness. Ignoring the stunned expression on his face, Anshumala said with concern, 'It is getting late. I would not like the Arya to be delayed any further. Besides, it is turning cold. With Arya's permission, I will ask the attendant to get the chariot ready.'

The two days Rudradhir had intended to stay in Mathurapuri, turned to three-and-a-half-months. He used every stratagem and every kind of argument to convince Anshu that she should return to Sagal as his wife, but she humbly expressed her inability and begged to be excused.

A frustrated and sorely disappointed Rudradhir came to bid farewell, on the eve of his departure for Sagal. His last words to Anshumala were, 'Devi, you are Brahmin-born. Even today you are supremely pure. I, Brahmin Rudradhir, of the family of the givers of the sacred law, declare that you are entitled to be the mistress of a Brahmin family. Your place is on the throne of my heart. This itself is a proof of your purity. Devi, the verdict given by the Brahmin, whose function is to interpret the law, is in itself a proof. Wait for me, Lakshmi, my goddess of good fortune. One day Rudradhir will come back to fetch you. The light of Sagal must return to shine in Sagal.'

Anshumala bowed her head and said with a polite smile, 'For the feelings of regard and kind consideration, your humble servant will ever remain beholden. With your blessings, your humble servant is quite content with her present condition.'

Sagal

AFTER A SOJOURN OF SIX YEARS, FOUR MONTHS AND SIX DAYS IN foreign lands, Acharya Pravardhan's son, Rudradhir, entered the city of Sagal through the eastern gate, on an evening forecast as auspicious by the astrologer. Rudradhir was dressed like an ordinary traveller and was seated on a tired but sturdy horse. He was followed on horseback by Mathura, his slave-attendant.

Rudradhir did not notice much change in the outward appearance of the city. Shops and markets hummed with early evening bustle and activity. Water had been sprinkled on the ground outside the shops to settle the dust. There seemed to be no lack of attractions for the evening's round of pleasure. Flower sellers, with garlands and bouquets of fresh flowers, were calling out to attract the attention of passers-by. The air was heavy with the scents emanating from the perfume shops. Citizens, gaily dressed and decked with flowers, promenaded in the streets in search of entertainment. The rich, in chariots, palanquins or on horseback, were on their way to the evening's entertainment to the garden by the lake or to the houses of dancing girls. Here and there, tonsured Buddhist monks were seen in their yellow robes.

Nobody paid any attention to the mounted traveller passing through the crowds, and Rudradhir was content for the moment to go on his way unrecognized.

Just as he was about to leave the main street and turn into the road leading to the Acharya's palace, Rudradhir heard

the sound of a trumpet. Through the crowded main street, an
outrider in military uniform was approaching, blowing on
a small silvery trumpet. The pedestrians stepped aside and
made room for his passage. Behind him, on the shoulders of
sixteen bearers, all dressed alike in colourful livery, came a
huge palanquin, in which, under a canopy and fan, sat a woman
gorgeously dressed, in a sparkling array of precious stones and
jewels. She looked like a courtesan. Rudradhir had some trouble
in recognizing her through her heavy make-up. On her right
rode young Sakrid, son of Kartavir, the noble, while on her
left was another youth on horseback, Mahendra by name,
son of Okris, the Greek noble.

Rudradhir was baffled. This was surely not Devi Mallika,
he thought. Even Ayurveda did not have the power to
change an elderly woman into a young one. Who, then, was
this new dancer who had graced Sagal and who was receiving
so much acclaim from the people, even more than Devi
Mallika had ever done?

The sound of loud applause fell on his ears. Rudradhir once
again looked back. In the shops, on the balconies of the houses
and along the pavement, cries of salutation went up: 'Long live
Mahadevi Seero! Long live Commander-in-Chief Prithusen!'

Rudradhir reined in his horse and stopped. It was Seero!
He turned away in disgust. In all the thirty-odd years of his
life in Sagal, he had never seen so ostentatious and so tasteless
a display. When he had last been in Sagal, the canopy and the
plumed fan had been privileges reserved for the exclusive
use of the President of the Republic or the Laureate of Art, the
Court Dancer, as a mark of honour. What could have happened
to produce a change in this time-honoured custom? Had that
son of a slave then become the President?

It did not take long for the news to spread that Acharya Rudradhir had arrived in the town. A stream of visitors, friends and relatives headed towards the palace. During the festivities attendant on his arrival, he started to enquire about the developments and the changes that had taken place during his exile. In no time the Acharya sized up the situation.

The ordinary people, however, had not noticed any great change in Madra or in Sagal. The horizon was clear of any threat of foreign invasion. The feuds, wrangles and jealousies among the nobles, that had been so common a feature during the Council's sessions, had also diminished. Trade and commerce were flourishing and there was prosperity all around. People were spending more time and money in the pursuit of pleasure. The inhabitants of Madra appeared to be happy, content and carefree.

One might say that in the garden of Sagal, while the small plants, vines and shrubs flourished, the tall trees—the nobility and the high families—stood silent and terrified. Mithrodus, the aged President and Commander-in-Chief of Sagal, was bedridden after a stroke. Acharya Pravardhan, heartbroken by the separation from his son, and thwarted by the machinations of Prestha, had died two years earlier after a prolonged stomach ailment. After his death the Republican Council had not been convened even once.

The President continued to hold the special rights and privileges with which he had been invested during the period of war emergency. While he lay helpless in his sickbed, the state seal was entrusted to his chief confidant, Prestha, the magnate. At the time of Kendras's invasion, there was not sufficient money for raising a strong army, even after the wealth of the nobles had been added to the state treasury. Prestha had advised the President to throw open the membership of the Council to the wealthier members of the community, on the condition that each candidate raised, equipped and maintained 100, 200 or 500 soldiers. Consequently, the membership of the Republican Council had almost doubled. Ten such members, enjoying the patronage of Prestha, were already members of the Council.

During the emergency, thanks to the manoeuvring of Prestha, wealth rather than caste, status or lineage had become the basis for the membership of the Council. Wealth keeps increasing and decreasing; it is the fruit of man's labour. Family and caste status, on the other hand, are bestowed by Heaven and, therefore, are unassailable. Now the low-born but wealthy people could also aspire and compete for the privileges that were exclusively enjoyed in the past by the nobles and the high-born. The prestige of the family began to wane. Filled with aversion at this denigration of lineage and caste, members of the nobility and high-caste dignitaries had begun to absent themselves from the meetings of the Council.

The effect of this indifference to the Council and the administration was that the President, in a state of failing health and senility, appointed Prestha, the magnate, to the office of the Chairman of the Council.

Prestha had attained this high position by shrewd diplomacy and opportunism, but his behaviour remained exceptionally humble. There was a time when Prestha, had been unable to become a member of the Council because of his low-born status. In a show of respect for the Brahmin families, he organized a number of yajnas, with animal sacrifices and festivals for the citizens of higher castes. He also paid homage to the Buddhist faith, which preached compassion to all living beings. To confer the same favours on the Buddhist faith as he had done on the caste religion, he returned to the monasteries and the temples the incomes, which had been appropriated by the state during the war emergency. Conflict between the votaries of the caste religion and of the Buddhist faith once again flared up in Madra.

The marriage between Commander Prithusen and Seero, the granddaughter of the President, had taken place with great pomp and ceremony. On that occasion, the whole of Sagal had celebrated and participated in the festivities. Having no male heir to succeed him, the President had bequeathed his entire property to his granddaughter and bestowed all the rights and privileges of the family on his chosen son-in-law. The stigma of low birth was washed clean from Prithusen, and he became the richest and most honoured noble of Madra. Because he had had to stifle the voice of his conscience he remained melancholy and disturbed. Feeling disgusted with himself and society, he shunned all contact with the public.

Noticing his son's mental condition, his father chided him affectionately, 'Son, what is there in the world that is beyond your reach? You should enjoy what you already have and develop in yourself the necessary strength to obtain things that are at present out of your grasp. Your foot is on just the first rung of the ladder. Neither Seero nor Divya is the ultimate object of your life. Life is full of variety. Son, it is cowardice to regard your life as already over, simply because you have not been able to marry one particular woman. Had Divya been alive, she too would have been within your reach. The sages have called that person foolish who ignores the present in remorse for the dead and buried past.'

Seero the granddaughter of the President of the Republic, Seero the daughter-in-law of the Chairman of the Council, and Seero the wife of the valiant commander walked with her head held high. She enjoyed the most enviable position in society,

but she was covetous of still greater conquests for herself. She
enjoyed the finest of pleasures and she expected the handsomest
of the young men to pay court to her. Nothing but the choicest
of liquors was allowed to moisten her carmined lips. She sought
distraction in the kisses from ever new pairs of lips. And there
was nothing more exciting for her than to be clasped in the
strong arms to the manly chests of young men.

Prithusen had stifled his conscience for the sake of Seero.
It was because of Seero's obduracy that he had lost Divya. By
losing Divya he had also lost the long-cherished dream of
his life. He could not tolerate Seero's blatant indiscretions.
Exercising his right as a husband he once rebuked her. Seero
burst into tears and denied the truth of the accusations. Then,
finding submission to her husband unbearable, like an angry
snake, she hissed back at him, 'I am no slave that you have
bought. It is you who are dependent on me. I am not a pet that
you can keep on a leash in your house. Nor am I a slave kept
for your physical enjoyment. Don't you sleep with prostitutes?
How many slave-girls have you to keep you company in bed?
There is no end to the women who do different things to
satisfy your desires! You're not the only man in the world.
There are many others like you, and better than you. I'm not
the slave-wife of a Brahmin family. I have the blood of a Greek
conqueror in my veins. I'm not a brood mare from whom you
can breed foals, so that they can pull the chariot of your family.
If you insult me, I can turn the whole community against you.
If I can have you appointed as the Commander-in-Chief, I
can find another to replace you. Oh, what will happen to me
when my grandfather is dead?' She began to cry bitterly.

Prithusen's eyes burned like hot coals. His fingers itched
to grab Seero's throat and throttle her. His hand dropped to the

hilt of his sword to cut off her head, but then, the image of his dispassionate, far-sighted father and that of the aged President, with his retinue of Greek nobles, appeared before his eyes! Prithusen heaved a sigh of impotent rage and resigned himself.

Seero was not somebody that he could crush in his fingers. The vast authority of the President of the Republic stood like a shield before her to protect her. Greek nobles were there to stand by her. She would not become docile under his authority. She was conscious of her strength and was prepared to exercise it against him. For twisting her neck, Prithusen would have to pay with his own neck. At the earliest opportunity, thousands of Brahmin swords would flicker like hot tongues, thirsting for the blood of Prithusen and his family.

For several days Prithusen brooded, sometimes his unseeing eyes fixed upon distant objects, at other times with his head bowed. At last he came to the conclusion that his wise and shrewd father was right; there was only one reality in life, and that was power. And the thing that would bring him satisfaction was the exercise of power. Power was the force that moved the world. Had he wielded absolute power, as the kings of the Maurya dynasty in Magadh once did, he would have had Seero burnt alive on a pyre for her sinful behaviour. No, tied to a post, a frightened Seero would have gazed on silently. He thought of Divya, as the First Consort, how she would have nestled in his arms. And he would have made Seero wash their feet!

The realization that underneath his outward show of power he was a helpless creature, nagged constantly at his mind. It was Seero who, in reality, held all power and status. As Seero's husband, he remained the nobleman next in line to succeed the President of Madra. Without her, he was only the son of a slave who had so far forgotten his origins as to aspire to receive the same respect as was given to the high-born.

Prithusen took to the dulling effect of heady wines to numb his mind. He tried to drown the voice of his conscience in the tinkle of the anklets of dancing girls and prostitutes. Yet he did not attain any peace of mind. He could not forget the reality of his situation. He would sometimes say to himself, 'This is only self-destruction, the behaviour of a weakling.' But then, another voice within him would cry, 'Power! Absolute power! On the advice of my father; with the force of my sword!'

He began to neglect Seero, but continued to behave as the privileged son-in-law of the President of the Republic. When he downed bowl after bowl of strong wine in the palace gatherings, when he ordered that nubile maidens be presented for his enjoyment, he did so merely to distract himself, and as something a man of his position and status was obliged to do. In his heart he remained as indifferent to these things as a Buddhist ascetic aspiring for Nirvana. Just as a bhikshu cares for his body only insofar as it is a means of achieving redemption, in the same way Prithusen looked upon all these physical pleasures as a means of attaining an ulterior objective. Power, and to be the absolute ruler of Madra, that was his only ambition.

In recognition of his services in the war, Prithusen had been granted an estate of ten villages by the Republic. In his own right, he was the commander of five hundred soldiers kept for the defence of Madra. He maintained another one thousand for members of the Council who enjoyed the patronage of his father. His command of this force of fifteen hundred trusted veterans was more satisfying to him than all other pleasures.

The people of Sagal were used to bowing before power and authority. While submitting to the mighty, they felt assured of protection. In the absence of King Milinda, the people had begun to pay their homage to President Mithrodus. Since the President suffered a stroke and became paralytic, the people were deprived of the occasion of offering their obeisances to him. So they began to hail the Pure of Soul, the Defender of the People, the Blessed of the Gods, the Son of the Chairman of the Council, the Son-in-law of the President of the Republic, the Destroyer of the legions of Darva, the all-conquering Commander Prithusen, addressing him as Commander-in-Chief and regarding him as the representative of the power of the state. And Seero felt that she deserved this public adulation more than Prithusen.

Vain and covetous and thirsty for attention, Seero insisted on keeping up her ostentatious lifestyle. The populace, dazzled and thrilled by their protector's affluence and grandeur, looked up to her more enthusiastically than before. The members of the caste society felt slighted by these exhibitions of personal glory, but finding themselves helpless under the circumstances, maintained a grim and disapproving silence.

To her husband, Seero had ceased to be a wife. Prithusen tolerated her, because in her capacity as the granddaughter of the President, she still had a place in his schemes. His mind was now preoccupied with a stratagem, one conceived by his father, of again declaring a state of war and thereby securing for himself the position of the Supreme Commander and Absolute Ruler of Madra. To that end, he was only awaiting a suitable opportunity.

Rudradhir had changed considerably during the six years, four months and six days of his exile, and this change had been noticed by his relatives and the citizens of Sagal. The warm

climate of Magadh had tanned his complexion. His father had
died, and the responsibility as the head of the family had given
him a new seriousness in appearance and behaviour. He spoke
less now. He developed a more penetrating and mature insight
into life. In Magadh he had seen the re-establishment of the
power of the caste system, freed from the stranglehold of
the Buddhists. He had also learnt how complex and violent the
process of capturing power was. He had seen the grand Buddhist
monasteries reduced to rubble and ashes. He had seen the caste
system resurrected and brought back to its former glory under
the leadership of Commander Pushya Mitra. Carrying the same
burning flame of the Brahminic sacrificial fire in his heart, he
had come back, and had taken a vow to spread it once again in
Madra for the redemption of the caste system.

Rudradhir saw that the caste families, frustrated by subjection,
had turned their backs on matters of state administration, and
withdrawing behind the walls of their palaces, were now lost
in isolation. He saw that Prestha, the magnate, had become
the Chairman of the Council and was running the administration
in the name of the President of the Republic, who was nothing
better than a living corpse. Prestha, through his cunning diplomacy,
was gradually depriving the twice-born Brahmin families and
the caste society of their authority.

He addressed himself to the caste families in order to alert
them: 'It is suicidal to turn away from this struggle and be
content with personal safety. He who loses himself in pleasure,
loses the right to pleasure, which can only be won through
struggle. The so-called republican principles are nothing but
a conspiracy hatched by the effeminate Buddhists to trample
upon the rights of the twice-born Brahmins. The twice-born
Brahmin is a portion of the divine. The exercise of power is
his attribute and obligation; to rule is his right. When fire

ceases to perform its function, even the insects take pride in treading upon it. The Brahmin, bereft of authority, fails in his duty. The king and his subjects are two entirely different entities. The Sudra who wants equality with the Brahmin is a downright sinner, and he brings sin upon the head of the Brahmin too. Rama, supreme among mortals, and supreme upholder of the law, by punishing Shambuk the Sudra, set the precedent for propriety of conduct. The code of punishment is the mainstay of religion.'

Rudradhir held secret discussions with the nobles Kartavir and Sarvarth, and Vishnu Sharma, the savant, devising an intrigue for overthrowing the authority of the low-born heathens and Sudras. His proposal was that they should catch their enemies unaware and destroy them. 'An ant awake is much more dangerous than a sleeping elephant,' he said.

The Brahmins of Madra, deprived of power and privilege and disheartened by the Buddhist dominance, sat back and waited, content with the offerings from the religious sacrifices. The army of Madra was under the control of Prestha, the magnate, Okris, the Greek noble and Commander Prithusen. In these conditions, the high-caste families and the Brahmin feudatory chiefs took no interest in the army. They were squandering the income from their estates on dissipation, instead of recruiting and maintaining soldiers. Prestha knew this and yet said nothing. Acharya Rudradhir understood how the Brahmin nobles, displaying a lack of foresight, were playing right into Prestha's hands.

The Acharya counselled the Brahmin nobles that outwardly they should pretend to remain indifferent, but in secret, set about raising an army of their own on their estates. As time passed, bands of soldiers began to infiltrate into Sagal in the guise of ordinary citizens. To counter the arrogant heathen belief about the equality of all castes, they decided to proclaim Sarvarth, the noble, of the ancient Paurav family, as the new President of the Republic.

Acharya Rudradhir came to know through his spies and informers that the Chairman of the Council had received intelligence that the armies of the neighbouring kingdom of Katha were massing for an attack on the western border of Madra. The Acharya gave deep thought to this news. He summoned his counsellors and said, 'There is no room now for delay. Surely, Prestha is anticipating the death of the ailing President in the very near future. Under the cover of the threat of invasion, he wants to bring his own soldiers into the town. Prithusen is certainly in the plot. By assuming the guise of protectors of the people, they want to frighten the people and win over their support.'

Devi Mallika got up from her seat to welcome Acharya Rudradhir after his long sojourn abroad. She made him sit next to her, and with particular regard offered him the customary welcoming hospitality of a betel-leaf and a bowl of wine. She expressed her condolences on the death of his father, and showed great curiosity and interest in his long stay abroad.

Acharya Rudradhir had little understanding of the fine arts, and even less interest in them, but he noticed the lacklustre appearance of Devi Mallika's entourage. She herself looked tired and dispirited. Signs of age had begun to show on her face and in her body. In the audience too there was neither the old gathering of art lovers, nor was much quality to be seen in the performances. Many of Devi Mallika's pupils had left her after completing their training. Those who remained were mediocrities.

Mallika asked the Acharya to stay for a while. A musical composition was being rehearsed. An aged singer, Mahul, was elaborating on the basic notes of a raga before the young pupils and a few casual listeners. Encouraged by the presence of the Acharya, the singer directed the full force of his voice towards him. 'A . . . aa . . . m . . . aa . . . dir . . . aa . . . ma . . . madir.' He seemed to be singing the one word over and over again.

Old Mahul's neck was craned upward like that of a camel straining to bite at the leaves of a branch a little beyond his reach. The veins of his neck and temples had swollen from the strain of singing. Drops of perspiration had appeared on his forehead, his eyes were bloodshot and were shedding tears. He stretched the last note as long as he could. Then, filling his lungs again with air, he opened his toothless mouth, reddened with betel juice and fringed with white whiskers, and began to intone the same word a little higher in the octave.

Mahul's once mellifluous voice had become tremulous with age and was jarring to the ear. But his eyes shone with the satisfaction of having done his best. His trembling fingers, gesticulating in the air, moved to emphasize the subtleties of his modulations. Mallika and one or two other connoisseurs nodded in appreciation. As for the Acharya, the fact that the end of the performance was nowhere in sight was an acute torture.

The old maestro kept at it for nearly an hour. Rudradhir did not know the subtleties of music and after having had to wait for so long, even his curiosity had subsided. After the prelude was over, Mallika and the other connoisseurs exclaimed enthusiastically, 'Bravo! How wonderful! How delightful!'

Finding the maestro looking intently at him, Acharya Rudradhir also expressed his approbation, 'Fine! Very fine! Very fine, indeed!' Encouraged by the appreciation, old Mahul once again filled his old lungs with air, opened his mouth wide and began to sing.

The Acharya felt dismayed and regretted his gesture of courtesy. He was reminded of the grandeur of Devi Mallika's assemblies in bygone days, when wealthy art lovers, men and women, not finding room to sit in the hall, would crowd the surrounding veranda, when in the midst of a large number of accomplished singers, Mallika would appear like the full moon in a sky full of stars, when the whole of Sagal used to resound with the tinkle of her dancers' anklets, when it was not necessary to search for the subtle beauties of art, because they would by themselves overwhelm the mind with their effect. And now, Mallika's assembly hall looked like a garden ravaged by frost and winter winds. In the singer Mahul, the choreographer Udumber, the old dancer Pritha and the musician Padma, there remained some link with the tradition, but the vibrant splendour and vitality of the past had vanished.

The assembly over, the Acharya sat down with Mallika in the veranda, 'Devi, what has come over your assemblies which were once the glory of Sagal?' he said ruefully.

'It is the wheel of time, Arya,' replied Mallika in a dejected voice. 'Or the will of fate! What can I say? My misfortune or that of Sagal! I am no longer young. The human body has limited capabilities. I have not been able to find a pupil who would carry on my artistic traditions. The public too has lost interest. You are a man with a head on your shoulders. Arya, you know that art thrives on refined and cultivated tastes. Ordinary people find it beyond their understanding. Besides, there are so many reasons. On whom can I throw the blame? It is my ill luck, you might say!'

'I heard that Madulika was the one who received your special attention after the great-granddaughter of the late Chief

Justice. It used to be said that Madulika would take your place
and keep you torch burning,' said Rudradhir, remembering
what he had heard about Madulika, a pupil of Mallika.

'You're quite right!' Mallika replied and heaved a deep
sigh. 'Madulika could have kept the tradition alive. After some
time, some other girl, more capable than her, could have been
found to add to its lustre. But, Arya, Madulika did not have the
self-discipline necessary for the pursuit of art. Then perhaps,
she was not to blame.' Devi Mallika said, and fell silent.

Her reticence and sadness piqued the Acharya's curiosity.
He leaned a little closer to her and asked, 'Did she commit
some serious indiscretion?'

Vexed by her memories, Mallika replied, 'You are a wise
person, Arya. You know that art is a demanding vocation. A
student can get nowhere without self-denial and self-discipline.
At the mercy of an unworthy pupil, art is disgraced and it
withers. Fourteen months ago, Commander Prithusen became
infatuated with Madulika. He did not have a moment's rest
without her. Madulika began passing her time with him
and absenting herself from her rehearsals. In her frenzied
state of mind she would not be able to distinguish between
harmonies and discords.'

Mallika's voice became agitated. 'I chided her. "Madulika,"
I said, "infatuation and dedication to your art do not go together."
I told her that she must in no case leave the precincts of the
palace. One day, Arya Prithusen came to my palace and
challenged my authority over my own pupil. He insulted me in
the presence of Madulika, "If the question before Madulika is of
becoming your successor so that she may inherit your wealth, I
shall give her double your wealth; if she is interested in becoming
the Court Dancer, then I have the power to appoint her as such.
Who is there in Madra that can flout Prithusen's wishes?"'

'What insolence!' exclaimed the Acharya.

'There can be no greater insult to art than that,' Mallika's voice rose higher. 'I ordered the doorkeepers to conduct Madulika out of my palace. To think that I had brought her up with my own hands, had taught her the intricacies of music and dance, and then to have to turn her out in that manner . . . It was as painful to me as separation from Ruchira, the child of my womb! But Arya, Mallika cannot bear any insult to art.' Her eyes filled with tears.

'Devi, when an undeserving person becomes ambitious, he crosses all bounds of decency. There is hardly a walk of life in Madra today in which disorder and insolence are not rampant. Whose honour is safe today? What institution is without blemish today? Devi, the greedy eyes of a Sudra weighs even the sacrificial horse and the sacred cow in terms of the value of their hide. Can justice and the well-being of the people ever be safe in such hands?'

'Art demands a well-ordered mind,' Mallika said, trying to suppress her agitation. 'But is there in Sagal anybody with a well-ordered mind? The high-caste gentry, the real connoisseurs of art, harassed and frightened, have withdrawn from society and are living in seclusion. Arya, in Sagal today it is the rule of jackals, and the lions, bewildered and confused, have withdrawn into their dens. The newly acquired wealth and power have gone to the heads of the low-born and they have all turned into debauchees. What appreciation can such as they have for the subtleties of art?

'And those who are disgusted with such dissipation and regard indulgence as the root cause of all wickedness, are no better either. They tend to seek refuge in Nirvana, hoping that they will attain peace in detachment. They get solace only in the call of the tonsured monks who invite them to join the Buddhist fold. In times of such confusion and disorder, how can art flourish?'

Finding confirmation of his views in the words of Mallika, the Acharya maintained his solemn demeanour. 'The well-being of society demands that this should be stopped. Devi, both the here and the hereafter are at stake. In Madra the offerings for religious sacrifice are being eaten up by the swine. The gods, enraged over this sinful behaviour, have cursed us. Devi, it has become imperative to rid Madra of this sinfulness.'

'But, Acharya, what can men do if such is the will of the gods, if fate wills it so?' Mallika replied in a disheartened voice. 'You have seen the times when Goddess Saraswati was worshipped with such veneration in this temple of art. It was blessed by her. And now, when the goddess has turned her face away, how desolate and harsh it has become!'

'The fire-tongued Brahmin is the representative of the divine on earth,' the Acharya said sharply. 'He represents the invincible might of the gods. The Kshatriya is his right arm. All goes awry if, instead of walking on his feet, a man is made to walk on his hands. With his legs and feet up in the air, the head and the arms have to bear the strain. It is the bounden duty of the people to install the Brahmin in the seat of power. Devi, I seek your cooperation for the establishment of a righteous order.'

'You have only to command me, Arya,' Mallika said humbly. The twin reflections of the oil lamp shone brightly in her eyes.

Gazing intently into her eyes, the Acharya asked, 'Do you promise, Devi?'

Mallika grew apprehensive, 'What does the Arya mean?'

'The objective is the re-establishment and proper protection of the caste religion in Madra. It is for this that your help and cooperation are needed,' the Acharya replied in a firm voice.

Mallika thought for a moment and said, 'I am at your service, Arya.'

'Is this place safe for a conversation?' the Acharya whispered cautiously. 'Even walls have ears.'

Devi Mallika assured him that no one could hear their conversation. The Acharya then gave her a detailed account of his plans in a low and secretive tone.

In a solemn voice Devi Mallika said, 'In the service of the gods, the Arya's commands shall be obeyed.'

Prithusen and Rudradhir

DEVI MALLIKA, THE COURT DANCER OF MADRA, THE LAUREATE OF ART, the Light of the Town, had lost her zest for life and for a long time had withdrawn from public events. Consequently, the gentry of the town were deprived of the pleasures of her art. On important festivals and other days, performances were organized at her palace, but they were more in the nature of formalities observed to keep up old traditions. There was little sparkle or enthusiasm in them.

The citizens of Sagal were, therefore, overjoyed to learn that on the night of the full moon, in the month of Kartik, a grand festival of music and dance would be held in Devi Mallika's palace. To this festival, the nobility, the members of the Council, the important merchants and traders, ladies of the nobility, and a number of reputed dancers had been invited.

The concert was arranged in the open air, under a clear sky flooded with the cool beams of a bright moon. White carpets had been spread; guests sat on white mattresses against white cushions; on all sides, white flowers bloomed; white fans were used, and even drinks were served in white crystal and silver bowls and vessels. The attendants, both male and female, were dressed in white. Mallika herself, her pupils, the musicians, the guest dancers, were all in white costumes. They had decked their bodies and hair with white flowers and strings of pearls.

The guests were thrilled to have been provided with such an event after so long an interval. Acharya Rudradhir,

Kartavir, the feudatory chief, Vishnu Sharma, the savant,
cavalry commanders Balabhadra and Dharmajit sat on one side,
making a crescent, with the great feudatory chief Sarvarth in
the centre. Sakrid, Indradeep, Vinay Sharma, Vasudhir and others
sat at some distance from them. Prestha, the magnate, Okris,
Martha and Pandit Ikrid, the Greek nobles, and Vardhak and
Gopal, the feudatory chiefs, sat on the other side. Commander
Prithusen, together with his friends and their womenfolk
sat close by. High-caste ladies accompanied by their attendants
formed their own set. Another group was formed by traders
who had lately acquired membership in the Council, their friends
and other prominent merchants.

Devi Mallika, although unable to give a performance on
account of her advanced age, thanked the guests for having
honoured her with their presence. Even though she had lost
her agility, she took part in the inaugural ceremonial dance.
Precious wines from Kapisha, Kandahar, Magadh and Drakshi
were served to the guests. When the moon touched the zenith,
the dancing girls, in all their finery, turned from the devotional
to the voluptuous and the provocative. The guests, instead of
sipping their drinks, began to gulp them down.

Seeing that the hands and feet of the guests had begun
to move to the beat of the music, Mallika suggested to the
nobility that they join in the raaslila dance. At a sign from Mallika,
Kusumsena stepped forward to take Prithusen's arm for the
dance. One by one, the other men moved up to the ladies
and dancing girls. The orchestra, consisting of veenas, flutes,
tambourines and kettledrums, struck up the raaslila tune. The
dancers stood in a wide circle on the concert floor.

At the end of the first round, those who had danced
well were showered with praise. Mallika complimented
Prithusen on the nimbleness of his footwork. Of the ladies,

besides the dancing girls Kusumsena and Vasumitra, Zola, wife of Martha, the Greek noble, and Amrita, Acharya Rudradhir's younger sister, and wife of Indradeep, were the recipients of special praise. Amrita had received training as a dancer under Devi Mallika, along with Divya and other girls from high-born families. Feeling thirsty after the dance, the guests drank many more bowls of wine. Over the rim of the wine bowl, Seero cast an inviting look at Mahendra, son of Okris, the noble. Mahendra moved up to her and addressing the assembly, said, 'Honourable citizens, we have to thank Devi Mallika for having provided us with this happy occasion after a long, long time. Let's forget everything tonight and lose ourselves in dancing.'

In response to this, Indradeep shouted, 'With the moon shining in the sky, if there is any such person who does not drink or dance, I would say he is a worthless fellow.'

The orchestra struck up another tune and the raas dance commenced once again. Zola came up to dance with Prithusen. At the close of the dance, Devi Mallika's slave-girls came in with fresh white towels, wiped the perspiration off the necks and faces of the guests, sprinkled perfume on them and cooled them with fans made of white swan feathers. Once again, bowls brimming with wine were served to the guests.

Sakrid, emptying his bowl at one gulp and handing it back to the slave-girl, said, 'Friends, shall we waste such a precious night in indolence? Such a night comes but once in a year.'

Old Ikrid, removing the bowl from his lips, expressed his agreement jocularly, 'And youth also comes but once in a lifetime.' His voice was heard only by Okris and Prestha who nodded their heads and smiled.

Sakrid had already moved up to Seero before Mahendra could. Seero laughingly stretched her arm towards him, but the influence of drink made her too languid to rise. She sat there sipping the ice-cold wine. Prithusen's eyes turned in her direction, but he looked away. He saw that the dancing girl, Vasumitra was looking at him in the hope of dancing with him, and that Amrita, Rudradhir's sister, was also coming towards him with the same intention. Prithusen moved forward and took Amrita's hand. His eyes fell on Rudradhir. He paused for a second and then started dancing.

Every few seconds Prithusen would steal a glance at Rudradhir and the other elders of the Brahmin community, who sat around Sarvarth, the great feudatory chief. They were constantly on his mind. As he had taken Amrita's hand into his, a suspicious gesture had caught his eye. Rudradhir's younger brother, Vasudhir, was infuriated and was about to object to his dancing with Amrita, but at a sign from his brother he fell silent. For a moment, every nerve of Prithusen's body became alert, and this alertness dispelled the fumes of drink in his head.

With fatigue and drink, Amrita was dancing slowly. But Prithusen was quite content. It was not so much the enjoyment of the dance as the mute acceptance of the situation by Acharya Rudradhir and the other high-caste nobles that gave him the utmost satisfaction. 'There was a time,' he mused as he danced, 'when in an attempt to lend a shoulder to the palanquin of a high-born girl, this very Rudradhir had insulted me. And today, right before his eyes, his sister has come to me of her own accord, and with her head on my chest and my arms round her, is dancing happily, and Rudradhir cannot so much as open his mouth. Such is the authority that power brings.' Drugged with the sense of power, he smiled. He even made it a point to show Rudradhir that his sister was dancing in his arms. The sense of satisfaction that he experienced came not so much from his contact with Amrita's body, as from the pride of power.

Zola was dancing with Dhriti Sharma, but she constantly followed Prithusen with her eyes. As soon as the round was over, she released herself from Dhriti Sharma's arms and moved towards Prithusen. She threw herself down on his mattress, breathless with fatigue, reclining against a cushion. On seeing that he had become the centre of attraction for the high-born ladies, Prithusen's heart again filled with a sense of pride.

Under the influence of drink, the guests began to show signs of listlessness. Mallika's slave-girls, however, continued to be prompt in serving bowl after bowl of wine. Prithusen felt proud of the fact that he received the most attention. Mallika herself had offered wine to him twice. This honour was reserved only for the highest nobles.

After the slave-girls had wiped their foreheads and sprinkled perfume on them, a number of guests, including some of the ladies of the nobility, feeling languid and tired, chose to sit against the cushions sipping their wine. Others went into the garden to find a corner to rest amidst the malati creepers.

When the orchestra began to play again, Prithusen gently touched Zola, who sat by his side, lazily reclining against him. Zola did not move. Prithusen bent down a little and looked into her eyes. She was not fit to dance any more. Prithusen too did not get up to dance. Mallika sent one of her slave-girls with two fresh bowls of cold wine to them. They thanked Mallika heartily, accepted the bowls of wine, and with their eyes resting on the dancers, snuggled closely together.

Zola's eyes wandered to where Seero was. She was sitting close to Mahendra, half-asleep, with her head on a cushion, while Mahendra had his arm around a dancing girl and was whispering something in her ear. Prithusen smiled as he looked at the dancers, who, in their drunken state, were dancing out of step.

The orchestra started a new dance measure. A number of guests, who had gone into the bowers to relax, came back to join in. The guests began to choose their partners for the next dance. Bowls brimming with wine were again sent to Prithusen and Zola. When Zola saw that Vasumitra was looking at Prithusen, she caught his arm in both her hands. Prithusen looked deep into her eyes; those eyes were more intoxicating than wine.

The guests were tired and fuddled and the dancing was gradually tapering off. Any time the dancers wanted to stop, they would unceremoniously break off in mid-step and walk towards the mattresses, while other guests would step in and take up the measure and the abandoned partners. The ladies were almost exhausted and many had gone to sit with their friends. The young men and the dancing girls were still up, whirling about with complete abandon, emitting cries and uttering whoops incessantly. Taking Zola, who was incapable of dancing, into his arms, Prithusen moved away towards a clump of bushes.

From the grove came the sound of heavy snoring. Holding up Zola, Prithusen moved towards another grove. Seeing that the place was secluded, Zola, who was unable to stand on her own feet, put her arms round Prithusen's neck. She was barely able to contain herself. 'Oh, dearest,' she breathed in his ear.

The musicians were playing away, while cheers and cries came from the young dancers. For Prithusen, everything was hazy and confused. Zola's eager whisper rang in his ears. In the darkness of the grove all he could see was her half-closed eyes, shaped like the petals of a lotus. Inert in his arms, Zola sent thrills of excitement through his body.

Zola responded by holding Prithusen in a tight embrace. Prithusen too, in the languor brought about by wine, was letting himself ride on the wave of excitement. For a moment he thought of returning to the concert floor, but his legs would not bear his weight. He vaguely heard a jumble of the sounds of different musical instruments and of merrymaking. Then a voice fell on his ears from the other side of the grove, which abruptly brought him back to his senses.

'Kumar, have you searched this side too?'

'Yes, Arya. This side, and also the other side.'

Prithusen recognized the speakers. They were the army officer Indradeep and Rudradhir's younger brother, Vasudhir. The stealthy behaviour of his old enemies filled Prithusen's mind with a sense of foreboding. Holding his breath, he waited to hear more. The footsteps of two more men were heard approaching the grove.

'Will all the preparation go for nothing?' It was Vinay Sharma's voice. 'The planet Devas will soon be aligned with the constellation of the Seven Sisters.'

'Prestha's palace must have been surrounded by Shvetketu and his soldiers by this time.' It was Balajit's voice, tinged with anxiety. 'They'll give a blast on the trumpet when they set fire to the palace. And here you've allowed that son of a slave to escape! What could have made him suspicious?'

Prithusen's body was covered with cold sweat. He did not think of Zola who lay huddled up on the stone slab beside him. He was all ears to every little sound. Even the throbbing of his heart pounded dreadfully in his ears. He trembled from head to foot.

'If that son of a slave succeeds in getting away, he can prove dangerous,' Balajit was saying. 'It may be that he's lying in some grove, sleeping it off after drinking heavily. Have armed soldiers been posted on the ramparts of the palace?'

'Yes, Arya, two hundred trusted soldiers have already entered the palace compound through the rear gate. One hundred more are hiding in civilian clothes in the dark lanes outside the rear gate. Two hundred more are hiding near the main gate. They are only waiting for the signal of the trumpet call.'

Suddenly the silence of the night was broken by the sound of a trumpet from the northern part of the town. Indradeep shouted the order at the top of his voice: 'Attention! Surround the assembly yard and proceed towards the main gate.'

Prithusen was familiar with the garden and the groves of Mallika's palace. Leaving the unconscious Zola, he wrapped his uttariya loosely around his head and face, and taking long strides, ran towards the rampart. A few armed soldiers coming out from behind the trees were moving towards the assembly yard. For a moment, Prithusen froze; then, going over to them he ordered in the manner of an army commander, 'Soldiers! Towards the main gate!'

As the soldiers turned obediently towards the main gate, Prithusen, with the help of a tree branch, climbed over the parapet wall and jumped down on to the road on the other side.

Unarmed and helpless, he stood on the road and thought for a moment, 'Where shall I go? Should I go towards the main gate where my bodyguard and chariot are waiting? . . . Towards my father? The two hundred soldiers of the enemy must have finished him by now. Shall I go towards my palace? The palace must have been captured by the enemy and set on fire.'

The sound of horses' hoofs, coming from the direction of the main gate, fell on his ears. He at once crept into a dark lane nearby. A band of riders appeared to be making a quick round of the palace. Prithusen went on walking further into the darkness of the lane. He took off his pearl necklaces and other precious ornaments, and one by one, threw them away. Covering his body and head with his uttariya, he tried to pass himself off as a commoner protecting himself from the weather.

The dark lane ended. On the main road, the moon shone as brightly as the sun and thus it was risky to go on to the main road. He shrank from going further and remained in the lane. Not far from where he stood were the palaces of the President of the Republic and of Okris, the noble. Prithusen thought to cross the road and proceed in that direction, for there alone he could perhaps find shelter.

Suddenly, the clatter of horses' hoofs was heard from that direction too. Prithusen stood in the darkness and watched. A group of horsemen, led by two Brahmin nobles, Agnikesh and Sakrid, with their swords drawn, swept by. Prithusen realized that the palaces of the President and of Okris had been surrounded by the enemy. It was no longer possible to seek shelter with friends.

He stood hidden in the darkness of the lane, breathing heavily. Every muscle in his body twitched, and he was bathed in sweat down to his heels. Like an animal surrounded by hunters in a forest, shivering and shrinking within himself, hiding wherever he could, he made his way towards the outskirts of the town. Every time he came onto the main road flooded with moonlight, he trembled from head to foot. Each voice he heard seemed to call his name, and his blood froze within him. Unarmed and hopeless, he was mindless with fear.

For a long time Prithusen lurked in the lanes. He despaired at the thought that after daybreak it would become impossible for him to save himself. At the same time, he did not understand why he should wander aimlessly from place to place, trying to save his life by hiding. With his armed soldiers behind him, he would certainly have overcome the insurgents. Had he been armed, even though alone, he would have fought to the bitter end and died honourably. Now there was no way out for him. He could either be killed like an animal or like a mouse save himself by scurrying from one hole to another. The effects of the wine had worn off, and he was feeling weak and exhausted in every limb. With an effort of will, he fought off the blankness that was clouding his mind.

The full moon dropped till it touched the horizon. The houses on the west of the road cast long shadows, enveloping the opposite side of the street in darkness. Without any clear sense of direction, Prithusen stepped into the nearest lane.

On the other side of the road he saw a man coming towards him intoning the words of a mantra. As the person drew near, Prithusen recognized him at once. It was the monk Cheebuk, the reputed physician. The monk's eyes fell on him. Prithusen had been a patient under his personal attention for well over two months. It was not difficult for the monk to recognize him, even without the rich garments he wore habitually.

'Where are you going, Arya?' he addressed Prithusen without hesitation. 'That way isn't safe. The riders looking for you have gone in that very direction.'

'Venerable sir,' Prithusen said, his voice full of despair, 'I have been betrayed and rendered helpless. I have nowhere to go. All roads are closed to me and all places have become dangerous. It is only a matter of time now. The butcher has caught me in his noose. In a short time his axe will be on my neck. Revered sir, being unarmed, I am helpless, shelterless; a dishonourable death awaits me.'

The monk looked intently at Prithusen. Even in that darkness, Prithusen could notice a glint of pity in his eyes.

'Son, if you are looking for shelter, there is the Buddhist monastery nearby,' he spoke in a low, sympathetic voice. 'Every applicant is granted shelter there. And it is beyond the pale of worldly conflicts and the bounds of state authority.'

'O blessed one, I shall ever be beholden to you for granting me shelter at this time.'

At daybreak, the citizens of Sagal were awakened from their sleep by the sound of the kettledrum and bugle. Frightened and amazed, people peeped out of doors and windows, or lying in bed, listened to the proclamation of the criers:

'His Excellency, the Master of Exceptional Virtues, the Shining Jewel of the Kshatriya Caste, the Defender of the Faith, the Great Noble, Sri Dev Sarvarth, having cleansed the earth of sin, with the consent of the caste society of Madra, assumes the sceptre of authority as President of the Republic of Madra. The office of the Chairman of the Council, with the consent of the members of the Council, is assumed by the Noblest of Acharyas, the one versed in scriptures, the Feudatory Chief, Mahapandit Rudradhir. With the consent of the caste society of Madra, the command of the defence forces is vested in the Feudatory Chief, Holder of Landed Estates, the Noble, Kartavir. The kingdom of Madra, standing on the laws of the caste society, shall henceforth be administered in accordance with the laws of justice. The entire Brahmin community, the Greeks, the Sudras and slaves, in the performance of their duty shall carry out the orders of the supreme authority.'

The full moon of the month of Kartik disappeared, and with it went the authority achieved by the rule of the low-caste people in Sagal. At sunrise, with the re-establishment of the caste-system, the authority of the Brahmins was restored. On the main roads, at crossings and other places, the weapons and helmets of the soldiers of the Brahmin feudatory chiefs glittered in the light of the sun. While this new splendour was a source of joy and a cause for rejoicing for one section of the community of Sagal, for others it was a source of terror. For ordinary citizens, it was a cause for fear mixed with curiosity.

The town was the same, its highways were the same, so were the lanes and byways, the palaces, mansions, lakes and gardens. People too were the same, only the form of government had changed. The Buddhist concept, that the same life force operates in all living beings, which had never aroused any enthusiasm among the high-caste Brahmins, and which encouraged self-assertion among people of the low caste, was now repudiated by the new law of the state based on the caste system.

The business magnates and merchants, who, with the power of money and with the diplomacy and patronage of Prestha, had obtained seats in the Council and the right to raise armed forces, were, overnight, stripped of their rights. With the exception of the Brahmins, all other classes were deprived of the right to revenue from landed estates. The landed property of the Buddhist monasteries was expropriated. The monks, often seen on the roads and in the lanes and bylanes with their shaven heads shining in the sun, had almost disappeared from view. Their voice, which so loudly brought solace to the people of low caste, was virtually silenced.

Prestha's palace and family were destroyed in the all-consuming fire. In place of large mansions guarded by armed soldiers, stood the bare skeleton of Prestha's palace, in black ruins, licked by the tongue of fire, amid a waste of ashes that spread on all sides. Prestha and other Greek nobles, who had shown sympathy for the Buddhist faith, were deprived of their landed estates and military rights. The President, stricken with paralysis, lay on his deathbed, listening without comprehension to the unfamiliar utterances of the Buddha, and waiting for Nirvana.

The soldiers of Acharya Rudradhir had combed every lane and bylane and palace grounds of Sagal, but had not been able to trace Prithusen. With Prithusen still alive, Rudradhir had no peace. After killing the serpent, if its young are spared, then in due course they too become full-grown snakes.

Shelter was granted to Prithusen in the Buddhist monastery. He spent the whole day in the dark meditation cell of Cheebuk, lost in thought, without eating a morsel of food. After midnight, he sought the permission of the monk to leave the monastery.

'Why do you want to go out, Arya?' the monk asked, his characteristic smile playing about his lips. He had guessed Prithusen's purpose.

'Honoured sir, how long can I go on hiding here like a frightened mouse, in fear of my life?' replied Prithusen. 'When I returned victorious from the battlefield, you were so kind as to treat my wounds and bring me back to health. Today, by giving me shelter when I am persecuted by my enemies, you have granted me my life a second time. I am beholden to you for two lives that you have given me. Permit me, sir, to go out into the dark and look for an opportunity to face my foes. I shall either vanquish them, or lay down my life in the attempt. I cannot destroy myself in humiliation.'

Cheebuk beckoned to him to come closer. 'Arya, it is not commendable to destroy oneself in humiliation. It is proper to think of defeating an enemy, but how can the enemy be defeated in the dark of night? In order to conquer the enemy, you must be able to recognize him.'

'I shall be able to recognize the enemy, reverend sir.' Feeling doubtful about the monk's meaning, Prithusen looked into his eyes.

'Then, recognize the enemy right here,' Cheebuk said, the constant smile playing on his lips.

'What do you mean, honoured sir?' Prithusen said, looking at the monk with wide open eyes, full of curiosity.

'Arya, the enemy takes birth in your thoughts.'

'Honoured sir, at this time, I am not in a fit condition of mind to follow metaphysical disputations. I am talking about the struggle to preserve life,' Prithusen said anxiously, after some thought. 'Pray, permit me to leave the monastery.'

The expression on the monk's face remained unchanged. 'Arya, it is precisely about the preservation of life that I have been talking to you. You were given shelter in the monastery to prevent bloodshed, since you were in danger, and not to enable you to wait for an opportunity for shedding blood.'

Speechless, Prithusen looked at the smile playing on the monk's lips. He recalled how, in his wounded condition, when he was struggling between life and death, this monk, with his infinite compassion, had brought him back to life. At that time, too, the same smile used to play on his lips. 'Arya, with every resource in my power, I shall try to save your life,' the monk had assured him at that time.

Prithusen remained silent. The monk called a bhikshu and asked him to bring some fruit. Prithusen had no desire to eat, but he could not disregard the monk's command, and, therefore, partook of some fruit.

During the daytime, the monk went out to different parts of the city, administering medicines to the sick. He told

Prithusen of the prevailing situation. There had not been much bloodshed, but the entire administration had undergone a radical change. Prithusen's friends and comrades were in no position to help him. It would be a grave risk for both Prithusen and his friends, if Prithusen tried to meet them. Rudradhir's spies were combing every lane, every path and every suburb in search of Prithusen. Their guess was that Prithusen had got wind of the conspiracy and after escaping from Mallika's palace, he had left that area of the city. They suspected that he had gone in disguise to those areas which he had conquered from the ruler of Darva, and it was in that direction that the spies were hunting for him.

Prithusen did not draw much consolation from what the monk told him. 'Honoured sir, am I to spend the rest of my life in humiliation and fear, hiding in this secret place like a crippled animal that has somehow escaped the hands of the hunter?' he said, in a voice of utter despair.

'Fear and despondency do not befit a brave person, Arya,' the monk replied.

'How can I sit idle in such a situation, honoured sir, simply because there is apprehension of bloodshed and violence? What other way is open to me except of fighting the enemy?' Prithusen asked impatiently.

'Arya, bloodshed is not an effective means of defeating the enemy. The enemy, of course, can be put to death with a weapon. You can subjugate the enemy for some time, but you cannot conquer him. He who has been killed, who has ceased to exist, cannot be conquered. A man prefers subjugation to death only in the spirit of cowardice or retaliation. As soon as the power of the conquering enemy is weakened, the defeated enemy once again tries to take revenge. Arya, such subjugation is not victory either. Sufficient blood has been shed in the world, but its result has never been victory over the enemy. A victory of this kind serves only as a seed from which grows the new plant of rancour and revenge. Arya, nobody is ever afraid of the dead body of an enemy. Tell me, wherein does enmity lie, in the body or in the mind?'

'In the mind, honoured sir,' Prithusen replied in a subdued voice.

'Then, Arya, victory lies not in subduing the body of the enemy, but his mind. You should, therefore, conquer Acharya Rudradhir in the same way as the Buddha conquered the mind of Deva Dutta, as Dharma Ghosh conquered the mind of the Emperor Ashoka, as the Buddhist Naga Sen conquered the mind of the Emperor Milinda.' Having said all this, the monk sat silent, looking at Prithusen with his smiling eyes.

Prithusen sat quietly, with his head bowed. Cheebuk continued, 'Arya, how many enemies does a man have? And who are they? Where are they to be found? Man does not know all of them. He cannot know all of them, either. How many of them can be killed with weapons? There was a day when the people of Sagal hailed you whenever they saw you going round on horseback. Today the same people, seeing you in your present condition, will not utter a word of cheer. Is it because they have become your enemies? In what way have you harmed them? At the time of the victory over Darva, you killed many soldiers of Kendras. Were they your enemies? You had never set eyes on them, nor had they ever set eyes on you. The cause of the enmity lay only in the mind, in the belief that they were your enemies. Enmity is a thing of the mind.

'Arya, the man who accepts defeat at the hands of the enemy and the man who goes to kill that enemy, are both hounded by fear of that enemy. Acharya Rudradhir is out to kill you, because he is afraid of you, because he trembles at the thought of you. Arya, the person who is afraid and admits that he is panic-stricken is not brave. The brave and courageous man is only he who is not afraid of anyone, who has no terror of anyone. Arya, you too are afraid of the person who is afraid of you. The powerful are afraid unconsciously, while the weak know that they are afraid. There is bound to be fear, if there is cause for fear. The only fearless man is he who is free from the cause of fear. If a person is afraid of your power, then his fear is the hidden seed from which your fear will spring. And this seed of fear can sprout at any time, when it finds a favourable soil and climate. Arya, such being the case, power is the cause not of fearlessness but of fear, of fear in others and in yourself. Such power cannot lead to happiness. Arya, the man who accumulates the means and causes of unhappiness, and hopes to draw happiness from them, is suffering from a grave illusion. Such a desire for happiness leads, like the dream of a pauper, only to misery.'

Every day, after returning from his round of the city to gather alms and visit the sick, Cheebuk would go to Prithusen and talk to him. Hardly a fortnight elapsed before Prithusen gave up the idea of going out of the monastery to plunge back into strife and struggle. He would put questions to the monk about non-attachment and perpetual happiness, and would later meditate over the monk's replies. From his face and appearance the look of perplexity and pain vanished. In its stead, there shone the calm of a well-ordered mind. The discourses of the monk no longer vexed and disturbed his mind. He would, on the contrary, listen eagerly to them, with joined hands.

One evening, soon after the monk's discourse, Prithusen said humbly, 'Honoured sir, your humble servant seeks, by accepting the spirit of Universal Brotherhood, to become a traveller on the path of everlasting happiness. Honoured sir, grant me the robes of the religion of the Buddha, accept me into the Threefold Shelter.'

The monk replied, smiling, 'Arya, for that too, your time will come. The happiness that one experiences on the path of renunciation, which one acquires without snatching anything from anyone, cannot be taken away from him. Young sir, the time will come for that too.'

On his own accord, Prithusen began to observe *vinaya* and *sheel*—humility and courtesy—the rules of conduct for a Buddhist bhikshu.

The physician monk, Cheebuk, on receiving a message from Dharma Rakshit, the head of the monasteries of Sagal and Principal of the monastic order, went to meet him one afternoon.

The Principal of the monastic order was extremely worried over the crisis that had overtaken the Buddhist religion. He had heard the town-crier announce with the beating of drums, the order issued by Sarvarth, the President, and it had distressed him terribly. The order of the President ran thus:

'Any citizen, who delivers to the state authorities, the son of a slave, Prithusen, the enemy of the caste religion, will receive from the state treasury the sum of five hundred gold pieces and a gift estate of one village. The citizen who flouts the law of the state and gives shelter to the low-born, the destroyer of religion, Prithusen, will be liable to the punishment of death, by the court of law.'

Monk Cheebuk, in accordance with the ritual of deference, greeted the Principal by prostrating himself in the five fold obeisance. Dharma Rakshit raised his hand in blessing and prayed for the health and well-being of the monk. Cheebuk went on his knees and asked for the Principal's command. At a sign from the Principal, Cheebuk sat down on a mat of kausheya grass. Surmising the reason for the Principal's uneasiness, Cheebuk did not open his mouth and waited for him to speak. Dharma Rakshit, in his agitation, put the matter briefly, 'May you have a long life. I believe you are aware of the crisis that has overtaken our faith.'

'Honoured sir,' Cheebuk replied, 'faith is never overtaken by a crisis. Only those men who subscribe to a particular faith get frightened and feel that the faith has been overcome by a crisis. Religion finds a place, sometimes in the hearts of many people, sometimes in a few. That is what this humble bhikshu thinks.'

Thinking over the reply of the monk, the Principal said, 'You are aware of the question that is causing anxiety to my mind. You must have heard the state proclamation.'

'So I had surmised, honoured sir. I have heard the proclamation,' Cheebuk admitted.

'For Prithusen, a person wanted by the state, to receive shelter in a Buddhist monastery is, in this abnormal situation, a source of danger both to the Monastic Order and to the religion. You know that Rudradhir is an avowed enemy of our religion.'

'Honoured sir, it was necessary to give asylum to one who came to seek shelter. The Monastic Order cannot refuse its sanctuary to such a person. Such is the order of our Faith.'

Lines of anxiety deepened on the forehead of the Principal. 'But, for the safety of the Monastic Order and of religion, we have a different duty at this time,' he said. 'A fast, normally desirable, may be disregarded when a person is ill.'

'Do I have your permission, honoured sir, to say something?' Cheebuk said, joining his hands and looking at the Principal of the order.

The Principal nodded assent, at which Cheebuk said, 'Honoured sir, just as water serves a special purpose when a person is thirsty, the observance of religious practices too, assumes a special significance in times of crisis.'

'But the safety of the Monastic Order is more important than the safety of an individual,' the Principal said, looking into Cheebuk's eyes.

'Honoured sir, Bodhisattva offered the flesh of his own body to save a poor homeless bird that had come seeking shelter. The proper use of his body, his wisdom, his religion lay in offering his own body to the shelterless bird. Honoured sir, my mind tells me that the safety of religion, the safety of the monastic order, has its importance insofar as it gives shelter to the shelterless. In this, even though the institutional structure of the Monastic Order may suffer, it will enhance religion. But refusal of shelter to a fugitive, even though it may save the institutional structure, will do grave harm to religion.'

After remaining silent for a long time, Dharma Rakshit said, 'It is laid down in our code of conduct that if there is difference of opinion among the monks, then the course of action is decided by an assembly of the monastic community. But on account of the prevailing conditions, it may be disastrous for the Monastic Order if this secret is revealed to the assembly. Out of regard for your religious zeal, however, I have said all that I had to say, in respect of my views and my recommendations.'

Cheebuk sat for a while with his head bowed, and then, offering his humble salutations to the Principal of the monastic order, took leave and returned to the monastery.

Monk Cheebuk's face, ever beaming with compassion and fellow feeling, for once became clouded. His mind, always free from uncertainty, was now torn by conflict. He could not flout the instructions of the Principal, and thereby violate the code of Buddhist discipline, but neither could he act against the moral instructions of the Bodhisattva. To steady his mind so as to be able to decide on his course of action, he sat meditating till late in the night in front of the image of the Buddha.

By putting himself in the place of the Buddha, and trying to see how the Buddha would have acted under similar circumstances, he was able to resolve his mental conflict. Gazing with rapt attention at the lustrous face of the Buddha, illuminated by the light of the lamps, the monk's face once again became free from anxiety, and lit up with joy. Before the image of the Buddha, he touched the floor with his head in a token of reverence.

Before sunrise, Cheebuk was standing before Prithusen's cell. Prithusen was lost in thought. Seeing the smiling face of the monk in front of him, he respectfully rose and offered his salutations.

'Do you have any doubts weighing on your mind, my son?' the monk asked, raising his hand in blessing.

'None, honoured sir, your teachings have freed this devotee of all doubts,' Prithusen replied with bowed head.

'Is there any fear left?'

'None, honoured sir.'

'Do you have any enemy?'

'With your blessing, I have no enemy left, honoured sir.'

'Will you go with me to the door of Rudradhir for alms?'

'Honoured sir, to the door of Rudradhir or to any other place that your worship may command.'

'Do you then apply to take the vows in order that you may enter the fold of the Buddha, of the Holy Word, of the Monastic Order?'

'Honoured sir, I submit myself for ordination into the Monastic Order.'

'Your wish shall be granted. Prepare yourself to receive it.'

Monk Cheebuk gave instructions to the monastery to make arrangements for the reception into the fold of a new bhikshu.

Before midday, Prithusen, his head shaven, dressed in russet robes, and holding a begging bowl in his hand, emerged from the door of the monastery in the company of the physician monk Cheebuk.

Monk Cheebuk, accompanied by another bhikshu, stood outside the heavily guarded gate of the palace of the lawgiver of the caste system, the Chairman of the Council, Acharya Rudradhir.

'Revered sirs, wait till the alms arrive from the kitchen,' the doorkeeper said to them respectfully.

'Today we desire to receive alms from the Acharya's own hand,' the monk replied, smiling, to the doorkeeper.

'Sir, the Acharya's instructions are that no one can enter the palace without his explicit permission. Please excuse me.'

'Pray, convey to the Acharya the blessings of the monk Cheebuk and his companion bhikshu,' Cheebuk said, still smiling.

When the command came back from inside the palace, Cheebuk, taking his companion with him, along with the doorkeeper, went into the audience chamber of Acharya Rudradhir.

The Acharya, with numerous palmyra leaves and birch leaves lying before him, was dictating orders to the scribes. Seeing the monks standing in front of him, the Acharya got up from his seat and, joining his hands, said to Cheebuk, 'Acharya Rudradhir, son of Acharya Pravardhan, bows before the eminent physician of Madra, the wise monk Cheebuk.' And bowing before the monk's companion too, the Acharya said, 'The unknown Buddhist monk may also kindly accept the salutations of the householder.'

As both the monks took their seats, the Acharya sat down too.

'Your reverence may kindly command what service I can do.'

'Arya, all that a bhikshu can ask for is alms,' the monk said. 'The Acharya may express his inmost wish.'

'I seek your blessings, honoured sir. When my body suffers from any ailment I shall seek the help of the honoured physician.' The Acharya smiled, and again joined his hands.

Cheebuk too smiled, 'Even when the body has no ailments, the mind may be ailing, Arya.'

'Honoured sir, what has that man to give who has himself renounced the world?' the Acharya remarked jokingly.

Cheebuk's smile did not fade. 'The Acharya is wise. Nothing can be renounced unless it is first acquired. No one can acquire the world and, therefore, no one can renounce it either. Acquisition and renunciation both are motivated by the same aim—that of contentment.'

'You are right, revered sir,' the Acharya admitted. 'A man of the world, who has to pursue worldly affairs, has always many reasons to be discontented. He has many worries.'

The monk sitting besides Cheebuk said, 'This bhikshu has come to relieve the Acharya of one of his many worries.'

Hearing the bhikshu's voice the Acharya raised his head and then gasped for breath in amazement.

The monk continued, 'I, Prithusen the bhikshu, having achieved the blessedness of universal friendship, shorn of all enmity towards the Acharya, have been freed from fear and anxiety. To relieve the Acharya also of fear and anxiety on my account, I have come to the Acharya in his audience chamber, to put myself in his hands. Receive Prithusen and give to the bhikshu, in charity, the joy of universal friendship.' The monk spread out both his hands in a gesture of self-surrender.

The Acharya opened his lips to say something, but after heaving a deep sigh, closed them again. He sat silently, with his head bowed. After a while, when the noonday gong was sounded, he raised his head. Addressing the guest monks, he said, 'Will the bhikshus kindly partake of some food?'

Cheebuk smiled and said, 'The Acharya, familiar with our code of behaviour, knows that the Buddhist bhikshus do not eat anything after midday.'

The Acharya was struck with remorse at the fact that the monks who had come to his house could not be fed, and begging their pardon, said, 'Honoured sir, the householder begs to be forgiven for this lapse on his part.'

'Arya, you need have no anxiety on that score,' the monk reassured him.

For a long time silence prevailed in the audience chamber. Then Cheebuk got up, took leave of the Acharya, offered his blessing, and made for the main gate, accompanied by Prithusen.

Acharya Rudradhir sat silently, with his head bowed.

Seeing the Acharya torn by anxiety, Vasudhir, his younger brother, said, 'Acharya, when the enemy eats the dust of the ground, the war ends. This is the law of the caste religion.'

Rudradhir looked up at his younger brother, but there was no peace in his eyes.

Mallika

Madra, the insolence and insubordination of the lower classes disappeared from the public life of Sagal. Devi Mallika, too, was satisfied with the re-establishment of the Brahminic regime. In her assembly hall she organized regular artistic events in accordance to proper traditional methods. But even then, the spontaneity that used to be so much a feature of the days of her youth, when pupils like Divya and Madulika were there to assist her, could not be revived.

Devi Mallika herself felt that there was something lacking. Art was still held in great esteem, but the public was not drawn to it. The knowledge of the nuances of art was there, but not the devotion to them. The cage was beautiful, but the songbird within lacked vivacity. Seasoned musicians like Marul, Apit and Lomak, would emit from their aged throats the purest of notes; the older dancer Udumber would, with his skeletal body, display many difficult, complicated postures, portraying different emotions; Pritha, too, would likewise give flawless expositions of her art.

To take delight in such art required knowledge, and an effort of will and taste, just as persistent practice was needed for meditation and reflection. This was pure art, unblemished by secondary considerations such as a sweet voice or a pretty face. But for the ordinary people art had become a lifeless formality. It was as arduous to enjoy it as it was to appreciate abstract discussions on the nature of the soul freed from the bondage of the body. Art lovers held Mallika in great regard, but sought satisfaction in the concert halls of Vasumitra and Kusumsena, which were vibrant with the breath of youth. The dedicated art lovers from far and near, however, still came to Devi Mallika's assemblies.

After the downfall of Prithusen, Madulika, feeling penitent and remorseful, came to Mallika to beg for forgiveness. Mallika, however, did not take her back. Art loses its purity and dignity in the hands of the unworthy who give precedence to physical pleasures.

After turning her back on Madulika, Devi Mallika began to feel more uneasy in her mind. 'When the caste system is being given its proper place, should the pursuit of art be denied its rightful appreciation?' she asked herself. Her lifelong effort and hard work had gone to give art a place of eminence and authority. Did this mean that with her death, her art would perish too? Was it that the throne of the Laureate of Art would be disgraced by some undeserving and unworthy person! That was as painful to her as seeing it all go to ruin before her eyes.

Wealth held no attraction for Devi Mallika. She believed that all the wealth she possessed was merely an offering made to the supremacy of art. She accepted the offerings as a living symbol of art. Mallika had not only accumulated possessions; she had also earned fame and the esteem of the art lovers. Wealth was only the tangible reflection of that eminence and repute.

In her young age, Devi Mallika had borne a child in the hope of leaving a successor. Having been blessed with a beautiful daughter, she dedicated herself to Saraswati, the goddess of art, and took a vow that she would not bear another child lest her interest in dance and music should flag. A cruel fate snatched that child away from her, but Devi Mallika did not break her vow. Fate was unkind to the devotee, but the devotee's faith remained unshaken.

Devi Mallika bore this unfolding of destiny with equanimity. A successor in the sphere of art, she thought, need not be a child of your own womb; she must be the child of your soul. She took comfort in the knowledge that Gopa in Taxila, Sulekha in Magadh, and Ratnaprabha in Mathurapuri were keeping up her tradition. But what had Sagal, once a place of pilgrimage and a seat of art, to offer now, to travellers who came there, attracted by her fame? The very thought of it made her suffer acutely. She had based her hopes on Madulika, but Madulika had proved unworthy.

Devi Mallika, renewing her faith in the beneficence of Goddess Saraswati, once again decided to seek her replacement. She made up her mind that in search for a successor, she would travel far and wide, to other kingdoms and states of Jambu Dweep. She made enquiries from travellers, pilgrims and traders of the various centres of art in different parts of the country. She learned all that there was to know about Taxila, Malva, Magadh, Mathurapuri and Dakshinapath. The one person who had been most highly praised in her hearing was a certain Anshumala, the pupil of Ratnaprabha of Mathurapuri.

Ratnaprabha had shown both talent and devotion, Devi Mallika remembered, but during the last four years her fame had begun to shine all the brighter. And that was because she had a pupil like Anshumala. Who could be more fortunate than a teacher who had such a pupil, a pupil who could turn the spark of knowledge into a burning flame? Thinking that Acharya Rudradhir must have visited Mathurapuri at the time of his return from Magadh, Mallika asked him about Anshumala. But the Acharya did not show much interest in the subject.

The Acharya's silence in this regard convinced Mallika that a dry-as-dust man such as the Acharya could not be expected to know much about the finer points of art. 'Come what may,' she said to herself, 'I shall seek out a successor for myself even at my advanced age.'

On the pretext of making a pilgrimage, Devi Mallika set out on a journey and visited numerous holy places, towns and cities, visiting the centres of art and culture, and at last turned up in Shursen. As she approached Mathurapuri, reports of Anshumala's fame reached her. Devi Mallika was convinced that her heart's desire would certainly be fulfilled in the abode of Nataraj, Lord of Dance and Music.

The news of the arrival of the Court Dancer of Sagal, the Laureate of Art, Devi Mallika, sent a thrill of joy and enthusiasm throughout Mathurapuri. As if vying with the eastbound current of the Yamuna river, the stream of people flowed towards the western gate of the city. The highway from the palace of Ratnaprabha to the western gate was decked with arches of plantain stalks, columns of painted earthenware pots, festoons of mango and jamun leaves and garlands of flowers. The façades of the houses and shops lining the path were covered by banners and pennants of various colours. The surface of the highway was decorated with patterns and pictures made from rice and parched barley. The air was thick with the fragrance of myrrh, frankincense and sandalwood. The terraces and balconies of houses groaned under the weight of the crowds of spectators. The air resounded with the notes of the veena, cymbals, tambourines and kettledrums.

Devi Ratnaprabha, together with Anshumala and other pupils, state officials, feudatory chiefs and business magnates, was present at the city gate to receive her teacher. As Mallika's chariot, its flag with the emblem of a crocodile flying, appeared in a cloud of dust, the sound of conch shells and other instruments filled the air and shouts of joy rose to the sky.

As Devi Mallika alighted from her chariot, Ratnaprabha welcomed her and performed the arati ceremony by moving a golden tray, laden with one hundred and one lighted lamps, in a circle round her teacher and presented her with a platter filled with jewels.

Smiling, Devi Mallika declined the offer. 'Daughter, a devotee of art does not desire jewels which shine with borrowed light. To her, only those jewels are precious which emit their own light. Today I have come to ask for such a jewel. Give it to me either as a present or as charity.'

For a moment, Ratnaprabha stood lost in thought. The gentry and the citizens looked on in surprise. Then, with bowed head and joined hands, she replied, 'Mother, you have only to command. Whatever I am, and whatever I possess, have been bestowed upon me by Goddess Saraswati through your grace.' Kneeling on the ground, she placed her forehead at Mallika's feet.

Mallika put her hand on Ratnaprabha's pearl-decked hair and blessed her, 'Daughter of the Goddess of Art, may you enjoy forever the blessings of knowledge, renown and wealth. Your teacher has come to ask you, to give her in charity, her pupil's pupil—Anshumala.'

Hearing Mallika's words, Ratnaprabha stood up. Taking Anshumala by the hand, she pulled her forward and sat her at the feet of Mallika, and in a voice choked with emotion, said, 'Mother, she too was bestowed by you. Who but Goddess Saraswati herself is capable of conferring a boon like her?'

A shout of joy rent the air. People cheered on all sides. Conch shells and the triumphal drums began to play. In the midst of that tumult, lifting Anshumala's head, Mallika looked at the face of the one for whom she had yearned for so long.

For a few moments, she stood transfixed. Her breath came in short gasps. Suddenly, her eyes welled with tears. Holding Anshumala tightly to her breast, Mallika cried out, 'Divya! Divya! My child, the child of my soul!'

To give up Anshumala was, for Ratnaprabha, like giving up everything. But just as a mother sending away her daughter after marriage lends to the pangs of separation a festive look, in the same way, Ratnaprabha handed over her friend, her sister, her daughter Anshumala to Devi Mallika, in the hope and confidence of a brighter future for her protégée.

With tears streaming down her cheeks, she went as far as the city gate to bid farewell to Anshumala. Huge crowds gathered on all sides. The entire population of Mathurapuri was saddened by its separation from Anshumala, but it had the satisfaction of fulfilling the wish of the foremost Laureate of Art, Devi Mallika. Anshumala's chariot was filled with jewels and ornaments presented by her admirers and the lovers of her artistry.

With her hand shielding her eyes, Ratnaprabha looked at the receding flag, as though her life depended on it. It became smaller and smaller, then a speck on the horizon. Long after that speck had disappeared from view, she continued to stand motionless, supporting herself on the shoulder of her pupil, Muktavali.

His Excellency Ravi Sharma, the Viceroy of Mathurapuri, tenderly roused her with a touch of his hand and escorted her to her chariot. Ratnaprabha returned to her palace with her face hidden behind the folds of her stole.

Divya

DEVI MALLIKA RETURNED TO SAGAL SUCCESSFUL IN HER MISSION, her pilgrimage having yielded the desired result. Her homecoming was an occasion for rejoicing for both the gentry and the common people of Sagal.

People were eager to see that jewel of an artiste who had proved equal to the demands of Mallika. Connoisseurs and lovers of art came from far and near to have a glimpse of her. Crowds of people gathered at the evening concerts in Mallika's palace. There was a great deal of elbowing and pushing for seats, but no one was able to see the fabled dancer. The heir to Devi Mallika's throne remained confined to the interior of the palace.

Finally, a day was fixed for the ceremonial investiture. Devi Mallika announced that a month hence, on the auspicious date of the full moon in the month of Phalgun, the ceremony would be held, and people would have the opportunity of seeing her successor. For the men and women of Sagal the waiting period of thirty days was full of eager curiosity and anticipation.

Arrangements were made for a grand sacrificial yajna for the propitiation of the gods. At the ceremony, one hundred priests and scholars recited benedictory hymns, and the seat of the head priest was occupied, at Mallika's request, by the Chairman of the Council, the noblest of Acharyas, Mahapandit Rudradhir.

The site chosen for the investiture of Devi Mallika's successor was on the bank of the silvery Pushkarni lake. In front of the dais, on a raised platform, sat the Master of Exceptional Virtues, the Great Noble, the President of the Republic, Sri Dev Sarvarth, and next to him, the Chairman of the Council, Acharya Rudradhir. On both sides of the platform, rows of seats were arranged in the form of a wide crescent, for the nobility, the heads of Brahmin families, the feudatory chiefs, members of the Council, and high-caste ladies. Behind them sat the monied families of Sagal, the merchants, the business magnates, and their friends and relatives. And behind them all, the soldiers and the vast concourse of people as far as the eye could see. Unable to suppress their curiosity, in spite of the professed indifference to worldly affairs, many Buddhist bhikshus were present, in their russet robes.

A contingent of Brahmins chanted auspicious mantras. A troupe of prominent dancers of the town and the pupils of Mallika performed the inaugural, propitiatory dance and welcomed the guests. The state astrologer prophesied eternal renown for Devi Mallika's successor.

At the auspicious moment, the new Laureate of Art was brought to the dais in a palanquin decked with white flowers. Mallika, with loving attention, helped her alight from the palanquin and escorted her to the seat of honour reserved for the Court Dancer. For this occasion, Mallika had dressed and decorated her successor with her own hands. The face of the successor was hidden behind a veil of strings of pearls. The people, with intense curiosity, were waiting for the ceremony to end, so that they might have a glimpse of the new Laureate of Art.

A Brahmin priest, reciting couplets from the Vedas, placed before Mallika a platter with portions of raw rice, sandalwood, a few blades of grass, and ceremonial rouge made from saffron and herbs. Devi Mallika, with the third finger of her right hand, anointed the forehead of her successor, whose face was still hidden behind the veil of pearls.

The sound of conch shells, kettledrums, trumpets and flutes reached a crescendo. Members of the gentry rose from their seats and, one by one, placed gift offerings on the dais for their first glimpse of the new Chief Courtesan.

After anointing her forehead, Devi Mallika knelt down and in homage touched her own head to the feet of her successor. The impatient crowd began to clamour for a glimpse of the new Laureate of Art.

At a sign from Mallika, the herald blew his conch shell. A hush fell on all sides. Mallika parted the veil of pearl strings and thus revealed to the audience the face of her successor. Facing the congregation, Mallika went down again on her knees and bowed her head in obeisance. Holding their breaths, people looked on at the new light of the town.

The silence had lasted for a few seconds, when a low murmur began to be heard from the side where the nobility was sitting.

'Divya! The great-granddaughter of the Chief Justice! Divya! A Brahmin girl! The granddaughter of Vishnu Sharma! Divya! A high-born girl! A Brahmin girl!'

Hearing the noise, Mallika raised her head and noticed the agitated confusion that had set in among the members of the nobility and the high-caste families. In a moment, a shout was heard:

'A Brahmin girl cannot be allowed, in Madra, to become a courtesan, a mere object of pleasure and entertainment for the people. She cannot be allowed to disgrace the caste religion!'

It was the voice of Acharya Bhrigu Sharma, who stood with his arm upraised, trembling with rage.

Like a thunderclap in a valley surrounded by high mountains, his loud protest began to echo and re-echo on all sides. In the ranks of the nobility, several swords had been drawn and were being flourished above the heads of the audience. Soon after, many more swords flashed in the sunlight.

Devi Mallika stood speechless, as though petrified by the rising tumult that surrounded her.

Divya sat silent, her head bowed.

Then Divya got up from her seat and walking calmly with measured steps, went to one side of the dais and stood before the audience. She raised her hand, indicating to the people to be silent. The tumult subsided abruptly.

'Please hear me, citizens, men and women of the caste families and others. I would request Acharya Rudradhir, the highest legal authority on matters relating to religion and social conduct, to give his ruling on this subject.'

Everyone turned towards Acharya Rudradhir, the Chairman of the Council.

The Acharya remained silent.

Waiting for his words, the vast concourse of people also held a breathless silence. The swords, drawn from their scabbards, hung motionless in the air.

With his head bowed in deep thought, the Acharya said in a faint voice, 'The laws of the caste religion are binding for all time; past, present and future.'

For a few moments, Divya stared at the Acharya, trying to grasp the meaning of his statement. Then, in a gesture of silent submission, she bowed her head and said, 'So be it!'

She stepped down from the dais and began to walk out. People drew aside to make way for her, just as water parts before the prow of a boat. With her head erect, without looking to either side, she passed through the audience.

Homeless once again, Divya walked along the highways of Sagal in her costume of a celestial handmaiden. A large crowd, unable to restrain their curiosity, followed her at some distance. She did not turn round to see who was in the crowd. She walked on, like the swan queen leading a bevy of swans.

She went out of the city gate. The sun had set. The full moon of the month of Phalgun had risen above the horizon; its early, faint light mingled with the last vestiges of dusk. Divya looked at the road leading towards the eastern horizon. Heaving a tired sigh, she turned her eyes towards the inn, which stood outside the city gate. For a few moments, she stood undecided; then with firm steps, walked towards the inn.

Travellers arriving at the city gate after it had closed for the night usually spent the night at the inn. Likewise, those who desired to begin their journey before dawn would also come to the inn in the evening and spend the night there.

Divya went in. She crossed the courtyard, and stepping across the veranda, sat down in a dark, unlit room. The curious multitude followed her. Gradually, the courtyard began to fill, and to hum like a beehive. When they found no room in the courtyard, the crowd gathered in the doorway and along the boundary wall. Drawn by curiosity, outrage or sympathy, and eager for excitement, they were debating among themselves the future of the dethroned court dancer.

The guard in charge of the inn, vexed and fuming, kept shouting to the people to clear the path and the courtyard for the travellers, but no one paid any attention to him. It was no longer possible even to shut the inn gates.

A bhikshu drew near the crowd and called in a loud voice, 'Citizens, permit me to go to the unhappy woman oppressed by society. Let me go to the dethroned court dancer. Pray, let me go to her. I have come to bestow on her some peace in her suffering.' The bhikshu's words were lost in the tumult.

In the shimmering glow between sunset and moonlight, a traveller came walking along the eastern road. Seeing a huge crowd surrounding the inn, and hearing the loud clamour, he slowed down and then stopped. The dust covering his hair, face, clothes and thick on his legs up to the knees bore testimony to the fact that he had been walking the whole day long. In that deceptive light, he strained to see and hear the reason for such a large and noisy crowd. All he could hear clearly were the words of the bhikshu.

Leaving the road, he went towards the crowd that surrounded the inn. 'Tell me, kind citizens of Sagal,' he said addressing them, 'has the investiture ceremony of Anshumala, the dancing girl of Mathurapuri, been performed? I have come a long way to see the ceremony. For a whole month I have been travelling as fast as I could. Kind folk, tell me, has there been any hindrance to her inauguration? I hope no harm has come to Anshumala.'

Only one person paid any attention to the traveller. 'Uh, sculptor Marish? Which Anshumala are you talking about? . . . The Brahmin girl? . . . The great-granddaughter of the late Chief Justice?'

'The same,' Marish nodded his head.

'It was Divya who desired to become the court dancer of Sagal,' the citizen corrected Marish. 'She has been disgraced by the caste society, and has left the town and taken shelter in this very inn. Are you . . .'

Not hearing the rest, the traveller went towards the door of the inn.

The bhikshu and the traveller were both trying to make their way through the crowd towards the inn gate.

'Gentle folk, kind citizens,' the traveller was saying,

'allow me to go into the inn. I shall give solace to that unhappy woman. Citizens, let me pass. For her sake, I have come all the way from Shursen. I have arrived this very moment.'

The bhikshu too was saying, 'Let me pass, citizens. I have come to take this oppressed woman into the bosom of the True Faith, so that she may know peace.'

The excited crowd was deaf to the words of the bhikshu, the traveller and also of the guard of the inn. The courtyard was so packed with people that no one was able to move. Suddenly, the sound of a gong was heard from the direction of the city gate, and a state official, standing on the rampart, shouted, 'It is time to close the city gate. Those who have to go into the city should enter now.'

The human tide began to flow from the courtyard and through the doorway of the inn towards the city gate. Being unable to resist this stream, the traveller and the bhikshu retreated.

Just then a bugle sounded and the tumult subsided. The crowd fell silent and people stood where they were. Four torch-bearers on horseback emerged through the city gate. They were followed by a bugler on horseback. 'Attention! Attention, citizens!' shouted the bugler, 'The Chairman of the Council, the Protector of the Faith, the Great Feudatory Chief, Rudradhir is arriving. Give way, citizens! Step aside!'

The people greeted the Acharya with cheers and shouts. A path was cleared for him. The Acharya stepped down from the chariot. The guard of the inn went down on his knees to salute him.

'Where is the dancing girl who came to the inn?' the Acharya asked in a solemn voice. 'Guard, show the way.'

The guard, escorting the Acharya, proceeded towards the veranda. The entire crowd stood motionless like wooden statues,

but the bhikshu and the traveller from Mathurapuri, seeing
their chance, followed the Acharya.

The four torch-bearers took their positions in the corners
of the room, which was now flooded with light. Divya, dressed
in her costume of a celestial handmaiden, was sitting on the
floor, her back resting against the wall. She lifted her eyes and
looked at the visitors, but continued to sit motionless. The
crowd, peeping through the door, stood in silent awe.

In a voice devoid of any emotion, Divya asked the Acharya,
'What further orders await this unfortunate creature?'

Sitting down on the mat spread by the guard, the Acharya
said, 'Devi, your place is not that of a dancer—courtesan. You
are of high birth. Your place is that of the mistress of a noble
family. I am here to offer you the place of the First Lady in the
house of the Acharyas. Devi, oblige me by accepting the offer.'

Her eyes fixed steadily on the face of the Acharya, Divya
replied, 'Acharya, the place of the mistress and of the First Lady
of a noble family is a rare honour. This destitute woman bows
her head before the offer of such a high position. But Acharya,
the mistress of a noble family is not a free woman; she is not
independent like a disreputable courtesan. Learned Acharya, the
honour given to the noble bride, the respect given to the noble
matron, and the authority given to the First Lady are there
because of the man who gives her protection. It is not an honour
due to the woman; it is an honour due to the powerful man who
owns her. Arya, this honour and respect can be obtained by
a woman only by willingly surrendering her inner self.'

After a few moments silence, she continued, 'Learned
sir, what is left of the woman who has given up her self?
The Acharya must forgive this humble servant. Even though
destitute, she wishes to live independently. By losing her self
she cannot remain alive.'

Realizing that his great authority would carry no weight, the Acharya sat silent looking at the inscrutable face of Divya.

Just then, the bhikshu approached the seat of the Acharya, and said, 'Devi, I, Bhikshu Prithusen, a devotee of the Buddha, am here to receive into the bosom of the Buddha the woman oppressed by society.'

Divya's eyes opened wide as she heard and recognized the voice of the russet-robed bhikshu standing in front of her. A shudder ran through her body. She heaved a deep sigh and sat motionless looking at the face of the bhikshu.

Bhikshu Prithusen raised his hand in benediction and said, 'Devi, by the mercy of the Buddha, it has been possible for you to realize that attachment and infatuation are only illusions. Devi, peace does not lie in riches, not in prowess, nor in the gratification of the senses. Everlasting peace lies only in Nirvana. Devi, no sorrow of the world can mar the beatitude that lies in Nirvana. The unhappy ones of the world, oppressed by society, find peace in the shelter of the Buddha, in the protection of the True Faith, in the protection of the Monastic Order. Come into the sanctuary of the Infinite Mercy.'

For a second, Divya's vision was clouded. In the room lit by torches, Rudradhir, the image of authority and power and the russet-robed bhikshu faded from before her eyes. She saw herself with her baby in her arms, an outcast in front of the closed doors of the Mahabodhi monastery in the town of Mathurapuri, under a tree, a destitute woman begging for shelter in the name of the Buddha, the True Faith and the Monastic Order.

Her eyes lit up again. In a voice trembling with emotion, she said, 'Honoured sir, what is the position of woman in the religion of the bhikshu?'

In a calm voice the bhikshu replied, 'Devi, the bhikshu's purpose is Nirvana. Woman represents temptation. As such, she is a hindrance in the path to Nirvana, and, therefore, has to be given up.'

'Honoured sir, then follow your religion of Nirvana,' Divya replied in a slow but firm voice. 'A woman's religion is not Nirvana but creation. Let the bhikshu permit her to follow her own path.'

When his chance came to speak, the traveller from the east drew near, and addressing Divya, said, 'I am Marish. I have come all the way from Mathurapuri to be near you, Devi.'

Once again Divya's eyes opened wide and lit up with wonder and curiosity. The traveller, covered with dust from head to foot, said, 'Devi, I cannot offer you the place of the First Lady in a royal palace; I cannot give you the assurance of the eternal joys of Nirvana. I live in the midst of the joys and sorrows of this world. Experience and reflection are my only assets. I can only offer to share those feelings and experiences with you. I am a traveller along the world's rough and dusty roads. On that journey, impelled by the desire for your womanhood, I offer my manhood to you. I want an exchange of support. In this fleeting life I can only offer a feeling of fulfilment.'

He paused for breath, and added, 'By reproducing my kind, I can try to add another link to the chain of human continuity.'

Divya sat quietly for a few moments, lost in thought. Then no longer needing the support of the wall, she stretched out both her hands towards Marish. In a tremulous voice, she said, 'Grant me the abiding shelter of your arms, Arya.'